VICTORIA FOX

'Lashings of scandal, shocking secret pasts and steamy romance'
New

'A proper guilty pleasure'
Now

'Oozes glamour and revenge. The ultimate beach read'
All About Soap

'If you think the *Made in Chelsea* crew live a glitzy life,
you ain't seen nothing yet'
Heat

'Just too exciting to put down'
Closer

'Always a fun read!'
Jackie Collins

'Pour yourself a glass of Pimms because this is
guaranteed to get you seriously hot'
Cosmopolitan

**Indulge yourself with Victoria Fox's
previous books**. . .

HOLLYWOOD SINNERS
TEMPTATION ISLAND
WICKED AMBITION
GLITTERING FORTUNES
POWER GAMES

Short Stories. . .

TINSELTOWN
RIVALS
PRIDE
AMBITION

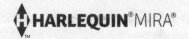

SANTIAGO SISTERS

VICTORIA FOX

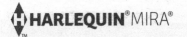 HARLEQUIN®MIRA®

First Published in Great Britain 2016
By Harlequin Mira, an imprint of HarperCollins*Publishers*
1 London Bridge Street, London, SE1 9GF

The Santiago Sisters © 2016 Victoria Fox

ISBN: 978-1-848-45395-1

Our policy is to use papers that are natural, renewable and recyclable products and made from wood grown in sustainable forests. The logging and manufacturing processes conform to the legal environmental regulations of the country of origin.

Printed and bound by
CPI Group (UK) Ltd, Croydon, CR0 4YY

For Charlotte
(when you're big enough)

Prologue

Winter, 2014

NYchronicle.com/News/US-News/Tess-Geddes-disappearance
Live Feed, 10.31AM:

Concerns are mounting over the disappearance two nights ago of Hollywood superstar Tess Geddes. Ms Geddes was last seen leaving her New York home at 21:00 on Friday 19 December and no contact has been made with her since. The vanishing is described as 'out of character', despite the actress's turbulent history. Friend and co-star Natalie Portis released this short statement yesterday: 'Tess is a fighter. We knew she'd suffered the year from hell—but she knows better than that. She wouldn't do anything stupid.'

It emerged this morning that Ms Geddes was accompanied by an unidentified female companion on the night of her disappearance. Police are now engaged in a hunt for this person, and witnesses are urged to come forward.

*

Her scent was deep: familiar and strange both at once. It filled the stairwell; savagery and glamour—one a relic from her old life, the other an emblem of her new.

Fear in her eyes, a pleading fear, begging for understanding. But it was too late for that. It was too late for sorry and too late for tears. She had arrived at her worst nightmare, and when that was over it would all be over: their history, their love, their hate; the cord that bound them unravelled at last. How to kill her? What method could rival her treachery, her greed, her betrayal; what could recompense her evil?

They should have stayed as one. They couldn't survive apart. It was fate, forever destined to come to this: from birth, to death; two halves of the same whole.

PART ONE

1994—2000

1

Argentina

She wondered, sometimes, if they had started off as one person. All things combined, until a silver blade entered their mother's womb and curled them apart. She pictured it dividing their heads, their shoulders, their hearts, their hands, and whether or not it had hurt. The change was immediate. Heat poured into her sister, red like fire. Cool stayed behind, with her, blue and quiet and longing for the warmth.

Calida Santiago dismounted her horse and knelt beside the wheezing *guanaco*. The animal was like a llama, with cinnamon fur and small, straight ears, and had broken its leg; the damaged limb was splayed behind the soft white pillow of its underbelly. She put her hand out to stroke it, and it flinched, fur trembling.

'Is it going to die?'

Diego, their father, tethered the horses. He secured the *guanaco*'s neck in the crook of his arm to stop it biting or twisting, while he felt the fracture and then the pumping strain of its heart. 'We should do what's right,' he said, removing the carved knife from his gaucho belt. Diego's riding trousers were stained with dirt and sweat, his face obscured by dust. The *facón* blade glinted in the dwindling afternoon sun.

'Take Teresita away.'

Behind them, Calida's twin sat sidesaddle on their shared horse. At ten years old, they should both have been children. But Calida, for all of her two-minute head start, would always be the elder. It was what life had decided: she had been built the sensible one, the one who looked out for and looked after. Occasionally she wished to be as carefree as her sister, to dare a little more, to risk, but it wasn't in her nature.

'I don't want to,' protested Teresita. 'I want to see.'

Calida took her sister's dirt-smeared hand, as native to her as her own. Grudgingly, knowing her father couldn't be defied, Teresita slid from the saddle.

'Papa will make it better,' Calida said. 'Come on, let's go for a walk.'

Teresita wore a dust-cracked scowl too determined for her years. She was wilful, stubborn, impossible once she set her mind to something, resolute to have her way no matter the cost: she was their mother's daughter through and through.

The twins picked their way through sun-charred bramble, Teresita trailing behind like a disgruntled wolf cub, and into a ravine that twinkled with water. Calida crouched to rinse her face. The dust got everywhere; it was the taste of home, grit that caught in their teeth and ears and powder that clung to their eyelashes. All around, the dry green Patagonian steppe rolled into the distance; sharp peaks severed the vista and then flattened into grassy plains, like the whipping surface of a vast and angry sea.

'What's Papa doing?' asked Teresita.

'Nothing. Forget it.'

But Teresita wouldn't. She always demanded to know, to find out. She was always asking these dumb questions that Calida didn't know the answers to.

'I can hear it screaming. Does it hurt?'

'No,' said Calida, putting an arm round her. 'Come here.'

She drew Teresita close. Her sister's hair smelled of the horses: the rich, solid scent of the saddlebags and the coarse rope of the reins, the leather stirrups, the tangy metal bit they put between Paco's teeth and heard him crunch on like an apple core.

The *guanaco* shrieked a final time. Teresita pushed against her; whether with fear or resistance it was hard to say. Calida had felt her twin's push from the very beginning: when they were born, a strength driving behind her, indignant at having been left behind. *Hurry up, come on, get out, it's my turn...* When she had been old enough to identify it, and recognise in Teresita's mop of black hair and huge jet eyes the sister she would love until the ends of the earth, Calida sensed that push so often in her life. Teresita's struggle when she was crying and didn't want to be comforted; her wishful gaze, reaching beyond the perimeter of the farm and into the frightening unknown; her resentment of gravity when all she longed to do was fly. Calida stayed on the ground, arms out, ready to catch her if she fell.

But there was a pull, too; a force of belonging that could never be changed and never be dimmed. It was blood, a mirror heartbeat, a laugh that echoed her own. At night, when they lay in their bunks, giggling in the dark or making hand shadows on the wall, whispering secrets that didn't need to be told because they already belonged in each other's hearts, Calida knew that this connection was a rare and precious gem. Faith. Trust. Devotion. Loyalty. No matter what, the sisters were there for each other.

'What's going to happen when we're grown up?' said Teresita now.

'I don't know. I haven't thought about it.'

'Mama says not to do what she did.'

Calida didn't reply. Instead, she said: 'We'll be together, though, won't we? So it doesn't matter. We'll always be together, you and me. Promise?'

Teresita ran a hand across the brittle earth. She blinked against the sun, and gave Calida a smile that warmed her bones. 'Promise. Can we go back yet?'

Calida went up the ridge to check. Diego was untying the horses. The *guanaco* was gone and she saw the slash of blood on her papa's *bombachas* and dared herself not to look away, to be the big girl Diego always told her she was.

Paco chewed lazily on a tuft of yellow grass.

'Come on, then,' said Calida.

*

Every day the sisters went riding with their father, while Julia stayed at home. It had been that way since time began. Their mother rarely emerged and the girls knew not to make noise in that part of the ranch, especially when Julia was resting.

Calida tried not to feel sad at how, on Julia's better days, she would invite Teresita into her bedroom; Calida would listen at the door, shut out of their exchange, desperate to hear and be part of the confidence, until she heard her papa's tread and shame directed her away. Julia spent hours brushing Teresita's ebony hair and singing her songs, telling her stories of the past and stories of the future, assuring her what a magical woman she was destined to become. Her mama adored Teresita, because Teresita was beautiful. The twins' division was responsible for this injustice, marking their physical difference: Teresita as exquisite and Calida as average. Calida knew there were greater things in life than beauty, but still it hurt. She wasn't special, or in any way extraordinary, like her sister. If she were, her mama would love her more.

Once upon a time, when Julia had first been married, she herself had been a magical woman. Calida had seen the evidence, photographs her father had taken when they had worked the land as a couple: Julia against the melting orange sunset, her head turned gently away and her hair in a thick plait down her back. The horse's tail had been frozen in time, a blur when it had swished away flies. Calida loved those pictures. This was a woman she had never known. She longed to ask her mama about that time, and what was so different now, but she was afraid of making Julia angry.

Julia told Teresita those things, anyway. At least she was telling someone.

*

Summer 1995 was unbreakingly hot. Sunshine spilled through open doors, the heat bouncing off wood-panelled walls. The twins were in the kitchen, paper pads balanced on their knees. Their home tutor was a harsh-looking woman called Señorita Gonzalez. Gonzalez was thirty-something, which seemed ancient, and the way she wore her hair all scraped back from a high forehead and her glasses on the end of her nose only made her more alarming. She wore heavy black boots whose tops didn't quite reach the hem of her sludge-coloured skirt, so that a thin strip of leg could be seen in between. In classes, Teresita would giggle at the black hairs they spied lurking there, and Calida had to tell her to shut up before they got told off. Gonzalez was strict, and wasn't afraid to use their father's riding switch if the occasion arose.

'I'm hot,' said Teresita, kicking the floor in that way she knew drove Señorita Gonzalez mad. Calida's own legs were stuck to the wooden chair, and when she adjusted position the skin peeled away with a damp, thick sound.

'*Díos mio, cállate!*' hawked Gonzalez, scribbling on the board. 'All you do is moan, Teresa!' It was only the family who called her Teresita: it meant 'little Teresa'.

Teresita stuck her tongue out. Since the teacher's back was turned, this failed to have the desired effect, so she tore off a sheet of paper, balled it up and tossed it at Gonzalez, nudging Calida as she did so, to include her in the game. But Calida didn't like to stir up trouble. The woman froze. Calida gripped the seat of her chair.

'*You little*—!' Gonzalez stormed, blazing down the kitchen towards them, whereupon she grabbed Teresita's hair and hauled her up, making her scream.

'Ow! Ow!'

'Stop it!' Calida begged. 'You're hurting her!'

'I'll show you what hurts, you disrespectful child!'

Gonzalez dragged Teresita up to the cast-iron stove and launched her across the top of it. 'That hot enough for you?' she spat. Calida felt the impact as sorely as if she were the one being assaulted: Teresita's pain was her pain. But her sister stayed silent, contained, her dark eyes hard as jewels and the only giveaway to her panic the lock of black hair that hovered next to her parted lips, blown away then in, away then in, flickering with every breath. Gonzalez took the riding switch from behind her desk and drew it sharply into the air. 'Time for a lesson you'll really remember!'

'*Wait*!' Calida leaped up. 'It was me. I threw the paper. It was me.'

There was a moment of silence. Gonzalez looked between the twins. Calida rushed to her sister's side and shielded her, just as the kitchen door opened.

'What is going on in here?'

Diego stood, his arms folded, surveying the scene. Calida felt Teresita squirm free, but not before she took Calida's fingers in her own and squeezed them tight.

'The girls fell down…' Gonzalez explained, in a different voice to the one she used with them: softer, sweeter, with an edge of something Calida was too young to classify but that seemed to promise a favour, or a reward. 'You know how energetic they are, rushing about… Honestly, Señor, I have my back turned for one minute!'

Diego approached and ruffled Calida's hair. 'There, there, *chica.*'

Calida clung to her father. She inhaled his warm soil scent. Diego held his other arm out to Teresita, but Teresita watched him and stayed where she was.

'Nobody's hurt?' he asked.

'Nobody's hurt,' confirmed Gonzalez. She narrowed her eyes at Calida and Calida thought: *We're stronger than you. There are two of us. You can't fight that.*

*

Winter came, and with it the rains. Teresita was staring out of the window; mists from the mountains pooled at their door and the freezing-cold fog was sparkling white. The reaching poplars that bordered the farm were naked brown in the whistling wind, and the lavender gardens, once scented, were bare: summer's ghosts.

'What are you thinking about?' asked Calida, coming to sit with her. Teresita always had her head in some faraway place, where Calida couldn't follow. She was forever making up stories she would sigh to her sister at bedtime, some that made her laugh and others that made her cry. Now Teresita reached to take her arm, looping her own through it, a ribbon strong as rope, and rested her head on her shoulder.

'The future,' she said.

'What about it?'

'The world… People. Places. What life is like away from here.'

A nameless fear snaked up Calida's spine. Privately, the thought of leaving the ranch, now or ever, made her afraid. The *estancia* was their haven, all she needed and all she cherished, by day a golden-hued wilderness and at night a sky bursting with so many stars that you could count to a thousand and forget where you started.

'But this is our home,' Calida said.

'Yes. Maybe. It can't be everything, though—can it?'

'What about me?'

'You'll come too.'

It was another dream, another fantasy. Teresita would never leave. They were happy here, happy and safe, and Calida comforted herself with this thought every night, locking it up and swallowing the key, until finally she could fall asleep.

2

Teresa Santiago would often think of her twelfth birthday as the day she left her childhood behind. This was for two reasons. The first was the bomb that exploded halfway across the world that same day in March, in a place called Jerusalem. They heard about it on the crackly television Diego kept in the barn, a small, black box with a twisted aerial that they had to hit whenever the reception went. Teresa tried to grasp what was happening—the flickering news footage, the exploded civilian bus, the hundreds of swarming, panicking faces. It seemed like it belonged on another planet. She felt helpless, unable to do anything but watch.

'It's a long way away,' reassured Calida. 'Nothing can harm us here.'

Her sister was wrong.

Because the second reason was that it was the day Teresa witnessed another type of combat, a different, confusing sort, which reminded her of two *maras* she had once seen scrapping on the Pampas. Only these were no *maras*: one was her father, and neither he nor the woman he was fighting with had any clothes on. Moreover, there was the faint inkling that this woman should be her beloved mama—and wasn't.

It happened in the evening. The twins were outside; shadows from the trees lengthened and stretched in the lowering

sun, and the air carried its usual aroma of vanilla and earth.
Calida was on her knees, taking pictures with the camera
Diego had given her that morning. She had been obsessed
with photography for ages, and had waited patiently for this
gift. '*You're old enough now*,' Diego had told her, smiling
fondly as Calida basked in his love, always her papa's angel.
He never looked at Teresa that way, or gave her such special
birthday presents. Teresa was too silly, too wistful; too girlish.
Instead Diego spent time with Calida, teaching her the ways
of the farm and entrusting her with practical tasks he knew
she would carry out with her usual endurance and fortitude,
while Teresa drew a picture he never commented on or wrote
a poem he never read. Calida would be the one to find them
later and tell her how good they were, and insist on pinning
them to the wall. Teresa remembered she had her mother's
affection. That, at least, was something Calida didn't have.

'I'm going to wake Mama.' Teresa stood and dusted off
her shorts.

Her sister glanced up. 'Don't.'

'Why not? It's our birthday.'

'She already saw us today.' Indeed, Julia had graced them
with her presence that morning, thirty minutes at breakfast in
her night robe, pale-faced and sad-eyed.

'She'll want to see *me* again.' Teresa said it because she
knew it would hurt. She loved her sister deeply, an unques-
tioning, imperative love, but sometimes she hated her too.
Calida was clever and useful and smart. What was she, in
comparison? The youngest, made to follow directions and do
as she was told. Why couldn't she have been born first? Then
her father would respect her. Then she could make her own
decisions. Jealousy, a nascent seed, had grown over the years
into creeping ivy.

'Whatever.' Calida pretended Julia's preference didn't wound her but her sister knew better. Teresa knew every little thing she thought or felt. 'I don't care.'

Teresa stalked past. It was as though the twins could argue on the barest of words, those surface weapons sufficient, like ripples on the deepest ocean.

Inside the house, it was cool and quiet. Teresa glanced down the hallway and decided she would take her mother a sprig of lavender, her favourite. She knew where the best of the purple herb grew, at the side of the stables, and went to find some. She imagined Julia's face when she handed her the lilac bouquet, and lifted at the thought.

A strange sound came upon her slowly. At first she thought it was an animal in pain, one of the horses, maybe, and she hoped it wasn't Paco.

But as she drew nearer, she knew it wasn't that at all.

Teresa stopped by the stable door. The scent of lavender enveloped her, heady and sweet, and from that day forward it would eternally be associated with sex. In her adult years, in fields in France or in gardens in England, in perfumed tea-blends or in Hollywood spas, it would carry with it an echo of that exotic, bewildering revelation, all the more tender for the age at which she had discovered it.

A primal reflex told her the sound was human, not animal: gasping, close to a scream, as if the person making it was being stifled. There was violence buried inside; but willingness, too, even begging. She picked out a contrasting tone, guttural, which punctuated the silence between the high-pitched yelps, like a pig grunting. Words, perhaps, although she couldn't be sure: *Yes*, she kept hearing, *yes, yes, yes*, and then *please*, and then *yes* again. Unable to desist, she drew the stable door wider.

Two figures wrestled on the hay-strewn floor. A bundle of clothes dripped from a rafter. The man, on top, was turned away, his pale, bare bottom pumping up and down. Each time it rose, a shadowy strip appeared between his cheeks, and a soft pocket of fruit, like an over-ripe peach, could momentarily be seen. His back was muscular, the ridge of spine glistening with sweat, and his thighs were scattered with hair. Gradually, the speed of his motions increased. He lifted the leg of the person beneath him and hooked it over his shoulder, pressing deeper, his hand clutching the person's knee as he tensed and thrust with an urgency that soon became manic. His grunts got louder. Teresa saw the soles of his feet, white, the toes braced on the dry floor. She wanted to call his name, but knew it was impossible. This could never be interrupted: the thought of interruption was somehow cataclysmic.

Abruptly, their position changed. Teresa stepped backwards, scared she would be seen, but she had no need for fear: they were utterly consumed by their task.

The woman, facing her now, straddled the man, her cheeks flushed and her breasts pale and heavy, the nipples large and black, drooping slightly. She had long, mahogany hair. Teresa had never seen the woman's hair down before, always scraped back off a high forehead, and she looked prettier than she normally did.

What alarmed her most was the clump of hair below Señorita Gonzalez's stomach. It was close to the man's belly, and she kept lifting it off him and going back down, and there was something connecting them, something swollen and weird that Teresa had heard only whispers about. The difference between boys and girls: the thing that grew hard. The man's hands gripped Gonzalez's waist then ran up to her breasts, squeezing them together, his thumbs on her nipples. Gonzalez threw her head back, all that mahogany hair falling free; her face screwed up tight and her mouth opened wide and the veins in her neck stood out as she released an ear-splitting cry, rocking back and forth and then, at last, she collapsed on to his chest.

The man kept going, raising his hips and thrusting. Gonzalez was thrown into an upright position, her breasts bouncing hectically, and Teresa almost laughed, but she was about to cry as well so it was confusing. In seconds, the man groaned.

It was over.

But that groan lingered on. It released something in Teresa, like a flesh wound in that pale instant before it splurges blood. All at once, she despised her papa. She despised his weakness. She despised his nakedness. She despised that pathetic, defenceless, self-serving groan. She despised him for liking her tyrant teacher, for choosing her over them. She despised him for loving her twin more than he loved her. She despised him for pretending that evil woman was her mama, who was tired and sick and ignorant of his sin. Teresa was filled with rage, but within that rage sat a nugget of conviction that smacked her with total clarity. Her father had committed a basic, unequivocal transgression that she would never forgive and never forget.

Gonzalez lifted herself and tied her hair back. They said something to each other, Teresa didn't hear what, and laughed softly.

She found herself staring at it. The thing was relaxing now, less stiff and angry than before, and smaller, almost shy as it rested against her father's thigh.

Soundlessly, Teresa retreated from the stable door. She stumbled back into the house, the lavender forgotten, and went to the bathroom and thought she might be sick.

Later, Teresa decided she would not tell her sister what she had seen. It was something she should keep to herself, a burden she alone must carry, and it would be the very first thing she ever kept from Calida.

*

Summer turned to winter and winter turned to spring. Skies were bracing and boundless blue, wisps of clouds drifting high in the ether, and far away the snow-capped mountains surveyed their kingdom of open plains. In the evenings, Teresa sat on the veranda to watch the horses run free, their manes wild in the hot wind.

She spent less time with her father, and resisted his embrace.

'*Chica*, what's the matter?' Diego would ask. But she couldn't answer him. She couldn't look at him. She kept remembering what she had seen—it came at her in flashes, accompanied by that pitiful, animal groan, and she could not bear to be kissed good night or even touched by him. In lessons with Gonzalez, she became surly and distant. Gonzalez smacked and mocked her—'What are you doing?' Calida whispered when their tutor's back was turned. 'Stop making her angry!'—and despite the number of times Teresa longed to put Gonzalez in her place and confess to what she'd seen, she never did. She was afraid of hurting Julia, of disappointing Calida, of Diego's denial, of the question she kept returning to: *Why didn't you run? Why did you stay and watch?* And the more she rejected Diego, the closer he grew to Calida, and the more Teresa felt the cool shawl of loneliness close around her shoulders.

What was there left for her here?

Her mama was right. Her mama told her she didn't belong on the *estancia*. She was fated for greater, more important things. She had outgrown this life.

How could Calida be content to stay? There were so many worlds to see, so much more to discover, beyond the gate at the foot of the track. Teresa felt the draw of possibility as a physical force, beckoning her, tempting her. *Stay here and you'll never amount to anything. You'll always be second best.* She imagined her existence twenty years from now, as unhappy as Julia, her hopes and dreams snuffed to dust.

Julia hadn't always been like this. Hers was a cautionary tale, so she said, as she combed Teresa's hair and gazed in the mirror at the decades between their reflections. Once, Julia had bathed in banknotes and showered in glittering coins. She had been raised in a mansion many miles away and, as the only daughter of a rich man, had had her every need catered for; surrounded by servants, banquets, and ball gowns, she was the girl whose hand every suitor sought to claim. Then Diego Santiago had swept into her life, so different from the polished men of whom her father approved, and they had fallen in love. Julia, as spirited and defiant as her daughter, refused to be cowed by her father's ultimatum. Given the choice between her family and her lover, she had chosen her lover. Teresa thought this romantic, but Julia was quick to clarify her mistake. She had been left with nothing. No money. No luxury. No furs or sapphires or silk sheets. When her parents died, they left it all to a distant cousin and not a peso came Julia's way. Her sacrifice lost her everything.

What Julia wouldn't give to swap her fortunes now! Look where romance had got her: a house that was falling apart, clothes that were tatty and shapeless, a husband who had changed, or so the story went, when he left to fight on the Islas Malvinas, leaving Julia behind with her pregnancy and a rapidly swelling depression. Now, her only refuge was in her romance novels, which she read to Teresa late into the night. *The Billionaire's Mistress, The Diamond Tycoon, The Handsome Magnate…*

She informed Teresa how her beauty would serve her well; it was a pass into an exclusive club beyond the reach of ordinary people, and it meant she never had to settle. 'These are the kind of men you must find,' Julia counselled. '*Rich* men.' She told Teresa that love was a trap only fools fell into. 'Men will let you down—all men, eventually, no matter how much you think you can trust them—but money never will. If you have money, you have power… and if you have power, you have everything.'

That night, watching the stars through the window, silver cobwebs in a deep and soundless purple, Teresa prayed for the courage to make her mama's vision come true. Diego's betrayal proved that this was a cutthroat, adult world, that the innocence of her childhood was over, and, if she intended to succeed, she couldn't hide away.

'Recognise fortune when it comes for you,' her mama said. 'And when it does, be ready.' Teresa was ready. She sensed it like a current at her fingertips. Something vital was about to change, something big: she could almost touch it.

She closed her eyes and took a breath, filling her lungs with promise. In the bunk below, she heard the yield of the mattress as Calida turned in her sleep.

3

London

Seven thousand miles across the sea, in a townhouse in Kensington, actress Simone Geddes faced the wall-mounted mirror as her husband drove into her from behind.

Shit, Brian was a lame fuck. He had never made her come—not once. His technique, if that wasn't too grand a word, was to pound as hard and as fast as he could until her groans of boredom could be mistaken for cries of ecstasy, and so when the time came for him to collapse on her back in a sweaty, sticky heap (three minutes later), he could feel satisfied that she had also reached climax. This made her suspicious that Brian had never made a woman come, because otherwise he'd know.

'That feel good, baby?' he growled, rutting away, lightly slapping her bottom.

Do it properly! Simone wanted to scream. *If you're going to slap me, give it some welly*! But as with everything with Brian, it was lame. Lame, lame, lame.

'Let me get on top,' she instructed. Her husband was close to spunking and she wouldn't be in with a shot unless she took matters into her own hands. As she flipped his pale, bloated-from-too-many-lunches-at-Quaglino's body between her thighs and clamped him into place, she thanked God for the mirror she'd had the foresight to install in the mansion's master suite. At least this way she could get off on her own image, and no one could deny she looked incredible. At forty-eight, Simone Geddes was the ultimate English screen siren: cool, composed, with a chiselled sort of beauty that could freeze even the most experienced co-star into submission. She wore not an ounce of fat. Her ribcage was visible, delicate as a toothcomb beneath flawless white skin. Her breasts were high and small, the nipples tight. Her thighs were long and lean, smooth as the curves on a cherished motorcar. Her bush was honey-blonde and waxed into a neat landing strip. Her arms were slender and sinewy.

'Baby, you are so sexy…' Brian echoed her thoughts. She watched his hands reach up to knead her tits, quickly followed by the back of his head, then the feel of his wet, insistent tongue lapping her nipples as she mused on how much hair he had lost from that area. It was turning into a veritable monk's patch!

'I'm ready, hot stuff,' he murmured—what were they living in, the 1970s? 'Can you feel me deep inside you? D'you want this cock to make you come?'

Brian's cock was mediocre. Simone would deal with it as one might a sticky gearbox, grinding it into position until finally she was cruising. She kept an eye on her own reflection as she hit orgasm, enjoying the pink flush that built and spread across her chest, and the way her breasts bounced and shook as she surrendered.

Brian shot his load a second later. He did this disagreeable wiggly thing with his hips, like he was stirring the contents of a mixing bowl with a big wooden spoon.

Efficiently, Simone dismounted. 'Time to get ready,' she ordered, stalking into the bathroom. Before entering, she called out, 'Wear the Armani, would you? And the shirt. That shirt's good. It's slimming.' She slammed the door.

Ugh. Doubts over her marriage were at an all-time high. At first, she had been seduced by the muscle of a big-shot director—not that she wasn't a big shot herself, but Brian Chilcott was one of the hottest names in British film and together they were dynamite. Of course she had hoped the sex might get better, but then, when it didn't, she'd given up. Brian did nothing for her, erotically. She didn't even fancy him. Had she ever? Or had she just been in love with his plethora of awards and the allure of being half of the UK's reigning power couple? No wonder she took other lovers. Men who knew where a woman's clitoris was located—who knew women *had* one, for a start—and would happily spend an hour down there sending her to the brink, until the marital sheets were crumpled and soaked. Vera, the Spanish maid, asked no questions. The day Vera did, Simone would fire her so fast her head would spin.

Simone ran a scented bath and climbed in. The hot bubbles soothed her and she applied her cucumber facemask and closed her eyes. Brian's latest movie was premiering tonight at Leicester Square and she had to look the part: they'd been married five years now and it was always around this time that the gossip columnists decided to speculate. A glowing joint appearance every couple of months normally did the trick. *Just remember to smile!* Simone told herself, attempting to practise underneath the mask, which had now set solid and cracked like cake icing.

She was beginning to relax when a caterwaul sounded from the bedroom.

'But *Daaaaad*!'

Brian's voice followed immediately: 'I said no, darling.'

'You are such a shit, Dad! All my friends are going. It's

only a fucking party—why do you have to be such a moron all the time?'

'It's only because I care—'

'No, you fucking don't. If you did, you'd fucking well let me go. It's like I'm a fucking criminal—it's like you're keeping me fucking prisoner!'

'Stop swearing.'

'Like fuck I will.'

That was enough! Simone rose from the bath and wrapped herself in a towel. Damn Emily Chilcott! The thirteen-year-old was the bane of Simone's life—she and her elder brother, the awful Lysander. Who would have stepchildren? Soon after Simone had moved in, Lysander and his friends had 'done a waffle' in the first-floor wet room, which involved defecating into the shower grill and, well, she couldn't bear to think of the rest. Vera the maid had been forced to clear it up. Simone had been appalled, but all Brian did was to roll his eyes and chuckle, 'Boys will be boys.'

Not on her watch, they wouldn't. Emily and Lysander were begging for a smack of discipline; if they were her own, they wouldn't get away with a second of it.

But they're not yours, are they?

And now you're a dried-up old husk. Barren. Shrivelled. Sterile.

Simone swallowed hard. She put her hand on the bathroom doorknob and stopped, watching her hand, focusing on it, because when she thought of that time, of that secret, it stole her breath away and it was all she could do to keep standing.

It wasn't like that. I had no choice.

Emily's tirade shattered her thoughts. '*I hate you!*'

Simone tore open the door. 'What the hell is this?' she demanded.

'Oh, perfect,' sang Emily, who privately loved Simone getting involved because that meant she could access her favoured armoury: the 'you're-not-my-mother' diatribe. 'Now your little bitch on the side is coming to tell me off.'

'Emily, no!' objected Brian, who was sweating. 'You mustn't say that!'

'Bloody well let me go to the party, Dad, or I'll say a lot worse.'

For a pretty girl, Emily Chilcott made an ugly mess of herself. Her permanent scowl erased the loveliness of her blue eyes, and her filthy mouth better belonged on a black-toothed hooker than an heiress to London's greatest film dynasty. She was attractive, but her attitude made her a grim proposition. The same went for Lysander. Since their mother had left Brian for a female German show jumper named Trudi (a well-publicised scandal ten years ago), it had all gone tits up: all four tits up, if you thought of it that way. Brian's *laissez-faire* attitude was one big long apology, and the kids took every advantage of it. When would he grow a ball-sack, for heaven's sake?

Simone met Emily's glare and raised it several notches. She would not lose.

'Don't you dare speak to me like that, madam.'

'Screw you, *Simone*.'

'You shut that mouth right now or I'll shut it for you!'

'Oh yeah?'

'With pleasure.'

Brian stepped in. 'Now, now, ladies…'

'Lysander's allowed to do whatever the fuck he wants,' raged Emily. 'He's in his room this minute getting high off his nuts and neither of you two gives a shit.'

'He's doing *what*?' Simone stormed into the hallway. Behind, Brian crooned, 'OK, let's everyone take it easy…'

Simone headed for Lysander's room and threw open the door. But the sight that met her eyes wasn't of Lysander—handsome, dark, rangy Lysander, with a curl to his spoiled, upper-class lip—skinning a joint or bent over one of his elaborate bongs; it was Lysander, butt-naked, reclining against his pillows and receiving a dedicated blow job from a redhead. Simone's lips parted in shock. She didn't know where to look. Lysander was coming hard. His eyes met hers as he ejaculated into the redhead's mouth. In the corridor, Emily giggled. 'Oops,' she trilled, 'my mistake!'

Post-climax, Lysander was unfazed. 'All right… Mummy?'

Lysander's accent was so sharp you could skewer cubes of meat on it.

'What on earth is going on?' Simone rasped. The redhead jerked up, clocked their audience and flung herself off the bed. She grappled for her clothes, her breasts jiggling as she tried and failed to cover her modesty. From the front Simone saw she was older than Lysander—quite a bit older, in fact. Lysander lit a cigarette.

Simone fought to keep her eyes off Lysander's dying erection. He made no attempt to conceal it. It was huge. Why couldn't Brian share *that* family trait?

'You're disgusting!' Mortified, Simone turned on her heel. 'Do not touch me, Brian!' She flapped him off. 'Whatever you do, *do not bloody touch me*!'

Before she disappeared back inside the master suite, she heard Emily wheedle: 'So, Daddy, can I *please* go to the party? See, I'm not as bad as 'Sander…'

And, predictably, depressingly, Brian's castrated consent.

*

'I just don't understand why you can't take control of them more!'

In the back seat of a blacked-out Mercedes rushing through Piccadilly, Brian placed a hand on his wife's knee. Simone resisted the urge to recoil against the window: after all, they soon had to put on a convincing show for the cameras.

'I try,' he said pathetically. 'You know how strong-willed they are.'

'Or how weak-willed you are.'

'They're yours, too, you know.' Brian said it as if he were sharing a prized chain of Umbrian holiday homes, not a host of cancerous growths in the armpit.

This time, she did flinch. 'They already have a mother.'

'But only one stepmother.'

God, it made her sound like some gnarled old thing in *Cinderella*. Oh, for a child of her own! Simone dreamed of it night and day. A girl—yes, a daughter, it had to be a daughter—whom she could mould in her own image. The girl would be her legacy, her gift to the world long after Simone's own legend died. She would raise her as the ravishing, well-mannered, and impeccably groomed young lady that Emily Chilcott wasn't and never could be. Simone wished for this immaculate creature so fervently that she thought she might explode. Yes, she had fame. Yes, she had riches. Yes, she had a wardrobe, and a stylist, and an army of fans that could topple the fucking monarchy, but all she yearned for was that most prized possession: a girl.

It would never happen. Simone was biologically unable, even before the first flushes of menopause. She hadn't always been. No, it hadn't always been that way…

'Here we are, baby,' said Brian, as they pulled up at the red carpet.

Their driver opened the door and the wall of sound that crashed in almost knocked her off her feet. Simone gripped her clutch and pasted on a smile. Cameras flashed and sparked. 'Simone! Brian! Let's see a kiss for the fans!' And so on.

Simone had picked out her outfit personally, a Versace emerald-green drape dress with scoop neckline. Everyone said that, after forty, one should cover one's décolletage, but Simone disagreed. She hadn't been using five-hundred-pound face and neck creams the last twenty years for nothing.

'You look tired.' Michelle Horner, Simone's manager and one of the most cutthroat women in the business, stole her at the end of the press queue. Simone had always thought Michelle resembled a whippet, especially tonight, in a grey trouser suit and pumps, her nose appearing even longer under the lighting. Michelle wore glasses on the end of her nose, amplifying the effect. 'All OK on the home front?'

'Same old.'

They entered the atrium, where champagne was circulating. Heads turned. In certain spheres Simone was known as The Ice Queen. She wasn't sure where or how she had picked that up, but it was certainly an easier façade to maintain than the poor joke-a-minute suckers who had cultivated a comedy precedent and had to spend the rest of their days working the room like a court buffoon.

'Terry Sheehan wants you for *January Fight*,' Michelle was saying. 'I told him we'd consider the script but it would have to be something special what with the Jonasses ringing off the hook and Sindy Reinhold at Paramour calling every hour of the day. I said, "Terry, we're not getting out of bed in the morning for less than ten, and if you don't like it you can bite me." Between you and me, he'll be scrabbling in his toilet bowl for coins. This is a waiting game and we'll wait.'

Simone was only half paying attention. Across the space, a fellow forty-something actress had arrived. The woman was single, attractive if not ragingly successful, and in her arms she carried a gorgeously sweet black baby boy.

'Where'd she get that from?' Simone cut in.

Michelle followed her gaze. 'The kid?'

'Of course the kid—I thought her husband ran off with that bit of fluff.'

'He did. She wanted a child, though. So she adopted.'

Simone narrowed her eyes. That sounded awfully simple. 'Is it awfully simple?'

'For ordinary people, I shouldn't think so. For her, maybe.'

'Where do you get them from?'

'That one came from Africa.'

'The internet? Are they in a catalogue or something?'

Michelle stepped back. 'You're not considering it, surely,' she said.

'Why not?'

'What does Brian think?'

Right then, Simone couldn't give a hooting crap what Brian thought. *He* wouldn't know what it was like to go through life with no child to call her own. *He* wouldn't understand. As with all else in their marriage, Simone would make the decision herself and then she would inform him of it. His opinion mattered not a jot. 'Michelle, I want you to look into it for me.'

Michelle was used to dealing with her clients' whims—this one would blow over in a week. 'OK,' she agreed. 'Do you want a brown one?'

'No.'

'A Chinese one? '

'No.'

'Mexican? Filipino?'

'I'm not ordering a goddamn takeaway. I don't know.'

'I'll get you some information.'

'Good. This could be the missing piece, Michelle. It really could.'

Brian joined them. On a happy impulse, Simone leaned in to kiss his cheek. A passing paparazzo captured the moment. 'Hello, baby,' he said, chuffed.

Hello, baby…

Except it wouldn't be a baby. She had her own reasons for that. It would be a child. Hello to the child who was somewhere out there, halfway across the world, waiting to be plucked from poverty to riches, from obscurity to the spotlight, from nothing to having it all. What little girl wouldn't want that?

She smiled. It would happen—and soon.

For, when Simone Geddes put her mind to something, she did not fail.

4

Argentina

In the autumn, without explanation, Señorita Gonzalez was fired. Diego appeared to make the decision overnight, and Calida didn't dare question it—except to her sister.

'What happened?' she whispered.

'I don't know.'

'Do you think he found out what she was really like?'

'Maybe. Who cares? She's gone now.'

Teresita was flicking through one of their mama's romance novels. Calida frowned: she could read her twin just as easily as the words on the page.

'You know something,' she said. 'About Gonzalez—I can tell.'

'No, you can't. You don't know everything about me.'

'I know you can't actually *like* those books. Come on, *A Prince's Affair*?'

Teresita bristled. 'What's wrong with them?' she countered.

Calida could list the reasons from the covers alone—plastic men in open shirts with chests like dolls, smooth and hairless, and bright white teeth; how Julia swooned over their aeroplanes and chunky watches and forgot about the life that was right here in front of her. Calida thought the books looked like nonsense, but she didn't say so, because she didn't want to prove her twin right. They *did* know everything about each other—and in that case Calida didn't need to explain what she disliked, nor Teresita what she enjoyed, so it seemed safer to walk away, and to try not to think about what Teresita was keeping from her, and why she hid it so deep, out of sight.

*

A month later, the girls were watching television in the barn when the phone rang.

Calida went through to the house. She lifted the receiver. 'Hello?'

The voice on the line sounded far away. It was a woman.

'*Es la policía,*' it said. 'My name is Officer Puerta and I need to speak with Julia, wife of Diego Santiago. Is that her?'

*

They manoeuvered Julia into the back of the Landrover with difficulty: she hadn't taken the car out in years and professed to have forgotten how—and besides, how could she operate a vehicle at a time like this? She was a wife in crisis.

'My husband,' she kept gasping. 'What's happened to my husband?'

'We have to get to him, Mama,' said Calida. She was terrified but she couldn't show it. She had to stay strong. She helped her sister into the passenger seat and held her hand. 'Don't worry,' she told her firmly. 'It will be all right.' Teresita gazed back at her with a stoic expression, and it was an expression Calida couldn't decipher. She couldn't find a way into it. It closed on her as firmly as the car door.

Calida had driven on the shrubland before, but never on the roads and never without Diego. She crunched the gears as they rocked and bucked down the pot-holed drive, and she tried to remember what her papa had taught her about checking her mirrors and coordinating her feet. It helped to hear his voice, guiding her.

Please be OK, Papa. Please, please be OK.

Eventually, they met the highway. Vehicles rushed past at speed. When a gap opened in the traffic she set the Landrover in motion and immediately stalled, trapping them across the oncoming lane. '*Move!*' screamed Julia from the back.

Calida floored the gas and the car lurched forward. Car horns screeched. The wheel spun in her fingers and she grappled for control, finally setting them straight.

She followed the police officer's directions. Everything was alien, sinister. Thoughts whirled as she turned south to the waterfront. Mauve clouds streaked the sky over the town lake. Calida could see the pulsing red beams from the police vehicles and the lump in her throat swelled.

You're going to be OK. You have to be OK.

In her heart, though, she knew.

All her life her father had been a rock, as solid and constant as the mountains of home—but lately, he hadn't been right. Since Gonzalez had left, Diego had become unpredictable, suspicious, checking up on the girls, calling them trouble, shouting at them for the tiniest thing. What had happened? What had changed? Once, he would never have left them at night while he went to town. Now, it happened more often than not. She had listened at the door while her mama spoke to Officer Puerta, watching Julia's knuckles grow paler by the second. There had been an accident.

They reached the blockade: a ribbon of tape, police talking grimly into their radios, and, beyond that, into the dark, dense fog of the night, a shape she couldn't make out and didn't want to see. Calida brought the car to a stop. They opened the doors and climbed out. Calida attempted to be close to her sister but her sister didn't want to be close. Instead, Teresita wrapped her arms round herself and turned away. Calida swallowed a lump of sadness. *I need you*, she thought. *Don't you need me?*

A woman saw their approach and crossed the tape.

'Come with me,' she told Julia. 'The girls stay here.'

Teresita was watching the police lights. 'What's happened to Papa?'

'I don't know.'

'Is he dead?'

The question stalled Calida. She knew the word that wanted to form on her tongue, the natural, logical word, but she couldn't bring herself to say it.

Calida would reflect on that moment and the tormented days that followed as frozen segments in time, as still and silent as the images on her camera. Diego pinned against the tree, the brief, ruthless frame of his body before he'd been covered; Julia with a handkerchief to her face, crying for him or for herself; Teresita refusing to weep, even once, and refusing her sister's sympathy and shutting herself away.

It transpired that Diego had been drinking. Not just that night but every night before. Calida didn't understand why. Her papa was a responsible man—not a drunk who got smashed in a bar and walked out into the middle of the road in front of a truck and got hit so hard his lungs collapsed and his heart stopped beating.

Diego had been her compass, her anchor and her ally. Now, he was gone.

Calida mourned him quietly and alone. Her mama's door remained closed.

*

'Are you awake?' she whispered into the dark.

Weeks later, in bed, listening to her twin's sleeping breath, Teresa shivered. She thought of her papa picking her up when she was five and swinging her over his shoulder, tickling her until she screamed with laughter. Tears sprang to her eyes.

You killed him. You have to live with that for the rest of your life.

Guilt and confusion hounded her every minute.

Papa died because of me.

Teresa had pushed him to it. In telling her father what she knew, she had set the wheels in motion. She had watched his face fall, heard his pleas not to tell her twin, delighted when he'd dismissed Gonzalez. She'd enjoyed that he spent more time in the bars, away from the farm and away from Calida. She hadn't considered that his shame had turned him into an addict, or that he would wind up killing himself.

How was she to know that?

'Are you awake?' She tried again.

Silence came back at her. Perhaps, if it hadn't, she would have told Calida the truth. Her sister would have kissed her and told her she wasn't to blame—it would all be OK; they would get through it together. But there the silence was, cold and accusing. Teresa sat and climbed down the ladder, her feet meeting the floor, pale toes against dark wood. Her nightdress was thin and her legs were bare. She crept into Calida's bunk and lay down next to her, felt the heat of her sister's body, and put an arm round her slumbering shape, using the other to pull the blanket up to her chin.

Calida moaned as a freezing ankle touched hers.

A yawn, a sigh, then nothing. Sleep.

Teresa longed for the same oblivion. She snuggled into her twin's back and held hard, thinking if she held hard enough they could be close again, like they had been when they were little. Everything seemed so complicated these days. It wasn't simple, like it used to be, when all that mattered was each other. She had kept her father's secret because she'd been scared—and then because she had wanted to shelter Calida in the way Calida had always sheltered her; she hadn't wanted her sister to lose faith, like she had, in the only man in their life. But the more time passed, the deeper this wedge drove—a point of divergence on the cusp of adolescence. Teresa inhaled her sister's skin, a scent she would never lose because it lingered on her own body, and wished she were more like Calida. She had thought she was doing the right thing in getting rid of Gonzalez—but since when had she been any good at that? Calida was the one who did the right thing, who fixed, mended, and made better.

Since Diego's death, Calida had set to with grit and purpose while Teresa hung back, thinking, *I'm twelve. I don't want this to be my life.*

Every time she looked at Calida, she saw her own failings—at having robbed them of their papa, at not wanting to stay and toil, at wishing she could be far away from their home—and the reasons why Calida would always be the better twin.

At last, she withdrew from the covers and left the safety of her sister's side. For a moment she stood alone in the gloom, the boards scratchy beneath her feet. Through the window, the gate at the foot of the track seemed alive, pulsing in the moonlight, lit up like a pearl. She returned to her own bed, her heart thundering.

I'll get away from here one day. I'll make Mama proud. I'll be rich and successful and all the things she wants me to be. Then I'll have done something right.

Comforted by this, Teresa reached for *Fortune's Lover* and

read it beneath the blankets for a while, until her arm started to ache from holding the torch.

When at last she surrendered to sleep, the story grasped for her unconscious and, in her dreams, she walked through the farm gate and kept on walking.

She dreamed of billionaires and red carpets, of palaces and yachts, of sparkling blue swimming pools and satin purses stuffed with notes.

She dreamed of the elusive heroes of her mother's novels, their shirts crisp and parted at the collar. So unlike any of the men she had encountered, these men were of a different breed, exotic and treacherous and holding out for her.

5

He arrived on a day in July, when the sky and earth and everything in between was enhanced, as if she was looking at it through her camera lens and could draw it into sharper focus. All week they had drowned in a storm—angry, grinding clouds dousing the soil and filling the lakes—and now it had cleared the air was silver-fresh.

Calida was inside. The door, loose on its hinges, trembled gently within its frame. She heard him before she saw him— the heavy bag that fell from his shoulders and hit the soil, the deep, single cough—and the sound of a man took her by surprise. It was a year since Diego's death. At first, illogically, she thought it might be him.

'Hello,' she said, stepping on to the porch.

The stranger was standing at the wooden gate, his back to her. Paco the horse was nuzzling the palm of his hand, and the way he leaned into the animal, and the animal into him, struck Calida as secretive and rare. When he turned, she caught it in stages: the lifting head, the profile, the crease in one cheek as he smiled. He was in front of the sun, making his hair blonder and his face darker, though his eyes shone like bursts of blue water on the arid steppe. He was taller than her, lean and muscular. He wore a grey T-shirt, the kind that's been used so much it becomes soft to touch, and faded blue jeans. The jeans were tucked into cow-leather gaucho riding boots.

'Señorita Santiago?'

He had a sure voice. Paco responded to it, nudging the stranger with his muzzle. A weird thing was happening to Calida's tongue. It seemed soldered to the roof of her mouth. She tried to unstick it.

'I'm here for the work,' he explained. 'I saw your ad.'

On her mama's instruction, Calida had pasted the fliers up months ago. Calida wasn't sure what she had expected—certainly not for someone to turn up out of nowhere, without warning, someone who looked like this: certainly not *him*.

'My name's Daniel Cabrera.' He put out his hand.

She experimented with the words in her head. The surname sounded like a kiss and a dance, maybe both at once. She took his hand. It was cool and strong.

'I got talking with Señor Más at the market and he said you were still looking for help. I figured it was better to come straight out here and meet you in person...'

She nodded. *Speak, for God's sake! Say anything!*

'I'm Calida,' she offered at last.

Daniel's smile widened. She guessed he was seventeen, maybe eighteen. His forearms arrested her—the colour of them: a deep tan; and powerful—on the outside was a scattering of light, fair hair, and on the tender skin closest to his body a strong vein was visible. His wrists were thick, and around one he wore a leather band.

'Your home is amazing,' he said.

'*Gracias.*'

'It's quite the legend in town, Calida.' How come no one else could make her name sound like that? 'People look out at

this land. They can't believe one family owns it all. It would
be a privilege to be out here every day, with you.'

Every day... with you... Calida blushed. Her eyes darted
to the ground.

'Beautiful horses,' he said. 'I used to work on an *estancia*
in the south—rides for tourists, that kind of thing. I grew up
with animals—they're my family.'

Calida struggled for something to say. If Teresita were here,
she'd have no trouble talking. 'What about your real family?'
she blurted, and instantly knew she'd said the wrong thing.
Daniel's face, formerly so open and friendly, fell into shadow.

'They live in Europe,' he said. 'Where I'm from.'

'Oh.' There was a pause.

He was looking directly at her. 'Calida, is your mother in?'

Just like that, the illusion of her maturity was shattered. Of
course Daniel saw her as a kid: she was only thirteen, even if
sometimes she felt twice that age.

'She's indoors,' said Calida. 'I'll take you to her.'

He smiled a smile she would carry with her forever.
'Thanks,' he said.

*

Daniel Cabrera got the job. Julia took one look at him and
hired him on the spot.

'A good solid man about the place,' she said, brushing her
hair for the first time in weeks. Calida noticed how her mama's
eyes lit up when Daniel walked in, and how she kept playing
with her hair and erupting into light, tinkling laughs.

'She likes him,' Calida confided in her sister.

Teresita was unfazed. 'You're only mad because you like
him too...'

'I do not!'

'Liar.'

'*Cállate*, shut up!'

'I've seen how red you go.' Teresita put on a silly voice and danced around: '*Oh, Daniel, you're so handsome! You're so perfect! I think I love you, Daniel!*'

Calida smiled in spite of herself. 'You're an idiot.' But she couldn't help her blush—and she couldn't think of anything else to say except to repeat her protest, but the more she repeated it, the more it exposed that Teresita was right. Daniel Cabrera occupied her thoughts twenty-four hours a day. Whenever she was alone, she pictured his arms around her, his golden head bowed to hers and his warm breath on her neck. They stayed like that in her imagination, just still, unsure how the moment moved on. Calida felt there was more, but it was reckless and adult and she didn't understand it, and to feel his embrace, if only in her mind, was, for the moment, enough.

But it wasn't Julia she should have been afraid of. It was her twin.

'Daniel should move into the outhouse,' said Teresita, after supper one night.

She delivered the suggestion with a careful insouciance that immediately rang alarm bells. Calida looked up, tried to find a way into her sister's countenance but, as happened so often lately, she could not. Her heart quickened. Teresita took a tight sip of her drink and in that moment she knew. She didn't know how she knew, but she did. They had been twins too long. Her sister wanted him, too.

'There's running water out there,' Teresita went on, 'and he could come up to the house for food. I'd like to have him close all the time... Wouldn't you, Calida?'

Teresita's eyes met hers, but, instead of the reassurance she'd been hoping for—that the proposition was for Calida's

benefit, a selfless act made in knowledge of her devotion—
instead she met a dead-on challenge. Teresita's gaze was one
of sheer resolve. *Turns out I'm into him. What are you going
to do about it?*

'That's a wonderful idea,' said Julia.

Calida swallowed her distress. She stood and cleared the
bowls. All night she refused to talk to Teresita, or even look
at her. 'What's wrong?' her sister asked. 'Are you angry with
me?' But Calida couldn't form her accusation. Teresita would
deny it, in any case; say she'd imagined it. But Calida knew
better. She had seen the confrontation in her sister's regard,
the glint of cunning. It made her want to give up, because if
she were ever pitted against Teresita in a game of love, she
knew who would win. Her twin was magnificent, and she was
ordinary. It was as simple as that.

*

And so it happened. Over the coming months, Daniel became
part of the ranch, as integral to Calida as the horses and the
mountains and the sunset. Slowly but surely, she fell in love
with him. She loved the fact he only spoke when there was
something to say. She loved his smile, which seemed to find
humour not just in the joke but in a private comedy that existed
only between them. She loved his focus as he worked. She
loved his passion. She loved his strength. She loved his silhouette as he rode off into the dust, the black shape of his cowboy
hat and his boots upturned in the stirrups.

She loved how he taught her bareback riding; and when
they went together to retrieve a wild pony that had strayed
from their neighbour's land, he showed her how to capture the
animal and rein her in, bucking and twisting, until she calmed.

Once, Calida witnessed him showering. It was dawn, and

he wouldn't have expected them to be up yet. She watched from her window, her blood pounding.

Daniel used an outdoor steel tub, a bar of soap, and a hose connected to a hand-driven pump. He removed his T-shirt. His chest elicited in her a confusion of feelings: desire at the map of taut, bronzed muscle, and the trail of hair that vanished into his jeans, but also a sharp tug somewhere deeper and more affectionate. She felt that she knew him, every part of him, even though she hadn't met those parts yet. She saw him as a stallion, wounded by a past encounter, untamed and untrusting, but that she might whisper to him and find she could gain that trust, and it would be a gem far rarer than the rarest treasure in the deepest well in the most distant part of the earth.

He pumped the handle, tendons in his back rippling, and the water came quick and hard. He bent over the basin, head bowed, and his hair turned light to dark.

Only when his hands went to his jeans and he started to unbuckle them did Calida look away, pulling the material over the window. Part of her wanted to peel it back and see, but the other part was stronger. It knew that one day it would be her hands on Daniel's jeans, her unbuckling, and she would wait patiently for that day because it would be perfect, and that as fast as she undid him he would be undoing her, unravelling and unravelling until she was a spool of silk in his fingers.

*

December arrived, and with it the first flush of summer.

In the kitchen, Teresita was up, already dressed in her riding gear. The sisters never went riding without the other, and Calida asked: 'Where are you going?'

'Cattle herding,' said her twin, as if this were something she did alone every day. Calida heard Daniel getting the horses

ready in the yard, and, in her own nightshirt, felt panicked
and unprepared.

'I'll come too.'

'We'll be fine on our own.'

Daniel came in. He smiled when he saw Calida. 'Ready?'

'Calida's not coming,' said Teresita.

'Actually, I am.' She recalled her sister's defiance over the
supper table and a flash of anger spurted in her chest. 'You'll
wait for me, won't you?' she asked him.

His smile widened. 'Sure.'

'It's a stupid idea.' Teresita scowled, folding her arms.

'I think it's a good idea,' said Daniel.

*

By nine o'clock they were crossing the steppe. The wilderness
was dotted with beech forests and glittering rivers. Calida
was uncomfortable on Diego's old *criollo*, and, despite the
extra sheepskin she had piled on top of the saddle, she lagged
behind.

All morning she was forced to watch Teresita up ahead,
riding alongside Daniel, as if it were just the two of them.

Approaching midday, the heat became searing. Dust swirled
in their eyes and nostrils, and they tied scarves around their
faces to ward off the worst. The horses' hooves picked a path
between rocks and boulders. Calida saw Daniel finish an apple
then lean forward, deep over his animal's mane, to feed him
the remains. When they stopped to rest, he tethered the horses
in the shade and, before fetching a drink for himself, he filled
a bucket with water from the stream and poured it gently over
their heads, working it through their coats and removing the
metal bits from between their teeth. Calida wished her father
were here, because Diego would have liked Daniel.

The herd was on the other side of the valley and they rode hard to reach it in the light. Mustering was one of her favourite things: the rush of the cattle as they swarmed across the plains and the beat of their tread echoing across the land; the chase the horses gave as they circled the drive—and how, when the job was done, the beasts poured like water through a funnel into the next prairie. When night came, they set up camp in a sheltered vale, by the remains of a fire all ash and dust from their last visit.

Daniel warmed *empanadas*, and cooked an *estofado* stew, which he prepared on a wooden board. The handle of his *facón* was silver and intricately carved, and Calida decided it was of personal importance to him—a gift, perhaps—and remembered the family he had mentioned, so briefly, in Europe. Who were they?

After they had eaten, Daniel lit a cigarette and lay back on the arrangement of sheepskin and leather that would serve as his bed. His features danced in the flames. He let smoke out in a thin plume that shot deep into the night.

'Daniel, will you help me?'

Teresita was struggling to lift the saddle from the ground, caught up as it was in her stirrups and reins. Calida sat on a log, her chin on her knees, and watched.

'Here, like this,' he said. Teresita giggled. Calida glanced away.

'Should I set up next to you?' Teresita asked.

'It's the best shelter,' he replied. 'Better to be under the trees.'

'Better to be private…'

The voice Teresita said this in was older, more adult, than her thirteen years. From where had she got this way of speaking—their mama's books?

Daniel didn't respond, but then maybe he didn't need to. Maybe he was looking at Teresita in the way Calida prayed and hoped he would one day look at her.

Unable to bear it, she got into her own bed. Normally, staying overnight, she and her sister would share, warm safety in the reassuring shape of each other's bodies. Safety? All she thought now, when she thought of her twin, was danger. She wanted to scream: *What are you doing*? They were meant to be allies, not rivals.

A tear slid out of Calida's eye. If only Diego were still here. Everything had gone wrong after he'd died. Teresita wasn't the same girl she had been.

'Calida?' Daniel's voice interrupted her thoughts. 'Come sit with us?'

'I'm tired,' she replied, rolling over. Daniel wouldn't be able to trace the upset in her voice, but her sister would. A small, silly part of her expected Teresita to come and lie down next to her, squeeze her tight until she fell asleep like they'd used to do when one of them was sad. But the bed remained cold. Teresita stayed out in the night, a sovereign queen. She had never needed Calida in the way Calida needed her.

Over at the fire, she heard the slosh of a bottle passing between them, and talking, but mostly her sister talking. Whenever Daniel spoke she strained to hear, grasping after his words like a desert after a drop of rain. It was unfair, so unfair, that she should be shut out on account of her being plain, and nothing special, and nothing remarkable, or anything that would make Daniel look at her twice. She pictured Teresita flicking her long hair, cat eyes twinkling in the night. The bottle passed again, followed by the catch of a lighter as Daniel lit another cigarette, enjoying the evening and wishing to prolong it. Calida longed to block her ears in case she heard something she could never un-hear—or, worse, *stopped* hearing things, because that meant they might be, they could be... No, Daniel wouldn't. He wouldn't.

Above, the stars were out in force. A warm breeze shivered on the leaves. Calida thought of the photographs she had taken of Daniel, back on the farm, without him knowing, ones she would pore over in private. What had seemed romantic at the time now seemed desperate and hollow, paper wishes that would never come to anything. He would never look at her and think she was beautiful—not the kind of beauty Teresita possessed. That power would forever be beyond Calida's reach.

In a depressing instant, Calida's life rolled out ahead of her, as average as the face she saw whenever she looked in the mirror. She would always be behind the camera... never in front of it. Teresita was different. She was destined for more. And in her mind's horizon, before she drowned in sleep, Calida glimpsed the ship that was coming to take one of them away, sailing stealthily through the night towards them.

6

At fourteen, Teresa Santiago's body was changing. Her breasts were growing—now, when she put her hands on them, their fullness filled her palm. She compared them with Calida's, glimpsing her twin's flatter chest under a smock, and wondered why some girls had them and others didn't. Her legs were lengthening and her waist was shapely. There was hazy fuzz between her thighs. It reminded her of Señorita Gonzalez in the stables: the mysteries of the body that played on a loop in her mind.

Today, the house was empty. Teresa ventured into her mama's bedroom and sat at the dressing table. It was a claw-footed thing in eggshell-beige with an oval glass top: a relic from Julia's former life, and at odds with the austerity of the rest of the farm. Above the dresser was a mirror, mottled where it met its frame, and in it Teresa appraised her reflection, the effect uncanny because she looked so like Julia in her younger years that it could well have been the same person. She reached for a brush and ran it through her hair, black as coal and sheer as silk. Her eyes were green, wide, and Cleopatric, and her brows were thick. Her mouth was a Cupid's bow.

Your beauty will serve you well… Julia's voice reached her—or was it her own? *It will be the thing that gets you out of here.* She clung to it, her pass, her ticket to freedom: the one thing she had that was all hers, not her twin's, not anyone else's.

Her reflection gazed back at her for so long that she began to lose her grip on which was the real version—the one here or the one in the mirror.

Quickly, she left the room.

*

Calida wasn't speaking to her. Teresa understood why, but the further she climbed in, the deeper she dug, the harder it became to turn back. She was testing her beauty; how far it would take her and the currency it held—and Daniel would give her her answer.

Every time she felt bad about Calida, knowing how her sister adored him, she reminded herself of the many things Calida had taken from her. Forever being the one in control, telling Teresa what she could and couldn't do, always making the decisions and treating her like a child. Being the apple of their father's eye, the one people trusted and relied on and respected. Being born first: the eternal offence.

What did Teresa have? Her looks. They were all she had.

Many times she wanted to forget the whole thing, say sorry to Calida and go back to how they were. But then she thought of the cracks in their companionship, and the glaring rift where she had kept the facts of their father's death to herself. Teresa felt wronged by it, made to protect his affair and then watch him die and feel responsible for it. Calida hadn't had to go through that, had she? Her memories of Diego were untainted. Teresa carried the burden and resented her sister for it.

Moreover, her father and Gonzalez had proven one unambiguous truth: that there was no justice, no integrity when it came to love. In an adult world, it was every person for herself: a question of survival. Realising that was just part of growing up.

Friday night, she made a decision. Daniel was in town—she had overheard him making arrangements to meet at *Luz de Las Estrellas*.

Teresa prepared carefully: her best outfit, lashings of mascara, high heels she had practised walking in. Finally ready, she stumbled into the kitchen—only to find that Calida had beaten her to it. Her sister was in the process of sneaking out of the door. Calida's face was painted with lipstick and eye shadow, badly applied, and with a pang Teresa thought of the dozens of times their mama had taught her to put on make-up and had never done the same for Calida. 'Where are you going?' she asked.

Calida was defiant. 'To find Daniel.'

'Oh. So am I.'

Calida broke out and went ahead down the lane. Teresa followed, seeing her twin's balled fists and tight shoulders and feeling sorry but at the same time proud.

Finally, here was something she could take control of. A judgement she alone could make. Besides, why was it fair that Calida got Daniel all to herself? Did she feel entitled, because she was older? Did that mean Teresa deserved only scraps for the rest of her life? In truth, she had no feelings for Daniel. He was a gaucho, not a billionaire, and he had Calida's soul, the soul of the ranch, the soul of Argentina…

Her own soul felt confused.

But she had to know if he liked her. If beauty was everything Julia vowed it was. Daniel was a test, the results of which decided her survival in the outside world.

The moon was whole in the sky, illuminating the track that led the half-mile to the highway. When they reached the road,

Calida looked like an abandoned child, shivering in her skirt and top, her arms wrapped round her waist.

'How are you going to get there?' Teresa asked.

'I'll think of something. I don't need you.'

Teresa put her arm out to hail a car. Calida slapped it down.

'Someone will stop!'

'That's the idea.'

It wasn't long before a truck pulled over.

'Hi.' Teresa leaned in the window. She looked older than she was: they could easily have been sixteen-year-old friends on a night out. 'Give us a ride?'

'Jump right in.'

She slid on to the back seat. Calida hesitated, before cutting her losses and joining her. The girls sat as far apart as possible, Calida staring resolutely out of the window at nothing, hating every perilous moment but unwilling to allow her sister to go alone. The man driving was middle-aged, with thinning hair. He wore a beige shirt and slacks. Teresa couldn't see his face, only his darting eyes in the rear-view mirror.

'Where you headed?' he asked as the car pulled away.

'*Las Estrellas*,' Teresa answered.

The man sneered. 'You old enough?'

'We're eighteen.'

His eyebrow lifted. 'Right,' he said. 'Something the matter with your *amiga*?'

'She's shy.'

'You're the chatty one,' he said. 'I like that.'

Teresa took her eyes from the man's. Her heart was beating like crazy. The way the man ogled her, like a bear in need of a meal. She could say or do anything and he would still want her. She could ask for anything and he would say yes.

Minutes later, their ride pulled up outside the club. Calida got out and slammed the door. The entrance was heaving. A crowd swigged from beer bottles, blowing smoke into the air. The deep, heady thrum of music leaked out to the street.

A guy on the door stepped forward. 'ID,' he demanded.

Teresa lifted her chin. 'I don't have mine. I'm eighteen.'

'Sure you are. ID, or you're not coming in.'

Teresa batted her lashes. 'Come on, give me a break…'

The man looked over her head to the next in line. Scowling, Teresa stepped to the side. Just as she was working out a Plan B she saw Daniel Cabrera emerge from the club, his arm round an attractive blonde. Behind her, Calida stiffened, appalled at the notion he had a girlfriend. Teresa stalked over without a backward glance.

'Hi,' she said.

Daniel was shocked. 'What are you doing here?' Then: 'Calida? Is that you?'

Teresa sensed rather than saw her sister approach. She stood her ground. 'We came separately,' she said.

'Does Julia know?'

'She doesn't need to know.'

'Hey, Dani, what's going on?' The blonde came over.

'Nothing,' Daniel said, stepping away from her.

'Who are they?'

'Girls I work with.'

'Shit, what are they, like twelve?'

'Too young to be out, that's for sure.'

Teresa glared. 'I'm still here, you know. I can hear just fine.'

'Well, you shouldn't be here,' Daniel said. His voice softened somewhat when he addressed Calida. 'I'm surprised you did this, Calida,' he said. 'You should have known better. Why did you bring your sister with you?'

Teresa wanted to scream. *Why do they have to treat me like a baby?*

All Calida did was to grimly lift her shoulders—and then, to everyone's embarrassment but most of all her twin's, a sob broke out of its carefully assembled cage. Calida sniffed and wiped her eyes, trying to contain it so nobody would notice.

Daniel extricated himself from the blonde and pulled her into a hug. Teresa heard her sobs honking against his sweater. Daniel held the back of Calida's neck tenderly, and the blonde became agitated. 'Are we going or not?' she said irritably.

Calida drew away. 'I'm sorry,' she muttered. 'I just… I'm sorry.' Her face was blotchy with tears and humiliation and the wound of an exploded dream.

Daniel led his girlfriend away and began speaking to her intently. The girlfriend sighed, rolled her eyes, then turned on her heel and went back inside.

'Come on,' he told the sisters, 'we're going home.'

'We don't have any money,' said Calida. She sounded utterly dejected.

'It's a good job I do, then, isn't it?'

On the ride back to the farm, they barely spoke. Calida was curled against the window. Teresa wondered if she was asleep, and leaned into the front so that her mouth was inches from Daniel's shoulder and she could smell the smoky scent coming off him. 'You won't tell Mama, will you?' she whispered.

Daniel waited a moment before responding. When he did, he reached into the back and touched Calida's knee. Perhaps he thought she was the one who'd asked it.

'I won't tell,' he said.

7

'Money,' said Simone Geddes' manager, as they took a car from the airstrip and began the long drive through northern Patagonia, 'plain and simple. Once we show these people the kind of cash we're carrying, it's a free pass straight to your kid.'

Simone opened her diamond-encrusted compact and reapplied SOS lip cream. Travel made her horribly dehydrated, and the trip from London had been exhausting; first the city-hop to Amsterdam, then the fourteen hours to Buenos Aires, then the final leg to this deadbeat part of the world that looked as if it had never seen a car on four wheels, let alone a Range Rover Lumma CLR with built-in sound system and a sun roof that allowed Simone's headscarf to whip prettily in the breeze.

'Well,' she turned to Michelle, 'I trust you know what you're doing.'

'Naturally. I've had my contacts working round the clock on this for over a year, Simone. I don't make mistakes.'

'I'm aware of that.' Simone lit one of her super-slim menthols—she was trying to give up, but these hardly counted. 'That's why you're my manager.'

Michelle Horner delivered a tight smile, the equivalent of a raucous laugh from an ordinary person, and consulted her papers. She passed a file to Simone.

'Six daughters, the right age, and a nice spread of light and dark.'

'I'd like one with dark hair.'

'I meant skin tone.' Michelle tapped a sharp red fingernail on the photo, which showed half a dozen grinning tweens holding hands on a farm. They looked poor, but happy. 'We've got everything from mocha to cappuccino.'

'I feel like I'm buying a puppy!' Simone trilled joyously.

'With any luck this one won't pee all over your floors.'

Simone flicked ash out of the window. Some of it blew back on her and without needing to be asked the driver activated the rear-seat ashtray; a crystal plate slid smoothly from the leather footrest. Simone tapped her cigarette into it.

'So, which has your vote?' Michelle asked.

'Hmm, I'm not sure. Maybe the one in the middle.'

'That's my favourite, too.'

'They're a bit scrawny, aren't they? Will they grow into their looks? It's important, Michelle. This girl is going to be my ambassador, among other things.'

'I understand that,' Michelle replied. 'I even had one of those photo-fit experts draw up estimates of what they'll be like in ten years' time, like they do for missing people.' She handed the printouts to Simone. 'Feast your eyes on this.'

Simone consulted the images. She thought they all looked a bit creepy, to be honest: half botched cosmetic surgery victim, half low-budget drag act.

She turned to gaze out at the sprawling rustic geography. *Argentina.* Who would have thought it when, all those months ago, she and Michelle had spoken of adoption for the first time? Since then Michelle had been true to her word. She had dispatched the finest team to every corner of the globe in search of treasure. After countless meetings, endless back and forth, and a spate of ugly arguments with Brian, who couldn't understand any of it and refused to try, Simone had settled on South America. She desired an exotic-looking daughter. The girl had to be poor, because poverty would make her grateful: Simone wanted to be thanked for this. They had narrowed their quest to an *estancia* on the Pampas, and a single father with six children to feed and not two pesos to rub together. Simone would be their saviour.

'Aren't our children enough?' Brian had complained, the day she'd told him.

Simone had bitten her tongue—hard. Never mind the fact that Emily and Lysander weren't hers, they were *hideous*. Especially Lysander, who had possessed the nerve to pinch her bottom by the swimming pool last Friday, in front of all her friends and during the barbecue she had put on as a charity fundraiser. *Hey!* magazine had been covering the event and Simone could only imagine her flushed, affronted face, spicy sausage hanging between the grill tongs, as she'd opened and closed her mouth like a goldfish. Oh, she'd wanted to slap him! Too quick, Lysander had dived into the water.

'I need to do this, Brian,' she had said. 'For me.'

'This new one won't be yours either.' It wasn't like meek, mild Brian to take that toxic tone and Simone had been startled. She had almost liked it.

'It will be as close as I can get,' she replied.

Brian had stared her down for a moment, but Simone always won a stare-off and predictably her husband cowed, his shoulders rounding, before he skulked away. How could she expect him to understand? He didn't know. She'd never told him. No child would ever come from her womb because her womb was incapable.

Hostile, they'd informed her. A hostile womb. Cripes.

Michelle brought her back to the present. 'This family is going to get the shock of its life when we turn up,' she was saying smugly. 'We told them who you were but of course they'd barely even heard of the bloody Beckhams.'

'Gosh, it must be remote.'

The car was slowing. 'Are we there?' called Michelle.

Their driver pulled over. He consulted the GPS.

'José, is there a problem?'

The man didn't speak much English. 'We are lost,' he said eventually.

'Lost?' Michelle snapped. 'How can we be?'

'Ah no, it is right way.' The car started up again. Michelle and Simone exchanged sidelong glances. *Does he know what he's doing?* mouthed Simone. She had visions of being driven to a hilltop plateau and sacrificed like a mountain goat.

Michelle nodded curtly, but didn't take her hawk eyes off the wavering GPS.

'We've lost signal,' she said, throwing her hands in the air. 'Typical!'

José had the indicator on. They came off on to a dirt track.

'Is this it?' Simone enquired. She was tempted to light another cigarette, but it was so overheated inside the car that she feared something might explode.

'I do not know. We follow trail, ask at house.'

Before they could stop him, José climbed out of the car and opened the gate, tying it with rope to a knackered wooden post. The sun beat down. Simone sighed.

'I want my hotel, Michelle. I'm tired and I'm cranky. I knew it was a bad idea to do this on the day we arrived.'

'You know what I say: strike while the iron's hot.'

'Everything's hot. Too bloody hot.'

José jumped back in. The engine gunned. They had barely

set off when a crunching sound erupted from the belly of the car, quickly followed by a burst and a hiss, like a balloon deflating. 'What was that?' shrieked Simone.

'Tyre is gone,' said José. 'Problem with tyre.'

'So fix it!' Michelle roared. She wound up the windows and blasted the air-con, as poor José sweated and heaved outside, attempting to jack the vehicle's considerable weight. Michelle assaulted her phone for a moment, fishing for signal. The networks were down. Simone rolled her eyes. This was hardly shaping up to be the glamorous entrance she'd envisaged, sweeping into the beggars' idyll like a fairy godmother. This broken-down heap of trash was hardly the ball-bound pumpkin.

José was out there for forty-five minutes. The women became crotchety. Simone finished her bottle of Perrier then admitted to needing the loo.

'I can't go here, what if somebody sees?'

'We're in the middle of nowhere,' said Michelle.

'Yes: a completely flat, no-damn-bushes-in-sight nowhere. What about *him*?'

'José?'

'Of course José—whom else would I be talking about?'

But Michelle lifted a thin eyebrow and nodded through the windscreen.

'Our knight in shining armour,' she said. A man of about twenty was riding towards them on a horse. He came in a cloud of dust, his blond hair reflecting the sun. As he neared the Range Rover, his horse began circling and stamping its hooves.

José stood, and the men conversed in Spanish. The stranger climbed down, tied his horse to a shrub and came towards the car. He had a rugged, tanned face and startling blue eyes. The word *gaucho* ran through Simone's mind, and it had the same effect as someone pinching the tender skin on the underside of her arm.

Michelle opened the door. 'What's he saying?' she asked José.

'He say we get help at farm. We leave car here.'

'And walk? You're asking Simone Geddes to *walk*?'

The men exchanged something else, and laughed.

'May I ask what's funny?' Simone got out and slammed the door. She removed her headscarf and held it over her mouth: she had never been anywhere so dusty! Dust was rolling across the landscape; you could see it churning like tumbleweeds. 'I am perfectly capable of walking, thank you very much—is it far?'

José pointed to a shack in the distance.

'Right.' Simone began to pick her way delicately across the rocks. 'Let's go.'

*

It was dusk by the time they made it to the house. Simone's feet ached and she was so thirsty it was as if someone had spent the entire afternoon sandpapering the inside of her mouth. At Michelle's insistence she had been persuaded on to the horse, which she found horrifying, because all there was to hold on to was a knotted leather rein. The gaucho had to heave her into the saddle, if a lump of rags and sheep wool merited that description, pushing her backside as she attempted to get a leg over, and, as Simone hung there, close to tears, she thought it was just about the most undignified position she had ever been in. The horse smelled. The reins made her hands black.

She longed for the Kensington mansion. For once, she longed for Brian!

'We are here,' said José at last.

'And where exactly are we *meant* to be?' Michelle demanded through gritted teeth. José talked to the stranger before replying:

'He say this place we need to go is other side of mountain.'

'We have to cross a *mountain*?'

'*Sí*. I take wrong highway.'

'Tell me something I don't know. You're fired.'

'I sorry.'

'Just get me inside and to a goddamn telephone.' Michelle turned to her client. 'I'm getting straight on to the agency and they'll send someone out here ASAP—in a fucking helicopter if they have to.'

The gaucho helped Simone off the horse. This way was slightly less unseemly, but only just. He sort of caught her arse in both his hands, and her legs churned air like a first-time swimmer without armbands. She thanked him in English, only afterwards realising she should have done it in his language, and he grinned and didn't reply. God only knew what he was thinking.

Simone was being led inside when something happened. She was alert at first to the sound: a sweetly hummed tune, sung by an angel she couldn't yet see. And then the vision appeared—a girl of about fifteen materialised around the side of the house with the languid, cat-like indifference that was the hallmark of adolescence.

Simone gasped. The girl was hands-down the most ravishing creature she had ever encountered. Her hair was long and sleek, her limbs slender and brown. Her eyes were huge and inky, the lashes impossibly thick. Her mouth was a rose bud.

The girl stopped singing.

'Hello,' said Simone.

Another child, nowhere near as appealing though clearly

related, came in her wake. She, too, was brought up short at the sight of the uninvited guests.

The gaucho said something to them. Simone held a hand out to the prettiest and tried not to let the other one's glower put her off. The other one looked feral.

'*Hola,*' she stumbled, '*me llamo Simone. Soy de Inglaterra. Cómo se llama?*'

There was a long silence. *Gently does it*, thought Simone, unwilling to blow the chance now it had arrived so conveniently in her lap. To imagine they were never even supposed to have come to this godforsaken place! But this was it. Here. Now. The One. And she saw it all clearly. She understood what was meant to happen, starting with securing this girl's trust. Like coaxing a fox in from the cold.

'Teresa,' the girl replied, at last.

Simone inhaled and exhaled deeply. 'That's a pretty name.' She turned to Michelle. 'She's it,' she said.

Michelle attempted discretion even though it was doubtful their company understood. 'One thing at a time, Simone,' she hissed. 'Let's not get carried away.'

But Simone had never felt less carried away. She felt totally level headed, as if all she had done was to walk into a fate that had already been mapped for her. Teresa was the one. *She was it*! The beauty would be returning with her to London, even if Simone had to swim across the Atlantic with the child on her back, like a giant turtle.

The gaucho led them inside. The kitchen was painfully basic, with a single wooden table, an iron stove, and a collection of battered pots and pans that hung from a rafter in the ceiling. Heavens! How did people live like this? Simone thought of her own kitchen, with her diamond-granite worktops and Sub-Zero Pro fridge freezer.

A woman—their mother?—emerged from the hall. She was dressed in a tatty robe, her hair limp, and her eyes sunken. She and Simone appraised each other, across time, across continents; in another universe, the woman the other might have been.

José addressed her. '*Disculpa, señora, perdóname, pero puedo usar su fono?*' The woman listened to the gaucho for a moment before pointing hesitantly into the back. Michelle followed, accompanied by José, until Simone pulled him to her. 'You stay here,' she commanded. 'I need you to help me talk.'

The woman, who would once have been beautiful but whose embittered expression robbed her of any lingering shred, eyed her suspiciously.

'I have a proposition for you,' said Simone, after introductions had been made. The air in that hot, Patagonian kitchen, glowing amber from the melting sun, seemed to vibrate with anticipation. 'One that could change your life.'

8

Over supper that night, Julia was in an unusually good mood.

'What a wonderful person Simone Geddes was,' she kept saying. 'And such good fortune that they should stumble across our lowly abode! I'm only glad that we were able to help—those poor women, breaking down in the middle of nowhere…'

Calida ate quietly, while Teresita quizzed her. 'Is she rich?'

'Beyond our wildest dreams.'

'Is she famous?'

'Oh, yes,' Julia said. 'Simone's an actress. She lives in a mansion in England.' Their mother lifted her fork precisely to her mouth and chewed carefully. 'We're going to stay in touch and then I might have some exciting news to share with you.'

Teresita danced up and down in her seat. 'What news?' she pressed, while Calida stayed quiet. Their visitor had unnerved her. It was as if the woman had deposited a trick in her wake, a sting in the tail, a nasty surprise, the nature of which would not be apparent immediately but would soon reveal itself in a horrible, startling flourish.

Julia closed her eyes, as if with the effort of concealing a truth too thrilling to keep at simmering point. 'Simone wishes to offer one of you girls a special vacation,' she said, 'as a way of thanks. To stay with her in London over the English summer.'

Calida didn't know why her mother bothered to make it a mystery. Maybe she wasn't just embittered, maybe she was cruel too, and wanted to make Calida believe she had a chance at taking the prize before snatching it out of reach. Calida knew she would receive no invitation. Simone would prefer Teresita. Everyone preferred Teresita. Did Daniel prefer her? Ever since their disastrous trip into town, her twin had made it perfectly clear where her ambitions lay. Calida had been stupid to think she could pull off a stunt like that, anyway—chasing Daniel into a world she had no place in, not once stopping to think about his reaction, or whom he might be with, or what he would say. Teresita could wing these things, but she couldn't. It had been so unlike her, her silly attempt to be more like her sister, and see how it had backfired.

Perhaps it wouldn't be so bad if Teresita went away.

'I can't wait!' Teresita could scarcely contain her excitement. Calida had seen the way her sister had eyed Simone's jewellery, admired her gleaming car, envied her chic wardrobe and, at one point, salivated over the bulging wallet that the actress had laid down on the counter, fat with banknotes. This was what her twin desired.

Afterwards, Calida stayed behind to wash the dishes. She recalled a phrase her papa had used, as they had lingered outside the store in town for her photographs to be developed. He'd stroked her hair and said: *Good things come to those who wait.*

She couldn't help wondering if bad things did, too.

*

Later, when Julia had gone to bed, Calida sat on the veranda and gazed up at the stars. *Are you there, Papa? Are you with me?* If Diego were alive, he would be on her side. She wasn't even sure what battle she was fighting, but she knew he would be on her side. Now, it seemed as if everything was slipping from her grasp, too fast, too much change, and she didn't know who she was any more. She didn't know who her twin was, and, in a lifetime of reflections, of using the other to define oneself, it was a question that frightened her to death. She longed to find a way to reach Teresita, to remind her that the bond they had was stronger than this. But she couldn't.

Her thoughts were punctured by the sound of laughter. She stood and followed. Who was her sister talking to? Julia had long since fallen asleep.

It was with a growing sense of dread that she arrived at Daniel's cabin, and heard Teresita talking inside. Her twin spoke animatedly and vivaciously—no wonder people liked spending time with her. Words didn't come so easily to Calida; they seemed too important, too permanent. She'd never be able to charm Daniel that way.

Anxious, she peered through the window, and saw the pair sitting at his table.

Jealousy boiled in Calida's blood. Her sister hung on to his every word, every so often touching his arm, or resting her chin on her hand in a way she had learned from their mother. *Sensuous*. The word, sinuous and sinister, sewed itself under Calida's skin with a sharp needle. *You'll never be sensuous. You're not pretty enough.*

'Calida's confused, you know,' Teresita was saying.

Calida froze, her heart wedged in her chest. She wanted to interrupt, but all she could do was stay and listen, her feet rooted to the ground, her breath held.

Daniel hesitated. 'About what?'

Teresita sighed as if she were about to expose a truth she would rather not. Calida saw their mother, again, in the mannerism. 'She likes this boy…' she began.

'Oh,' said Daniel. For a crazy second, Calida thought her sister was going to do the right thing, at last, to tell him how Calida felt, describe her unwavering commitment; although the prospect was appalling it was also a kind of relief—perhaps it took a soul as brave as Teresita's to make it happen. But then she said:

'It's this boy in town. She's obsessed with him. That's why we came to *Las Estrellas*. I kept telling her she should give up. She can be so desperate sometimes.'

Calida began to tremble. Her ears rang, high and sharp.

'She should set her sights lower,' Teresita finished.

Daniel looked confused. Disappointed. No, she couldn't work out his expression. 'I don't think your sister needs to do that,' he said.

'She likes him because he's rich. Money's really important to her. Once, I suggested that you two might have a thing… but the fact is you're not her type. Calida wants someone who can treat her—buy her things…'

No! Calida silently stormed. *No! That's you! That's all you! That's not me!*

'Not like me,' said Teresita, on cue. She put a hand over Daniel's.

Mud filled Calida's mouth and lungs. Heat prickled her fingertips.

'I really like you, Daniel.' Teresita's beauty was amazing in this light, her huge, soulful eyes glittering. 'I've never kissed anyone before. Will you teach me?'

Calida could hear no more. Without knowing how, she

stumbled to the outhouse door, her vision splintering and a roar in her throat, and knocked.

'I need Teresita at the house,' said Calida, when Daniel answered. She was stunned at how steady she sounded. She even smiled for her sister. 'It's important.'

Teresita shot Daniel a lingering look before slipping out into the night.

'You can't control me for ever, you know,' she slammed, striding ahead through the dark. Calida didn't respond. She was mute with hurt and fury.

She watched the back of her sister's head and for the first time ever, hated it. Calida had disliked her in the past, envied her, coveted her, but she'd never hated her.

Only when they were in their bedroom, and Calida shut the door behind her, did she cough up the rope that was strangling her. 'How dare you?' she spat.

'What?'

'I heard everything. The lies you told Daniel.'

'So?'

'*How could you*?' Calida choked. 'I know you like him. I know you don't care that I do as well. I might not understand it, but I know it. But how could you lie?'

Teresita turned away, started fumbling pointlessly with her belongings.

'Don't you dare turn your back on me,' Calida seethed.

Her twin whirled round. 'Don't you dare tell me what to do! I've had enough of you telling me what to do!'

'You knew how I felt,' Calida said, her voice shaking, 'how I feel.'

'Am *I* not allowed to have feelings?' Teresita lashed. 'Have you got first dibs on those too? Tell me something, Calida: just what *do* I have that wasn't yours first?'

Calida blinked. 'I don't know what you mean.'

'I'm sick of it.' Teresita's voice skidded, a flicker of vulnerability, but she caught it. 'I'm sick of playing second. I'm sick of you deciding what my life should be. Can't I have a little *fun*? Can't I be my own person? Or do I have to ask your permission every time?'

'It isn't like that.'

'It's always been like that. And I thought you knew every little thing about me, Calida. You know me better than I know myself, right? That's what you always say. Have you ever stopped to think about how that makes me *feel*? Like I don't even have that. I don't even have *me*, because *you* got there first!'

'How can you say this? After everything I've done—'

'I didn't ask you for any of it! Just because you chose to hold my hand doesn't mean I have to be grateful for it. You thought you were helping but all you were doing was holding me back. So, what, I'm supposed to kiss your feet for the rest of my life? Thank you for stifling my dreams? Carry a debt I never even wanted?'

'I thought I was looking after you.' Calida tried to understand, to see things from another point of view, but her thoughts jammed. 'I'm your sister—'

'No.' Teresita looked deep into her eyes, that steely resolve the last remnant of the twin Calida recognised. 'Let me tell you who *you* are, for a change. You're someone I'm not sure I even like any more. You're someone I've already left behind. You're someone I don't have anything in common with except the misfortune of a birthday.'

Calida opened her mouth but no words came out.

'Daniel's not interested in you, Calida. I was doing you a favour. The longer you carry around this pointless torch, the more embarrassing it's going to get.'

Calida's eyes filled with tears but she kept them from falling.

'But he's interested in you… right?'

'He was an experiment,' said Teresita. 'To see if I could.'

That was the worst part. At least if she cared, it might have made sense.

Calida's face burned. 'So all this was for nothing.'

'Not for nothing: he was a decent enough distraction.'

'You don't know a thing about him.'

'I know more than you. I know he likes pretty girls—like me.'

It was the first time their physical difference had been acknowledged: even at this hour, a cheap, callous shot. The words hit Calida like a punch.

'Shut up,' she whispered.

'Why should I?' Teresita threw back. Now the flame had been lit, an inferno galloped in its wake. All the suffocated hurt, the petty jealousies, the spite, all the hidden scars and buried grudges and smothered indignations, it all came tumbling out. 'For once I won't shut up when you tell me to—I won't do a thing you say. I'm tired of doing what you say! And do you know what, Calida? If you'd given Daniel five more minutes, he'd have kissed me—and he'd have liked it. I'd have told you and loved every second, because finally *I'd* have something *you* didn't have—I'd be the winner, not trailing behind, being told she's too small or too precious or whatever you use to tie me down. I hate it here! I hate it! Can't you see that?'

Calida felt herself disintegrating, like a pillar of salt in the wind.

There may have been a moment when Teresita could have reached out, like a hand over a cliff edge, and hauled them both to safety; a point at which it was still salvageable, the damage could be explained, taken back, remedied with trust and confidence and time.

The moment never came.

Calida saw red, then. She thought of all she had done for this person, loved and cared for her, put her first and kissed away her tears—and this was how she was repaid? Suddenly she was across the room, she didn't know how, and her arm was in the air. She struck her twin round the face, sharp and clean, pushing her into the wall with a loud, sickening thump. Calida hit her again, and again, this perfect princess who had turned into a monster, her blows carrying the weight of a thousand soldiers.

'I wish you'd just disappear,' said Calida, when she was done.

The words hung between them, growing in the silence, and the longer they hung there, unrescued, untempered by an antidote, the huger they became.

'Simone Geddes is going to choose me,' hissed Teresita. 'You do realise that, don't you? And when she does, and when I'm gone, I hope I *never* come back. I hope I never see you or this dying shit-hole ever again. I'm going to make it, Calida. Do you understand? I'm going to make it, far away, without your help or any fucking thing you do for me. I'm going to make it *on my own.*'

Calida didn't stay to hear any more.

She turned on her heel and slammed the door behind her.

9

A week later, Teresa left for England.

Simone Geddes organised her travel, starting with the glimmering car that collected her from the *estancia*, and a suited driver who touched his cap when she climbed in. It was cool inside; a citrusy fan that came from vents in the front. The seats were made of leather, polished and smooth and the colour of vanilla ice cream.

The road dissolved in a blur as the car hurtled towards the airport.

Teresa held the locket around her neck, its pendant clutched in her palm. It was pebble-sized and gold. Diego had given both his daughters identical ones when they were small; she remembered the day she and Calida had unwrapped them, delicate in tissue, and had helped each other tie the catch. Packing the last of her things for London, Teresa had thought twice about bringing hers, had fastened it only at the last moment, a final, muddled grasp at the sister she didn't say goodbye to.

A tear slipped out of her eye. Fiercely, she wiped it away.

She would not cry. She would survive. She didn't need Calida.

A sign flashed past. AEROPUERTO 10KM.

Teresa closed her eyes. Simone's invitation was a chance

at the life she craved. A chance to leave the slums behind and head for the starlight…

Besides, she would be back in a month—and it would all feel like a dream. She would confront her sister then. For now, she wouldn't think of her at all.

But it was her mama's face that stayed with Teresa, then and all the way to England. How Julia had clung on tight as she'd said farewell, hardly able to speak through her tears. How she'd said to her: '*I'll always love you. This is for both of us.*'

10

December 2014
Night

She woke with her hands bound. They were bound at her waist, the fingers clasped as if holding an invisible bouquet. Her ankles were tied, too. She kicked out and both legs moved together on the hinge of her knees. A dry expulsion, half breath, half groan, seeped from her throat and hit a damp, mysterious wall. Instinctively, she bit down. Her mouth was stuffed with cloth. Her lips were sealed with tape.

At first it was pitch dark, then, as her eyes adjusted, she became aware of a faint, pulsing orange. It shone from high and crept across the floor in a ladder. She imagined climbing it, unsure which way was up, and escaping that way.

Escaping what?

The question emerged with little sense of urgency. She lived each second, gradually, one second then another, deciding whether or not she was alive.

Sounds filtered through. A city siren, screaming to loud then fading to quiet then gone; a dog barking; a man calling to another man, their voices passing at an unknown distance. She wondered where they were going, if she could go with them.

Soft things pattered at a window, then her eyes adjusted

and she saw white flakes, thick white flakes of winter tumbling through the black night like moths.

It was Christmas in New York. The idea was an anchor, some reminder of where she was and where she had come from. Out on the street, passers-by would be wrapped in coats and scarves, mittened hands holding another's, noses red and hearts warm as they planned their trip home, to heat, to friends, to safety.

She closed her eyes. Perhaps if she fell asleep a while longer, she was so tired, so very tired, and when she woke up she would be home... Home...

And then she heard a voice, pulling her back from the brink of slumber:

Get out.

It was clear and precise and she trusted it.

You're in danger. Move. Get out. Now.

She tried to push herself up on her elbows but her stomach couldn't take it. Ropes inside her twisted and pulled; she whimpered, growled, writhed in anger.

The door opened.

She blinked, drinking the room in, desperate to see more.

Footsteps.

Someone was with her, standing right there, over her, looking down. She froze. The person stood very still. Time stopped.

She tasted terror.

'Hello,' *said a voice.* 'I'm glad I found you. Are you glad to see me?'

PART TWO

2000–2005

11

London

Teresa Santiago woke to the sound of shouting. It was in a language she didn't understand, and the ferocious, high-pitched squawks shot back and forth like two cats scrapping in a yard. One belonged to Simone, a literal far cry from the dulcet tones in which she addressed Teresa. The shouts were coming from downstairs, a concept she was only now getting used to since she'd only ever lived in a single-storey dwelling. She got out of bed and stood in her silk pyjamas, wondering if it was safe to emerge.

After a while, the screams died down. There followed a series of stomps and the bang of a slamming door. Teresa pictured the other girl who lived here, the blonde with the upturned nose, throwing herself on the sheets and bawling.

She stretched, and the room yawned with her. It was enormous. The ceiling stood at three times her height, with delicate cornicing like the icing on a birthday cake. A glinting chandelier hung from a central floret. The curtains were duck-egg blue and billowed gently against the open windows, of which there were three; huge and as perfectly rectangular as if they belonged in a dolls' house. Through them, the hum of London swam up on the breeze. Her four-poster bed was swathed in peach satin, plumped with dozens of pink cushions, and the mattress was as deep and squidgy as the honeyed brioche Teresa was occasionally served for breakfast.

It was a princess's bedroom. At lights-out, Teresa would lie still and wait for her eyes to become accustomed to the dark, and when they did she would test herself by closing and then opening them again, half fearing that the room would have been swallowed up, and she would find herself back at home in Patagonia, Calida asleep on the bunk below and the moon looking in through the window. She couldn't believe that all this was hers. OK, it was on loan, it wasn't forever, but boy was it something else. London was another universe. Simone Geddes' mansion was incredible. At the beginning she had got lost every hour, exploring the furthest reaches of the house and then forgetting her way back. Simone had a loft, a cellar, a games suite, and a spa; they had a library and a music room and a reading room; they had a separate area where they ate their meals and drank their drinks and the lounge alone was bigger than the entire farmhouse back in Argentina. All the floors were piled one on top of another, like a stack of pretty boxes. When Teresa first arrived, she'd hurt her neck looking up at them all and Simone had laughed affectionately and stroked her arm.

'Welcome to my world,' she'd whispered.

It truly was the realm of her imaginings. Everything she had hoped for and dreamed of. Her old life ceased to exist. Poverty, struggle, longing. And Calida…

Teresa pushed away thoughts of her twin. She suffered a tangle of emotions whenever she thought of her: anger, hurt, frustration, and sadness; it was easier to bottle them up. Calida had wished her gone. She would be happy back on the farm, with Daniel, who was the only person who mattered to her anyway.

I wish you'd just disappear…

Though the bruises had faded, the scars were still tender to touch. *Fine*, Teresa thought, *you got what you wanted. See if I care. I'm having the time of my life.*

There was a knock at the bedroom door. 'Ms Santiago?'

The maid stepped in. Vera was a kind, plump, Hispanic woman. Once or twice they had chatted in Spanish, but Vera always cut it short because, she explained, she wasn't meant to converse with the household. 'I'm not the household,' Teresa said, 'I'm a guest.' But Vera had backed out of the room and stayed quiet on the matter.

Privately, Teresa wondered if the maid was content working here. Simone spoke sharply to her, as did the other children. The blonde girl, Emily, acted as if Vera didn't exist, yet had vicious words to impart when her trail of bubblegum wrappers, cigarette butts, and empty bottles of cola failed to be cleared promptly from the side of the swimming pool; while the boy, Lysander, with whom Teresa hadn't had much contact because she found him daunting, but thrillingly so, liked to make her blush.

Now, the maid wheeled a silver trolley across the carpet, which she brought to a stop at the foot of Teresa's bed. She bobbed a short curtsey.

'*Gracias*,' said Teresa, marvelling at the sight.

'*De nada*—can I bring you anything else?'

'No, thank you.' Teresa had never been treated with such reverence: she felt she could ask for anything—a bicycle, a sandcastle, a unicorn—and it would be brought straight to her, with apologies for the delay. Vera nodded and left the room.

The breakfast was sumptuous. Teresa lifted the metal cloche and underneath was a spread of eggs, bacon, mushrooms, and tomato, diamonds of toast with the crusts cut off, a pat of butter in the shape of a seashell, a bright glass of orange juice and a

goblet of fresh yoghurt topped with blueberry compote. She
wolfed the feast.

Excitedly, she dressed. Simone was taking her shopping
today and she couldn't wait. She'd heard so much about luxury
clothes and seen Simone's own dazzling wardrobe, and could
picture the stores with their polished displays and glossy sales
people; the buzz and zing of money as it flashed in and out
of the till.

In the hallway, she stopped. Emily was blasting music from
her bedroom and a sign on the door read: KEEP OUT: BITCH
WITHOUT A MUZZLE.

Emily's room was forbidden territory and Teresa knew she
wouldn't be welcome. Since she'd arrived, Emily had barely
said two words to her. Frequently she caught the girl scowling at her, and once Emily had brought her friends over and
Teresa knew they were giggling and gossiping because they
kept looking over and then hiding their smiles behind their
hands. Teresa wished she could speak English because then
she could explain that Simone had invited her and, since she
was here, they might try to get along… It was only a couple
more weeks, after all.

Holding the banister, she descended the staircase. It was
wide and carpeted, its lofty white walls adorned with giant
photographs of Simone at work; Simone in the director's
chair, mingling with co-stars or donning a variety of glamorous wigs. Down in the vestibule stood an impressive cabinet
of awards. Julia had said that Simone was famous, but Teresa
was beginning to see that for the severe understatement it was.

In the kitchen, the actress was stirring coffee and gazing
out of the window to where a pool boy was raking leaves
from the water. She was muttering something ominously to
her husband, and Teresa identified the sound of Emily's name.

Noticing their guest, Simone's face lifted. She turned, arms outstretched.

'Good morning, sweetheart!' She gave Teresa a hug. Simone was very affectionate for a hostess and Teresa never quite knew what to do, so she hugged her back and this seemed to be the right thing. Over her shoulder, she spotted Brian eating toast messily at the counter. Brian Chilcott was a director, which meant he told people on movie sets where to go and how to act. He was overweight, and had a florid, disinterested face, and wore ties that looked uncomfortably tight at the neck.

He delivered a wink to Teresa. Diego used to wink at her sometimes but this wink was different; there was something latent in it, a threat too cloudy to name.

'Are you ready for our shopping trip?' Simone encouraged.

Teresa didn't understand. Brian put in: 'Are you going to teach her English?'

'Shut up, Brian. Keep your booze-addled nose out of it.'

Teresa didn't grasp what they were saying, but she heard the bitterness in Simone's voice. Brian put down his toast and shrugged on his jacket. On his way out, he pecked Simone on her cheek. She turned away but he wouldn't be deterred.

Teresa's eyes widened as she saw Brian clasp Simone's backside and squeeze it hard. Images of Gonzalez and her papa made her shudder. Nausea bubbled in her throat, a sick feeling that took root in her stomach and threaded up like weeds. She remembered her father's nakedness, his cowardice, and his surrendering groan. Did Simone and Brian do the same thing? Did Emily do it? Did Lysander? For some reason, the thought of Lysander doing it made her insides clench, not unpleasurably.

When Brian had gone, Simone relaxed.

'English lessons might not be a bad idea,' she mused. She

repeated the suggestion to Teresa, enunciating each word as if she were a dunce. 'English… you learn… yes? Soon. I will organise.' She fumbled for the same thing in Spanish. Teresa wondered why they should bother, if she was going home at the end of the month.

*

The afternoon passed in a glorious whirlwind. Teresa was on cloud nine from the instant she stepped into Simone's car and they whizzed through the city maze, ducking and diving past shining red buses and gleaming black taxis, over the magical bridges and past the masses of people. When they stopped at the first shop on Bond Street, a crowd surged forward and screamed Simone's name. Teresa was alarmed. She thought they were being attacked. Simone's bodyguard drew them safely inside.

'That's nothing, darling,' she giggled, 'you should see me at a premiere!' Then she leaned in, a glimmer in her eye, and added, 'It'll be you soon, you know.'

Over the next four hours, they tried on every garment in that shop and the next, and the next, and the next, until they collapsed in a heap of happy exhaustion. Everywhere they were treated like royalty: Teresa questioned if, perhaps, Simone Geddes *was* royalty. She was urged to try on dresses and skirts, blouses and boots, and had no concept of what they cost except for clues from the ladies at the cash desks, who positively trilled when the sums came up. The assistants grovelled around Simone; nothing was too much or any kind of trouble, and every time Teresa emerged from the changing rooms in an exquisite new combination the party flattered and fawned, saying how perfect and beautiful she looked. With her wild dark hair and striking almond eyes, she oozed untamed beauty that, at fifteen, was on the cusp of exploding into something phenomenal. At one point, Simone wept. '*Que linda*!' she spluttered, dabbing a tissue to her eyes. Teresa beamed. She felt like a million dollars.

They arrived back at the Kensington mansion weighed down but cheerful.

'Thank you,' Teresa said in English, meaning it, as tentatively she gave Simone a hug. Simone needed no encouragement to return the gesture.

'You're welcome, my sweetheart,' she said, her voice choked with emotion. 'If you enjoyed today, you just wait for what's coming.'

*

Over the next fortnight, Teresa saw and did more than she thought she would pack into a hundred years. She visited majestic palaces with men standing outside in big fur hats that looked like bulrushes. She drifted round museums where the floor was so polished that it shone like silver water, and you could hear the soft, expensive pat of people's shoes as they walked across it. She went to the cinema, which had a huge TV screen and she ate buttery popcorn that made her fingers salty. She stood on Waterloo Bridge and gazed at the golden spires of Parliament and the pale dome of St Paul's, which reminded her of a pearl on one of Julia's old necklaces. She partook in Basic English lessons, and found she had a flair for the language. She posed for a string of daylong photo shoots alongside Simone. She spent nights in the home theatre, where she asked to watch Simone's movies, and, after a half-hearted show of reluctance, the actress put on her award-winning effort in *Two Dozen Men at My Feet*, in which she played a rebellious countess who seemed to cry a lot behind closed doors.

On Friday, Simone issued an announcement:

'We're having a party. This evening. I want you to dress up.'

Teresa found Vera and asked her about it. 'Her ladyship wishes to show you off,' said Vera in Spanish. 'It's a party in your honour.'

'Is it a goodbye party, because I'm leaving soon?'

Vera returned to buffing the marble in Simone's bathroom.

'Who'll be there?' asked Teresa.

'Ms Geddes has many friends,' said Vera. 'They will want to meet you.'

Three hours later, the household was teeming with staff. The terrace was strung with fairy lights that danced against the stars and a fountain of sparkling water gushed from a cherub's trumpet. Guests trickled through, the men in crisp, sharp suits that reminded Teresa of the men in her romance novels: the billionaires. The women drifted like angels in their floor-length, sweeping gowns, slowing to pluck a flute of champagne or a miniature morsel of food. Cloying perfume hung in the air.

Across the veranda, Emily Chilcott shot her an evil glare.

Simone told her she looked wonderful, in a damson Moschino creation that skimmed the patio, her jet hair tumbling free, and kept a proprietorial arm round her the entire time. Occasionally, she would step back and gesture towards Teresa as if she were an item in an exhibit. The guests nodded approvingly, the men regarding her in the same voracious manner as the driver she had hailed back home to take her and Calida into town—a galaxy away, it seemed. They spoke too fast to keep up with, but Simone's reassuring smile told her she was doing well. She revelled in the spotlight, all the more precious because it would not last, and soon she would be back in South America in the rags she had grown up in and it would all seem like a fairy tale.

Afterwards, Simone kissed her. 'You were perfect, just perfect.'

Teresa was exhausted, exhilarated, elated. She didn't need to speak English to understand that these people were important. Power had wafted off them in great, intoxicating clouds. Producers, agents, directors—but what did they want with her?

She scarcely dared think it, but as she prepared for bed that night she allowed herself the luxury. For whatever reason, Simone wished to ingratiate her with the industry, to impress them. Was it possible that when she returned to Argentina, it would be with news that she was going to become an actress? That she was relocating to London, to Milan, to Hollywood? Or might Simone ask her to stay on? Would she teach Teresa the ways of wealth and success, and give her a key that would open the door to her own destiny? She told herself off for fantasising—always her weakness. Most likely the party had been a farewell, just as she had thought. Most likely…

She fell asleep the instant she hit the pillow, and dreamed she was swimming in a deep, deep sea, and on the seabed was a diamond, sparkling, beckoning. Someone was calling her name, but the further she swam, the quieter the voice became.

*

The day before Teresa was due to go home, Emily Chilcott waltzed into her room. Her eyes were shining and eager and there was a bounce in her step.

'Hi,' she said sweetly, 'are you ready to go?'

Teresa found Emily's smile disturbing. She zipped up the last of her bags.

'I expect you'll miss me,' said Emily, 'since we've become close.'

Teresa sat on the edge of her bed. She didn't trust Emily.

Several times she had consulted her translation dictionary after receiving a snide comment or sarcastic aside. Emily had said some toxic things: Teresa was a brat, a misfit, a bitch; she didn't belong here. The other day she had seen Emily kick the family puppy when it got in her way. Only somebody truly horrid would be able to hurt an animal.

'So I thought I'd give you a goodbye present,' Emily went on. In a flash she withdrew a glinting pair of scissors from behind her back, brandishing them up high. 'Time for your makeover!' She beamed, clicking the scissor blades, her eyes mad.

Teresa didn't have time to back away before Emily advanced, grabbing a clump of Teresa's hair and, with a sickening snitch, lopped it off.

'Oops!' said Emily gleefully. 'Better make it even!'

Teresa was so surprised that she couldn't speak. Automatically her hand went up to meet the amputation and all she felt was bare neck. She tried to escape, but Emily pulled her back. With appalling speed and efficiency, the scissors snipped and chopped. '*Para*!' Teresa cried, distraught. '*Basta*!' She tried to wriggle free but Emily had her whole weight bearing down and now she was cropping and slashing and slicing great swathes of hair, cackling giddily as it fell to the carpet, and she hacked more and more, until Teresa's glossy waist-length locks were up at her ear, bitten and chewed and scruffy. She started to cry. Emily seized her fringe and she tried to pull back but it hurt so much that she couldn't do anything apart from sit there with her hands in her lap, quivering, as with every devastating slice she became balder. '*Por favor, no lo hagas*,' Teresa howled, '*Por favor*! *Para*!'

But Emily didn't listen. When she was done, she leaned to whisper in Teresa's ear. Teresa could see their joint reflection in the mirror: Emily flushed with excitement, her pixie face alive with delight; and she, tatty and ugly, threadbare and tear-blotched.

Emily's voice was a hiss: 'You'll never be part of this family,' she said. 'Go home, little peasant. Get out of my house and my country. Or this is only the start.'

She replaced the scissors on the dresser, and quietly left.

*

Simone Geddes went insane with anger. She slapped Emily round the face and shook her like a ragdoll. Through it all, Emily remained calm and composed, satisfied at both her offence and at Simone's reaction. Teresa hadn't uttered a word about who was to blame, but it hadn't taken a genius to figure it out. Brian, when he came in from work, chided Emily in a bored fashion before sitting down with a sherry and *The Times*.

Hysterical, Simone gathered Teresa's butchered mop under a cap, grabbed her hand and led the way upstairs. Vera was cleaning Teresa's bedroom.

'I cannot believe that little harlot would do this!' Simone was raging. Her whole body convulsed with anger. 'That girl is vile! She is the devil incarnate!'

Simone barked something at the maid and obediently Vera translated. Teresa could understand Simone's fury, for what was Julia going to say when she saw the state of her daughter? Vera explained that Simone would be hiring London's most exclusive hairdresser to pay a private visit in the morning.

'But I'm going home in the morning,' said Teresa, in Spanish.

Vera relayed this to Simone.

Simone had her back to her, and turned round slowly. A glance passed between her and the maid. As if reaching an important decision, Simone steered Teresa to a chair and sat her down. She took Teresa's hands and held them.

There was a long pause, before Simone said, 'You're not going home.'

Vera's fingers fastened in her apron. At Simone's command, she translated.

'I hate having to be the one to tell you,' Simone went on, swallowing hard, 'but I must... This isn't a vacation, darling. Your mama told you that because we thought it would make things easier. It was never a vacation. It's permanent.' A beat. 'I've adopted you, sweetheart. You're going to live with me now, and be my daughter.'

Teresa didn't move, didn't speak.

Vera interpreted each of Simone's words. As the revelations unfolded, one layer after another, the maid's voice became quieter. Not once did she look at Teresa.

'Your family do not want you any more,' Simone said, licking dry lips. 'They asked me to take you away. Your mama needed the money. She... She sold you.'

There was a strange sound in Teresa's ears. She struggled to process what was being said. She felt as if she was floating several feet above her body, rudderless. Her past, her life, her identity: all of it collapsed beneath her like a house of cards.

Her first thought was: *It makes sense*. She had asked for this. Told Julia she wanted it. Jointly, they had mapped her future, as far away from the *estancia* as possible. Simone would have paid handsomely. Everyone was happy.

But it hurt. It hurt. Julia had lied.

She didn't want me.

'You've had a nice time here, though, haven't you?' Simone was saying, nodding at her encouragingly. 'Would it be so bad to live with me, in London?'

Something stuck. Something wasn't right.

'Speak, sweetheart.' Simone squeezed her hands. 'Please… say anything.'

There was only one word that made sense: 'Calida.'

It took a second for Simone to connect the dots. The sister. The twin. The one she hadn't chosen. Her expression faltered a moment before righting itself.

'Calida knew about this, too,' Simone explained gently. 'She and your mother *both* made this decision. Together. For everyone's benefit.'

Vera's rendition confirmed it. In a reel of sun-kissed images, her childhood with Calida flashed before her eyes. The closeness, the connection… the drum of her twin's matching heartbeat… the horses, the land, the dust, the laughter.

She had run from it all. Run far and run fast and never looked back.

I wish you'd just disappear.

'They don't want you,' Simone said again. 'Your sister chose to give you away as freely as Julia did. *I'm* your new mother now. *I'm* your new family.'

A flood of emotions washed over her.

Here it is, she thought, *your new life*.

She had prayed for this outcome, and now it was here.

So why was there this glaring hole in the centre of her heart?

'You're Tess Geddes now,' Simone said. 'My daughter.'

All night—that long, lonely night—the stranger's name floated in her half-consciousness like a phantom, daring her to step into it, to let it swallow her up.

To hell with you both, she thought. *I don't need you.*

I'll show you just what I'm made of—and then you'll be sorry.

12

'Looking great, everyone. And… action!'

Simone, or rather her character Miranda Fenchurch, stepped out of the Royal Courts of Justice in a navy pinstripe suit, faced the wall of cameras, and delivered the gut-wrenching oration that would conclude the most anticipated political thriller of the year. As with all Simone's scenes, they canned it in one.

'You're a special lady, you know that?' the director told her afterwards, as the first spots of rain began to fall and an assistant ushered her under cover.

'Don't patronise me, Greg.'

'I'm sorry, I didn't mean—'

'What a dreadful sycophant that man is,' Simone muttered to her aide, once the director had skulked off. 'Calling me a lady—who does he think he's talking to, Camilla Parker Bowles? God forbid.' Privately, however, Simone knew that she *was* special. Playing Miranda Fenchurch in *An Eye For An Eye* was a departure from her usual: she was embodying a cutthroat, hard-nosed barrister who wasn't afraid to rattle the cage. The awards cabinet at home had better make way for a shiny new addition.

On the way to her car, a female co-star flagged her down. 'It was wonderful meeting Tess at the party,' the woman said. 'What a beautiful girl.'

'Isn't she?'

'When will you be announcing the adoption?'

'When the time is right,' Simone replied. 'It's a complex process, you understand.' She could picture the headlines already: SELFLESS SIMONE RESCUES TEEN FROM POVERTY. GEDDES GIVES GIRL A CHANCE. Any star could traipse halfway across the world to buy a baby, but there was something unusual and intriguing about Simone's decision to make that difference for an older child.

The media would lap it up like piglets at a watering hole.

'It must be,' said the woman. 'Is she finding it hard to adjust?'

Simone thought: *None of your damn business.* But she felt compelled to say, 'Not a bit. She loves it here. She loves her new life. She loves me.'

With that, she climbed into the Mercedes and shut the door.

*

The mansion was quiet, which meant no Emily. So much for Brian's pledge to ground her. She found her husband in his office. 'Where's Tess?'

Brian turned in his chair. 'Still in her room,' he replied.

'No change?'

'No change.' Brian got up. He looped his arms around Simone's waist and she did her best not to wince. She could feel Brian's gut pressed up against her gym-toned stomach, and endeavoured to focus instead on the wall-mounted shots of him mixing with the power set. That was what had drawn her to him in the early days—how was she to know that under-neath the façade lurked an overweight spineless doormat? No wonder Brian's first wife had left him for a woman. If it weren't for Brian's bi-weekly ruts she would begin to doubt if he possessed anything between his legs at all.

Simone went upstairs and knocked softly on Tess's bedroom door.

'Tess, sweetheart?' she called. 'Can I come in?'

It had been like this for weeks. Tess emerged only to wash and eat. She didn't speak. She didn't engage. She held herself stiffly, as if she were made of glass. What was going on in her head? Anger, sadness, shock; which was the overriding emotion?

It would take time, Simone knew. A bit like training a dog. She was able to close her heart to Tess's plight because once, many years ago, she too had been forced to make a sacrifice, one for the good of a child, and it had made her tough. If she could get through it, then the rest of the world ought to be able to as well.

She closed her eyes and swallowed hard, to stop herself gagging on the past. When she thought of it, she could still feel the weight of the baby in her arms.

The baby...

Taking Tess was karma. Simone deserved her child.

'Still pissed with you, is she?' Lysander passed her in the hall. He wore peppermint shorts and a polo shirt with the collar turned up, and looked offensively handsome. Wasn't he meant to be at college? 'Can't say I'm surprised.'

'You know nothing about this, Lysander.'

'I know it's abduction dressed as Armani.'

'It is nothing of the sort!' Simone was aghast.

He grinned.

'You just stay away from her,' she said. 'Do you understand?'

Lysander took a step closer. He put a hand on the small of

her back and her entire body tingled. 'What,' he whispered, 'like you told me to stay away from you?'

Blushing wildly, Simone turned and flew downstairs. The sooner Lysander moved out of the mansion, the better. He was a diversion she could well do without.

13

Argentina

Calida's sixteenth birthday drowned in all the other days.

If she had been capable of feeling, she would have felt her twin's absence. She would have known that this was the first birthday they had ever spent apart. She would have touched the wound, the searing wound where Teresita had been ripped from her side in the same way she had been ripped at their inception. She would have looked at her hands, her arms, her knees, her chest, heard her breath and her pulse, and questioned what their mirror reflections were doing at this moment, the precise minute and second they had emerged, as two, into the world, sixteen years before.

But she didn't, because it was any other day, and every day was submerged in the same numb disbelief so that it became impossible to make distinctions.

Her sister had gone. She wasn't coming back.

Julia admitted it a week into the so-called vacation, unable to hold her tongue any longer. 'Teresita begged me to let her go,' she explained, as she exhibited another new acquisition: satin shoes, expensive perfumes, watches and jewels. Calida had thought it strange that Simone had been so generous—but she hadn't known then the product she had paid for. 'She begged Simone to take her. Told us she was ready—she was desperate. It's permanent, Calida. Your sister's been adopted. She's gone to live in England. The sooner you come to terms with it then the easier it will be.'

Calida's body was kicked and punched by her mother's words. But her mind remained steady, and told her, quite calmly, through the noise: *Of course*. It was what Teresita had sought: to get away, to flee her humble beginnings, to forge her fortune.

Calida remembered every poisonous sentiment that had spilled from her twin's lips on the night they had fought and in a ghastly way it added up. Being adopted by a movie star was the opportunity of a lifetime. Teresita hadn't cared what she was leaving behind—it was no sacrifice to her. *When I'm gone, I hope I never come back. I hope I never see you or this dying shit-hole ever again...*

After the news, when the shock moved from sky-collapse to mere earth tremors, Calida wrote dozens of letters. Unable to extract Simone's details from her mother, she instead located her manager online: a Michelle Horner, who had an office in Mayfair, London, and an address to go with it. On searching for the actress, pages brimmed with doppelgangers of the sweating, dishevelled woman who had graced their ranch that day: this one was ravishing. There were stills from her films and onstage; snapshots from articles and interviews, some of a young, wide-eyed Simone, and others where she was older and standing next to a suited fat man, or posing with a blonde girl and a black-haired boy, and looking a little less pleased with herself.

In her letters, she pleaded with Teresita to come home. She said she was sorry for the spiteful words they had exchanged, vowed that their friendship was worth more and had to be saved. No matter what… right? No matter what, they were there for each other. She wished to explain that there was a way back. There always would be. She wasn't mad with Teresita for the decision she had made—it would have been a decision borne of the hurt and frustration of their showdown, and she understood.

Calida didn't know what she had expected from initiating correspondence—but whatever it was, it wasn't what she got. Silence.

Each one of her letters went unanswered. She waited every day at the gate for mail, hoping for change—but nothing. She imagined Simone and Teresita scrutinising the notes, her increasingly despairing tone as she implored her twin to reconsider, to come home, and laughing cruelly at her efforts. Though she tried with all her soul to deny it, she knew she had to face the truth. Teresita had closed the door on her family—what was left of it, anyway—and had no intention of opening it again.

She had always possessed a harder heart than Calida. But to read those letters and not be touched by any of it, or moved to reply, if for nothing else than to cement the choice she had already made? To ignore the twin who asked for understanding, for help, for forgiveness; not stopping once to acknowledge her part in the collapse of their relationship?

It wasn't the sister she knew… or thought she had known.

It was a stranger.

*

The year 2000: a new millennium, a new start. Instead, it felt like an end. As the days passed and turned into weeks, Teresita became a ghost in her mind; the sudden ring of her sister's laugh or the mischief that danced in her eyes assaulting her from nowhere, like a ghoul from the shadows. She couldn't eat. She couldn't sleep.

Calida's sadness solidified into fury. Right now her twin would be in London, loving every moment, living out the fantasy that she and Julia shared, the fantasy that had always turned its back on Calida because she couldn't understand it. How could she be so unfeeling, so pitiless; and for what—a palace of fakery? Yet despite Calida's indifference to the glamorous lifestyle, and the painstaking denials she made to herself that she desired anything whatsoever to do with it, she couldn't help the worm of envy that burrowed its way into her heart. Why hadn't Simone taken her? Was she not pretty enough, lovely enough, exciting enough? What was it about Teresita that drew people like moths to a flame, while Calida stayed in darkness?

One day, Julia came to her and said: 'I'm leaving. You're sixteen now. You'll live. I've renewed a friendship in the city and I'm going to stay there for a while.'

Calida's mouth fell open. 'What? But what about…?'

'The farm?' Julia swished a silk scarf over her shoulder. 'Tell you what, Calida: it's yours. You always did like this place better than I did.'

'I can't look after it on my own.'

'You've got Daniel.'

'Mama—you can't. It's not…' Her throat closed, making it hard to speak. She felt like sand in an hourglass, time rushing through her fingers. 'There isn't—'

'Come now, Calida. You're an adult. Teresita's started her new life. You can't expect me to hang around here for the rest of my days playing the doting mama.'

And, just like that, the next morning, Julia left. Just like her daughter, she was able to turn away from her past and her responsibilities without a backward glance. She left behind no cash—but Calida wouldn't have wanted it anyway. It was blood money, testament to the devil-sent pact the three of them had orchestrated, the abomination of that unholy exchange. Calida would have nothing to do with it.

Alone, she summoned Diego's voice. *Speak to me, Papa. Tell me what to do*. And she heard his reply: *Every path has an ending. Every problem has an answer*.

It was the same guidance he'd bestowed on her when she took her pictures, telling her to be still and quiet and at peace, because only then was she truly able to see. Calida had become a lone pillar in a sandstorm, after the rest of the building had blown down. All her life she had been taught to be self-sufficient, to rely on no one but herself. Now, after the dismantling of her family, she understood for the first time how crucial this independence was. The way forward was to become the pillar; to lean on no other supports, neither props on either side nor a foundation beneath her feet.

*

Winter blew in. It was the harshest season Calida could recall, sleet lashing and winds crying, and some nights the gale threatened to tear the wooden farmhouse from the ground. The land froze and with it the ghosts of their crops. Food was scarce. The old roof leaked and dripped, and as fast as they repaired one fissure, another appeared. Calida lined up buckets on the kitchen floor, the slow seconds counted by the *pit-pit* of water as it spat into the tin. Each day she prayed for sun, a sliver of promise in the clouds, but the sky churned grey and limitless as a deep, livid sea.

Paco the horse became sick. It started with a waning in his eyes, a burning ember reduced to a flickering wick. He became

listless and depressed, and lost his appetite. 'Strangles,' Daniel
called the disease.

Calida couldn't survive losing Paco as well. She floundered
against his illness, unsure what steps to take. But Daniel knew.
He said: 'I know how much he means to you—it will be all
right,' and in the same grave, capable way as he tackled so
much else on the farm, he did what was required to save Paco's
life. Calida questioned why Daniel was still here; the pay had
long since dried up, but he never graced her with a response.
Just once, he asked if she would refrain from enquiring again.

'I'm part of this,' he told her. 'That isn't going to change.'

But what had changed was the lost ease of their companionship, when Calida's youth had excused her bumbling infatuation and Teresita had never said those wicked things. *She can
be so desperate. She should set her sights lower.*

She cringed whenever she thought of it. Calida yearned to
unpick it, correct it, tell Daniel there was no boy in town that
she liked; Teresita had lied about everything. But if she did
that she was confessing to having eavesdropped, and admitting
to him her true feelings. Why couldn't she admit it? What did
she have left to lose?

Teresita would tell him, she tortured herself. *Teresita would
dare.*

'Do you miss her?' asked Calida one afternoon, as she
hung up Paco's reins, stopping to rinse her hands beneath
the outdoor tap. The water choked a splurge of brown before
clearing. It was accompanied by the sharp stench of iron.

Daniel didn't speak for several moments. She was wondering if he'd heard, when at last he said: 'You know, Calida—I'm
glad it's not you who went away.'

Calida wasn't glad. If she had gone away, she could have
proven her sister wrong: she *could* have an adventure; she

could take a chance… The trouble was, a chance never took her. It stung that he hadn't answered her question.

'She really wanted to go, didn't she?' said Calida.

Daniel faced her. 'Sometimes, if you're unhappy, you have no option but to leave. It's self-preservation.'

The wind moaned in the rafters. Calida examined the nail on her thumb.

'She hated it here that much?'

'I don't know,' said Daniel. 'She's young. She doesn't know what she wants.'

'I do. And I'm the same age.'

'But you're…' Daniel smiled a little, with compassion, humour, she didn't know what. 'You're different, Calida. You're not like other girls.'

'You left your home,' she said. 'Do you think about your family?'

His blue eyes held hers. Calida could see him about to open up, the last bud in spring, but then his face fell into shadow, as it had on the day they'd met.

'I'll never go back,' he said bluntly, turning from her. 'That part of my life is over. There's nothing left. I can never return.'

'You never talk about it.'

'There's nothing to say.' Daniel started stacking saddles on the barn ledge; the weight of sheepskin and the tangle of reins. 'But the more distance there is between that place and me, the happier I am. I'll die before I cross that ocean again.'

He stopped, then, and said, 'It's not the same for Teresita. I swear to you. I know that much. You're too important to her. This place is too important. She doesn't realise it yet, but she will… She thinks she wants more—that whatever's out there is better, that it'll solve her problems, answer her prayers. It won't, because the problem she's trying to figure out isn't this place—it's her. No matter how hard she tries, she can't leave herself behind. One day soon, she'll look around at her new world and consider what she swapped it for… and then she'll see her mistake.'

Calida bit back tears.

'I don't want anything to happen to her,' she said. 'I can't help it. What if it does, and I'm not there? I've never not been there.'

Daniel came to her, put his hands on her arms. A spark raced up Calida's spine and set fire to her blood. 'It's nice that you care so much,' he said.

She nodded. There was a long pause.

'I broke up with my girlfriend,' he said.

'Oh.'

Daniel waited for her to speak, as if he had offered a hand-shake and she'd left him hanging, unsure when to pull away. He returned to ground they'd been on: 'I know what it's like to be parted from your family. It hurts… but you'll find a way.'

She nodded. A flush of shame crept up her neck.

He feels sorry for me. I can be so desperate sometimes…

'Thanks, Daniel,' she muttered, and hurried back inside.

14

Paris

Tess Geddes mounted the wide stone steps of the Collège de Sainte-Marthe de Paris and gazed up at the building. From the bell tower, a deep clang resounded.

In the heart of the Quartier Latin, Collège de Sainte-Marthe de Paris was the most prestigious and exclusive boarding school in the French capital, if not in Europe. It was set apart from the standard education system and reserved for those with elite money and standing, a finishing school to prepare young ladies for world domination.

Pretty, polished students wearing knee-high socks and frilled skirts dashed ahead of her, glossy manes bouncing and leather satchels slung elegantly over one shoulder. Tess watched them, appraising the challenge. *I can do this*, she thought. *I can do anything.* When Simone had informed her she was going to Paris, it made no difference. England, France, wherever it was—as long as it wasn't Argentina, with people who didn't want her and who got rid of her the first chance they got.

Simone stood back as her staff hauled the baggage: a huge buckled trunk with gold studs that resembled a coffin. Tess thought, *I know who's buried in there.* She wondered, if she sprung it open, whether she would find, instead of daintily laid blouses scented with pockets of fragrant rose pomander, the body of her old self, curled up in a ball like a kitten in a straw nest, hair brittle and eyes closed.

'You'll make so many friends,' Simone was saying, as she pressed a tissue to her nose. Several other parents glanced over at this show of emotion, their attention snagged by Simone's sizeable entourage and the incognito dark glasses that marked her out as a celebrity. Although, judging by the throng of gleaming four-by-fours parked at the school gates and the ranks of bodyguards talking grimly into Bluetooth headpieces, Simone wasn't the only VIP on the premises. Their audience glanced between Simone and Teresa, who couldn't have looked less alike, and smiled politely.

'And you'll even have Emily for company!'

Simone could barely choke out this sentiment, but she made a valiant effort. Up ahead, Emily Chilcott was linking arms with a fiery redhead and shooting Tess death glares. Emily had been attending Sainte-Marthe for three years, one thing Brian *had* insisted on, and was apparently Queen Bee of the dormitories.

'Mademoiselle Geddes, I believe?' A middle-aged woman was walking towards them, one arm held out, as pale and goosebumpy as a raw chicken thigh. 'I'll take you to your lodgings, shall I?' she said in English. By now Tess had a competent grasp of the language. Simone's lessons hadn't been fast enough so she had taken matters into her own hands, devouring every book and magazine she could, reading it alongside her dictionary into the small hours of the night. 'See if we can't get you settled in. My name is Madame Aubert and I am your house mistress.'

Simone kissed her farewell. 'I'll see you in a few weeks, darling…'

As Tess followed Madame, she eliminated the echo that rebounded through her brain. *A few weeks*... That was exactly what Julia had said as she had been driven away from Patagonia. *Fuck them*, she thought. *They don't deserve my tears*.

The school was like a cathedral. Stained-glass windows spilled red and gold on to the cool, chequered floor. Baroque pillars ran to a huge glass dome, ornate with gold, and weeping religious figures. 'This is where chapel is held in the morning,' said Madame Aubert. Through that space they emerged into a giant courtyard—'*La Cour Henri Jaurès*'—which was marked with white and red lines and a vertical pole at each end that was capped with a net. The surrounding structures were high and arched and, above, through little square windows, excited squeals could be heard drifting from the dormitories, against a blast of music. Up a set of winding stairs, Madame Aubert led her down a corridor and pushed open the farthest door.

'Here we are,' she said. 'Your home from home.'

The room had ten beds, five down each side, each pristinely made with the sheets pulled tight, and with an accompanying side cabinet and closet. Madame Aubert informed her that supper was at six in the dining room and left her to unpack.

It was eerily quiet. Tess went to the window, which faced away from the courtyard and towards the rest of the school: a collection of grey-slate rooftops, still slick from the morning's rain. She removed the items from her trunk and laid them on the shelves, like someone else's belongings. With a jolt, she realised she had left behind the diary she'd been keeping, tucked behind the bed at Simone's mansion.

The diary had become her steadfast friend, and she had spilled into it her innermost emotions—about Julia, about Calida, about the life she'd left behind; about her regrets and hopes and the strange land she now found herself in, unsure which way was forward, afraid of her own powers because she had implored the gods for this providence and somehow they had answered. She fingered the locket around her neck. Every time she went to take it off, something stopped her. She wanted to rip it from its chain, stamp on it, toss it from a cliff, but somehow she was unable to.

She was distracted by a burst of giggles at the door.

A clique of girls tumbled in. They stopped when they saw her. Leading the pack was, of course, Emily Chilcott, resplendent in her power zone, and at her side stood the redhead Tess had seen at the gates. The redhead had the most incredible-coloured hair Teresa had ever seen—bright, flaming orange, with golden highlights around the top like a halo. Emily said something in English—Simone had explained she was 'too thick to get a handle on French'—and they all laughed again, but not in a way you could join in with. Tess decided they could bitch and laugh at her all they liked. She had been through worse than anything Emily could throw at her.

The group paraded down the aisle between the beds, showing off lithe, tanned legs and releasing a mist of musky scent. With a sinking feeling, Tess realised they were her roommates. Madame Aubert had probably arranged it, thinking she would want to be with her family. Emily, her family? That was some joke.

'I'm Tess,' she told the redhead, deciding to ignore her stepsister. But Emily was having none of it. She charged forward, blue eyes flashing, and like a magnet drew the others into formation. She smiled openly and said:

'They don't care who you are. They're *my* friends, and you're the impostor. Rest assured, *Teresa*, you won't survive here. I'll make sure of it.'

As the redhead passed, her slanted green eyes narrowed

in malice. Tess felt a sharp yank at the back of her neck, so quick as to be unsure whether it had happened. Her locks were scarcely mended after the attack. Despite Simone's efforts, Emily's scissors had triumphed. 'Nice hair,' said the redhead unkindly, and closed the door.

It was easy enough to stay away from Emily during the day—Tess spent most of her time in Fast-Track French and was scheduled to join the main curriculum at the end of spring term—but, at night, there was no escape. Emily's clique clustered into one another's beds after lights-out and giggled and tittered under the sheets, sucking on illicit squares of bitter chocolate and sipping from bottles of Orangina, which Emily's outside contact had supplemented with vodka. Sometimes they would throw things at her in the dark—nothing that hurt, just a sock that one of them had worn in Games, or a balled-up note written in French that she couldn't understand and, sometimes, Emily's favourite, a tampon or a sanitary towel from the supply under her bed.

The redhead's name was Fifine Bissette, but everyone called her Fifi. She was the only daughter of France's premier power couple; her father was a renowned surgeon whose services graced only the affluent, while her mother was an ex-model-turned-socialite. A running joke at Sainte-Marthe was that Fifi's *papi* had once borrowed cold-blooded Fifi's heart for another patient and forgotten to replace it.

She and Emily made the perfect match.

Through it all, Tess forged her vendetta. Slowly but surely, her plan took shape, and became the fuel that kept her going. She used her hatred for Emily as a way to endure the monotony and loneliness of the days at Sainte-Marthe, in which she got up alone, dressed alone, and ate breakfast alone; in which she withstood her solo French classes with

Madame Fontaine and saw no other girls, then when she did felt too unsure of the language to attempt a friendship, and the longer she left it the more difficult it became and the stranger they decided she was. She used her anger as a passage through the emptiness of the night, the moonlight and the taunting laughs, as she lay still as a corpse because then they might leave her alone.

Every moment, she was thinking. She was plotting.

It was risky, but the risk was worth it. Tess had no fear. She had nothing. In the days and weeks since the adoption revelation, she had shut out the world. It had been necessary, a method of reassembly, of digging inside herself and cancelling out all those weak parts, the parts that cried for her twin and longed to be held by her.

She had wiped the slate clean and started again—with the person she wanted to be: strong, intrepid, powerful. Emily deserved it. She deserved her revenge.

*

The following week, before chapel, Tess approached Fifi in the waiting line. The other girls backed away: breaking rank was the ultimate offence.

'Where's Emily?' Tess asked in French.

'None of your business.'

'I wanted to wish her luck.'

Fifi was sceptical. 'With what?'

'The song,' Tess widened her eyes, 'for Monsieur Géroux? Oh, no, don't tell me she forgot. Aubert will go crazy—she told us about this ages ago!'

'Told you about what?' Fifi was impatient, but Tess detected a sliver of anxiety, of wanting—no, *needing*—to do right by Emily. Not to mess up.

Tess sighed. 'Look, I know Emily's been skipping Fontaine's classes.'

'She doesn't need to speak French,' Fifi jumped in, and the clique nodded in agreement. 'She's going to Hollywood to become an actress. So it's irrelevant.'

'I know,' Tess was all sympathy, 'but you know what our mother's like…'

It felt weird saying it, but she had to remind Fifi of their allegiance. That she *did* have a connection with Emily, and it might stand to reason, despite Emily's bullying, that she should wish to help her. Anyway, it was true. Emily was meant to attend Madame Fontaine's lessons. Instead she spent the entire time smoking around the back of the music block. What wasn't true was that Tess actually gave a shit.

'Aubert told us weeks back that Géroux was leaving,' Tess went on. Monsieur Géroux was their music teacher. He caused quite a stir among the pupils, due to being thirty-six, inoffensive looking, and in possession of all his own hair. He was moving to Switzerland to take up another position. 'She asked us to prepare a song,' she lied, 'with Fontaine's help, to perform for Monsieur today. As in now, in chapel.'

Fifi looked horrified.

'Oh dear,' said Tess. 'I worried this would happen. She hasn't done it, has she? Aubert will go mad! Not to mention Simone… Emily really is going to get it for this. Like, big time. I wouldn't be surprised if she was suspended.'

Fifi stumbled. 'I don't think she's done any song—she hasn't said anything…'

'*Alors*,' said Tess, handing over a piece of paper, 'just give her this, OK?'

'What is it?'

'It's the piece I wrote.' She waved her hand, as if it were

no big deal. 'I don't mind if Emily shares it. We can pretend we arranged it together. I'll go tell Aubert now. Just make sure she gets it, OK? Or it's going to be majorly embarrassing for her in there.' *Oh, she'll get it. She'll get it all right.*

Fifi clutched the paper. 'Why are you doing this?' she asked suspiciously.

Tess lifted her shoulders. 'Fifi, we're family. Haven't you heard of loyalty?'

Satisfied, she turned on her heel and went inside. Quickly, she located Madame Aubert and tied up her ploy. Tess explained that she had wished to perform a farewell song for Monsieur, and would it be OK if she and Emily interrupted morning service for a few moments to do so? Aubert thought it was a wonderful idea, and no doubt couldn't wait to report back to Simone on how well her girls were getting along. *Ha*, Tess thought as she took her place in the pews, *if only you knew*.

Minutes later, the assembly was called into chapel. Tess spotted Emily looking suitably worried. She was frantically reading through the sheet of handwriting, and each time Fifi or one of the others attempted to peek over her shoulder, she swiped them away, unwilling to admit she hadn't a clue what words were written there. Emily could barely introduce herself in French, let alone tackle the complex structures Tess had toiled hard on, looked up in the library, and double-checked with a bunch of geeks in an online forum. Excitement surged in her chest.

She didn't have to wait long. After the school refrain had been sung in its usual dispassionate drone—*'Aujourd'hui, nous sommes graines; demain, nous sommes des arbres'*— and an announcement had been made about the forthcoming hockey tournament against the rival girls' academy, L'École de Françoise Barbeau, it was time for Tess and Emily's performance. Across the pews, Tess shot her a sweet smile.

'Beloved Monsieur Géroux,' crooned Madame Aubert from the lectern, as there was a general expectant shuffling in the ranks, 'our girls in Special French wished to say goodbye to you in the way you taught them best. I think this is a lovely gesture and proves how much you mean to them—and to everybody here. So, without further ado, please welcome them to the stage: Tess Geddes and Emily Chilcott!'

Emily hesitated and, for a horrible moment, Tess thought she wasn't going to fall for it—but, at the last moment, she shuffled up to the front. She shot Tess a strange look, half gratitude and half loathing. *It serves you right*, Tess thought, remembering how her hair had been slashed, and every cruelty and unkindness she had suffered at Emily's hands. *You underestimated me. You all did.*

Tess saw Monsieur Géroux in the pews, his expression open with happy surprise. The piano struck up a lively tune. The song began.

The first verse went without a hitch. The teachers beamed through all Tess's carefully constructed sentences, praising Monsieur's delightful teaching style and prowess on the instruments, and Emily mumbled alongside her, finally falling into the tune. Then something strange happened. As they hit verse two, Tess's voice gradually receded. She turned to stare at Emily, a practised mask of disbelief on her face, as Emily continued to belt out the words, her cheeks flaming with the effort of her botched—but still, lamentably, understandable—pronunciation, and when she realised she was singing out of kilter with Tess she sang even louder to make up for it.

'Emily…!'

An elfin blonde named Claudette squeaked from the ranks,

as Emily's clique, including Fifi, turned ashen, along with the *professeurs*. Emily, thinking the shout had been some show of support, continued to sing as clear as a bell, her voice ringing out above the music, before suddenly, at Madame Aubert's signal, the piano stopped. Emily's voice travelled alone to the end of the refrain, and then fizzled out.

The congregation was staring, appalled. A few nervous laughs rose up from the chapel. Madame Aubert rushed over, red and flustered. Without a word she snatched Emily by the elbow and led her off the stage. Tess followed. On the way down they passed Monsieur Géroux, whose eyes were trained on the floor. The tips of his ears were bright red. Tess could sense the gaze of every girl boring into her.

'*Vous horrible fille!*' Madame Aubert lambasted Emily when they reached the courtyard. 'What were you thinking? Was that some kind of joke? *Allez au bureau de la directrice, immédiatement*! Until then, consider yourself a month in detention!'

'But—'

'No buts, young lady.'

'I don't—' Emily turned to Tess, but Tess gave her nothing. 'But she… I—'

'Go. *Now!*'

When Emily had scurried off, Tess said, 'I'm sorry about that, Madame. I don't know what got into her. It must have been some prank she and Fifi thought up. I mean,' she blushed, 'not to wrongly implicate anyone, it's just I saw them talking outside and giggling over something. Emily was fine in rehearsal.'

Madame Aubert, who hadn't been sure whether or not to be cross with Tess, thought a moment then shook her head. 'Don't worry, *ma chérie*, it wasn't your fault.'

It was only later, when Emily Chilcott returned to her dorm and dusted off her long-neglected French dictionary, that she realised what she, alone, had been singing.

'Monsieur, we thank you for looking up our skirts and letting us suck your big clarinet... Monsieur, we thank you for playing on our G-strings...'

From that day on, among staff, Tess Geddes remained the perfect angel. Among her class, she became something of a legend, having admitted to a carefully selected band of corridor gossips that she, in fact, had been responsible for Emily's humiliation. It was little wonder that wherever she went in the school, that month and every month after, she was followed by a tentative wave of admiration: the new girl who had taken on the year's tyrant—and won.

Emily, meanwhile, was reviled by her tutors and made fun of by her peers, for falling for such an obvious trap. Furious beyond the ability to speak, she immediately requested a room transfer and took her clique with her. She scowled and scowled and hated and bitched, but she never dared cross Tess Geddes again.

Needless to say, Tess considered it a job well done.

*

The horror of the annual swimming gala blasted into the summer term with all its attendant anxieties: fear of getting undressed, fear of changing-room snarkiness, fear of coming last in every race. As always, Teresa attempted to do the whole undressing thing entirely behind her towel. It took some skill, but she had it perfected. Her own body seemed so much... womanlier than everyone else's. That was the only way to describe it. Her breasts were large and round, and capped by dark buds. Meanwhile Emily and Fifi stood in open splendour, showing off their perfect breasts with compact, pink nipples, and the neat flash of the hair between their legs. Why weren't Tess's pink like theirs? And why were her hips pear-shaped, instead of streamlined?

'Oh my God!' came Emily's taunting shriek, all of a sudden. 'Look at her!'

For a second Tess thought she was the one being addressed, before remembering that Emily didn't go there any more.

Instead their target was a short, dumpy girl by the showers whose name she didn't know. The girl wore braces. Her hair was dark and she had a fringe.

There followed a burst of shocked whispers. 'Oh no! I can't believe it! That's gross! How *embarrassing*. Ugh, that's disgusting!'

The girl was blushing from head to toe, confused, blinking like a rabbit behind her glasses. Tess didn't know what they were talking about either.

'Sat in some red paint, have you?' Emily giggled. 'That is *rancid*, Ferraris. Someone get her a nappy!' More giggling. More revolted gasps.

Quickly, the girl patted her behind. Tess had never seen the colour drain so quickly from someone's face. The girl vanished into the nearest loo cubicle and slammed and locked the door. Emily was quick to follow, her fist battering the door.

'Come out, Little Red Riding Hood! We know you're in there!'

Tess understood. Weirdly, she had her period, too; it had to be true what they said about girls getting in sync with each other. She was about to intervene and tell Emily to stop being such a poisonous cow when a terrible crash came from inside the cubicle, the sound of the girl's head hitting the tiled floor, right before she passed out.

*

Tess went up to the medical ward before afternoon prep, where the *infirmière* showed her to Mia Ferraris's room. 'Hi,' she said, hovering at the door. 'I'm Tess.'

The girl with the fringe smiled weakly. 'Hi.'

'How are you doing?'

'OK. I just fainted, that's all.' She looked mortified.

Tess felt sorry for her. The whole school would know by now, and doubtless Emily had embroidered the tale to make it extra dramatic and gruesome. Mia would be paranoid every time she walked down the corridor. It had been a nasty thing to do.

Tess set down a supper tray. 'Want me to sit with you for a while?'

'You don't have to.'

'That's OK.'

Mia struggled up on the pillows and picked dejectedly at the fish cake. The sauce on it was congealing. 'Forget about Emily,' said Tess. 'She's a cow.'

Mia didn't reply.

'I hate having mine…' offered Tess, 'if it's any consolation.' Mia looked up. 'Not the fish cake,' Tess said, and smiled a little. Mia smiled back. 'But that too.'

Mia forced a forkful into her mouth. 'It's horrible.'

'I know!'

'It tastes like a fish I've been carrying around in my pocket all week.'

'You carry fish in your pocket?'

'No,' said Mia. 'I don't know why I said that. It just popped into my head.'

Tess laughed. She wondered why she had never seen Mia

Ferraris around before. Probably because Mia was one of those people who blended into a crowd, knocked into obscurity by the glossy bling of Emily Chilcott and her crew.

Mia's eyes were lovely, Tess thought; green but flecked with gold. Kind eyes.

'I thought what you did in chapel was cool, by the way,' said Mia.

Tess raised an eyebrow. 'Monsieur Géroux?'

'Yeah! It was so funny.'

Tess caught her eye and they exchanged a naughty grin.

'Did you see the look on his face?' she asked.

'*Playing on our G-strings*, ha ha ha!' The explosion of Mia's happy laugh made Tess join in too, and she realised it was a long time since she'd done that.

'Why do you think Emily has it in for me?' Mia said.

'She only made fun of you to get people to stop picking on her,' Tess replied. 'That's how it is with girls like Emily. She feeds on other people's misfortune. She tried with me and it didn't work, so now she's on to someone else.'

'And that someone's me,' uttered Mia miserably.

'Don't worry,' said Tess. 'I can handle Emily.'

'You know, I was always afraid to talk to you,' Mia said, 'because I thought you were too pretty to bother with me. Before you started, Emily was the prettiest girl in school. Next to you she's about as feminine as Claudette Perault's *brother*!'

Tess didn't know what to say. She thought Mia was funny. And maybe she was on to something. Was that why Emily reviled her, because she felt threatened? Was that why Calida hated her? Her sister had always strived to keep her down, to put her back in her place, to discourage her from exploring her potential. In essence, she was just like Emily. *They're as bad as each other. I don't need either of them.*

Tess swallowed the lump in her throat. She forced herself to brighten.

'Are you going to eat that?' She prodded Mia's chocolate tart.

Mia smiled and offered her a spoon. They shared it.

15

London

Simone had known that Sainte-Marthe would do her good. When she had chosen the exclusive French school, she'd thought: *This is what will set my daughter apart.*

By the time Tess became ready to embrace the power and prowess of a movie career, she would have ten times the culture and sophistication of every other actress on the block. Of course the press was in rapture over the broadcast. Nobody seemed sure about how the adoption had unfolded, but any lingering queries were quickly extinguished by the magnetism of Simone's addition. Tess was a raving beauty: on the cusp of womanhood, her age was riveting. Why hadn't Simone selected a younger child? Because, said Simone, she wanted to help those who were so often overlooked.

That was bullshit. Nobody except her knew the real reason.

Just as everything was looking as close to perfect as could be, at the start of the summer holidays, someone fucked up. And what a fuck-up it was.

Had Simone not been wearing her sea courgette face pack when she found the letter, her features might have betrayed some iota of the shock and horror that washed over her like a bucket of sick. As it was, she calmly knelt to the doormat, flicked through the pile of mail her PA had dropped, and released a dainty gasp.

'Vera!' she squawked. The maid came running. 'Tell me what this says,' she thrust the ream of pages into Vera's hands, 'word for word—leave *nothing* out.'

Vera did as she was told. Simone clutched the banister as each phrase assaulted her. '*Teresita, please come home. I'm sorry for what happened between us and I want to make things right. I love you and I miss you… I need you back here…*'

'Jesus Christ!' screeched Simone after Vera had concluded her translation. She grabbed the letter: it was dated months ago, must have been sitting in Michelle Horner's in-tray all that time like a silent assassin. She ripped it up, then, deciding that wasn't enough, stormed into Brian's office and fed it into the shredder.

Immediately she got her manager on the phone. She was aware of Calida Santiago's countless notes to Michelle's office, all of which had been destroyed on receipt. Everyone there had strict instructions *never* to allow such a missive to arrive on Simone's doorstep: the last thing she needed was for Tess to start believing there was a long-lost twin out there pining for her return. Who had disobeyed the rules? Who had been idiotic enough to forward it to the house? Supposing Tess had seen it?

'I don't know how this happened,' Michelle said, uncharacteristically flustered. 'I hired a new assistant, she's learning the ropes, perhaps she—'

'What's her name?'

'Sarah.'

'Sarah what?'

'Sarah Quentin.'

'Fire her,' Simone spat. 'Do you realise that Tess could have been here? Thank God she's out with Lucie today.' Lucie was Simone's personal shopper.

'I'm sorry.'

'Sorry doesn't cut it,' said Simone crisply. She banged the phone down.

The courgette facemask was a waste of fucking time. So much for a de-stress compress! She scrubbed it off. Action was the only route. She stormed up to Tess's bedroom and started rifling through her belongings. Then… *A-ha!*

There it was: her daughter's precious diary. Opening it, she scanned the Spanish and shouted to Vera, thrusting it into her hands. 'Tess is back at four,' she drilled. 'I want you to read the whole damn thing, do you understand? Then give me what I need: something only Tess would know. Something entirely personal to her.'

'Like what?'

'I don't know, do I? Use your goddamn imagination. Report to me in an hour. If you fail, you can consider yourself fired.'

Simone wanted to fire fucking everybody. She wondered whom else she could fire today. She'd like to fire Brian. Fat lot of good he was! And 'fat' really was the word. Right now he was out lunching with his producer buddies. When was he going to run another project? It had been years. Brian's name was flagging, while hers was on the rise. She could see her husband now, tossing back mounds of caviar and quaffing a vat of red wine as he loosened the notch on his belt. He was so fat!

Simone had to relocate to the Japanese garden in order to calm down.

It's OK. The letter was a blip, and easily rectifiable. They would forge a response to that Argentinian hillbilly, copying out Tess's handwriting and relying on Vera for the words, and that would spell the end of it. Goodbye, long-lost sister.

On the rim of the koi pond, she trailed her hand through the emerald water. It looked pale and ghostly, as if it didn't belong to her. Fish darted through lush green weeds, a flicker of red and a glimmer of white. Simone closed her eyes.

In a flash, she was back there: Surrey, 1966.

Her grandparents' house, dark and austere... The sharp stench of cabbage... Looming clocks that ticked mournfully in dimly lit corners. Floors echoed and boards creaked. A mausoleum, and not just in bricks and mortar: this was a couple in mourning. Their only child, Simone's mother, had been snatched in labour, and they had been charged with raising the girl, a killer in their eyes. They never forgave her the crime of her birth. Each time they saw her, they saw the woman God had swapped her for.

As Simone blossomed into her teens, the comparison became more striking.

At fifteen, she had fallen pregnant—a stupid mistake. She tried to conceal it, hid her sickness and concealed her bump... But, months in, by which time it was too late, her grandparents found out. They were enraged. They consigned Simone to the attic, kept her prisoner. In the end, she bore the child there. Her grandmother laid towels on the wooden floor. The agony had been extreme. It was pain beyond pain.

Afterwards, exhausted and half dead, Simone had held her son and kissed his tiny head. Not for long. Her grandparents were unwilling to face the scandal. The baby was prised from her arms, whisked away and put up for adoption. Simone had held her son for mere moments, but those moments she would remember for the rest of her life. Days later they told her she had done the right thing, and now they could sweep it under the carpet, forget all about it. That baby was best off without her...

Later, when Simone finally escaped her grandparents'

clutches, she found she could not get pregnant. Initially it had been a lottery, an amusing game—how many men could she sleep with before it eventually happened? But then the doctor told her. The trauma of her childbirth had dried her up inside. It had left her barren. *Hostile.*

That was it for her. Simone buried herself in her acting career, and eventually in Brian. She had hoped that Emily and Lysander might fill the void, but they didn't. Simone wanted her own child, just like the one she had been forced to surrender.

When it came to it, she could not face a baby again. Or a boy…

And so here was Tess. After it all, didn't Simone deserve her second shot?

She was giving another child up over her dead body. Not again. Never again.

*

She found Lysander in the basement gym. 'Fuck me,' she ordered. 'Now. Do it hard.'

Simone needed it—the thrill, the release, the reminder that she was in control. She hated him and she wanted him; she despised him and she desired him.

Lysander was topless, his shorts damp with exertion. He replaced the weights, stood from the pull-down and wiped a towel over his glistening torso.

'Don't mess with me, Lysander,' she said. 'I'm not in the mood.'

'Who's messing?'

'You're making me wait. I'm not waiting. Do it now. Fuck me.'

Lysander's handsome face fell into a satisfied grin. He

was used to their spontaneous liaisons, and it was always on his stepmother's terms. She was a horny bitch and he was a motherfucker—literally. The wrongness of it made it so right.

Roughly, Lysander pushed her down on to the sit-up bench. She faced away from him, her legs either side of the leather, waiting. He lifted her skirt.

'Come on,' Simone instructed, 'I need you. I need your big, fat, hard cock. Fuck me harder than you've ever fucked me before.'

She was so wet she thought she might slip off the bench. Lysander tore down her knickers. Without preamble, three fingers entered her from behind. She slid on to his wrist, the gym silent apart from the husk of their breathing and the warm sucking sound of her body joined with his. 'Fuck, yes,' she snarled. In the mirror she clocked his dark, concentrated face as he kneaded her to climax. Only at the point where she began to feel like a cow with a farmer's arm up its backside did she instruct him to produce his erection. Boy, was it huge. Lysander's dick sprang from his shorts.

'Make it hurt,' she commanded. 'And slap me. Slap me till I scream!'

Her stepson didn't have to work long for that. Plunging into her in one triumphant stroke, Simone released a yodelling sound from deep in her throat.

'Do it!' she cried. 'Yes, yes, harder—! Come on, is that all you've got?'

Lysander grabbed her hips and drove her ferociously against his root, his balls slapping the neatly waxed fuzz between her legs. He pulled her hair and smacked her arse until a patch of pink began to flower there. 'You like that?' he rasped.

'No, it's fucking terrible. Fuck me harder.'

He slammed deeper, hotter, faster, her pussy drenched around him.

'Get your tits out,' grunted Lysander, who was partial to tits.

Simone managed to unbutton her blouse. Lysander yanked down her bra, revealing one breast. His gaze went syrupy at the sight and he caressed the pouch, still perky despite her age. She arched beneath his touch, lithe as a cat.

'You know what's going to make me come,' she moaned, on the brink of ecstasy. 'Make it happen, you dirty fucking bastard. Nail me there.'

He didn't need to be told twice. Obediently, Lysander coursed down to that rim of skin, fingers still soaking from the honey pot. He eased his index finger inside, then his thumb, feeling her tight passage loosen around him.

'Whatever you say…' he murmured, '… *Mummy*.'

Simone cried out.

Wow, she must be pissed at something. The only time Lysander had gained rear entry was last winter, after his dad had backed the SG1 Range Rover into the front-drive ornamental fountain. Marvelling at the bulging tip of his cock, Lysander poised it against the knot of her arsehole and then, like a knife, sank in.

'Oh my God, yes,' sighed Simone, as they fell into rhythm.

This was what she needed. She needed to hurt, to be punished—to be a bad girl and a wicked wife. Nobody told Simone Geddes how to behave.

She would do whatever and whomever she wanted. She'd earned her right.

16

Argentina

Calida

Do not contact me again. I have no desire to hear from you.

Everything in your letter reminds me of why I hate it there and why I love it here, and Simone taking me away was the best thing that ever happened to me. I have a new name now, and a new life.

*You told me that you never wanted to see me again. Well, you got what you wanted. Why should I care how you feel? I meant every word I said that night. Daniel will **never** look at you because you are desperate and embarrassing—and ugly. That's why Simone chose me, not you. That's why she's my new mother. She knows you're ugly. Everyone knows you're ugly, including Daniel. When I flirted with him, he told me as much. You should give up, Calida.*

And you should give up writing to me. I don't want you. I'm not your twin sister any more. If this doesn't prove how I couldn't care less, you're even more deluded than I thought.

Don't write again. I won't read it.

Tess.

*

Every afternoon, Calida rode the bus into town, and found refuge in the place she always had: her photographs. At the library, she hid with a book, focused on it utterly and lost herself in its faces. She had come with Diego once; they had borrowed this volume and taken it home and looked at it every night. The pages were thick and shiny, the images huge—of cracked golden deserts and lush, tumbling waterfalls, of the ice-white Arctic and the glinting green ocean. But the ones that captured her most were the portraits; the mix of distrust and fascination those subjects held against the camera. For that instant, Calida was looking right into those people's souls and they were looking back. They were *seeing* each other. It was time travel. It was magic.

Leaving the library one evening, she sat on a wall by the wide-open *lago*. Across the turquoise water, the crags of her family's land rose in white, snow-capped peaks against the crystal sky. But there was no family left. It belonged to her alone.

My land.

Strange to think of it that way—and, as she did, an uncomfortable sensation came over her. She felt surrounded; tied to the dying acreage against her will, drowning in it, suffering for it, carrying its weight on her seventeen-year-old shoulders and buckling beneath its demands. Meanwhile, Teresita had escaped. She was released, freed from responsibility and able to forget it in the blink of an eye.

It wasn't fair. Nothing about this was fair. Calida had never been so aware of her limitations. Her inadequacies. How she would always play second to her gorgeous, terrifying sister, and always be the one left to pick up the pieces.

Teresita—Tess—had made that clear. How stupid she had been to rip open that letter with such excitement, such hope, when all it contained was poison.

*

Calida made her decision at the start of September. It was the only way.

On recent nights, she had taken to sleeping outside. It was too painful to stay in the bedroom she'd shared with Teresita; remembering, as children, their conversations long into the night, shushing each other and tittering beneath their blankets whenever they heard their papa passing outside. Under an empty, star-crusted sky, she could let the earth cradle her, its vastness swallow her up. She closed her eyes and imagined Daniel coming to her, lying down next to her, more addicted to him than she had ever been—worse, stronger—and finding her soul at peace only within these imaginings.

Tonight, in the shadow of the veranda, she closed her eyes. She pulled the covers up over her waist and parted her knees beneath, sighing as she tumbled into her fantasy. Her hand travelled down to the soft nest between her legs.

Come to me, Daniel, she silently begged, picturing him so clearly.

She could feel the warmth of his body alongside hers, as if it were happening; could feel his fingers on her back as they traced a languid circle. His breath warmed her neck. Calida would turn her head, just a fraction, until their mouths found each other in the silent, sweet-scented dark. Daniel's kiss would be hot and taste of the rain. She could feel his teeth and the mystery of his tongue, which hesitantly touched hers, and then, finding encouragement, filled her mouth. Daniel's hand would move from her stomach, down behind the ridge of her jeans. Deftly, he would unbutton and tug the denim down. His palm hovered over the mound of her cotton knickers.

Calida's finger plunged into the pit of her heat. She lifted her hips to meet it.

Is this OK? She could hear his voice. See his eyes, full of concern.

Yes. Oh, yes.

Have you done this before?

No.

Do you want to?

God, she did. Calida plunged her fingers deeper, rocking back and forth on the tingling bud that sent her wild. *I want to*, she pictured herself saying; *yes, I want to…*

Daniel would start kissing her neck, his lips soft and slow, practised and confident. She summoned the feel of his penis, rock-hard against her stomach, as his mouth found a path to her breasts. In her dream she was as generously endowed as Teresita. Daniel would suck, squeeze, and lick her nipples. His hair would be near white in the moonlight and she would run her fingers through it, draw it in so she could inhale him, felt the soft shells of his ears and the bristly stubble of his jaw.

You're beautiful, she heard him say. He would look right in her eyes, and she would know that he meant it: even if he were wrong, he meant it. *So beautiful…*

Calida gasped beneath her touch. She could feel his cock filling her palm, solid and strong and pumping through her fist. She needed it inside her.

Daniel kissed her stomach, moving lower, until finally he met her wetness with his tongue and she eased on to him, his lips soldered and his tongue swirling in deep circles. Her moisture doubled, running and dripping between her legs.

Over every ridge and cleft he tended until she was blind in a fever, her head spinning.

I want to have sex with you...

Calida was ready to come. Her fingers shook and her hips bucked and thrashed. She imagined Daniel kneeling between her legs, his thighs spread, his cock stiff, and her pale ankles hovering on either side. Throwing her head back, she reached for him and drew him down. Daniel would put a hand there to guide himself.

Clasping his backside, she pulled him in.

They would fall into a fast, pounding pace—he driving through her in heroic strokes, lifting her buttocks to draw her closer, pulling back so he was upright on his knees. He would clasp her breasts and massage them together, leaning over to draw one stiff nub into his mouth and then the other. In her mind, she watched, fascinated, from this angle able to see his hard-on engaged with and then withdrawn, engaged and withdrawn... Daniel would push himself up on his elbows, increasing his pace, finding a new angle and shattering her with it. Calida gripped his wrists.

She could feel them. She could feel him.

She was coming.

The sky vanished, the land flew away, the ocean crashed over her and it was all chased by a brilliant, dreadful sensation that she was powerless to stop. Bucking against her own fingers, she smothered the urge to cry out his name as she toppled one surge over the next, plummeting her into spheres of pleasure that killed her over and over until she was panting for breath and every part of her body was sated.

She blinked to the sky, catching her breath, waiting for her vision to restore.

Minutes passed.

'OK if I sit?'

His words threw her bolt upright. Daniel, the real Daniel, came round the side of the house. How long had he been there? Had he seen?

Panic engulfed her.

No. He couldn't have…

'Sure,' she croaked.

Daniel lowered himself next to her, his elbows hooked over his knees. She could tell from his expression, lost elsewhere, that he hadn't witnessed her actions. Relief didn't come close. She watched his back, the sliver of skin between his jeans and T-shirt, and thank God it was dark because her cheeks flamed at the memory of what she'd been doing. 'I have something to tell you,' he said. 'About Teresita.'

Oh no. Calida didn't think she could take it. *Tell me you didn't…*

'It was my fault,' Daniel said. 'Teresita came on to me that night in my cabin. You interrupted us. Do you remember?' Mutely, she nodded. 'I told her afterwards that nothing was going to happen between us. I liked someone else. I can't help feeling that's what drove her away—or played a part in it, anyway.' She heard him swallow. 'I wanted to tell you. I don't want to keep anything from you, Calida. Ever.'

Calida digested this. There was someone else.

Of course there was.

'It was nothing to do with you,' she told him. 'My sister made her own choice. Nobody forced her to do it. Besides, I wasn't blameless. Teresita hated me.'

'Don't say that.'

'It's true. I ruined her life. That's what she told me.'

There was a long silence. 'I know what it's like to be told that,' Daniel said.

Calida waited.

'My father used to tell me that, pretty much every day. That I was a waste of air—that I'd never amount to anything… He beat me up so bad he broke my arm. That's why I ran from home and why I'll never go back. He beat up my mother and then when she left he beat up on me. He beat me up every day. He was a drunk.'

Calida pushed herself up to a sitting position. Daniel's admission was a sheet of glass between them and she didn't want to say anything in case it broke.

'Then, when I turned sixteen, my father hit me and I didn't fall. For the longest time, I just kept standing. It hurt, just like all the other times, but I didn't let him know. So he backed off. And I went to him and I lifted him against the wall, and I came close and I said to him, real slow: "That is the last time you hit me. Do you understand? If you hit me again, I will kill you." I meant it. I meant every word.'

Calida held her breath.

'He had a temper,' finished Daniel. 'That was all.'

'How badly did he hurt you?' she asked.

'He put me in hospital. Pulled a knife a few times. It wasn't anything compared with what he did to my mother. I don't blame her for going. I would have.'

She touched his arm. He flinched. 'Why didn't you leave before?'

'I stayed for her. Without me, she'd have died. Then, when it was just the two of us, he beat me more than physically. He made me believe I would never succeed, never matter to anyone. I shouldn't have been born. I was nothing. No one.'

In the dark, a tear escaped from Calida's eye. 'And did he?' she asked.

'What?'

'Hit you again.'

'No, not after that—he knew the next time would be the last time. He never hit me after he realised I was big enough to hit back. He was a coward.'

'Is he dead?'

'I don't know. I don't want to know. I haven't heard a thing since I left that place and that's fine by me. Sometimes you have to get out to save yourself.'

Calida closed her eyes. Was that what Teresita had done?

Daniel lay down next to her, and took her hand. He took a deep breath, exhaling as if this was a truth he had kept inside for too long.

'I'm glad I told somebody that,' he said.

'I'm glad, too.'

*

Calida stayed awake, Daniel beside her, unable to follow him to dreams.

She gazed up at the host of bright stars, the stars of her home, until the sky turned from pitch to purple to lilac, the lip of the sun rose above the horizon, and dawn broke over the rugged orange peaks. All night, a storm swirled in her head.

You're desperate and embarrassing and ugly.

Daniel told me as much.

You should give up, Calida.

The shame of her masturbation mocked her, the idiocy of it. How when Daniel had lain beside her, confided in her, it had been so like her fantasy that for a moment she almost believed he might kiss her. But she was a friend to him—nothing more.

She never would be.

No man would ever want to make love to her like that. No

man would ever do those things with her... least of all the man she wanted most in the world.

There was nothing to stay for. Nothing left.

Careful not to disturb him, Calida rose and went back to the house. She dressed, showered, and quickly, quietly, packed a bag.

Then she stepped outside and watched him a while.

Remember this.

It was easier not to say goodbye. It hurt too much.

She recalled the *guanaco* her papa had spared, that day she had taken Teresita away so she didn't have to see. This was a sacrifice, just like that.

She opened the gate and started walking.

17

Paris

Life at Saint-Marthe improved with Mia Ferraris by her side. Mia was quirky and irreverent, she was funny and silly; she posted notes through Tess's locker, poems about Madame Fontaine's beard or her attempts at a slowly improving self-portrait, which she knew made Tess laugh. In lessons the girls teamed up together, and in Games they dragged their heels around the netball court and gossiped in goal about how often they ought to shave their legs, and whether boys liked shaved legs or hairy ones. Mia seemed convinced that they liked hairy ones, but Tess wasn't sure.

Mia was the only person she confided in about her real family.

'They did it for the money?' Mia was incredulous. 'How could they?'

Tess shrugged. 'Who cares? I don't.'

'You must, though. You must feel sad.'

'Why should I? They made their decision. They didn't want me. It's fine.'

'Aren't you upset?' Mia frowned.

'No.' She lifted her chin. 'I'm better off without them.'

Just before autumn term began, the school was rocked

by news that two jets had crashed into the Twin Towers in New York City. Images of burning skyscrapers and billowing smoke filled TV screens; weeping masses and blackened faces.

'My God,' cried Mia, as she and Tess watched the grim bulletins unfold.

Tess thought briefly of Calida. She didn't know why— Calida wasn't in New York—but the disaster roused old instincts: the urge to reach for her twin in times of crisis, to make sure she was still there, still OK, her other half, or the ghost of it.

*

In the spring Tess Geddes turned eighteen, she was sent to stay at the *appartement* of a Parisian socialite named Madame Hélène Comtois. All the girls at Sainte-Marthe were referred to similar posts during the Easter holidays, the idea being to learn the refinement befitting their social standing: the poise, finesse and general *savoir vivre* that marked the difference between girls and ladies. Madame Comtois lived in the 16th arrondissement at the top of an ornate Belle Epoque building, whose interior was bigger than Simone Geddes' London mansion, only on one floor instead of seven.

In her youth Madame had been a fashion model, and was now married to an eminent member of the *Parlement Français*. She was unusually thin and tall, with cropped dark hair and grey, feline eyes, which were obscured by green-tinted circular spectacles that she kept on a chain around her neck. She smoked constantly.

'While you stay under my roof, you live by my rules,' Madame told her when she arrived. But, three weeks in, there didn't seem to be many rules to live by. Aside from her evening tutelage in comportment, conduct, and carriage, and the obligation to speak to Madame exclusively in French, Tess was left to her own devices. She took herself to museums by the Place du Trocadéro, and read her book (*Le Comte de Monte Cristo*, given to her by Madame) in the Bois de Boulogne. She wandered the avenues off the Place de l'Étoile and took the Métro to the Basilica in Montmartre.

Mia Ferraris called every day. Her best friend was being instructed on La Rive Gauche and her madame was a tyrant. 'She looks like a steamed pudding,' said Mia.

Tess smiled. But even as she wanted to lean on Mia, to rely on her completely, she held back. She kept a part of herself protected, a part that no one could touch.

'She's wild,' Tess heard Madame Comtois say into the telephone one night, during one of her many conversations with Simone, 'but her beauty is *divine*.'

The following week, Simone flew to Paris. She arrived with Madame shortly after midday, complaining about the trouble she'd had with changing her euros. 'Why ever you let the franc go I *do* not know. We'll never lose the pound!'

She had been there ten minutes when she asked to speak to Tess—alone.

'Sit down,' said Simone matter-of-factly, when Madame had gone next door.

Tess watched as Simone peeled off a pair of leather gloves and placed them neatly on the cabinet. Her lips were painted red and her recently highlighted locks were pulled back in an elegant chignon. She observed Tess before glancing away.

'I was informed this morning that Julia and Calida are dead,' relayed Simone in a peculiar, disembodied voice. 'There was a robbery at the store they were in and they were shot and killed at the scene.' She blinked. 'I'm sorry, Tess. The farm, its contents, and the land will be sold. There's nothing left. I thought you should know.'

The wave that hit her was silent. Momentarily, it stole her breath.

'It's a terrible blow,' said Simone, 'but never mind. It's over now.'

Tess waited for the tears to come, but her eyes were dry. She just kept staring at the floor, at the gold swirl on Madame's carpet in the shape of an oil lamp.

They didn't love you. They didn't care about you.

They're nothing to you any more—just two strangers who died.

She swallowed the tidal wave of despair, a trace of salt on her tongue.

'Come along.' Simone sat next to her, and placed an arm round her shoulders. 'I'll take you to breakfast. I know a charming little place by the river.'

*

In June, Madame Comtois confirmed her attendance at the annual *danse d'éntrée*. The ball was a mingling ground for the city's elite sons and daughters. Madame had sent her protégées there since day one, and Tess was to be no exception. 'It sounds lame,' she protested in her dorm at Sainte-Marthe, as she was made to pack for the weekend away. Madame Aubert was obliged to sign girls off for their debutante reception.

'You kidding, right?' Mia spluttered. 'I'm soooo jealous! Mine isn't coming up until winter—and even then I bet Madame Pudding won't let me go…'

'Want to take my place?'

'Don't talk rubbish. You'll have a great time.' Mia beamed

and buoyed Tess's spirits and by the time the evening came around, she was almost convinced herself.

'Remember,' instructed Madame Comtois as she deposited Tess at the grand entrance to L'Hotel Aquitaine, 'the secret is *la modération*: grace and restraint at all times. You are a lady now, and a lady has a reputation to uphold.'

Another group of so-called ladies was clustered round the portico. Emily Chilcott and her gang resembled a nest of flamingos, dressed as they were in varied shades of pink. 'Look who it is,' Emily muttered, '*la petite orpheline*.'

'Piss off, Emily.'

'I didn't know Madame Comtois had such pretty curtains or I would have made a dress of them myself!' The clique sniggered. Madame had chosen her gown, reams of floaty chiffon with a nipped-in waist, but while it mightn't have been Tess's first choice, she conceded the colour suited her: against her bronzed skin and tumble of jet curls, she looked dangerous and alternative, a far cry from the rest of them.

Emily's own hair was bandaged up in a sleek yellow top-knot, secured so tightly on the crown of her head that it was tugging her eyes to her ears. Her dress clashed badly and Tess considered telling her, before remembering Madame's words: *grace and restraint at all times*. Emily might not possess them, but she did.

Alone, Tess went inside, where a porter took her coat. Music drifted out of *la grande salle*. In the bathroom she killed time, sampling hand lotions and dozens of perfume spritzers, which she dabbed on her wrists and ears as she had seen Madame do. After a while, she emerged. Beneath the domed vault of the impressive ballroom, rings of whispering girls eyed squads of posturing boys and occasionally a representative of one would pair off with a member of the other. First kisses, first fumbles—Tess knew she was a late bloomer compared with the others girls at Sainte-Marthe (even Mia had crossed that elusive bridge, spending the night with her brother's best friend during the autumn half-term, although she was adamant they hadn't had sex), but, even so, she wasn't sure this enforced mating ceremony was necessarily the best place to do it.

'Uh, excuse me…?'

Tess turned. The boy had gel-soaked curtains plastered to his forehead and the frightened eyes of a hare tangled in chicken wire. She could sense his blush, wafting out of him like an open oven. 'I'm Gilbert Toupin,' he stumbled. 'You can call me… uh… Gilbert. Would you like to dance?'

She had heard the Toupin name. Old money. Their ancestral home was a sprawling château in Bordeaux and the parents were reclusive aristocrats.

Over by the drinks, she observed Emily and Fifi pointing and giggling. Gilbert saw it too. Ashamed, he bowed his head. Tess took his hand. 'I'd love to,' she said.

Throughout their dance she was aware of his erection pressed against her leg, and was too afraid to move in case it did something unexpected, or it got caught or she hurt it, and Gilbert, for all his bumbling ineptitude, would expose her own glaring inexperience. She thought of the bravado she had worn on the farm, the foolishness of her flirtation with Daniel. If it had gone any further she wouldn't have known what to do. She would have feared ending up like her father, in the stables with Señorita Gonzalez. Even now, she could hear his groan. Could smell the sickly lavender…

Gilbert's embrace was clamped around her.

'You're so pretty…' Gilbert mumbled into her ear. When the moment came and he adjusted his head to kiss her, homing in like a missile, she at last broke free.

'I'm going to get a drink,' she told him. 'Back in a second.'

'I'll come with you—'

'No. It's OK. You wait here.'

Tess spent the rest of the night doing all she could to avoid Gilbert Toupin. She hid in the loos, she disappeared outside; she smoked four cigarettes with a girl in her History class who everyone said was anorexic. Miserably she watched the clock, praying for the time to come when she could escape this torture, when all at once someone produced a bottle of vodka. Finally, the chance to get drunk; as the alcohol coursed through her bloodstream Emily's acid scowls barely registered and, when Fifi Bissette cornered her with a lecture about how liquor didn't suit fat girls because it made them believe they were pretty and thin and then they made idiots of themselves, Tess frowned, nodded seriously, and then smiled nicely and said:

'Go fuck yourself, Fifi.'

She had just refuelled for the umpteenth time, she'd lost count, when, turning, she knocked into somebody; the liquid splashed out in a silver arc and spilled all down his pristine white shirt. '*Lo siento*,' she gasped. 'I mean, *excuse-moi*! I'm sorry!'

The man touched the material. She saw his hands; wide, capable hands, the fingers long, and the light covering of dark hair that escaped his wrists.

'It's no big deal.'

She put her glass down and started dabbing his shirt with the drapery of her skirt. A blue stain started to spread. 'Oh dear.'

'Leave it. It's fine. It was an accident.'

Tess glanced up, but, instead of the hostile reception she was expecting, the face that met hers was gently amused. He had dark hair and a soft mouth, a square jaw, and the chest she had slammed into was warm and hard.

'Alex Dalton,' he said, holding out his hand.

She shook it. 'That sounds English.'

'American, actually.'

'Then why are you speaking French?'

'Because you are,' he replied. 'We can speak Spanish, if you prefer.'

'I'm not Spanish. I'm Argentinian.' She tried to focus through the blur.

'Oh,' the man said, smiling a little. '*Lo siento.*'

'Are you at school here?' she blurted. She didn't like the way he was looking at her, as if she was funny. She wasn't funny.

'What do you think?'

'I think you're as rich and spoiled as everyone else.' She would never have been so rude had she been sober, but in saying the words she realised she meant them. Tess wasn't like them, or him, however much she kidded herself. She was slurring now and she could see two Alex Daltons, one overlapping the other.

'Aren't you?' he challenged.

'No. I was sold and kidnapped. I don't belong here.'

Alex Dalton laughed. 'Well, I ran away from home and now I'm hiding in a jewel thief's cellar, and he only lets me out after dark. So I work here, as a waiter, filling up glasses for all these rich, spoiled kids. People like you don't normally speak to me, so it's a really special night when someone spills their illegally smuggled vodka all down my uniform. Do you need some fresh air?'

'I'm fine, thank you.'

Haughtily Tess moved away, but as she did her foot got caught in the hem of her dress and she tripped. Alex Dalton caught her. She straightened, smoothed her skirt, and, filled with shame, shrugged him off and stormed out on to the terrace.

Fresh air hit and with it arrived a slam of nausea. Her tummy flipped and her mouth filled with saliva. Panicking, Tess located the nearest plant pot—an elaborate Roman basin filled with bougainvillea—and hurled a spurt of raw alcohol into it.

Someone was holding her hair back and for a crazy moment she believed it to be Mia, before remembering Mia wasn't there. 'Are you all right?' came a voice.

'Ugh! Get away from me! Can't you see I'm being sick?'

'Yes, I see,' said Alex Dalton.

'Go away. I feel terrible. Leave me alone.'

'I'm taking you home.'

'I can get home by myself.'

'Come here,' he held out his jacket, 'put this on.'

'I'm not cold.' But when he came close to wrap it round her shoulders, she didn't object. 'Sorry if I smell,' she said meekly.

'Actually,' he said in English, 'you smell like a florist's. Do you always wear this much perfume?' Tess thought of all the samples she had doused herself in earlier, in the bathroom. How rude of him to comment on it! She pushed him away.

'I'm teasing,' he said. 'Come on. I'll bring a car round.'

'Aren't you working?'

Alex frowned, as if he didn't understand. Then he smiled. 'They'll manage.'

The ride back to Madame's *appartement* was hell, every swerve and turn causing her to grit her teeth and blanch a shade whiter. Alex instructed the driver to pull over by the Parc de Buttes-Chaumont so she could puke again.

'Madame's going to kill me,' she despaired as she climbed back into the car.

Alex thought about it. 'I have an idea.'

Moments later they stopped outside the Café Convivial,

round the corner from Madame's. Alex forced her to drink three espressos in a row and go to the bathroom so she could splash her face with cold water. When she emerged, she felt better.

'You know you never told me your name,' he said, when she sat down.

'It's complicated.'

'How can it be complicated? It's only a name.'

'It just is.'

'Parents divorced?'

'No. My parents are dead.'

Alex stalled. 'I'm sorry. I didn't realise—'

'It's OK. My name's Tess.'

'You look like a pirate.'

'You say weird things.'

They sat in silence. Alex watched her. 'So who kidnapped you?'

Tess scratched her nail around a check on the red and white cloth. She looked up into Alex's green eyes and couldn't decide if he was laughing at her or inviting her to laugh with him. She didn't know why, but she told him; something in her craved to tell a stranger so she could try the story on for size, see how it sounded out loud, all at once. She told Alex Dalton everything, from the beginning, through Simone's first visit to her being taken away, from London to Paris, from news they had sold her for cash to news of the robbery and the obliteration of her family and her home. She could talk about everything and keep her emotions in check but when she said Calida's name she choked. She was tormented by every bad thought she'd had against her twin, every bad thing she'd said. It was no wonder she'd wanted to get rid of her.

I wish you'd just disappear…

With each revelation, Alex's expression sank. His eyes lost their humour and his brow tightened. He didn't interrupt; he listened.

'I thought you were joking,' he said quietly, when she'd finished.

'About what?'

'When you said you were kidnapped.'

'I suppose I wasn't kidnapped,' she admitted. 'I told myself that because I couldn't face the facts. I couldn't accept that they did this thing to me.'

A tear rolled out of Tess's eye and plopped on to her skirt. 'Why didn't my sister want me?' she whispered. 'Why did she let me go? Now she's gone and I...'

Alex took her hand. She thought how small hers looked, under his.

Alex wanted to say something meaningful, something that would help, but there were no words big enough. He kept his hand there, with his thumb stroking the back of hers.

'Come on,' he said eventually. 'You're tired.'

He walked her back to Madame's. Outside, on the steps, she hoped he wouldn't try to kiss her. But all he did was to touch his lips briefly to her cheek.

'I'm sorry,' she said, rubbing her nose. 'I'm a mess. You must see so many girls like me, in your job—you must be sick of sorting them out.'

'There aren't any girls like you,' Alex said. 'Good night, Pirate.'

Tess was through the door and straight into the glare of an anxiously waiting Hélène Comtois, before she realised he hadn't asked for his jacket back.

18

Argentina

Calida arrived at the coach station and bought the first ride out of there.

'I've got one headed for Mendoza,' said the woman at the counter, tapping on her keyboard. 'Leaves at three. You'll have to be quick.'

'I'll take it.' Calida fumbled in her bag and pulled out a stash of loose change. She handed it over, coins spilling across the desk.

The woman counted it. 'That isn't enough,' she said.

'It isn't?'

'No. You're two hundred short.'

Calida scrabbled in her bag for more, even though she knew that was all she had. 'Do you have anything cheaper? I don't mind where I'm going.'

The woman frowned, but checked the system again. 'Not until tomorrow,' she said. She folded her arms. 'How come you're so desperate to get away?'

'I'm not desperate.'

'You look it.'

Calida started scooping the coins back into the palm of her hand. The woman watched her, then covered the remainder and swept it into the kiosk.

'*Aca tienes.*' She peeled a ticket out of the machine. 'Platform 9.'

Calida's hand shook. '*Gracias.*'

'Keep the rest. But do me a favour? Get something to eat.'

*

The journey was long. Calida's eyes threatened to close but each time she jolted herself awake. Night fell over the road. Miles vanished as they sailed up the *Ruta Nacional*, the landscape changing from green to ochre and finally to black. They passed farms and lakes and forests, crossed bridges and wove between mountains, carved a line across open plains and rugged lowland. Calida had never been out of her region and the enormity of her country rolled away from her in all directions. The towns fascinated her, buildings filled with people and lives; dramas, hopes, and fears just like hers. She couldn't decide if this was a comfort or not; there was a sense of entitlement over her anguish and she wasn't sure yet if she wanted to share it.

They stopped to refuel. At the side of the road a young boy found her eyes through the window. His feet were bare and he was holding a bucket out for change. His T-shirt was ripped and his arms were thin and brown. Calida couldn't see his parents, or that he was with anyone. She smiled and the boy stared back, uncertain.

They moved on. Sunset deepened. Melting gold seeped across a wide mauve sky. Shades of coral chased the fading blue and a heap of bloodshot clouds gathered on the horizon. Calida held her camera to it but the motion of the coach made it difficult to capture. A few people in the surrounding seats threw her curious glances and she wished she could take their pictures as well: the cracked-leather face of the old man

opposite or the smooth-browed child making her dollies kiss.
It made the moment she was in real and concrete, permanent,
rocks in a sea of relentless change.

*

She arrived in Mendoza just after nine. Her neck ached from
the deep well of sleep she had toppled into as dawn was
rising, unable to fight it any more. Dreams of Daniel hung
on, intoxicating, the night she had spent lying next to him just
one moon passed but at the same time impossibly far away,
surreal, as if it had never happened.

By now he would be wondering where she was; maybe
he'd even be worried. But sooner or later Daniel would forget
about her. He would find a new girlfriend—maybe he already
had one—and Calida's face would quickly fade from memory.
He would understand there had been no future for her on the
farm, in spite of how much she had loved it. Her papa was
lost. Her sister was lost. So was her mother. The last person
she had clung on for, the final string of hope, had been lost
to her all along.

'*Esta es la última parada.*' A steward was holding an open
litterbag and picking a wrapper from the adjacent seat. 'This
is the last stop. Are you getting off?'

Calida blinked from her daydream. She was the only one
left on the coach.

'*Sí. Gracias.*'

Grabbing her bag, she descended the steps and retrieved
her suitcase from the luggage handler. She heaved it up the
concourse and took a sweltering breath.

Mendoza was furiously hot. The coach station was packed
with travellers, teenage groups with their arms slung round
each other and clusters of excited backpackers, tired mothers

fanning themselves and families passing round food packets, the younger ones asleep on their parents' laps. An old woman on a bench was sucking a *mate* straw and eyeing her beadily. Music played from a snack kiosk.

Calida went inside and washed her face. In the terminal, she joined the ranks of tourists checking the Departures board. Two magic words danced out at her:

BUENOS AIRES.

The elusive capital… There, anything was possible.

Calida checked her cash: enough for a sandwich and a drink but that was all. She had to turn her fortunes around. She had got this far only by chance, and from here on in had to forge her own luck. Resourcefulness had always been on her side—that same nature that Teresita had dismissed so cruelly. Teresita might have had the dreams, but Calida had the brains. All she had to do was come up with a plan.

Feeling light-headed, she found a stall and bought a packet of crackers and a bottle of water. She should save the rest of her money. Calida was no stranger to sleeping under the stars, and as she emerged on to the street and began her enquiries at every shop and bar in town, every booth and garage, asking after any opportunities for work, however sporadic and however thinly paid, and received only refusals, she prepared herself for sleeping rough over the next few weeks. Come late afternoon she was exhausted and found a park to collapse in, the grass, by now cooling, a welcome cushion for her weary bones. The park was emptying, day-trippers trickling out and the stone fountain dwindling to a stop. Calida laid her bag and coat beneath a tree.

That night she slept soundly, the day's upheaval plummeting her into welcome oblivion. But the next day was the same, and the next, and the next.

Then, on the fourth night, something happened. Calida was on the cusp of sleep, starving after her funds had run dry, and, when she heard their voices through the onset of sleep, creeping closer, she thought they could be part of her dream.

The kick to her stomach put paid to that. It was sharp, sudden, an unbelievable shock. The boys began to beat her with unfettered enjoyment. She curled up in a ball with her arms wrapped round her head as they beset her back and legs, bruising her shoulders and slamming their heels and fists into every scrap of trembling body they could find. They took everything, her bag and her case, all but the clothes she wore. The only item they left was her camera. Before she passed out, Calida heard one of them say, 'Piece of shit,' before tossing it to the ground. Comatose, she grabbed the neck strap, held on to it like a lifeline, and watched them rush away into the dusk, laughing and hooting like dogs, while tears of pain and humiliation soaked her face. Later, she would feel satisfaction at imagining them opening their spoils and finding so little. A few pesos she had been saving—that was all. She hoped it was worth it.

Next morning she woke, every part of her aching. A kind face hovered.

'Are you all right? *Díos mio*, you poor girl…'

Calida fell back into unconsciousness. The ground shook with approaching footsteps and a seam of new voices threaded around her, like a host of angels.

*

Her recovery unfolded on a vineyard outside town, owned by a man named Cristian Ramos. It was a pretty, hidden estate off a country lane, next to an ivy-covered church, and Cristian was a jovial, generous-hearted winemaker, who had been out walking his dog at dawn when he had come across a bruised and battered eighteen-year-old whom at first he'd thought was dead. Cristian was a gentle, honest man, father to three young boys and husband to his wife of twenty years.

'Stay here as long as you need,' the couple told her, after listening to her story.

Calida protested, as much as her depleted state would allow, but they would hear none of it and said she could earn her keep by working on the vineyard. So she spent her days amid the vines, rows of pink-skinned grapes that panned as far as the eye could see towards the crust of the Andes, perspiring beneath the sun and picking until her fingers were stained. The grapes discoloured and roughened her hands, dark juice engraved her palms, while the riper fruits, ready to burst, left their skins beneath her nails. Now and then she startled at a noise that turned out to be a flap of wings or a stir in the plants, and tensed, the ghosts of her attackers always at her back.

Gradually, she made progress. Those scars that could heal healed. The others, the invisible ones, she kept to herself, and tried to avoid touching them.

Weeks turned into months and the season changed. Cristian hooked her up with a contact of his who owned a restaurant in town. Calida started waiting tables there during the evenings and slowly her pockets filled. Cristian and his family refused to take any of it, though she tried to press it on them.

One day, Cristian called her in from the vineyard to tell her she had a visitor.

It was Daniel.

He was in the living room, his back to her, looking at a picture of Cristian and his wife on their wedding day. Part of her wanted to drop to her knees with happiness and beg him to take her home; another, stronger, part kept standing.

'How did you find me?'

Daniel turned, and a series of emotions crossed his face like the wings of a dark bird: sorrow, heartache, confusion, relief—and finally anger. He looked different at Cristian's house, smaller somehow. 'You've been gone three months,' he said. His voice was steady but his eyes gave him away: hopeful, yet guarded, like the *guanaco*. 'Three months, Calida—do you have any idea what you've put me through?'

No, was the answer, because she had chosen not to think about it.

'I'm sorry.'

'You're sorry? That's it?'

'I don't know what you want me to say.'

'You can start with an explanation. Tell me how you could—' Daniel's jaw set. 'Without even an explanation, just vanishing like that. Coming out here all alone.'

She disliked that this proved him right; that after all she was clueless, unable to survive anywhere but on the farm, naïve to the point of risking her own life. Teresita could survive in the big bad world—she was special—but Calida? No way.

Daniel's blue eyes searched hers. 'At first I figured you couldn't have gone far, but no one in town had seen you. In the end I tried my chances at the coach station. That woman remembered you, said she felt sorry for you, gave you your fare.'

Frustration sparked in her belly. *Why do I have to answer to you?*

Teresita didn't have to answer to anyone. Teresita never had. Not like Calida. Good old boring, reliable Calida, who never did anything out of the ordinary.

'When I got here,' said Daniel, 'I checked the hospitals. I

was convinced I would find you and that would be it. Then your name came up. The doctors told me a man had brought you in. From there I found Cristian's address.'

'Go back,' she said.

'What?'

'Go back to the farm. You've found me now, haven't you? And I'm fine.'

'I don't understand—'

'I can't stay there,' she told him, coldly. 'There's nothing left for me.'

'And there is for me—without you?' Daniel took a step towards her, then a warning flash as her head rose, and stopped. 'Did I do something wrong?'

'No.'

'Why, then? I thought… Calida, I'm not someone who has to do this. I'm not someone who talks about things—I just… I just *do them*. After what I told you,' he searched for the words, 'it took a lot for me to tell you that. I haven't told anyone else. There are two people in my life that I trust, and one of them's myself.'

Calida closed her heart to his words.

Daniel will never look at you because you are desperate and embarrassing.

'I trusted you,' he said. 'I trust you. And then you ran out on me.'

Calida was sick of being trustworthy. Trustworthy wasn't exciting or sexy or daring. Trustworthy was a friend, not a lover. 'I'm glad I left,' she said.

'*No te creo*. I don't believe you.'

She was measured—she stepped into Teresita's shoes for a moment and let herself be hard. 'I don't want the ranch any more and I don't want our friendship.'

The edge of compassion in his voice evaporated. 'You don't, huh?'

A beat elapsed in which she could have spoken, but didn't.

'You get to run away while I stay behind to pick up the pieces?'

'That's what Teresita did.'

'That was different.'

'If it pains you to go back then don't,' she lashed. 'The farm doesn't belong to you anyway—Julia only took you in because she felt sorry for you.'

There was a terrible silence. Calida knew she was being vicious, but now the poison was spilling she found she couldn't go back; as if this exchange was happening with her sister, all the hate and upset stacked against Daniel because he was here, because he could take it. It was easier to drill deeper than to turn back.

'Get rid of it,' she said, 'even if you have to give it away. See if I care.'

'You do care.'

'No, I don't. Why should I?'

'You can't cut me off like this.'

'Like she did?'

'It's nothing like that.'

'I never want to see that place again. OK? I never want to see you again. Who knows, Daniel, if you'd never come into our lives none of this would have happened.'

'Calida—'

Daniel reached for her, a last attempt. She backed away. In that instant, she knew she had lost him for good. His body closed. 'If that's how you feel,' he said.

'It is. I hate that place.'

'Just like you hate me?'

She looked him square in the eye. 'Right now, a little less.'

Daniel absorbed the final blow. In his gaze she saw a stranger reflected and, even now, especially now, registered some satisfaction at her reinvention.

At the door, he lifted his head a fraction, as if he were about to say something more, something that would unpick this and make it right. Anything.

'Goodbye, Calida.' The door slammed.

*

Calida saw her sister again just before Christmas 2002.

She had finished eating with Cristian and his family and made her excuses for bed. The children were next door with the TV on. The Ramoses' television wasn't the sort they had owned on the ranch. This one was huge and in colour, with dozens of channels. Calida was passing through when suddenly, there it was—a flash of red, a delectable smile; an impossible glimmer, like a butterfly almost caught then gone.

'Wait.' The children, confused, stopped the remote.

Simone Geddes assailed her first, a brittle smile locked in place for the cameras. It was as if Calida had seen the actress yesterday, no detail lost, that same ruthless, serene expression, polished beyond humanity. Simone was attending a film premiere in London, swathed in diamonds and a velvet dress the colour of midnight.

And then the butterfly: *Teresita.*

Calida gripped the back of a chair. The breath dried in her throat and a cool ribbon spooled down her neck. The siren onscreen bewitched her—her sister and a stranger. She wanted to reach in and pluck her from this fantasy, to dig and dig until she found the girl she had lost—but, thousands of miles across the ocean and an infinite distance beyond, she understood, finally, why Teresita didn't want to return.

Her twin shone. That was the only word for it. She had entered paradise. Her black hair had grown into liquid sable, piled high on top of her head. Calida knew that head: she had kissed it good night and smoothed its brow; she had pulled that hair when she was mad and held a fistful in her sleep when she was afraid. Emeralds the size of plums dripped from Teresita's ears. Her gown was red and pooled to the floor.

Simone did the talking, her arm held proprietorially round Teresita's waist. Teresita just stood there, and smiled and smiled. Why shouldn't she? She had it all.

Calida bolted upstairs. She lay on her bed, listening to the air as it filled her lungs: Teresita, Daniel, the world that had exploded in a thousand showering lights.

Cristian's wife knocked on the door. She couldn't bring herself to answer it.

Catching her image in the glass, she surveyed her tatty clothes, her bitten nails and her earth-smeared skin. Never had she felt so plain. All the while she had been pining, Teresita had been out there, living a stolen life and basking in her fortune.

When had the sword fallen? When had they come apart? When had it all gone wrong? She had thought it was Daniel, but saw now he'd been merely the catalyst. When Teresita was an infant, squirming like a kitten, fighting free; when she was five and broke out of Calida's arms to run alone across the prairie; when they went riding together and her sister, strong and wild as the horses, galloped ahead without a backward glance? Calida had taken for granted that they would always be part of each other, sewn into each other's lives, inseparable. She had been wrong.

Tess Geddes was a pitiless creature.

Ambitious. Cruel. Nakedly unkind.

Bitch, Calida thought, and with the word came a rush of unexpected heat, like fire rushing through a window. She said it again, this time out loud.

It tasted good.

Her anger came apart. In dismantling it, she took the useful bits and hid them, like treasure. Determination. Grit. The indomitable heart of the wronged.

Selfish bitch. You think you've ruined me.

Guess what? I'm only just beginning.

*

In the morning, Calida said goodbye to Cristian and his family. At the station she knew without hesitation where she was heading, and bought her fare without difficulty. She slept soundly on the coach, dreaming of what was to come.

Teresita had made it the easy way, cheating her pass into wealth and success. Calida intended to match her dollar for dollar—the difference was that she would work for it. And when she had, when she was equally as rich and renowned as her twin, she would look Tess Geddes hard in the eye and demand to be recognised.

I'm your worst nightmare.

In the gloom of the carriage, Calida smiled.

I'm your dark horse. And I'm coming for you.

19

St Tropez

'I've missed you so much!'

Tess arrived at the Port Grimaud villa just as Mia Ferraris stepped out to greet her. The friends embraced and an assistant took Tess's bags. The waterside retreat was bright and cool, an open kitchen skewered by an ornate spiral that rose to three upper floors, and, at the far end, where a spill of Côte d'Azur sunlight washed in, a forty-foot sailing yacht was tethered in the marina as casually as a car parked on a drive.

Mia's shoulders were burned and there was a livid strip of pink at her waist. 'Ugh, I know,' she said. 'I've been trying all week for an even tan, you know how I have to rotisserie myself or else I miss a bit? Then I fell asleep on one side.'

'It's her own fault,' came a woman's voice, floating downstairs. 'I wish you wouldn't spend so much time in the sun, *chérie*, it isn't good for you.'

'*Bonjour*, Madame Ferraris,' said Tess. She had met Béatrice and her husband Anton at the Sainte-Marthe open day. All the parents had been invited—strange that she should include Simone and Brian in that bracket, but what else were they?—as the students prepared to move into one of Paris's *Grandes Écoles*. This seemed a *grande* waste of time given Tess's impending assignation with LA, and, as far as she was concerned, to hell with the rest of her education. By now she was frantic to reach the big league: Hollywood. Movies. Rich, powerful billionaires... Simone called every day to inform her of meetings being set up, power lunches being booked in, and a meticulously selected troupe of agents already waiting in the wings. Whenever Tess returned to London she was flaunted at some glittering event, while Emily Chilcott looked on with an acid glare. Emily's envy was a delectable bonus. Brian had sent his daughter to Sainte-Marthe to become a doctor or a lawyer—but that wasn't what Emily wanted. Emily wanted what Tess had... only Emily couldn't have it.

'*You think you've got what it takes, huh*?' Emily hissed. '*Dream on.*'

Tess stayed quiet. She knew she was ready—everyone else could bite. She didn't plan to become just any actress, oh no: she planned to become the most talked-about, magnificent actress of her generation. *That'll show them.* She only wished Julia and Calida were alive to see it, tortured by guilt, wishing they'd never done what they had. How much had she been worth, she wondered—a thousand, a million, a billion, more? Whatever, she would earn ten times that amount. A hundred times.

'Call me Béatrice, please!' Béatrice smiled. 'None of this Madame, it makes me feel ancient. How are your mother and father?'

'*Ils sont bien.*'

'We should have invited them out here... *La prochaine fois.*'

Tess didn't like the sound of this reunion one bit. At the school open day, once Simone had finished griping about

Concorde's imminent closure ('I suppose I shall be taking the Boeing bus along with the hoi-polloi!'), she had slyly murmured that Béatrice was a 'hippy', and that she shouldn't be wearing Lanvin because it clung to her 'motherly shape'. Just because Béatrice had a different allure—a natural one that didn't appear as if she had been hung out on the washing line for three days by her ears—it didn't make her any less attractive. '*Peut-être*,' Tess said. 'Maybe.'

Mia handed her a beer. 'What are we waiting for? Let's hit the beach!'

*

The vacation was as enchanting as Mia had promised. The girls spent their days reading and sunbathing, taking the dinghy out to nearby coves, and wandering idly through the old town to pick up bric-a-brac. Tess ate like a queen: fuzzy pink peaches for breakfast, baguette with chocolate spread for lunch, then pizza at midnight.

'I'll permit this holiday so long as you *promise* not to put on weight,' Simone had dictated before she'd left. 'I've got Maximilian Grey-Garner III interested in representation and I guarantee you now he will *not* take on a walrus.'

The idea of Maximilian Grey-Garner III was at once terrifying and fabulous (although including him in the same phrase as 'walrus' would have a lasting and troubling effect). With a name like that, he had to be big league. Tess couldn't wait to impress him; to use him, his people, use whomever she had to, to climb to the top.

On her final weekend, Béatrice and Anton sailed the yacht down the coast to moor at St Tropez. Tess and Mia sat on the bow, their legs dangling over the edge. They each sipped a glass of chilled rosé as the yacht slapped up and down on the waves, feeling giggly as they compared tans. Tess had gone right off alcohol following puke-gate at the *danse d'éntrée* but was now in full recovery.

Before lunch they swam in the sparkling sea. Mia dived to look for fish. The snorkel bunched her hair into a muffin-top while squishing her top lip out. She made silly kissy faces while Tess laughed so much that she struggled to stay afloat.

'Time to eat, you two,' called Béatrice from the stern, her kaftan fluttering.

Anton detached the inflatable from the back of the boat and piloted it to shore. The beach shuddered closer in the hazy midday heat, a strip of gold peppered with flickering white parasols, beneath which neat-suited waiters hurried with piled-high plates of lobster and mussels. They took a table by the water and ordered *jambon cru* and melon, *steak-frites* and salad, and bottles of wine and Badoit. Tess was stuffed.

'Why don't you girls walk into port?' suggested Anton, as they debated the possibility of swimming after such a big meal. So the girls set off for the marina. St Tropez was a hive, crammed with shops and bars and holidaymakers posing in designer beachwear. The quay was stage to an unbelievable parade of gleaming super-yachts, monsters of the sea with elevated sun decks and upholstered patio furniture. Tess thought: *One day, I'll buy one of these. I'll buy ten.* On one, a three-tiered giant named *Le Grand Mystère*, a woman in a gold bikini was reclining on a velvet chaise.

'Oh, shit.' Tess stopped, digging an elbow in Mia's ribs.

'Ow!'

'Do you see who it is?'

Mia squinted. Joining the gold-bikinied woman were two girls: one with an elegant corn-blonde topknot, the other boasting a fiery mane. 'Emily and Fifi!'

Tess yanked her behind the nearest tree—but it was too late. 'Yoo-hoo!' Emily sang. 'Don't think you can hide, Mia Ferraris, that tree isn't nearly wide enough.'

'She is *such* a bitch.' Tess balled a fist. 'I swear to God I'll—'

'Ignore it,' said Mia, pulling her back. They heard a weakly chiding response from the gold-bikinied woman, whom they surmised to be Fifi's mother.

'Are these your friends from school, darling?' the woman enquired, removing enormous Prada sunglasses and beckoning them over. 'Come join us, do!'

As Tess climbed aboard *Le Grand Mystère*, Mia trailing reluctantly behind, the woman went to greet them. At the same time, Fifi cried out: 'Oh my God, *don't* stand up, *Maman*! I can see, like, *all* your rolls of fat when you stand up.'

'Sorry, *ma petite fleur*.' The woman shrank back down.

'I told you not to get that bikini. You look like a whale in it.'

The woman chuckled, rolling her eyes. 'Darling, behave...'

'I suppose you'll be in good company now that Mia's with us. Good job there are life rafts on this thing, otherwise we'd be underwater!'

Emily snorted a burst of unkind laughter, while Fifi's mother tutted: 'The way you youngsters speak to each other these days...'

'What are you doing here?' Tess asked Emily.

'Fi invited me.' Emily folded her arms. 'It's fucking dead at home.'

'We always come when Papa needs a rest,' put in Fifi. 'He's in town right now, screwing everything in sight. Right, *Maman*?'

Maman's face cracked like sheet ice. 'Don't be absurd, sweetheart.'

'I wanted to bring Claudette, too,' Fifi said, 'but my stingy bastard parents wouldn't let me. Thank God for the party over at Plage d'Aqua tonight, hey, Em?'

'There's a party?' said Tess.

'You'd hardly fit in,' sniped Emily. 'This is the big league. Not like you deserve to know, but rumour has it Alex Dalton's in town.'

Maman couldn't help but stir. 'Alex Dalton!' she trilled.

'Shut up, *Maman*,' said Fifi. 'You're embarrassing yourself.'

'I met him,' said Tess. She practically heard Emily's jaw drop. Next to her, Mia couldn't contain her gasp. What was the deal? He was only a waiter.

'Nice try, loser,' Emily sneered. 'Like, *nobody's* met Alex Dalton.'

'I have. I met him in Paris, at the dance.'

Emily's expression tightened. Everyone knew the *danse d'éntrée* was a sore point for Sainte-Marthe's golden girl because she had wound up kissing a boy with no thumbs and locking herself in the portable loos for the rest of the night, sobbing.

'I don't know what you're getting so excited about,' said Tess. 'He was waiting tables—just seemed like an ordinary guy to me.'

The relief on Emily's face was palpable. 'Well, you can bet *your* Alex Dalton was *not* the AD I'm talking about. *The* Alex Dalton is heir to, like, the biggest oil company in America? His dad's Richard Dalton? Fuck, you must have been living under a rock. Alex is the ultimate bachelor. And *I'm* planning to bag him.'

'Em can bag any guy she wants,' said Fifi loyally.

'That's right, darling,' said *Maman*. 'Just like I bagged your father.'

'Er—it's nothing like you actually, *Maman*? For starters, you're old and ugly.'

Maman giggled, loving the joke. 'So you girls will come, *non*?'

'Oh, we—' said Mia, at the same time as Emily spluttered, 'Over my dead—' and Tess smiled sweetly and accepted with a, 'Yes, we'd love to.'

*

Plage d'Aqua was the realm of the Beautiful People. The club comprised a wicker canopy over a doughnut-shaped bar, in the centre of which a team of impossibly attractive cocktail-makers rattled metal shuttles and tossed bottles of tequila high into the air. Soft white sand coasted down to the Med, fading to cobalt in the dusk. Some of the glamorous clientele had come directly from their loungers, clad as they were in beach-come-evening-attire, an impression only the seriously moneyed could pull off.

'Wow,' said Mia, as she helped herself to a drink. 'See who's playing!'

Thumping beats emanated from down the shore. 'Who?' asked Tess.

'Felix Bazinet, the DJ—I'm obsessed with him. He's *so* hot.'

'I've never heard of him. Want to say hi?'

'We can't!' choked Mia.

'Why not?'

'I don't know, we just... we can't! He's famous!'

Tess grabbed her hand. As they approached Felix's booth, she saw that he was tall and dark with an appealing rash of stubble. Her tummy did a flip in time with the music, but with fear, not excitement. *Get a grip*, she told herself. *You've got to do it sooner or later. Tonight's perfect. He's perfect.* She had to be the last girl in her year to lose her virginity—not that anyone apart from Mia knew. Felix would be the ideal rehearsal. She had to do it before Hollywood and the men she truly wanted to impress.

'Hey,' she said, 'I'm Tess—and this is Mia.' Felix liked her confidence—she could tell. Knocking back her drink, she decided alcohol was the way to go.

In the end, they wound up hanging round the DJ booth like groupies. Every so often, between sets, Felix glanced Tess's way and shot a lopsided grin.

'Did you see that?' Mia elbowed her. There was no jealousy with Mia—if Felix was interested in either of them it was considered a win. 'He's totally into you!'

'Maybe.'

'OhmyGodhejustlookedoveragain.' She spun round. 'Do you think this is it?'

'What?'

'*You* know…'

Tess swigged back the last of her glass and didn't answer the question.

'Another?' she asked instead. Mia nodded.

Alone, she padded across the sand. Lights strewn around the bar liquefied her vision and she stumbled on the uneven beach. *Sober up or they won't serve you.*

She was waiting in line when someone said from behind: 'Hello, Pirate.'

To her surprise, Alex Dalton appeared next to her. He was wearing a white T-shirt and his skin was tanned. It made specks of blond appear in his eyebrows.

'I thought you were never drinking again?' he teased. He spoke to her in English, and now she could hear his American twang.

'I lied,' she said. 'Why are you here?'

'I come out every summer.'

Tess was about to strike back with 'On a waiter's salary?' when she became aware of something strange happening in her peripheral. Every girl was gazing soupy-eyed at Alex, whispering in groups and biting their lips. An aura of space surrounded him, as if people were afraid to come too close. And there, sure enough, was Emily Chilcott, wearing a barely-there skirt and looking as if she'd swallowed a wasp.

You can bet your *Alex Dalton was* not *the AD I'm talking about...*

It made sense. Tess looked at him and said: 'You're not a waiter.'

'You're not a pirate.'

She wanted to bat back a smart response but nothing came. His conceited handsomeness left her at a loss for words, and she hated admitting he was handsome, because right now it was in that irritating way of a friend's older brother who liked to constantly remind you that you were nothing more than a mildly entertaining kid.

It occurred to her that Alex was exactly the sort of guy she should go for. Rich beyond measure, good-looking, heir to a massive fortune. But, after that first meeting, and it made her want to wither and die whenever she thought of it, she could never contemplate it: she'd given far too much of herself away. Besides, where did he get off being such a smug bastard? One look in his eye and she couldn't stand him.

'I left my jacket behind,' he said.

'I know.'

'Can I have it?'

'Funny, I didn't bring it with me.'

The barman took her order. At the last moment Alex added to it, saying, 'I'll get these.' She caught his aroma, expensive and clean.

'I can pay for it myself,' Tess said.

'Don't get tetchy about it.'

'I'm not.'

He turned to her and smiled. The way he gazed right into her, just as he had over their table in the Café Convivial, pissed her off. Why had she told him all that stuff? Why had she splurged her secrets? The confession swam back in dazzling, mortifying bursts; how she had spilled her guts—quite literally, when she'd barfed into that plant pot—then barfed again on the ride home, then he'd had to sober her up and she'd sat before him, tear-streaked, mascara-clotted, and confided her woeful story in detail she hadn't shared with anyone, not even Mia. Alex's swagger was a stark reminder of the cards he held. She was the meek, pathetic creature he'd stooped to save, Prince Dalton in his glittering castle, surrounded by a moat full of oil.

The girl he'd sat opposite that night was Teresa Santiago. Not Tess Geddes.

I'm Tess Geddes now. Teresa's dead. Fuck meek and fuck pathetic.

'You look beautiful, by the way,' Alex said, matter-of-factly, as if he were commenting on the weather. Her beauty was, to him, a given truth, an indisputable fact, such as Sunday followed Saturday, or the price of a loaf of bread.

'Whatever.'

'You been to *Plage* before?'

'No.'

He looked at her quizzically. 'You're very defensive, you know.'

'You're very rude.' Her eyes flashed.

'Just being honest.'

'Don't bother.'

Tess was desperate to get away but had to wait for her order.

'Thing is,' Alex said, 'I kind of liked the honest you. It's OK to be real. You shouldn't feel… I don't know, embarrassed, or anything. It was fine. It was nice.'

She pulled a face. 'You sound like *Dawson's Creek*.'

He grinned. 'Only trying to say what I mean.'

'And failing.'

Alex held his hands up. 'You're harsh, Pirate.'

Finally, thankfully, the drinks came. 'Do me a favour,' Tess said. 'Forget that night, forget we met, forget everything I said. I was drunk. I made it up, anyway.'

'What, you're ditching me?' He seemed surprised. She was glad.

I'm not part of your fan club, Alex. Go get Emily; she's your kind of girl.

'I've got someplace to be,' she said.

She walked across the sand until she could no longer feel his eyes on her.

*

Someplace, it turned out, was with Felix Bazinet. Tess returned to find Mia chatting with a black man whom she introduced as Felix's friend. 'This is Henri,' Mia said, clutching her. 'Isn't he sexy?' Her breath was sweet with pineapple and rum.

'Felix thought you'd left,' said Henri.

'No way,' said Tess, emboldened by the liquor. 'We're only getting started.'

Felix's set ended and he joined them for a dance, his lips flirting with the back of her neck and his fingers snaking round her waist. The drunker Tess got, the more reasonable it seemed to kiss him. It might be OK. It might be better than she thought.

'You wanna get out of here?' he growled.

Tess let herself be led down the beach, Felix's hand in hers a silent promise of what was to come. *This is good*, she thought. *It's safe. It's good that I do this*. They walked until the crowds faded and the moon shone brightly on silver-pale sand.

'Hey.' Felix pulled her down on to the beach. 'Come here.'

His lips found hers. He leaned her back until she was lying flat. 'Relax,' he told her, 'you're tense.' His lips didn't feel as she'd expected—softer and wetter—and he tasted of cigarette smoke. Tess tried to close her eyes but it made the sky wobble.

Felix's hand found her breast. She let out a gasp and, taking it for enthusiasm, he plunged his tongue deep into her mouth. Tess almost choked. She wanted to say, 'Stop, wait a minute, slow down,' but she couldn't. Suddenly her breast was exposed and Felix was tweaking and pulling her nipple. Next he started kissing it.

She wondered if this was how her papa and Señorita Gonzalez had started that day in the stables. The thought made her muscles tense with revulsion.

Forget that. You're not there any more. You're here.

But she couldn't. Felix's body was too like the body she'd seen, transfixed, afraid, peering round the stable door, and it was associated with violence and death and deceit. Felix lifted her skirt and licked his index finger. 'You'll like this.'

He drove this finger inside her.

'Ah!' She winced in pain.

'Relax… There you go… See? You like it really…'

It was a strange sensation, neither pleasurable nor

unpleasurable, and Tess felt detached, as if she was watching Felix change a car tyre. Occasionally he would go too far and it made her sore so she moaned, but this only encouraged his attentions.

'If you like that, you'll want something bigger,' he whispered. His lips hit hers again, and this time they felt too big, too fleshy, and she fought the urge to bite down.

He pulled away before she could. Against the lapping waves she heard the sound of his belt unbuckling and the shiver of material as he worked it down his thighs. A hard rod landed between them. Felix grabbed her hand and clamped it round, working it up and down. 'There you go,' he groaned, 'that's it, stroke it…'

The stench of lavender hit her nostrils and she struggled.

'Ready?'

'No, I don't—'

A searing, burning pain cut her off, as Felix sliced his erection into her, carving her insides out. She screamed. A gush swelled between her legs.

'It's OK,' Felix murmured in her ear. 'I like a virgin. I like that you're tight.'

'It hurts.' Hot tears rolled down her cheek. 'Please stop.'

'Give it a second…' But, instead of slowing his pace, Felix speeded up, rocking and bucking on top of her. 'You'll get used to it in a second… Lift your hips, baby, that's it,' he grabbed her ass and hugged it to his pelvis, 'that's it…'

All Tess knew was that she hated it. Sex was the greatest lie ever told. Lying here with a man she didn't know, his face pursed above hers, squeaks escaping his lips as his bottom rose and fell, until finally, thankfully, he ejaculated.

Tess heard him groan—an echo of that naked, cowardly groan she had witnessed in the stables on her twelfth birthday—and only then did she realise how stupid she had been. Felix flopped out, and started dressing.

'Thanks for that,' he said. 'Not bad for a beginner.'

She watched his figure recede up the beach until he vanished from sight.

Argentina

A storm was breaking in Buenos Aires. Warm rain fell and thunder crackled hotly inside a dense bank of cloud. Calida rushed through the capital, clutching her bag to her chest. The city was electrified, living, beating, thrumming with opportunity, and as she sheltered beneath an awning and waited for the deluge to stop, she thought:

I've arrived.

Cristian had advised she try the Hostel Lima on Avenida Rivadavia, owned by an ex-employee. She took the bus and enquired after a room. It was modest but ample: a bed, a lamp, a desk, a window from which she could glimpse the famous Casa Rosada, and a shared bathroom. She paid a week upfront and unpacked.

After lunch, she explored the city. The buzz, the energy, the unrelenting motion of Buenos Aires was intoxicating; the people, the vibrant bursts of tango that erupted on the street, the protests that marched past with their banners held aloft, the yellow taxis beeping and weaving, the bustling cafés and ripe scent of cooking and pollution, the wide, leafy boulevards of Palermo, and the cobbled, colourful Plaza Serrano—immediately, she fell in love with it. At Puerto

Madero she saw the giant sailboats and the clusters of fragrant passionflowers that adorned the waterfront restaurants. She entered cathedrals, their quiet, liturgical interiors warmed by the glow of Christmas candles, each exquisite *Virgen María* radiant in her glass case.

That night, the first in many nights, Calida went to sleep with a smile on her face. She had purpose. Things were changing. Her adventure had begun.

*

The following day she found work in a pizza bar on the square. It was a casual affair, waiting tables as she had done in Mendoza, and she slotted in quickly. It paid enough for her to extend her stay at the hostel while she found somewhere permanent to live.

Daniel sent notice, via Cristian, that the farm had been sold. She searched his missive for a shade of affection or clue of regret but there was nothing. Calida let the news wash over her in a thick, sad wave, leaving her breathless before rinsing her clean. Her home was gone. It belonged in the past. She found it too painful to think of the land and the horses, so she didn't. Too painful to think of Daniel, so she didn't.

She bundled the note in a drawer and closed it.

It was a friendly gang at the pizza place and Calida was open enough to secure their trust but not so much as to give herself away. She protected her story as if she were a fugitive, which in a way she was. The girl who had left Patagonia was not the same as the one who donned a cap and uniform every day for work, who drifted up and down San Telmo market on a Sunday, who visited the Recoleta Cemetery with her camera, photographing pre-Raphaelite angels in states of contemplation, who ate *bife de chorizo* at her favourite steakhouse and drank beer in the bustling *plaza*.

Early March, a small apartment in Belgrano came up on a six-month lease. She moved in straight away. It felt good to have her own space again.

One night, out by herself and ambling down Honduras, an eager queue of people caught her eye. The line trailed outside a tall stone building, strewn with climbing plants that soared to a ladder of delicate, twisting balconies.

The café name was emblazoned above its arched entrance in red Vaudeville letters: EL ANTIGUO SALÓN. Everyone had heard of Antiguo, the ultimate *porteño* café. Built in the nineteenth century, it had been home to the creative thinkers of the age; writers, artists, and philosophers gathered here to sip Fernet and smoke *cigarros*.

Calida crossed the avenue just as the grand doors opened and the line trickled inside. Fascinated, she followed them in. The salon was a dimly lit cavern of gleaming circular tables, chequered floors, and a ceiling embroidered with *trompe l'oeil* skylights. The walls were covered with framed paintings and snapshots of the Antiguo set through the decades. Calida ordered a *café cortado*. Waiters in starched cream aprons rushed to take orders and a jazz record played fuzzily. She could have stayed for hours, but the popularity of the place meant there was already a chain forming and she ought to ask for the cheque. The waiter laid it down with a flourish.

'Not staying for tango?' he asked.

She must have looked blank, because he smiled and said:

'Through the back.' The waiter nodded towards the rear of the room, where a thick, scarlet curtain was pulled. The curtain seemed to pulse, a vital, breathing thing, calling her. 'Rodrigo Torres is dancing tonight. Show starts in ten.'

A middle-aged woman wearing masses of gold jewellery crossed the floor, flicked open the curtain and disappeared behind it. The material parted for a moment before shivering back into place. Calida stood and went towards it. The rest of El Antiguo Salón receded around her, the conversation lulling to mute, until there was nothing but her tread, one foot in front of the other, and the curtain coming closer.

She peeled it open, was struck by a smell of old leather and musk, some citrusy aroma draped over years of cigarette smoke, and stepped inside.

It took moments for her eyes to adjust. A girl was flitting between glass-topped tables, lighting candles in jars that flickered orange and gold. A shaft of white funnelled on to the empty, black stage, like a divine message spilling through clouds.

Calida took a chair, and waited.

Slowly, the room filled. Calida kept seeing the gold-jewellery woman, at one moment vanishing backstage and the next greeting customers. Above her own table was a picture of a young girl with her hair in a plait, mid-tango, her elbow at a sharp angle and her head turned, and her leg stretched behind her in that classic, sensual pose. Calida decided it was the same person. She wondered if the woman still danced.

A steward came to collect money and the lights went out, making that pool of white almost blinding. A reverential hush descended. Calida was mesmerised.

The music began. Spiky, seductive rhythms heralded the arrival of the dancers with such urgency that Calida felt the need to sit up straight. When the pair strode onstage and she saw him—Rodrigo Torres, the man they had come to witness—she breathed in so sharply that a woman on the next table turned and caught her eye.

Rodrigo Torres was a vision. His silhouette was neat as an artist's outline, the way he moved more liquid than flesh and bone. He wore tailored black trousers and a white shirt buttoned halfway up his chest, his hair oiled and his hips winding. Fluently he led the dance, steps stroking the floor and caressing that surface in the way he might caress a concubine, his feet hooking and licking and kicking up invisible dust. Never was there more than a sliver between the dancers, the heat and hunger almost too intimate to watch. Raw sexuality pounded off their bodies, as real and unstoppable as the tempo. Calida was spellbound. Watching him, a strange, hot tingling rippled between her legs. *I want to do that*, she thought. *I want to do it with you.*

Teresita's voice came at her, telling her she couldn't. She shouldn't even try.

How monstrous it had been to see her twin at that premiere, glittering and wicked. How cruel it was that one path should lead to gold and the other to dust.

I can do whatever the hell I want.

*

The next night Calida came back, and the next, and the next. She discovered that Rodrigo Torres performed at El Antiguo for a week every month. Each time she grew more addicted to his performance; it sated her like water and filled her like a hot meal and it did something else to her, too. When she got home after a night watching Rodrigo she touched herself in bed, her fingers working beneath the sheets until she arched her neck and shuddered to climax, her hips raised, panting and fevered.

Think of all the things he could teach me…

Beneath Rodrigo's touch, she could become as bold as Teresita. She could learn the ways of her body, the ways of

pleasure, all those things she had never felt worthy of. Rodrigo
was nothing like Daniel: there was no risk, no danger.

She started taking her camera. Then she could steal Rodrigo
home with her, even if he was caught in motion like a moth on
a pin. But the images were far from static: Calida was stunned
at how much movement they conveyed. Rodrigo was fierce as
a bull yet tender as a lover, as he bathed in a lake of light. She
examined the sexy, earnest concentration on his face. These
were the best pictures she had ever taken.

One evening, the woman in the gold jewellery stopped her.

'What are you doing?' She snatched the camera from
Calida's grip. The show had ended, the crowd filtering out.
'It is forbidden to take photographs in here.'

'I'm sorry.' Calida reached to claim it back. The woman
scrutinised her. She had piercing eyes and was wearing a
shawl around her shoulders. At her throat was a pink gem that
reminded Calida of the grapes she had picked on Cristian's
farm. It looked edible.

'Do you work for De Tanturri?' the woman asked suspiciously.

'I don't know what that is.'

The green eyes narrowed. After a pause she granted, 'All
right, I believe you,' and passed back the camera. 'Though I'm
not sure why. De Tanturri is our rival. They are always spying
on us, seeing how we do things and trying to steal our clients.'

'I can't imagine anywhere rivalling this place.' Calida
couldn't resist saying his name. 'I mean, Rodrigo... he's
incredible...'

The woman's expression softened. 'Ah,' she said, understanding. 'I see.'

'Oh, no,' Calida was quick to clarify, 'I don't just take
pictures of *him*...'

Then, suddenly, she had an idea. Her photographs were miles better than the ones on the wall. 'Here.' She dug into her bag and withdrew a stack. 'Look.'

The woman took some time flicking through the images.

'These are good,' she said. '*Son muy buenos.*' She regarded Calida differently this time. 'I am Paola Ortiz,' she said. 'Manager of this place.'

Calida gestured to the picture on the wall. 'Is this you?'

Paola's expression became wistful. 'A long time ago.'

'You were a brilliant dancer. I can tell.'

'I was a young girl, then. Flying to the stars.'

She took a chance and said: 'A bit like me.'

'Oh?'

'One day I might even reach them—if someone gives me a shot.'

Paola smiled. 'What is it you want?' she asked.

Calida lifted her chin. 'A job.'

*

It was a paid evening slot, once a week. Calida captured the dancers' movements, the drama and poise of the ritual, fluid and sharp and always irresistible. Once the photos were developed, Paola, with much admiration, selected the best. These were framed and put on sale in the tango hall—where they stayed for all of half an hour. Each time, Calida's pictures sold out. She couldn't think why she hadn't considered it before. She was *good* at this; she could make a living from it. Probably because she'd never imagined making a living. Her life had been the *estancia*... but that was gone now.

A month passed before she approached Paola again. She'd had the idea of taking the audience's portraits; gifts or souvenirs to carry home at the end of a show. Her suggestion was welcomed, and coincided with Paola introducing Friday night beginners' dance classes, and soon enough Calida was spending all her time outside the pizza café either at El Antiguo or developing her pictures. It wasn't long before her work was fed into the famous salon gallery; the very one she had sat and admired not twelve weeks before. She thought of Diego, and knew he'd be proud.

'*Adios*, De Tanturri!' Paola sang as she counted up the club's takings.

Calida lived for the nights when Rodrigo was back. He danced at other clubs in town, but Paola liked to proclaim that his heart belonged to this place. Taking the ultimate portrait of him, the one that captured him absolutely, obsessed Calida. Nobody saw the flaws she did in her pictures—the angle of Rodrigo's head, slightly too low, or the shadow on his cheekbone, a touch too deep—but she came to know her subject's face as thoroughly as her own. Everything about him pulled her.

Teresita would like him.

That thought enticed her. The notion that Rodrigo had never met her twin—nobody here had, and thus had nothing against which to compare—was thrilling. For the first time, Calida was unique. There was only one of her. Her sister would never meet Rodrigo: she'd never be able to ruin him for Calida in the way she'd ruined Daniel. But the thought of her liking him, that invisible competition, drove her on.

You think I can't be with a man like Rodrigo? Think again.

One evening she stayed late, slowly and deliberately packing her kit, and listening out for his movements. Finally, he emerged from his dressing room.

Just as she'd planned, they collided on their way out. The scent of his body was dizzying. White teeth sparkled in a deep-tan face.

'Hello,' said Rodrigo Torres. 'So you are the photographer.'
Calida nodded. Rodrigo's stare burned into her.

'What's your name?'

'Calida.'

Lightly, he touched her arm. A shiver travelled up to her collarbone.

'Well, Calida…' His voice was deep and commanding. 'You must have passion in your soul to love the tango this much. I see you out there every night.'

Rodrigo put a thumb to her chin and lifted it. The gesture was achingly intimate. 'I see passion in your eyes,' he said, 'and I like it.'

Calida returned his stare. She fought the urge to go weak, to surrender to her nerves. But she stood strong. As strong as him. She was passionate, all right.

'What do *you* like?' Rodrigo asked, so quiet it was almost a whisper.

'I'd like to do what you do,' she said.

21

London

Tess closed her textbook—*American Political History: A Concise Encyclopaedia*—and yawned. She reached over the bed for a cigarette and speculated on how any tome over eight hundred pages long could possibly call itself concise.

Final exams were hurtling towards her at breakneck speed. After a year of neglecting her studies, giving attitude to *les professeurs* and generally not bothering with school (Madame Hébert had insinuated that if it weren't for *la réputation de sa famille* she would already have been expelled), she had to play catch up if she stood any chance of passing. Personally she couldn't give a crap if she did or not, but Emily Chilcott had been swotting like mad and Tess refused to give her the satisfaction.

Blowing out smoke, she lay back on the pillows. Ordinarily she could count the seconds before Simone's tread ascended the stairs and a sharp voice cawed, 'Put that damn thing out!' But, today, Simone was otherwise occupied. She and Brian were attending a restaurant opening in Marble Arch and so she was busy with stylists.

Instead, another stomp of footsteps approached. Tess was stubbing out her Marlboro when the door slammed open.

Simone had removed the lock at the start of the holidays. The other day, Tess had found a glossy in Simone's bedroom, open on an article entitled YOUR TEENAGER AND YOU. Item one on a list of 'Ways to bond with your child' was 'Remove barriers. Banish secrets. Open your door—and theirs.'

Emily Chilcott swept in. Her pastel-pink cut-off boasted a smooth, tanned belly, pierced with a diamond stud. At Tess's dresser, she began ransacking jewellery.

'Looking for something?' asked Tess.

'You shouldn't smoke in here,' carped Emily. 'I'll tell Simone.'

'She knows anyway.'

'Because you're such a *grown-up* now…' Emily smiled meanly. 'Right?'

Tess decided her time at Sainte-Marthe had at least served some purpose. It had taught her all she needed to know about survival among bitches—and that with a little ingenuity and a lot of balls she could climb the greasy pole of social hierarchy as well as anyone else, wherever she'd come from. Simone liked to spout off about education but, as far as Tess was concerned, that was all the education she needed.

All the same, she couldn't wait to get away from Emily and London. She was done with Europe; she wanted America. She didn't intend to be like Lysander, inexplicably shackled to the mansion and raiding the family coffers despite failing to do any work of his own. Lysander talked about his plans to go abroad and pursue a career in landscape gardening, but so far nothing had come of it. Lysander talked well about a lot of things, Tess noticed, but did little about converting them into action.

'It's a waste of time, all that,' commented Emily breezily.

At first Tess thought she was referring to Lysander. 'What?'

'Books. Exams. Getting grades. Simone's got other plans.'

Tess enjoyed the note of resentment in her voice. 'Maybe. But it's my life.'

Emily snorted. 'Bullshit. You'll do whatever she says. You're her pet, don't you realise?' How quickly a note became a symphony. 'You'll get everything. All this crap about how much Simone wants a daughter, blah-di-fucking-blah, and here I am all along and she never fucking notices because *I* don't fucking count. She'll make a star of you, Tess. But when *I* asked for acting lessons? When *I* told her I'd go to that junket thingy when you were away?' She honked a laugh out of her nose. 'Fat chance.'

'You don't need her permission.'

'Bullshit I don't. She's beyond the law. I'll never get anywhere in this or any other town. All it takes is a call and I'm dead meat. After all, I'm not her *daughter*.'

Tess shrugged. 'Neither am I.'

'You'd better not let her hear you say that.' But Emily's tone had waned and she regarded Tess now with a tentative solidarity. 'Get on the wrong side of that witch and you've had it. Look at my dad. He might as well have his balls in storage.'

Tess smiled at this because she'd never heard Emily speak like this before. In fact, she'd never heard Emily speak at all without slagging her off.

'He's no help, but then what did I expect?' Emily sat next to her. 'I've always wanted to be an actress, and Dad's, like, "One day, honey, soon." He's like a fucking dog on a chain when it comes to that bitch. Maybe she's holding the BJs to ransom.'

Tess knew what it was like to dream of riches and celebrity. Before, they had represented escape. Now, they represented vengeance. She *needed* them.

'You think you know half of what's coming?' Emily sulked.

'You think going to a party or two qualifies you as a celebrity? Wait until you get to Hollywood and some fit A-lister's screwing you in a bath full of Cristal and you're high off your tits and you're crapping hundred-dollar bills and then tell me it isn't the most extreme, thrilling, fucked-up-bloody-amazing ride of your life. Dad got me a movie when I was twelve, some dumb thing about an alien dog. It was shit but it was enough to give me a taste. I *know* it's the life I want.' Emily reached for the pack of cigarettes and flicked two out. She switched the light and caught them both at once. She passed one to Tess.

Tess took it. The girls smoked in silence. Vera called up that supper was served and Emily ground hers out and made for the door, their confidence broken.

*

'So there's this thing called Facebook,' Emily told Tess the following week. 'All my girls are on it. It's a way to connect with people, see what they're doing, who's dating who, that kind of thing.' They sat in front of Brian's Mac. 'Here. It's easy. Sign up.'

Tess began typing her name.

'No, you idiot! Not your real name, duh.'

'What, then?'

Emily typed in TITTY MCSHITTY and giggled behind her hand, before Tess smacked her and told her not to be a dick. She corrected it. 'How about this?'

'Tessa Chilcott,' Tess read. 'But no one's going to know it's me.'

'Exactly. Look.' Emily clicked her profile. 'This is how it works. You find people you want to link with then you message them to say who you are. Otherwise you're going to have every fucking sad case in England checking you out.'

Tess was pleased to see Mia pop up. *Check out my pics of St Tropez!!!*

Tess suppressed a shudder when she scrolled through them: her and Felix, drunk at Plage d'Aqua, Mia and Henri kissing... She had never been honest with Mia about what had happened on the beach because she couldn't work it out herself. After she'd lost her virginity she'd felt used and filthy, and had gone back to Mia's parents' house and shut herself in the bathroom and cried silently into so much loo roll that Béatrice had asked next morning if anyone had disagreed with the seafood. Only when she was back at Sainte-Marthe, lying awake one night in the dorm, did it occur to her that Felix Bazinet had raped her. Clearly, she remembered saying no. *Please stop...* And he hadn't. She'd sourced a pregnancy test from a girl in the top year in exchange for writing an essay on Foucault and thank God it had come back negative.

'Shit a brick, is that Felix Bazinet?' Emily's eyes turned to saucers.

'It's no one.' She closed the picture.

'You know, Tess, you should totally ditch Mia. She's a loser. I was talking with Fifi and Claudette and we agreed you could join us... so long as you ditch her.'

'Piss off.'

Emily didn't ask again.

On cue, Facebook threw up Fifi's profile. They were met by dozens of images of the flame-haired princess posing and pouting in a variety of outfits. In some she was dining with her parents on *Le Grand Mystère*, her mother's arms draped around her corpulent, indifferent father, while Fifi sat by with only an untouched paella for company. Tess decided that Fifi had an unhappy life. How weird popularity was.

'You'll live your whole world through this,' Emily promised sagely.

A week later, a message flashed up in Tess's inbox. It was
from Alex Dalton. His name made something flutter inside
her, but she quickly clipped its wings.

Hello, Pirate. How's the parrot? I hope your wooden leg isn't
causing you too much trouble—I've heard they can get stiff
this time of year. So, I'm back in Texas, at my dad's place.
His girlfriend's staying with us—at least I think she's his
girlfriend, she was just kind of here when I turned up. She's
got this dog called Mitzy that's so small it has to qualify as
a rat (my buddy Aaron nearly sat on it). I don't even know
why my dad's into her—she's twenty years younger than
him, she takes her dog to *get its hair done*, and the other
day, when I said I'd been living in Europe, she asked in all
seriousness, 'Where's that?' I think he only dates women
who are the complete opposite of Mom. Mom was smart.
I wonder if he misses it, sometimes, the conversation and
stuff. I do. Anyway. What else? I'm writing a book. When I
say 'writing', what I actually mean is 'watching movies for
research and drinking beer to get ideas.' Not that they're
coming: I don't know what it's about yet. I'm making it up
as I go along. All I know is there's this girl in it; she's a bit
like you actually. Maybe you can read it some day. So… OK.
Write back. *Hasta luego.* Alex

Tess scrolled through his photos. Alex had a ton of friends.
There weren't many pictures of him, which surprised her
because most rich boys spent their lives taking pictures of
themselves. A couple of Alex with a man she supposed to be
his dad. One of him as a kid, which made her smile, dressed

as a wizard and missing one of his front teeth; and one of him as a baby, being held by a woman, his mother.

So sorry, dude, read the comments below. *Didn't realise it was today, thinking of you. Gone but never forgotten. Call if you need anything* ☹.

Tess digested this. She returned to the message and was about to tap out a reply when a voice startled her from behind. 'You thinking of moving in here?'

Brian was in the doorway to his office, an affectionate leer on his face.

'Sorry.' Tess clicked the computer off.

'The girls at Ace are arriving any minute,' he advised. 'Best get upstairs.'

'Oh, yeah.' She was accompanying Simone to tonight's awards ceremony, a hot-pit of paparazzi and fans. Team Geddes, Simone's harem of make-up and wardrobe gurus, would be descending. She went to the door but Brian blocked her.

'Not talking to boys on there, are you?' he said.

'No.'

Brian's watery eyes appraised her. She could see tiny veins around his nose and mouth, and there were sweat patches at the armpits of his shirt. 'The internet's a dangerous playground. I don't want you getting mixed up in anything nasty.'

'I won't.' Tess tried to push past but he stopped her. Suddenly, his body was uncomfortably close. She could feel his belly pressed up against her side.

'You're a beautiful woman now, Tess.' Brian's voice was strained. 'A sexy woman... Men will want you. They won't be able to help it. Especially those whose wives have lost interest.' Tess kept her eyes trained on the floor. Coffee breath gusted into her face. 'Those who still have so much to give but their wives are getting it elsewhere. Older men, experienced men who could show you a trick or two…'

'I have to go,' said Tess. But Brian didn't move. Instead his hand brushed across her bottom, at the curve where it met the backs of her legs, and squeezed.

At last, he stood back. 'Have fun,' he murmured.

Tess bolted from his office and didn't look back.

*

Despite missing out on her Best Actress award to a twenty-something newbie who made a long and embarrassing speech about her 'timeless rock' of a husband, Simone considered the night to be a success. Tess had easily been the most fabulous creature there (the only living person to whom Simone would concede the title) and the press had gone manic for her, fascinated by her resplendent looks and her tragic story.

My daughter, Simone inwardly glowed, *is set to be a star*.

Thankfully, her plan to get rid of the twin had worked a treat. They hadn't heard a peep since Simone had forged that triumphant letter, using Vera's findings in the diary as bait. That entry had been platinum; the sisters' fight exactly the kind of fuel she needed to explode their relationship once and for all. It had presented some challenges, namely revising Vera's Spanish vernacular into authentic Argentinian, and the accuracy of the writing, but it was worth it. Tess was absolutely hers, with no one threatening to steal her back. What's more, she believed they were dead. Perfect.

Afterwards, Michelle Horner persuaded her into the bar. 'Two dirties with extra olives,' she instructed her PA. 'Pimento-stuffed—and keep the riff-raff *out*.'

Simone was musing on a problem. 'Tess needs a boyfriend,' she said.

Michelle polished her spectacles on her shirt. 'Why?'

'She never talks about boys. I'm starting to wonder…'

'Plenty of girls don't talk about that with their mothers. I didn't.'

Simone took a moment to savour this truth. She loved to hear the maternal relationship corroborated: it made it real. Occasionally she liked to forget Tess was even adopted, just edit that whole part out. 'But look at her, Michelle. She's *divine*.'

The cocktails arrived. 'She might be picky.'

'As she has a right to be…' Simone played with her olive, bobbing it up and down in the vermouth. 'You don't think she's a…' she leaned in, 'a *lesbian*?'

The idea had occurred on Sunday as Simone was firing the pool boy and now she couldn't scratch it out. She wanted precision for Tess in Hollywood: it would all be shot to hell if it transpired that a biker dyke in a strap-on was boning her daughter. Simone didn't know any lesbians, which explained the ignorance of this picture.

'Of course not! Don't be silly…' Ironically, Michelle was a lesbian. This meant Simone did know a lesbian; she just didn't know it.

'I've decided to set her up,' said Simone. 'Obviously she's still a virgin.'

'How can you tell?'

'I just can.' Simone had always been in tune with sexual energies. She could see them floating around in the same way other people saw auras. Tess had no interest in sex at the moment. Brian had even less. Lysander, on the other hand…

Simone's crotch sparked as she recalled the hand she had taken her stepson in that very morning. They had collided in the bathroom, Simone half-awake, her hair a mess, when

Lysander had wordlessly forced her grip around his pumping cock and spunked inside sixty seconds all over her silk peignoir. It shouldn't have been erotic, but, oh, it was. After a quick change of clothes she had returned to Brian in the bedroom. Her husband was propped against the bedhead reading the *Financial Times*.

'Who are you thinking?' asked Michelle.

'I'm not thinking about anyone,' Simone snapped, affronted.

'For Tess's set-up…?'

'Oh. Right. Yes.' She composed herself. 'Hugo Winthorpe-Myers.'

'Lady Annabel's son?' Michelle made a face. 'He's a bit of a sap, isn't he?'

'All the better for Tess's initiation.'

'If you're sure…'

'I'm never wrong, Michelle. You wait and see.'

*

Tess arrived for her date with Hugo Winthorpe-Myers and knew instantly that should the planet explode in a nuclear apocalypse and all humanity be wiped off the face of the earth save for herself and this man, she would never, ever consider him a match.

'Hi,' Hugo drawled, meeting her at the door to his ancestral home. He was dressed like someone three times his age, in a brown tweed waistcoat and toffee-coloured chinos. He had a slight facial tic that jerked his ear to his collarbone.

Give him a chance. Objectivity was everything. Hugo was wealthy, check. He had property, check. He had a title, bonus check. Tess was incapable of finding that thing called love— she couldn't even enjoy sex: how was she ever going to love anyone?—but she was OK with that. After all, love was a trap only fools fell into.

Brightly, she smiled. 'Come in,' Hugo wheedled, stepping back. He winked at her, though that could have been the tic. A gust of musty air assailed her from the grand hall. Through it, the dining room was enormous. Hugo pulled out a chair at one end of the table (which could have accommodated thirty people) and helped her in.

Rather than sitting next to her, he loped to the opposite end and flicked out his napkin. 'Wine!' he screeched, and the goblets were brought. 'To us,' he said.

'What?' She couldn't hear a thing this far away.

'I SAID TO US,' he shouted.

The starter was mushroom soup. Tess's heart sank when she saw she had sets of cutlery for four courses, and a grandfather clock in the corner taunted her by spitting out the seconds agonisingly slowly. The soup was grey and thick.

'Do you study?' Tess asked.

'I beg your pardon?'

'DO YOU STUDY?'

Hugo dabbed the corners of his mouth with a napkin. 'I don't need to,' he replied smugly. 'Hartleigh Manor is my future. This house will be my business.'

'Have you always lived here?'

'Of course!' he spluttered. 'Don't you know anything about the gentry? This estate has been ours for centuries. My great-great-grandfather was the Duke of Bassett. My father is the Earl of that same name and one day *I* will inherit the title.'

Above Hugo's bowed head, which was busy attending to the soup, was a framed portrait of a man in breeches. Nearby, in a glass cabinet, a stuffed eagle spread its dead wings.

'Do you have any brothers or sisters?' she asked.

'No, Mummy and Daddy only wanted me. Good job I was a boy, the old man says, or they'd have had to keep going.' Tess waited for Hugo to return the question, and was relieved when he didn't. She should know better than to ask stuff like that.

'How did your mother meet Simone?'

'Some party or other.' Hugo slurped. 'Mummy's always out making friends. Trouble is, everyone takes advantage because everyone wants to know an aristo.'

The main course arrived—stuffed quail with dauphinoise potatoes and buttered carrots—and Hugo elaborated on the lifestyle the house awarded him, the fleet of classic cars he was looking to collect (despite the fact he hadn't yet acquired his licence, 'but Daddy will sort that for me'), and the shooting expeditions he would undertake as part of Hartleigh Manor's Grand Business Plan. 'Stag dos, you know,' he pitched through a mouthful of macerated bird. 'They come out here to see how the other half lives before returning to their hovels. Only of a type, you understand.'

'What type?'

Hugo picked something out from between his teeth. 'Put it this way, sweetheart: I don't want a bunch of reprobates tearing up the taxidermy.'

After a pudding of apple crumble, chased up by a final course of melting Camembert and celery sticks, finally, and not a moment too soon, it was over.

At the door, Tess realised he hadn't asked her a single thing about her life.

'It was great learning all about you,' Hugo said cordially, leaning in to kiss her cheek. He stuck his tongue in her ear. It was so alarming that she shoved him away.

'What do you think you're doing?'

'Come on,' his tic went into overdrive, 'you know you want it. Nine ladies out of ten positively wet their knickers at the mere suggestion of my title.'

'They pee themselves?'

He was thrown. 'What?'

'Seriously, I'm interested. That is what you mean, right?'

'You know precisely what I mean,' Hugo said acidly.

'Well, then, I guess I'm one out of ten.'

Hugo backed off, furious. 'One out of ten might be generous,' he said snidely, before floundering a moment and delivering a parting shot. 'And for the record, you're too fat for me. I like girls like Mummy, who watch what they eat. You devoured that cheeseboard so fast it was like sitting opposite a Hoover nozzle.'

Tess wanted to punch him in his pimple-pockmarked jaw. Instead, she turned on her heel and stormed down the steps. The BMW was waiting.

'Enjoyable evening, Ms Geddes?' the driver asked as he whisked her away.

'Fine,' she answered, biting her lip until she tasted blood. Money or not, they were all the same. No matter their means, men were all bastards inside.

Look at her father: he had taught her everything she needed to know about the opposite sex and a lot more besides. She'd killed him for the privilege.

It wasn't my fault. It wasn't meant to happen that way.

Had she killed her mama and her sister, too? A cursed child, a poisoned cup…

Perhaps this was her punishment. A life of frigid misery, sold and paid for and carted across the ocean like a sack of sand because inside she was rotten and they'd longed to get rid of her. Tess choked on a wave of hopelessness before pulling herself back to shore. *Stop it. You're stronger than this. You're not a crier—don't start now.*

By the time they reached the Kensington mansion, she had pulled herself together and translated her tears into pounding, unstoppable energy. She might not be able to prove to Julia and Calida the woman she'd become, but she could damn sure prove it to herself. Tomorrow, she would pack her bags for Hollywood.

22

Argentina

Calida woke in her apartment in Belgrano, Rodrigo Torres' magnificent body warm alongside hers. He was sleeping, his lips parted and his dark, severe brow a reminder of the thrilling commands he had issued the previous night. Rodrigo was her teacher. She was his student. It was an electrifying journey to enlightenment.

Calida's defences had been stripped after her first week of tango lessons, months ago now. He had been patient, generous, leading her deep inside the music to explore its strange new rhythms, winding a path through its burning territory. '*You are a natural,*' he breathed into the coil of her ear, as he pressed his hips against hers.

It was only a matter of time before they had pressed their hips in a different way. Calida had known it would happen. Through dance she cast out her insecurities and stepped into the shoes of another woman—a ruthless, fervent woman who would stop at nothing to get what she wanted. And she wanted Rodrigo. At nineteen, she had been adamant about losing her virginity. While she had always thought she would give it to someone she loved, someone like Daniel, it was liberating to choose another route. That was what old Calida would have done. New Calida followed her body.

Their sex was intoxicating.

Too long she had pleasured herself by her own hand, not believing that any man would do those things with her. Why would they, when there were women like Tess Geddes in the world? But Rodrigo told her she was gorgeous—he adored her shape and her strength; he didn't want a girl who would snap as soon as he touched her. Calida wondered what it had been like for Tess. Her twin would have shed that badge years ago, with a dashing film star or a London pretty-boy, and by now would consider herself a connoisseur. Sex would be Tess's forte: she would trail her lovers on a string, just as she had Daniel, and would relish the power it gave her.

Calida had assumed the sisters would share this landmark, embark on it as one, confiding their secrets and conquests. Not any more. She locked these feelings away and buried the key, and decided she didn't care. Calida might have been born first, but Tess had stolen an advantage in everything else—beauty, boys, travel—and now it was time to catch up. The look on her twin's face when she finally did, tapping her on the shoulder and whispering, '*Hello, remember me*?' was what kept her going.

'You're the only girl I know who tastes good in the morning.' Rodrigo grabbed her and pulled her down. His erection grew against her belly and Calida opened her legs, ready to take him, no foreplay necessary. He held his tip against her.

'Do it,' she begged, craving the release, the oblivion. 'Do it hard…'

Rodrigo fired her his irresistible grin and turned on his back. Calida knew what he wanted—and she wanted it too.

It gave her a feeling of such control, to bring a potent man down, leave him quivering and crying her name. Lowering her head, she began kissing his balls, flicking her tongue out and then enclosing one between her lips. She licked the root of his penis in the way he'd instructed, working her attentions up the shaft, little by little. When she reached the thick flower of his crown she pouted her lips around it, driving against the cushion of her tongue. When he was almost there, she clasped her fingers around his dick and worked in tandem with her mouth, increasing her speed and bringing him as far into her throat as she could manage.

'*Sí, por favor, cógeme...*' Abruptly, Rodrigo took her head. He flipped her round on the sheets so he was fucking her mouth from above. His balls crushed against her chin. All at once he emitted a thin, high yelp and her mouth was filled.

'Your turn,' he murmured, before seconds later she felt his breath between her legs. Working his tongue on that spot that drove her crazy, Rodrigo sent her hurtling towards orgasm in less than a minute. Grinding against him, Calida pulled his hair and dug herself against him and then she came. His tongue tasted her even as she rode one wave after another, further out into the thrashing, limitless ocean.

On the tango floor, Rodrigo Torres was an expert. In bed, he was a matador.

Each time Calida slept with him, she opened up a little more towards the sun. Anxiety turned to confidence. Uncertainty turned to courage. Fear of the future turned to an absolute need to meet it and make it hers. Her flesh caught fire and with it her soul, her ambition awakening after endless seasons in the shade. Sex was proving to her once and for all that she was worth just as much as her twin. She didn't have to believe her mama's lie that she was nothing special and no one significant—because Rodrigo Torres proved otherwise. He proved that it was good to be Calida Santiago, and that knowledge implanted deep inside her, rare and precious.

*

On Calida's twentieth birthday, Rodrigo invited her to a Mexican restaurant on Santa Fe. The owner gave Rodrigo a brotherly clap on the back: 'Your usual table?'

'You've been here before?' Calida asked as she slid into the private booth, enjoying how her new red dress clung to her curves and its daring, plunging neckline. She could feel Rodrigo staring at her. She could feel other men staring at her.

'Not often,' said Rodrigo evasively, and consulted his menu.

It made a change to be out in public. Normally Rodrigo elected to stay in her apartment, the blinds drawn and the phone off the hook, 'Because then I can make love to you whenever I like.' Tonight, it felt more like they were a couple. It occurred to Calida that she should be pleased at this development, but the truth was she didn't want to be his girlfriend. Rodrigo captivated her, he obsessed her, he had her craving him like a drug… but she didn't love him. She couldn't. She would never love a man, not truly, unless he was a blond-haired blue-eyed gaucho called Daniel Cabrera.

'Doesn't she look exquisite, Nico?' Rodrigo said as their waiter came to take their order. Nico nodded and asked: 'Is it a special occasion, Señor Torres?'

Rodrigo started to shake his head, just as Calida said: 'It's my birthday.'

'Can we help you celebrate?'

'No, no,' Rodrigo jumped in, 'we'll keep it low-key, won't we, *mi vida*?'

When Nico had gone, he reached across the table and took her hand. 'You understand, *cariño*—it's only they'll bring out a cake and a song, make a spectacle of it, draw unwanted attention… I'm a celebrity, and I'd rather not be spotted.'

Calida drank her wine, observing her lover carefully over the rim of her glass. While things were casual, she couldn't see a reason for such secrecy. Even at El Antiguo, Rodrigo pretended they had no connection, avoiding her eye when he was onstage and she was in the shadows, zooming her lens on his performance.

'*Don't you see it turns me on*?' Rodrigo would murmur, later, when they were alone. '*It's role play, Calida; it makes me want you even more…*'

As they ate, she noticed how his eyes kept darting to the door. How he didn't quite focus on her while she was talking. How hastily he requested the check.

What game are you playing? Calida thought.

After the meal, Rodrigo followed her into a taxi and kissed her all the way back to Belgrano. '*Me volves logo,*' he whispered into her neck, his hands roaming her breasts, 'you drive me crazy.' He took her fingers and guided them to his cock, encouraging her to rub its stiff length through the material of his trousers.

The taxi pulled up and he threw a bundle of notes through the window.

Up in her apartment, they didn't even bother turning the lights on. Rodrigo unbuckled himself and hitched up her skirt and screwed her ferociously against the wall. Straightaway, she came. Shattered by her orgasm, she let herself be spread on the floor and when that wasn't enough he told her to get on her front and lift her ass in the air. From this angle, the penetration was intense. Rodrigo gripped her buttocks, his thumbs hooking her wide, as he thrust himself towards an explosive ejaculation. Calida climaxed again, seconds before he did, tensing and shuddering around him.

'How was that, birthday girl?' he crooned as he lay next to her.

Calida watched him for a long time, in the dark, until she fell asleep.

*

Things came to a head in December. It had been quiet enough at the pizza café for Calida and her staff to spend most of the afternoon out back in the manager's office, scrolling through profiles on Facebook. Everyone was on it, it seemed. She didn't get it. 'Why would you want to spy on people?' asked Calida.

'It's not spying,' said her friend Alicia. 'It's keeping in touch. Come on, there must be *someone* you want to find?'

'Not really.' But after the others had left, Calida typed in her sister's name: Teresa and Teresita and her occasional nickname, Tere. Nothing.

She tried 'Tess Geddes'. Nothing. No one.

Of course there wasn't. She wished she hadn't tried.

Tess Geddes wouldn't be thinking of her, would she? She'd be too busy loving her new life. Why should Calida bother? The only time she wanted to think of her selfish twin was when she pictured the moment they would meet again. Tess Geddes wouldn't recognise her. She'd be a worm against what Calida had achieved.

Rodrigo was meant to be picking her up at six. He preferred to meet her at the rear doors so they could slip into his car unseen. 'Paola has eyes all over town,' he said, counselling that Paola didn't like romances to blossom in the workplace.

Today, he was late. When seven o'clock came and went Calida ditched him and began the long walk home. All night she watched the phone for a call, or kept an ear out for the buzzer downstairs. Where was he? The annoyance she felt at having asked Paola for a night off, only for it to be wasted, was soon replaced by concern. Nine p.m. and still no word. On a whim, she rang El Antiguo. Paola answered immediately.

'Is Rodrigo there?'

'He isn't working tonight. Is that Calida?'

'Yes... I'm meant to be meeting him.'

There was silence on the end of the line. 'Hello?' she prompted.

'Calida, stay away from Rodrigo outside of hours—do you understand?'

'Why?'

She heard Paola speak to somebody else, then a door clicked closed and the buzz of the salon receded. 'You're dating him?' Paola asked wearily.

'Yes. Although—'

'He doesn't want anyone else to know.'

Calida held the phone a little tighter. 'Actually, he says—'

'He says it's more exciting that way.'

'Have you been talking to him?' She was furious.

'No,' said Paola. 'But I have been in your shoes.'

Calida was shocked. 'You've been with Rodrigo?'

'*Bella*, who hasn't? He's taken you to *El Horno Mexicano*? He always wants to meet at your place? He'll only go near you in private? Rodrigo's a player. He's a stud. He's keeping twenty beds warm as we speak. Every girl thinks she's the only one—believe me, because I got scorched. If it weren't for his ability to pull in the crowds I'd have abandoned him years ago. He hurt me. In the end, he hurts all of us.'

Calida tingled with anger. Misgivings she'd had since her birthday solidified and she couldn't bear the humiliation, the disgrace. *How dare he?*

She banged the phone down. Immediately it rang back but she pulled the cord from the wall, glowing with fury, and resisted the urge to stamp on it.

She had suspected there could be unfinished business—an ex-girlfriend, perhaps, someone he hadn't quite ended it with—but tens, dozens, more? *Paola*? She thought of his cronies at the salon, the way they looked over as she was going through her pictures, the sideways leers they delivered to Rodrigo. Who did he think she was, some easy lay who would smother him in kisses and tell him it didn't matter; she was lucky to be with him at all so he could go right out and screw who he liked because she'd be happy with any scraps she could get. *I'm better than that. I deserve more.*

Calida fixed a drink and downed it in one, and realised she felt quite calm. Paola's revelation confirmed only what she had known. It didn't wound her. It made sense. Rodrigo was using her, sure… but hadn't she been using him, too?

She'd never had feelings for him—only fascination. Rodrigo stood for every man she had been convinced would never find her attractive; every man that should have belonged to her twin, not to her. Beneath his tutelage, she had gone from shy, inexperienced ingénue to sexually poised siren—and she wouldn't take his shit.

The flurry of a TV news bulletin distracted her attention. Images of a raging inferno filled the screen, unfolding live downtown, as they reported a fire breaking out at República Cromañón. Bodies were being brought out on stretchers. Journalists recounted to camera. She poured another drink, not taking her eyes off the screen.

Suddenly the door erupted in a battery of knocks. Rodrigo swept in, his arsenal of alibis at the ready. '*Cariño*, I'm sorry. I've had a hell of a journey…'

'Where have you been?'

Rodrigo nodded to the TV. 'Good, you don't need me to fill you in.'

'You were there?'

'No, but the streets are chaos. It took me an age.'

'What,' she consulted the clock, 'five hours?'

He splayed his hands in a gesture to be calm. 'Go easy on me, baby. I've had a bastard of a night. I need a brandy.' He shrugged off his coat and went to the kitchen.

'I had a conversation with Paola Ortiz tonight,' said Calida, following him in. She saw him tense and thought: *Coward*. 'Are you seeing other women?'

Rodrigo stayed perfectly still. In that moment he was no longer the formidable tango dancer every woman coveted; he was a boy caught with his pants down.

'What makes you say that?' he asked. He was a terrible liar.

'I already know. You might as well come clean. You've been with a woman tonight. You weren't anywhere near those poor people at the fire.'

Rodrigo paused; thought about whether or not to deny it. 'It was the only night she could squeeze me in,' he said eventually. It was an unfortunate choice of words.

'You're a fucking asshole,' said Calida. 'Get the fuck out of my house.'

'Wait, *cariño*, I can—'

'Explain? Deny it? Don't bother.'

'I care about you.' He reached for her. 'I want to be with you, Calida. Forget the rest, they're nothing. We'll be together, just the two of us—what do you say?'

Calida looked at him, eyes pleading, arms outstretched, and all she felt was sorry for him. Rodrigo had given her what she needed and now she could walk away. Not so for him: he'd be stuck with himself for all eternity, facing a cheat and a liar every time he looked in the mirror. 'You've given me all I wanted,' she said coolly.

'So have you,' he was hopeful, 'I feel like that too—'

'It's over,' she said. 'Go home.'

'I could stay. I—'

'No, you couldn't.'

There was a moment, and Rodrigo's face froze, caught somewhere between shock, fury, and respect. Unused to rejection, he grabbed his coat. 'Suit yourself,' he spat. 'But don't come running when you change your mind—this was your chance.'

There was no risk of that. It was clear, now, what she had to do—and she should have done it a long time ago. For the first time, Calida was strong enough. She was a woman who could own up to her desires, tell the person she loved how she really felt: that there would be nobody else but him as long as she lived, and she could spend her life running from that fact but it would always hunt her down.

'There's only one chance I have to take,' she said. 'And it isn't with you.'

Rodrigo banged the door behind him. Before Calida could

change her mind, she rescued the phone from the floor and fixed it back into the wall.

Breath held, she dialled his number and waited for him to pick up.

Please be there, Daniel.

Tell me it isn't too late.

23

Los Angeles

The second week in July, Tess boarded a flight to America.

Simone sat next to her in First Class, alternately sipping champagne and buffing her manicure. 'Are you ready for this, sweetheart?'

'I was born ready.'

Simone plucked two silk eye masks from her carry-on. 'Get some sleep,' she said, passing one to Tess. 'You're going to need it.'

They touched down at LAX early evening. Simone was anxious to reach the Malibu beach house she had purchased over the phone (*'Over the phone?'* Tess had gasped when she'd learned of this news, 'You mean you haven't even seen it?' to which Simone had replied, 'I use a trusted buyer out there, darling: sometimes you've got to know when to delegate') and instructed their driver to go there immediately.

Tess was tired after their flight. In the end she had stayed up, too wired to sleep, and watched back-to-back movies. But there was no way she was closing her eyes now. Through the car window, the balmy boulevards of gleaming Los Angeles melted past in a gorgeous, golden-hued haze. LA was one of those cities she felt she already knew, from Simone's gilt-edged gossip, from films, from girls at Sainte-Marthe who returned from its sun-soaked beaches and A-list bistros brimming with tales of the illustrious Hollywood Hills... but seeing it in real life was something else.

It truly was the Beautiful City. Every street was a runway, every corner a photo shoot. Nobody was bigger than a UK size 8 and there was a sense of everyone checking everyone else out, if for nothing else than to check out the fact that they were being checked out. Men and women bragged their physiques: tiny butt-clinging shorts whizzed past on roller-blades; perky breasts and honed pecs burst from vest tops; toned legs wrapped round a throbbing motorbike; tresses of sun-kissed hair blew in tousled perfection from an open-top Jeep. On the sidewalk, a woman who made Simone's plastic surgery look like a particularly kind chemical peel trotted past on Barbie-pink heels, the dog on the end of her spangly lead wearing a fuchsia cape.

'You're in a different league, honey,' said Simone. 'Believe me.'

The heat, melting out of the day, was sugar-scented. Palm fronds rustled against a stained mauve sky. Tess could smell the ocean, a mix of salt and coconut tan lotion. The air buzzed with promise. Excitement surged. *I'm here. I made it*.

Half an hour later, the car pulled on to an oval drive. Tess got out and gaped in amazement at the villa. It was enormous. Lush green lawns ran in an immaculate slope to the entrance, sprinklers raining diamonds on the grass. A white stone façade sparkled like chalk. Twin verandas were capped with arched hoods. Through a copse of trees, Tess spied the swimming pool, a sheet of lime, and next to that a tennis court.

'Well?' Simone was in her element. 'What do you think?'

Tess found her tongue. 'I thought it was an apartment.'

'You don't like it.'

'I do! Shit, I mean of course I do. It's incredible…'

Simone clicked her fingers and the driver produced their bags. 'Let's go inside,' she said, 'get a feel for the place.' She tapped a code into the security gate and they were admitted. Padding around the cool interior, with its marble surfaces and ornate furnishings, was like being in a museum. Five bedrooms, three showers, and two wet rooms, two freestanding claw-footed bathtubs, a kitchen fitted with Sub-Zero and Gaggenau, a gym and sauna, a Jacuzzi, a masseur's slab, a library and movie theatre, and, just when Tess thought she had seen it all, another floor, another room, another staircase—but then she didn't need to take those, because there was a lift.

And then, at the back of the house, the *pièce de résistance*: they were right on the shore. Tess held the railing as if she were on the prow of a steamer, open water before her, yawning to an unknown horizon. Endless Pacific Ocean shimmered in the dusk, as far as the eye could see. On the caramel strip of sand that banked on to her terrace, a couple walked hand in hand. Further up the beach, a man ran with his dog.

'Well?' Simone stepped up behind her. 'Can you see yourself living here?'

'I love it,' Tess replied. She really did.

*

The month passed in a maelstrom of meetings, castings, parties, and power play.

Tess met every mover and shaker in LA, and it turned out her adoptive mother's discrimination had succeeded in making Tess Geddes a sought-after commodity before she had even arrived on American soil. No one wanted to be left out—even industry titans. All who met her fell beneath her spell. Simone had promised them beauty, but they had never seen a woman like Tess. Her sensuality was raw, free from affectation or decoration; her colouring was gorgeous; her accent was sexy yet fragile, the burned sienna of Spain mixed with the ripe husk of France, polished off by an expensive pout of English regality. At twenty, she was beyond stunning. Never mind the face that launched a thousand ships—Tess Geddes could launch a million.

Simone helped things along by draping her protégée in designer finery: a spot of Balmain here, a dash of Elisabetta Franchi there. Tess was papped everywhere she went; she was mobbed on the street, targeted as she exited a car and rushed into whatever studio or restaurant she was visiting that day—would she wear this bracelet, these sapphire drops, this exclusive brand of mascara? Simone cherry-picked the best, and relished every minute: she had long been hot property this side of the Atlantic, but, having Tess at her side, the girl who put all others in the shade, *her* girl, was a pride like none she had known. 'You've never looked better,' Simone's friends in London flattered whenever they saw her. 'Motherhood suits you.' And Simone would smile, aglow in the certainty that they spoke the truth. For starters, she looked years younger. She had energy. Purpose. Focus. She laughed easily. She no longer let snide remarks in the press get the better of her. She could now look back on her troubled past with detachment, as if her horrible pregnancy and the terrors of that Surrey attic hadn't happened to her but to some other unfortunate woman. She could move on.

Tess, meanwhile, loved it all. She embraced her role with a vigour and dedication Simone could only have prayed for. They were going straight to the top.

*

On Friday night, Tess attended a supper soiree at Maximilian Grey-Garner III's mansion in the Hills. She was tense about meeting him—her teenage years had played out to a soundtrack of 'Once Maximilian takes hold of you' and 'Once we get Maximilian on board' and there was much to live up to—but she knew she would impress. Maximilian was the man who would make things happen. Tess was hopeful that such a connection might win her distance from Simone. Now she was here, she intended to work on her own. She wanted the prize to be hers and hers alone.

'Well,' Maximilian bellowed when they arrived, striding in from the starlit patio where the rest of his guests were mingling, 'here she is.' He air-kissed Simone and did the same to Tess. His cheeks were heavy and sweating, clammy as they touched hers. He had a thatch of grey hair and his shirt was open at the neck and decorated with a garish floral print. On his feet he wore open-toed sandals and his ankles were slightly burned. Maximilian didn't look as professional as she'd assumed, more like someone's dad lolloping off across the beach to fetch ice creams.

'Understatement equals power,' Simone had counselled on the way over. 'They're the ones who don't have to try.' Tess reminded herself that Maximilian was, despite appearances, the most influential agent in Hollywood. His list was a phone book of big hitters. If she signed with him that would be it: the mega league.

'You have an amazing home.' Tess returned his smile.

'Oh,' said Maximilian, waving a hand, 'Scott deserves the credit for that. He's the designer round here. I make the money—he spends it! That's what we always say. Come on through, darling, I want you to meet everyone.'

As Tess followed Maximilian outside, she judged that he was honest and direct, didn't suffer fools, and that those qualities would serve her well. It was Sainte-Marthe all over again, just on a bigger scale: who was useful and when; who could be employed for what, and then how hard would it be to drop them? Everyone did it. It was endurance, the long slog to the top, and she wasn't here to make friends.

Heads turned as she emerged on to the terrace. Women took a step closer to their husbands; men's eyes flitted across her with appetite. Maximilian noticed, too. 'Simone wasn't making it up,' he said. Flutes of pale champagne passed by on a tray, and Maximilian lifted two. 'I hear you're causing a stir with the studios.'

'I'm trying.'

He narrowed his eyes at her. 'I sense when you try, you normally succeed.'

'Not normally: always.'

'Then the signs are good.'

'For…?'

'For us, of course.'

Simone joined them in that immaculately timed way she had, looping her arm through Tess's and smiling up at Maximilian. Tess wished she could negotiate this on her own. She understood Simone's investment and all the preparation she had done, but Tess didn't intend to spend the rest of her days paying this woman off.

Just like Calida was paid off.

'You *are* on my team, aren't you?' Maximilian raised an eyebrow.

Tess met his glass with a little too much force. 'You bet I am,' she said.

*

Simone announced the following week that the Chilcotts were flying over from England. 'Brian needs a break,' she said, and then, in a slightly strangled voice as if Tess had disputed or challenged her on that fact, 'and so does Lysander.'

Days before, on the seventh of July, London had been rocked by a series of terrorist bombings, three explosions on the Underground and a fourth on a double-decker bus. It hadn't occurred to Tess to worry for Simone's brood, not just because the tragedy was unfolding so far away but also because they rarely, if ever, took public transport. Even so, it had been a relief when Simone reached the mansion and learned that everyone was safe. 'And the kids?' she'd demanded shrilly. 'They're both OK?' Her white-knuckled grip had relaxed on the phone. The extent of the household's involvement had lain with Vera, who had been passing Tavistock Square moments before the bus detonation and had stayed behind as an eyewitness.

The Chilcotts arrived on the morning Tess was due at her first casting: for Caitlin Wood's new movie, *White Candle*. Caitlin was LA's number one female director, having hoarded a net of awards and acclaim at last fall's festival season: at Cannes she was incandescent, at Tribeca she was tremendous, at Sundance she was sensational. Tess was ready for it. She had practised the script, knew it by heart. There was never a question in her mind that she wouldn't deliver. She *had* to deliver.

'Whoa, check this place out!' Lysander led the brigade into the Malibu villa. 'This is sick!' He dumped his bags. 'Hey, Tess, looking hot as always.'

Simone flushed an angry shade. 'That is your *sister*, remember?' she hissed, folding her arms, but she accepted his peck on the cheek all the same. Tess noticed that she touched her stepson's elbow very gently as he did so. The gesture shouldn't have stood out, it was so tiny, so fleeting, but it did.

Emily skulked behind, determined to remain unimpressed. 'Bit of a cliché, isn't it?' she said boredly, flumping down on the white leather couch. 'Nowhere near as cool as the warehouse I'm moving into with Fi…'

'Right,' said Lysander, 'the Hoxton Squatters. That place is a shit-pit.'

'Fuck off, 'Sander.'

'Such a lady.'

'Such an *arsehole*.'

'Come on, you two.' Brian was struggling through the door with the remainder of the luggage. 'I've had this bickering the whole trip!' Simone stood by the counter, looking pained, her mouth set in a line of mild distaste. He approached Simone and held her stiff shoulders, before leaning in to kiss her closed mouth.

'You'd think they'd have some perspective after what's happened,' Brian went on. 'Lysander's friend Raoul was two stops from Edgware Road.'

'Raoul's fine.'

'But others aren't. Have some respect.'

'I do have respect! Christ. What do you want me to do? Life goes on, Dad.'

Brian heaved his suitcase. Tess went to help him, since no one else was.

'Thanks, love,' said Brian, as they reached for the handle at the same time and his rough skin brushed against hers. 'You're a good girl.'

Tess flinched. Ever since Brian had cracked on to her in his office, he'd made her skin crawl. He looked up at her now with a sad longing. Was it any wonder? He hadn't had a job in months, the kids disrespected him, the whole family treated him like an unwanted Labrador, and she had no doubt Simone lived up to her Ice Queen name in the bedroom. Tess questioned what life would be like being married to a titan like Brian. She could pinch him right from under Simone's nose if she chose to.

'We've got to get moving,' said Simone brusquely. 'Tess has an audition.'

'Audition?' Emily snorted, picking at the stitching on the couch. 'Don't know why she's bothering—the part's already hers, right?'

'Shut up, Emily,' said Simone.

'Isn't that how it works? Never mind about actual fucking *talent*—'

'Now, now,' said Brian, 'let's keep things peaceful.'

Emily rolled her eyes. But she gave Tess a reluctant '*They're such losers*' look that confirmed her attitude was directed at them, not at her stepsister.

In the end, the Chilcotts tagged along. Simone tried to tempt them into a siesta by the pool or into exploring the boutiques at the Colony Plaza, but Brian wouldn't be dissuaded. The others were too busy squabbling to form a persuasive protest.

'How long are you staying?' Tess asked Emily in the Escalade.

'Dunno,' she sighed, 'I didn't even want to come…'

'That's a heap of crap,' chipped in Lysander, his handsome lip curling. 'Em reckons she'll get spotted by some casting couch perv and they'll give her a job on a porno. You'd like that, wouldn't you, Em—a nine-to-five fuckathon?'

'You're disgusting.'

'Lysander, behave!' came Brian's voice from the front.

'All right, old man, don't give yourself a coronary.' After a moment, he asked: 'Would you, Tess? Do a guy onscreen?'

'No.'

'A girl, then.'

'Lysander—please!' Simone's rebuke choked out of her.

'I'm only asking. You've never done it… have you, *Mummy*?'

There was a long, loaded pause. Brian continued driving and Emily scrolled down her iPhone. 'Certainly not,' said Simone quietly.

'Not even in the old days? When you were getting started?'

'You go too far, Lysander,' warned Brian.

'She hasn't answered. Come on, it's not like we keep big bad secrets in this family, is it?' His question hung on a tantalising, torturous thread. Simone blurted:

'I'd never do that kind of film. Never. That's the end of the discussion.'

Lysander, satisfied by this exchange, wound down his window and sat back.

It was a relief when they reached Maximilian's office on Broadway. Simone grabbed Tess and hauled her inside, barking at some poor receptionist that Caitlin Wood was expecting them and fiercely jabbing the elevator call button.

Upstairs, Brian and the others hovered in the waiting area. Simone produced a mirror and had Tess check her reflection five times, a spot of gloss added and a quick rearrangement of her hair, before she was ready. 'You,' she barked at the Chilcotts, 'wait outside.' Then, to Tess, she whispered: 'Go for it.'

They stepped through the door and introductions were

made. The great Caitlin Wood sat between Maximilian on one side and two producers on the other.

'When you're ready, Tess.'

She took a breath and centred herself; found the opening line. The scene was a family reunion, Tess's character vulnerable yet proud, a girl whose parents disown her after they find out she is pregnant. She stumbled through the first part, slipping on the words and then struggling to regain focus, and Caitlin remained inscrutable, her cropped hair and slash of red lipstick ever-present in Tess's peripheral.

And then something crazy happened.

Although Tess was accustomed to the words, speaking them aloud changed them. For the first time, she was *there*; she *was* this person, it was happening.

Rage, unchecked, spilled out of her. Tess allowed her emotions to run away, knowing she should rein it in but unable to—she had come too far and the pain was too deep, too real, and there was no way of containing it. As she drilled into the climactic scene, the confrontation with her family, the moment she had waited for and wanted for years, she all at once forgot she was in a casting room. She was with Calida, raining hurt on her, hitting her, shaking her, begging her for answers but all along knowing her sister could not give them because her mouth was forever silenced.

Fury and bitterness she had kept in check broke free in a tidal wave; the hatred, the sadness, the heartache, it all came out. None of it was hard to bring up.

She would never be able to say these things in real life. It was too late for that. The people she needed to say them to were gone, their deaths sealing shut any chance of a way back, and now she was cut loose on the ocean of her future, no land in sight, no place calling her back, faintly, faintly, in spite of how she stifled it. She would never be able to express her torment, the soreness and upset that had nowhere to go except here, now, into this audition, in front of faces she scarcely knew. These people witnessed her heart and soul, crushed as those things were, pour on to that floor with absolute release. When she finished, nobody spoke. Even Simone was mute.

Tess took a second to come back into her body, to remember where she was. She felt cleansed, controlled, fundamentally altered. As if she had expelled a demon.

She clutched the script to her chest, waiting.

Caitlin and the panel conferred.

'Simone, could you give us a minute?' said Maximilian, nodding to the exit.

When the door had closed behind her, Caitlin spoke.

'That was impressive, Tess,' she said. Her eyes were sparkling. 'I've never seen anyone like you—especially not at a first audition. How old are you?'

'Twenty.'

'You read like an actor with their whole life behind them. It was outstanding.'

'Thank you.'

Minutes later, Tess went out into the lobby. She leaned against the wall, exhaling a lungful of air. Her blood was hot. Her mind was alert. Her pulse was racing. The ball of anger she had held in that room warmed her stomach, her chest, her neck, her whole body. *I earned this. I'm entitled to it. It's mine.*

Too long she had buried her feelings, guilty at hating her family because they were dead and that was the greatest karma of all. But now she saw she was permitted her wrath. She should let it grow. She had a right to hit back against the injustice of it, the heinous decision they had made, even if there was nobody to hit back against.

Calida wished me gone. My twin, my sister, my friend... She sold me.

It was with some surprise that, on reaching the elevators, hushed voices disrupted her thoughts. She had thought the Chilcotts had been relegated down on to the street. 'We have to tell him,' a man hissed, out of sight. Despite his low pitch, Tess recognised him immediately as Lysander. There was a scuffle, like someone escaping an embrace, before the woman replied. Tess's stomach lurched.

'Are you insane?' Simone shot back. 'This is my marriage. He's your *father*.'

'It has to be soon. I can't do this any longer. All the pretending, it's doing my bloody head in. I can't stop thinking about you. I'm mad about you.'

'Don't say that!' Another scuffle; this one combined with a moan. 'Please...'

'You know how I feel—'

Tess dropped the script. *Mierda*! The voices stopped just as abruptly.

Simone popped her head round the corner and turned on a mega-watt beam. 'Darling!' she cried. 'What did they say? Are we celebrating?'

Her adoptive mother looked wired; her eyes were wild, as if she'd emerged from a wind tunnel. Lysander nicked his chin with his thumb and hung back. Tess caught his gaze and this time there was no cocky retort or self-satisfied sneer.

'They gave me the part,' she said.

'That's wonderful!' Simone locked her in a hug. She smelled of Lysander's aftershave. 'Let's go and find the others, shall we? This calls for champagne!'

Tess followed Lysander out. As she stepped into the sunshine, watching the back of his head, the hot tips of his ears and the flush of colour spreading down his neck, she sensed that her life wasn't the only one about to change beyond recognition.

24

Argentina

The first few attempts, he didn't pick up. Calida couldn't blame him. After what she'd said to him at Cristian Ramos's house, she didn't deserve his time.

When finally she got through:

'I'm going away,' Daniel said. 'I won't be back until the New Year.'

'Where?' she asked.

His answering quiet told her it was none of her business. She no longer had his friendship. Remembering how he had let her inside that door, a glimpse behind the shield he kept so solidly in place—*I trusted you, and you ran out on me*—made her shrink with regret.

The weeks crawled by impossibly slowly… waiting for him.

Calida handed in her notice at the club.

'You've brought this place up from its knees,' said Paola, who was sad to see her go. 'I will miss you—but I understand.' Her contract obliged her to work a remaining two weeks. On the nights Rodrigo tangoed, she avoided him.

In a stroke of luck, Calida's exit from El Antiguo coincided with the pizza place opening another shop across town. Calida jumped at the supervisor's role. The money was double what she'd previously earned and over the coming weeks she watched the funds in her bank account climb, slow but steady, to the point where she was able to skim the top off her income and save every month. Next came news that her landlord was seeking a quick sale on the Belgrano apartment: was she interested in buying? Yes, she was. Property was a sensible investment, a home in her name, and the place had potential. She could do it up, sell it on, the market was rising…

All the while, one man stayed in her mind. Calida yearned to show him all she had learned. She fantasised about spending the night with him—but, instead of the inexperienced child who had lain next to him, trapped in the wanderings of her mind, she would take him in her arms and make love to him for real.

When they saw each other again, it would be OK. It would work out. She needed Daniel at her back for where she was going. She needed his support and his love. When she met Tess Geddes again, she had to know he was on her side.

She only had to be patient.

*

In January, Daniel contacted her to say he was visiting Buenos Aires and could arrange to meet on his way through. He didn't volunteer why he was in town and Calida didn't ask—she chose to believe he was coming for her. When the day came, she dressed carefully, discarding outfit after outfit. She wanted to look nice for Daniel but she didn't have to impress him. She wanted to resemble the girl he had trusted.

The apprehension was agony. Calida thought of all she had been through with this man, how he knew her better than anyone. He had known her as a girl, he had known her home, and he had known Teresita. No other lover would have known her twin. How could she give herself to someone else when there was this hole at the centre of her identity? Daniel was precious but this made him priceless.

Though she knew the knock on the door was coming, still it made her jump.

She answered, and all at once Calida wasn't twenty-one; she was thirteen, the age she'd been when she had first laid eyes on him. Daniel hadn't changed; those blue eyes hadn't changed. He was the same wind-tousled cowboy she had fallen for.

'Hello.' Such a small word, for all it meant.

Calida wanted to hug him, bury her face in the softness of his T-shirt and the hard assurance of his chest, but his body language told her no. It was too soon.

As they made their way down to the street, Daniel avoided looking straight at her. He checked his watch a couple of times. He was on edge, too.

'Thank you for coming,' said Calida, as they took a table in the square. A gang of kids knocked a football around on a patch of grass, and, in the distance, a band started up. A waiter came over and they ordered two *Quilmes*.

'Of course I came,' Daniel replied. 'You said it was impor-tant.'

'Still, you didn't have to.'

'I wanted to. We're friends.'

Calida smiled. 'That's a relief,' she said.

Daniel shifted in his seat. He looked older, the crinkle of lines around his eyes testament to his life outdoors. She wondered how he had suffered as a boy, in the looming shadow of his tyrant father; the fear he'd known as he cow-ered from the blows, and then, as he got older, the bravery in defending his mother. How could she have left him, after he'd opened up to her like that? Selfish. Her pain and longing had driven him away—but what about his pain? What about his longing?

'The thing is, Calida,' he said, 'I have something important to say, too.'

Daniel's voice was clipped. She could tell he was about to lay it on the line.

'Let me go first.' Calida put her hands on the table. 'Please. I deserve everything you're about to hit me with but let me say this first. I'm sorry. That won't make up for what I did but it's where I have to start. I was wrong. I made a mistake and I regret it every day. I didn't mean those things I said. I was confused, and angry, and sad, all those things, but they're not an excuse because whatever I was, I should never have taken it out on you. The truth is, I wouldn't be here if it weren't for you. Not here,' she gestured, 'I mean… You know what I mean. You saved me, over and over. I never thanked you. I'm sorry, Daniel. I really am. I'm sorry.'

Calida watched the drops of condensation on Daniel's bottle of beer and then his strong fingers as they closed around it. He drank and then replaced it on the table, where it stained the paper cloth with a thick grey ring. The movement incited a trace of his scent. He smelled so good, of all she missed and loved.

'It's OK,' he said.

She waited for more but it didn't come. 'No, it isn't.'

'I said it is, and it is.'

This time he did look at her. The electricity of his gaze made her spark, the same way Rodrigo had looked at her right before he tore the clothes from her body, but at the same time different. Tender, gentle—sad, almost.

'You got my note about the farm?' he asked.

'Yes.'

'I had no choice.'

'I know.' She felt ashamed at shirking her responsibilities. 'Who took it?'

'Americans.' Daniel dug in his pocket. 'Here. This is why I came.' He passed a cheque across the table and Calida's mouth fell open when she took in the amount. 'This guy offered way over before anyone else got the chance to take a look, said he wanted it taken straight off. He bought the horses, the land, the lot.'

'But...' Calida was shocked. 'It was falling apart. It isn't worth this.'

'This guy thought it was.'

'Clearly.' She couldn't believe the amount. This was enough to...

'Take it,' she said, passing it back. 'It's yours.'

'No, it's not. It was your home. It's your money.'

'I can't. You earned this. We owed you. You deserve it.'

'I don't need your money.'

'I know, but—'

'I would have sent it before but it seemed safer to deliver it in person.'

Calida nodded. 'Daniel, I don't know what to say.'

'Then don't say anything.' The note of affection in his words compelled her to glance up. They smiled at each other. His smile was like the sun.

It made her take a leap of faith. 'I guess I was hoping...' A beat, before she blurted it. 'I guess I was hoping we could share this... for us—for our lives, maybe, together. What you said in Mendoza about how you felt, that maybe you still feel the same way, because I do. I didn't say it then, I didn't know *what* I was saying then, but I can't count the times I've wished I could go back and change every word. I can't stop thinking about you, Daniel, *siempre pienso en ti*. No one else compares. I don't care what it takes—I don't care about anything apart from being with you. *Te extraño*. I care about you so much. I've made a living for myself here—and with this,' she lifted the cheque, 'we could be happy. I know we could. I could make you happy.'

It wasn't a perfect speech, but there it was. She'd said it. She'd laid her heart on the line, on the table between them, and Daniel sat looking at it, his face grave.

'Well?' she asked softly.

'I'm married.'

The force of his announcement made her sit back, as if she'd been struck. Her mouth formed around words for every outcome except this and no sound escaped.

'I tried to tell you. It happened last month.'

A stone hardened in her stomach. 'To whom?'

'A local girl.'

'Who?'

'Does it matter?'

'Yes.'

'Clara. We're on honeymoon. She's always wanted to visit Buenos Aires.'

There was only one question. 'Do you love her?'

He continued to stare at the table, at the heart she had put before him. She wanted to reclaim it, fold it back inside her and get up and leave, but she couldn't.

'*Sí*,' he said.

'Look at me when you say that.'

He did. Well, she'd asked for it. '*Sí*,' he said. 'I love her.'

'Why?'

'Don't do this, Calida.'

'Tell me why. She's not a mess like me, is she?'

And you told her your secrets and she didn't run out on you.

'She's nothing like you.'

'And that's why you love her.'

'You turned me away. It was definite, as I remember.'

She couldn't deny it. She had no right to be angry or upset—she'd had her chance and she'd blown it. 'Congratulations,' she said, pushing her chair back. 'I'm sure you'll be very happy together. I hope you understand but I have to go.'

'Calida—'

'No.' He reached for her but she shrugged him off. 'Don't make this worse than it is. Forget we ever met. Go back to your wife.'

She felt his eyes on her the whole time she walked, but she didn't turn back.

*

A month later, Calida was in a bar on Santa Fe when a celebrity bulletin caught her eye. TESS GEDDES ATTENDS CHARITY GALA IN LA. She hadn't seen her sister since Cristian's house. Tess looked like a million dollars as she sparkled in front of the cameras, glittering eyes and shining teeth, her perfect face a mask of sympathy.

The reporter spoke in Spanish: '*If you recognise the name, that's because gorgeous Tess Geddes is the daughter of Hollywood queen Simone. The pair visited the Brentwood Children's Ward on Saturday, where Tess was named an honorary patron. With filming in full swing for Caitlin Wood's new production* White Candle, *it's a wonder that Tess can take time out for her charity work. Tess is tipped for stratospheric success here in Hollywood and we can't wait to watch her star rise.*'

Calida held her glass in one hand and swirled the ice around in the bottom, listening to the cubes crack and slide against each other like splits on a frozen lake.

Her sister. Her nemesis. *How I despise you.*

If it hadn't been for Tess Geddes, Daniel would still be hers. Her twin had failed in taking him that night on the farm—but she hadn't stopped there. Oh no. By running from them, by chasing her own self-serving instincts, her insidious poison had ensured Calida would lose him another way. If Teresita hadn't left, they would still be there, Calida would still know him, maybe he would never have met his wife.

Bitterness filled her like tar. Daniel was gone. There was nothing left to lose. Hate was stronger than pain. Revenge more productive than sadness.

Calida stood from the bar. *You can't get away with it, bitch. I will not let you.*

She grabbed her coat, paid for her drink, and vanished into the night.

25

December 2014
Night

The person stood before her, a black, faceless, nameless shape.

'Who are you?'

But the words didn't form. They came up her throat and hit the back of her mouth but they didn't make it. Instead they were absorbed by the hot, saliva-soaked gag, and she screamed, but it was hard to scream and breathe at the same time and her heart pounded wild and fast, beating so hard she thought she would pass out, or die, and she hoped she would die because this wasn't her life, this wasn't her life...

A hand reached down, soft and hairless, and loosened the gag. It fell from her in a sticky, chemical-scented mess. The feel of air on her tongue was like water.

For a few seconds, she fell for the trick. Then she gasped.

'Water.' Her mouth was parched. 'I need water...'

The person moved at leisure in the dark, no rush, and she strained to catch any clue she recognised. She detected a familiarity in the way they moved, something deeply reminiscent, like the forgotten touch of a long-ago lover's hand.

Light pooled at the person's feet, teased her by glowing, and then vanished.

The water was brought. The person knelt but not too close. She fought to catch something from their body, warmth or scent, because she knew them.

She felt certain she knew them.

She gulped the water but the glass kept moving out of reach. Helpless as a newborn, she nodded after it, begging for more. The liquid travelled into her like life; she sensed it move down her throat and into her belly and through all the veins and arteries that kept her body moving. She loved and hated it for keeping her alive.

'What do you want?' she managed. Her voice was rusty, clogged with the fog of her unconsciousness. A question sur-faced in her mind: How long have I been here?

'I want to talk to you,' the person said.

Her captor sat with their back against the wall. Now they had spoken again, any last doubt was eradicated. Fear surged. Fear and need, and longing...

'I'm sorry—' she began, anything to make it stop.

'It isn't enough.'

For the first time, her kidnapper's emotions got the better of them. The person remained in the dark, head bowed. The words came again. 'It isn't enough.'

'We can talk,' she pleaded. 'Please, there isn't any—'

'I don't want to talk.' The tone changed. She shrank back. Her head was pounding. Snow continued to dust the window-panes, an endless suffocation. In the corner loomed the sharp and piercing shape of a tree, undecorated.

'Let me go,' she managed. 'Please, just let me go.'

'I'm afraid I can't do that,' said the voice. 'You did a bad

thing to me—and I don't like people doing bad things to me. If someone does a bad thing to me, I have to do a bad thing back.' The person's face came close, their breath, hot and hungry, on her neck. 'I'm going to hurt you now. But don't worry: it won't last long.'

PART THREE

2006–2010

26

Los Angeles

The man had been staring at her all night. Plenty of people admired Tess Geddes, some more surreptitiously than others, but few had the confidence to eyeball her.

Her first premiere—at least for a movie she had starred in—was held at the Fernbank Theater on Sunset. Every big hitter in Hollywood was involved in the run-up to *White Candle*. Tess and Simone arrived on the red carpet to a barrage of roaring fans. Thousands of eyes roamed her fishtail Monique Lhuillier dress, drinking in the vision that had set this town alight, and Simone's hand guided her like the protective mentor and mother she was. Tess had been the golden girl of LA for the past twelve months, but this was her moment. Tonight marked her official arrival.

Tess held her head high and bathed in their praise and adulation. She was proud of the venture and her work. She loved to read the rave reviews: *Tess Geddes isn't just a pretty face... Her beauty surpassed only by her talent... You think her looks are all she's about? Then you're mistaken...* She relished the idea that the girls at Sainte-Marthe would see this, that Madame Aubert and her *professeurs* would be pleased, that somewhere, perhaps, Señorita Gonzalez would watch her debut movie and it would chew her up inside. She only wished that Calida could see it.

See what you gave up.

The screening went brilliantly. Caitlin Wood could put no foot wrong, and, with Tess's chrysalis-to-butterfly transformation, her performance was lifted from marvellous to masterpiece. The audience of VIPs laughed in the right places, fell reverentially silent where they should, gasped at the twist where Harry Duvall's character confesses his love for Tess, and, at the end, erupted in ear-splitting applause. Tess and her cast were encouraged to stand to receive their praise.

At the after-party, she returned the man's scrutiny. A flicker of a smile danced on his lips. If he wanted a staring match, fine, she would give him one.

'Hello.' He took this as an invitation to come over. 'I'm Steven.'

'I know who you are.'

Steven Krakowski was an illustrious producer. At thirty, after a string of box-office triumphs, he had just gone into partnership with Miller & Mount, one of the biggest studios in town. He had neatly cut ash-blond hair and handsome features.

'Tess,' she said. They shook hands.

'Congratulations. You're an immense talent.'

'Thank you.'

'I bet your mom's angling for the awards circuit.'

'I don't need her to win an award.'

Steven liked her spunk. 'Why don't I doubt that?'

Tess smiled. Her mind was working. Tonight's attention, the glory she was receiving as an actress, it was all well and good—but she craved more. She could achieve more. She saw what Caitlin Wood had, the other kickass female producers and directors in LA, and she wanted it. She didn't have to be someone's puppet.

Predictably, Simone appeared at her side. 'Tess, may I have a word…?'

'I'm busy.'

'It won't take a minute.' She was shooting Steven daggers.

Steven was diplomatic. 'I'm due a refill,' he said. 'Ladies?'

Tess shook her head. Steven smiled cordially and moved off. 'What was that about?' Tess asked through gritted teeth. She was sick to death of her adoptive mother interfering. What now—Steven needed the Simone Geddes Seal of Approval in order to warrant being spoken to? Courtesy of Simone, the year had seen a reel of industry guys come knocking on the Malibu villa. She was determined to snag Tess a boyfriend and each time Tess tried to squirm out of it—'We didn't have much in common' or, 'I couldn't make him smile all night!' when in fact her date had spent all evening talking about himself or had no discernible sense of humour—Simone would pout, wounded. How could she explain that she would *never* find a man who made her spark? That she was incapable of that? She was ruined, frigid, frightened of sex?

'I hate that man,' said Simone.

'Why?' Steven seemed perfectly decent to her.

'There are whispers in this town. I don't like it.'

'What kind of whispers?'

'Krakowski has his fingers in too many pies. You figure it out.'

'You mean he's a young guy tearing up Hollywood and your old-school buddies don't like it? I'll be making my own mind up about Steven.'

'Don't get lippy with me, young lady. You take my advice.'

'I'll see who I like.'

'Oh, you're seeing him now, are you?'

'He strikes me as friendly, honest, and respectful.'

Simone spluttered, 'You've divined this after two minutes of talking to him?'

'And you've divined your opinion based on rumour and hearsay?'

'Trust me: rumour in this town is as good as fact.'

'I'm sure.'

'You just keep away from Steven Krakowski, Tess. Do you understand?'

Tess brushed past her in search of the bar.

*

Simone's veto succeeded only in making Steven an attractive prospect. Tess didn't have the hots for him, the thought of sleeping with him brought her out in the usual psychological rash, but then that was no change. *What's important*, she instructed herself, *is what Steven can do for you*. And Steven could do plenty of things. He was at the beating heart of the movie business. He could make or break a career with the click of his fingers. Befriending him would inject her straight into the core of the power set: a set that had nothing whatsoever to do with Simone Geddes. Tess had imagined herself with an actor—but why choose that when she could go straight to the cogs of the machine? Acting would only sustain her for so long. She wished to produce, to create: to be the woman in charge. Steven could help her achieve that.

And so she agreed to a date.

Steven picked her up from the villa on Friday night. He seemed anxious, which she found endearing, and, rather than the usual prescribed supper of chickpea *panisse* at Château Marmont, he took her down the informal route and to a cosy table at Casa Vega. Despite it transpiring halfway through the meal that Steven had chosen the place because he thought she was Mexican, it was the most agreeable first date she'd had. Steven was intelligent and articulate, interested in her, fascinated by all she had to say and attentive to her thoughts. He welcomed her ambition: he himself had come from humble beginnings and not a day passed when he didn't count his blessings and thank God for how far he had come. Tess offered him an edited version of her life, Simone's version, where she was the grateful orphan and Simone the beneficent donor. She decided she would wait to tell him the truth... if she ever did.

As the wine went to her head, Tess reflected on how refreshing it was to meet a man who didn't put beauty first. So many men did. Alex Dalton, for one. Shallow. Vain. Predictable. Last week she'd read that Alex had begun dating a Victoria's Secret model. Before that it had been a catwalk queen, before that, a darling from London Fashion week who had stolen the headlines for walking the runway in a see-through Marc Jacobs. Each time Tess clapped eyes on him, yachting in Italy with his girlfriends, partying with A-listers or attending some function in Boston, she wished so hard that she could take it back. Her confession. Her weakness. It was as if Alex carried with him a tiny, vulnerable piece of her, whose existence threatened all she had built. Only he knew the chink in her armour. Only he had seen her at her worst.

I'm not making that mistake again.

She didn't have to. In Steven's eyes, she was a strong, capable woman: a woman who would grab this town by the throat and make it her own.

'Well, would you…?' Steven was saying.

Tess blinked. 'Sorry, I was miles away.'

'Argentina,' he prompted. 'Would you go back? My friend has a ranch down there—I know it well. Outside Bariloche.'

'Oh.'

'We should head out there some time.'

'Sure. That'd be nice.' She necked the rest of her wine.

Over the next few weeks, Steven embarked on a dedicated campaign of wooing. Simone caught wind of it and screeched her disapproval down the phone, but was unable to do a thing about it. Her censure made Tess enjoy it more. *See? You're not my boss.* Enormous sprays of flowers arrived at the Malibu house, together with jewellery, purses, exquisite tiered boxes of cocoa-dusted truffles.

She was flattered. Hundreds, thousands of women hankered after Steven, yet he saw something different in her: she wasn't just a *Vogue* cover. Moreover, there was nothing about Steven that made her afraid. Thus far her experiences with men had all been variations on a theme: the perpetrator and the victim, their bodies, solid and overpowering, backing her into a corner and bringing her out in a panic. On the contrary, Steven was patient. After their second date he kissed her chastely on the lips. After their third, he kissed her again, for a bit longer this time. After their fourth, he put his tongue in her mouth, gently and softly, not unpleasantly. Like wading little by little into a cool sea, the water creeping gingerly up her knees, he persuaded her.

The first time they slept together held no surprises. Steven took Tess back to his mansion and she had known what was going to happen. He fixed her a drink, lay down with her on the couch and began to kiss her, his hands roaming her body and his fingers peeling the dress straps off her shoulders.

He treated her tenderly, reverently, and not at all like Felix Bazinet. He consulted every inch of her body, a piece at a time, tracing his tongue across her breasts, sucking her nipples, pressing his lips in a chain down her stomach until he reached the mound of hair between her legs. He groaned at this, commenting on how nice it was that she was 'natural', and dipped his head. Tess had never had a man go down on her before. Mia had raved about how hot it was, and Tess had read that it was a man's ultimate expression of devotion, but right then it just felt a bit gross and wet. Steven's tongue seemed huge as it lapped her in wide, upward strokes, his breath hot and the liquid click of his saliva punctuating each movement. Several times he circled her opening and then dipped the tip of his tongue inside, as if this were a die-hard successful trick he had learned, but really it achieved nothing. Tess faked her engagement because there was nothing else to be done. Every so often she caught Steven looking up at her to gauge her reaction.

When he entered her, she pinched with pain, but quicker and lighter than with Felix. His erection wasn't as big as Felix's and, even when he thrust as deep as he could, she was only letting him in a few inches. Steven moaned on top of her, rocking back and forth, the palm of his hand sliding beneath her ass and lifting her hips to his. She caught his aftershave, a trace of lavender, and her eyes stung with tears.

Steven took this for approval and whispered in her ear, 'I know, baby, I know…' as he quickened his pace and the arm of the couch slammed against the wall.

He ejaculated in a series of quivering spasms, and then slumped on top of her. He was very heavy and Tess adjusted her weight to support him. He was holding one of her breasts like a security blanket, fascinated by it, saying over and over how amazing she was and how she had just blown his mind. All she'd done was lie there. 'We're so compatible,' Steven murmured. 'I've waited for this connection, Tess. I feel like I can be anything with you. I feel like I can tell you anything.'

At last, he withdrew. His cock had shrunk to nothing, the condom hanging off the end of it resembling a sock on a peg. He shrugged out of his trousers and padded naked to the bathroom. Tess listened to him whistle as he started the shower.

What mattered was that Steven was a good and decent man. He signified escape from Simone Geddes. He could engineer great things for her in America, in excess of her former goals: true, lasting power, what it meant to win her own fortunes and not someone else's. *Money is power. If you have power, you have everything.* What Julia hadn't said was that the money could be hers. The power could be hers.

It didn't have to be a man's at all.

*

In February, on Valentine's Day, Steven surprised her with a trip to his beach house in Santa Barbara. He had instructed her to meet him at his LA home; he'd be a little late coming in from the studio but would be there as soon as he could. Waiting at the mansion was an explosion of white roses. Tess was touched. She hoped he would like the Cartier watch she had picked out, and hadn't gone to more extravagance.

At six o'clock, she heard a rumbling in the distance. Tess stepped on to the terrace, her hair and skirt whipping up in the wind. The noise was deafening. As the helicopter came to land like a giant dragonfly, the lawn below shivered and flattened.

Once it had landed, a man stepped out and saluted her. She thought Steven might jump out after him, or even, at one stage, the president. The man handed her a white card:

My darling,
Your carriage awaits... and so do I.
S

She had never been in a helicopter before. As the craft's nose dipped, hovered, then soared off into the sky, she looked down at Steven's mansion becoming smaller and smaller until it was swallowed by the grid of the Angel City. It was tight in the cabin, but exciting. Through a set of headphones she could hear the pilots on their frequency, liaising with each other and Air Traffic in codes and coordinates she didn't understand. Soon after, they began the descent over Santa Barbara. She spotted Steven on the headland, yet more white roses cradled in his arms, grinning madly.

'You came!' He ran to her and locked her in his arms. It was reminiscent of the end scene in the movie she was filming, where two lovers reunite after years torn apart by war. She and Steven had been torn apart by a sunny day in LA.

'That was... unbelievable,' she said. 'I loved it.'

'I knew you would.' Steven piled the bouquet into her arms as though he was offloading a puppy. 'Wait until you see what I've got planned.'

She hadn't been to his place in Santa Barbara before, but he wasn't interested in showing her round. Instead Steven led her down to the water, to where a sleek fifty-metre yacht was moored. As twilight blossomed, the sky turned to peach Melba. Indigo water lapped at the boat's flanks. 'Climb aboard,' he encouraged.

Soft music played. Tess marvelled at the polished deck, pristine and sparkling, outrageously expensive, and through the double doors a swathe of luxury furniture and glinting chandeliers. Steven guided her through the interior, waiting slightly peevishly as she put the flowers in water, and out the other side. On the bow, a white-clothed table looked out at the ocean, laid with silver cutlery and elegant stemmed glasses. Candles flickered shadows across the deck. She could smell cooking, flavours in tune with the salt and depth of the sea. Steven pulled out her chair.

'What's all this for?' she asked.

'It's Valentine's Day,' Steven said, helping her in, 'and I love you.'

It was the first time either of them had said it. Steven delivered the sentiment with unselfconscious ease, as simply as he might say them to his mother or his sister. Tess, for many years, had agonised over this exotic triumvirate of words, imagined the many scenarios in which she might voice them, the possible suitors she might find the courage to express them to, and now, sitting here, she had absolutely no impulse to say them back. Thankfully, Steven's carefree comment didn't require it.

The vessel began to move, a rumble as it backed out of the harbour, then, as it crossed into open sea, gaining momentum, slicing through the violet sheet. When land was out of sight, a waiter brought their first course. The feast was sumptuous. Fried shrimp with hunks of bright lemon and saffron cream; swordfish fillet with crunchy fennel, vivid orange and plump black olives; then vanilla *panna cotta* to finish, which Steven insisted on feeding her. Throughout, he talked happily about a new project the studio had signed, every so often reaching under the table to stroke her knee, or across to clasp her fingers. Afterwards, she felt full and content.

'Thank you,' she said. 'You shouldn't have gone to so much trouble.'

'Are you kidding?' Steven's eyes glittered in the dark. He tossed down his napkin. 'Come on,' he murmured. 'Time for another surprise.'

He darted off into the night, down a set of steps, and, by the time she followed and reached him on the lower deck, he was stripping off. His trousers were in a heap, then his tie was loosening, tugged off, dropped, then his shirt. Finally he stepped out of his underwear, scaled the low safety rope and flung his body into the black ocean.

Seconds later, he surfaced, shaking his head. 'It's beautiful!' he called, his face pale against the inky water. Above, in the sky, a whole moon shone down as perfect as a pearl. The Big Dipper swung above them, huge and ancient.

Tess peeled off her dress, bra, knickers, and went in after him. The water was freezing and had the same effect as being tickled, making her catch her breath.

'You're incredible,' said Steven, kissing her. His hands cupped her ass and lifted her so her knees hitched around his hips. He was working a thumb inside her and she tried to take pleasure from it, pressing against him. Encouraged by this, he drove harder, pushing deeper as he nibbled and grazed her collarbone. It felt strange to be opened up in the sea, but at the same time made urgent, primal sense; Tess felt her body being returned to the water, some place it had always belonged.

Treading water, it was hard for Steven to get purchase. Knowing their goal, they swam to the boat and Tess clasped the bottom rung of the ladder, then turned away from him, as he prodded and bucked against her back. Water slurped beneath the prow, sinking her ass one minute and lifting it to the surface the next. With one hand Steven gripped the ladder and with the other he guided himself inside her. It had stopped hurting by now, but Tess still felt that familiar squeeze of discomfort as he broke through and began to rut. She was thankful he wasn't more generously endowed. Finally, it was over. Steven came silently, intensely, and the second he pulled away she felt him spill out from her into the sea. She had decided the female orgasm was a myth. 'I love you,' he said again, and this time it wasn't so casual. The moment hung for her to say it back, and instead she kissed him, deeply, to make up for it.

Back on board, Steven fetched them towels. They sat, huddled together, beneath the stars. 'This is the most amazing night of my life,' said Steven.

'It's wonderful,' agreed Tess.

Abruptly, he got up, vanishing inside for a moment before he returned, and then everything that followed seemed to do so in a blur. First, Steven dropped to his knees, the towel around his shoulders falling with the motion. Then he knelt, naked, one foot flat on the deck. At last, he produced a box. Small, crimson, unequivocal; she fought panic. He opened it. A diamond the size of a grape blinked up at her.

'Tess Geddes…' he said, and in that moment she realised that another girl was being proposed to, not her, not the real her, not Teresa Santiago. 'Will you marry me?'

*

One small word gave way to a media frenzy. Every paper wanted an exclusive. Every channel craved coverage. Every site demanded an interview. The press went into overdrive, reporters camping outside the villa, Maximilian's office ringing off the hook, designers and artists trampling over each other to pitch their ideas. Tess and Steven became the most photographed, talked-about duo in Hollywood. They were royalty. Before, she had been popular; with Steven Krakowski, she was gold.

Simone flew in and spent a couple of days playing the role of Dejected Mother, for which she could have safely added to her awards collection, before grudgingly partaking in the preparations. After all, she was a woman who embraced the limelight. In all her painstaking plans for Tess, she could never have rehearsed such a windfall. 'As long as you know what you're doing,' she counselled.

'Of course I do.'

'Steven's… an acquired taste.'

'I guess I've acquired it.'

Simone gave her a strange look, but promised to bite her tongue from now on: Steven was to be Tess's husband and he deserved the family's respect. Instead she took it upon herself to organise every aspect of the big day, while Tess gritted her teeth and humoured her as best she could. Steven smiled indulgently as the women went about their daily meetings, comparing fabrics, favours, and menu cards.

Tess wondered what Simone's own wedding day had been like. If she ever thought of marrying again; if she thought of marrying Lysander… After Tess had overheard their dialogue at the *White Candle* audition, Lysander was rarely, if ever, spoken of: a glaring elephant between them. The UK tabloids reported difficulties in the marriage with Brian, having not seen the couple together since a premiere in the spring. GEDDA LOAD OF GEDDES, one declared, on capturing Simone chatting quite platonically with a man who wasn't her husband. CHILCOTTS' MARRIAGE BLOWS COLD. Maybe that explained Simone's unwillingness to push the

Steven issue. Tess had an ace in her hand and she sure as shit couldn't be made to play it.

One day, a note arrived from Alex Dalton. Tess was surprised to receive it.

> *Congratulations on your engagement, Pirate. I hope he makes you happy, because you truly deserve it. Alex.*

The note should have made her smile; the sentiment was kind, but for reasons she didn't care to analyse, it didn't. She hated his pitying tone, his consolatory words: the inference that she was some poor foundling who deserved a break. *I'm making my own breaks, thanks very much. I neither need your sympathy nor welcome it.*

At the weekend, Mia flew out. Her friend was into her second year at Zurich's most prestigious Art Institute and full of tales about the guy she was seeing. Tess was elated to see her. 'Would you be my bridesmaid?' she asked one day over lunch.

Mia hugged her hard. 'I'd love to.' Then she pulled back, concerned. 'Hey, why do you look so scared?'

'I am scared,' Tess admitted. 'Of everything.'

'Don't be. Everything's going to be great for you. I know it.'

But that night, like every night, the past surfaced in dreams. Those things Tess wanted most to be rid of were the same that inched their way towards her in the dark. She had always thought that Calida would be with her on her wedding day. It had been a safe assumption, a given that as twins they would in some way share the most momentous day of their lives. Calida would never have the chance to get married.

Instead, she had been shot dead on a store floor and left to bleed to death.

It serves her right, a voice told Tess. And when she thought that, she was strong. She was filled with hate and hate kept her going, like coal in a fire.

Other times, Tess dreamed of her twin. That she was still alive.

She dreamed of the life she might be living.

27

New York

Calida Santiago travelled to New York on a sweltering hot day in June. The city was alive and insistent: corridors of skyscrapers, metallic and towering, a maze of mirrors that reflected their neighbours in silver-sharp angles, doubling and tripling her vision—she was disorientated at being unable to see through or over them; the cauldron of streets; the surge of Manhattanites rolling in a relentless wave down Fifth Avenue, in suits, on phones, carrying coffee, and the tourists, like her, out of sync as they gazed up at tiers of life piled one on top of the other. High above, mosaics of clear blue sky danced between spires. Calida took one look and thought: *Yes. It's here. This is mine*.

Paola Ortiz had a cousin who lived in Belmont and had arranged for Calida to housesit a couple of weeks while the cousin was away. The apartment was tiny but cosy, a flavour of her beloved Argentina on every wall and in every picture frame.

One day, in a busy café on Mercer, she noticed a girl flicking through apartment rentals on her phone. Calida slipped in opposite her.

'OK if I sit?' she asked, without waiting for a reply. The girl nodded.

Calida stole a glance at her companion. Early twenties, like her, with blue eyes, pale candyfloss hair, and a large, straight nose that she touched every so often, in the way of someone who wears glasses and keeps checking they haven't slid down. She was locked on her phone and, when after several fraught minutes she released a huge, exasperated sigh that couldn't go uncommented on, Calida put down her book.

'Everything OK?' she asked. The girl glanced up, put down her phone and sighed again. It was a wistful, romantic sigh, one that belonged in a black-and-white love story, or a rooftop in Vienna, or a Casablanca beach, not a bursting café whose barista was getting yelled at for putting too much foam in a cinnamon latte.

'I'm officially homeless,' the girl admitted. Calida placed the accent—a warm, southern twang. 'And this coffee tastes like shit.' She took a sip and cursed it when it was too hot. 'I'm, like, *this* close to getting my Brooklyn share,' she pinched a slice of air between her thumb and forefinger, 'and my best friend, who by the way *isn't* my best friend since, like, nine o'clock this morning when she called to say she was moving to freaking *Philadelphia*—I mean, hello, who the fuck goes to Philadelphia?—was meant to come with me. That was the condition. It's a shared room, see.'

Calida had a solid grasp of English from her work in Buenos Aires, inevitable since most of the tourists she had dealt with spoke not a word of Spanish. She nodded at the girl's plight. 'I'm Calida,' she said. 'What's your name?'

'Lucy. Lucy Ackerman of Austin, Texas. You're pretty, Calida. I like your eyes.' It was said perfunctorily, in precisely the same tone that Lucy had announced that the coffee was shit. 'You know what it's like to be so *near* to something you really, really want, then it gets ripped away, and there's nothing you can do about it?'

'Yes. I know that feeling.'

'What do you do about it?'

'You make it happen. If you want something, you go after it.'

Lucy rested her chin on her hand. 'So here's the story,' she said. 'One of the guys in this house, he's the hottest guy *ever*. He's an artist and his name's Brandon and I've liked him for ages, ever since I went to one of his shows and for some crazy reason he got talking to me. I don't know, maybe he saw something in me that no one else does. And just because I don't dress like his friends, like I'm not a hipster or whatever, it doesn't mean I'm not smart…' She shook her head. 'Sorry. We only just met and listen to me. I mean, *stop* listening to me! I've got diarrhoea.' At Calida's expression, she clarified, laughing, '*Verbal* diarrhoea—meaning I talk too much.'

Calida seized her opportunity. 'I need a place to stay, too. I travelled from Buenos Aires. I'm in New York to make it. Money, fame—I want it all.'

'Everyone says that.'

'I mean it.'

'Do you have a boyfriend?'

'No.'

'Have you been in love?'

'Yes.'

'I think I'm in love with Brandon. Is that even possible? I barely know him.'

'Of course,' said Calida. 'You don't have to know every-thing about a person to be sure they're right. You just… *know*.

Take you and me. I can tell inside five minutes that we'll be friends.' As she'd planned, Lucy glanced up, her expression open. 'Let's take the room together,' said Calida. 'Solve both our problems.'

Lucy's blue eyes brightened. 'Seriously?'

'Sure, why not?'

Lucy blinked, then beamed. 'I can't think of a reason! OK, I guess—yes! God, I can't believe it, this is going to be so much fun!'

Calida smiled back. 'You're right about that. Lucy, you're going to be glad you met me today. You, me, all of this, it's meant to be.'

*

The Williamsburg share was everything Lucy had promised: a six-storey brownstone sheltering a collection of self-conscious creatives, who spent their days drifting in and out of communal areas where they indulged in lengthy conversations about socialism and the evils of religion, and then locked themselves away for hours on end in their bedrooms with the aim of producing 'work' but never elaborating on what that work was. The most Calida saw were a couple of Danish Johann's poems stuck on the refrigerator, one of which began with the line: '*I am an apple, you are a bowl; I sit in state in the cup of your hands.*' Calida thought she was missing something.

'They love you,' Lucy encouraged during their first week, as they sat over bowls of spaghetti at the little wooden table in the kitchen. Calida didn't mention that neither girl's presence seemed to have registered with the housemates; on the whole they were ignored, but she was happy with that. Moreover, she wished to spare Lucy the realisation, which surely must have occurred, that Brandon Carter had barely sent two words in her direction since they'd arrived. Calida could see Brandon's appeal: he had the loveliest, darkest skin she had ever seen. His art—sketchy charcoal impressions that he exhibited at nearby galleries, and that Calida, with her devotion to the illuminating, absolute photographic image, found good if a touch frustrating—gave him an extra dimension. He was kind to Lucy, but clearly had his radar trained on another of the housemates, an elfin, French beauty named Evie.

Lucy was oblivious. 'Did you hear Brandon ask me out?' She sucked up a string of pasta. Calida liked that she ate with gusto, and wasn't prissy like the hipsters with their lentil salads and rye crackers that resembled rectangles of carpet.

'To the warehouse party?' Yesterday, they had walked in on Brandon making plans for a downtown birthday celebration. He'd been obliged to extend the invite.

'Sure! You are coming, aren't you? I can't go on my own.'

'I thought you wanted to be alone with him.'

'I do—but not at first. I can't turn up by myself.'

After a week of pestering, Calida finally agreed. She liked Lucy and wanted to help her, but equally she was aware that every night spent partying with rich kids who pretended poverty and acted like they were the Next Big Creatives but in fact were heading nowhere was going to wind her up just the same. She had to find a path in. Manhattan, the money and the mission: some channel that would lead her to her twin.

The warehouse was on Fulton Street and was packed with Brandons and Johanns. Chilled beats throbbed through the space and an array of beers, drugs, and smoking paraphernalia littered each surface, around which saggy armchairs and burst-leather benches were gathered. Everyone was thin and beautiful, and slightly tortured.

'There he is!' Lucy grabbed her arm.

Brandon's impressive Afro could be seen hovering by the decks. He was talking with a guy in a neon baseball cap who was languidly putting on records that nobody recognised but were too embarrassed to admit they didn't recognise.

Calida urged her to hang back, wait for Brandon to come to them, for it struck her as uncool for Lucy to be falling at his feet. But Lucy wouldn't be discouraged.

'Brandon,' they sidled up next to him and Lucy's voice turned into a purr, 'what's up? Great party.'

'Oh.' Brandon looked surprised to see her: perhaps he had forgotten the invitation. 'Hey. Yeah. Cool.' He perked up a bit when he saw Calida.

'Like your boots,' he commented.

Calida had thrown on a black dress and her old gaucha boots, which she wore on bare legs. 'Thanks.'

His handsome face broke into a smile. 'Want a drink?'

'Just a beer.'

'Sure.' He held her gaze.

Calida turned to Lucy. 'You want the same?' Lucy nodded, stricken, and when Brandon departed she wailed: 'He was flirting with you!'

'No, he wasn't.'

'I know flirting when I see it. God! I feel like hurling.'

'Don't be stupid. I don't even like him that way.'

But, to be safe, she spent the rest of the night avoiding Brandon. Instead she got talking to Johann, if the term could be applied to the intermittent grunts that emerged in between tokes on a joint. He was grudging and only passed it to her twice.

'What's Denmark like?' Calida asked.

'It's cool.'

'How long have you been in New York?'

'Three years.'

'Do you like it?'

'It's cool. I guess. Though, sometimes, it can be uncool.'

For a man who wrote on fridges about apples and bowls and cups made of hands, Johann had a surprisingly limited vocabulary.

At midnight, someone started letting off fireworks. They climbed a stepladder and, out on the roof, Calida found Lucy clinging to Brandon and gazing so dotingly at him that she missed the show. It was a spectacle: showers of red, pink, and green raining down on the Manhattan skyline, framing the Brooklyn Bridge and shimmering off the water. *This is my city*, thought Calida. *I'm going to fucking well take it over*.

Lucy staggered up. 'I think this is it,' she slurred. 'He's into me. I can feel it.'

Calida was about to ask how drunk Lucy was and if maybe she ought to go home, when, over her shoulder, she spotted something problematic. Brandon and Evie were pressed against each other, kissing like their lives depended on it. She tried to distract Lucy and lead her away, but it was too late. Lucy saw, and was silent.

Watching her friend's eyes fill with disappointment, she was reminded of the night she had sneaked into town and found Daniel at *Las Estrellas*. How it had felt to see him with that other girl. Now, he was married to another girl, a girl who got to have him in her bed every night, feel his body, wake up to his face every morning.

She put her arms around Lucy and held her. 'I'm sorry,' she said.

'Can we go?' Lucy asked in a small voice.

'Yes,' said Calida. 'Of course we can.'

That night, she told Lucy her story: about the farm where she'd grown up, about Daniel, about Julia, and finally about her sister. She told her how she had sent the money from the sale of the *estancia* to Cristian Ramos and his family, and in doing so had put their struggles to some good use of which her papa might be proud.

She stopped short of making the Tess Geddes connection, instead referring to her twin only as Teresa and saying she was living somewhere in England but she didn't know where. She couldn't risk Lucy's loose tongue leaking it to Brandon, then Evie, then Johann—and where would it end? No. She must keep it to herself.

They drank vodka, shared a packet of cigarettes, and stayed up until five, when the sun was bleeding over the river. She told Lucy because she thought it might cheer Lucy up, make her see she wasn't the only one for whom life was hard, but she also told her for herself. To remind herself why she was here and what she had to do. To refresh the hatred she checked in on every day, feeding it, keeping it warm, so that when the time came she could unleash it. Watch it savage the thing for which it was bred.

*

In time, Lucy got over Brandon. She had to, given that every day she was confronted by him and Evie draped over each other, giggling and kissing, and darting off for shared showers in the middle of the afternoon. It was painful, but at least it made an effective cure for her crush. Despite this, Calida wasn't immune to the occasional flirtatious comment from Brandon—whose sly advances corroborated Lucy's suspicion that he did indeed have it bad for her—and even a stoned offer one night to draw her naked.

'You'd make the perfect subject,' Brandon said, leaning in, eyes red-rimmed, 'kind of lost and sexy… I'm really into you, Calida. Evie and I have an understanding… she's cool about other girls. What do you say we make this happen…?'

Flatly, Calida turned him down, before getting up and going to bed.

'Hey,' he moaned at her retreating back, 'you could at least suck me off?'

'Suck yourself off, dickhead.'

The next morning Brandon attempted to retract his advance, mortally embarrassed, and make out like he'd been so out of it he hadn't known what he was saying. 'I thought you were Evie,' he wheedled. 'You won't tell her, will you?'

Calida had no intention of mentioning the slip to Evie but she chose not to tell Brandon this. It was useful to own a piece of him—especially since he'd begun work at a studio in Manhattan and was returning to Williamsburg each night brimming with stories about the city's power clique. Brandon was the key; she felt it. Now she only had to keep her eye out for the door—and, soon enough, that door appeared.

Brandon and Evie became closer, exacerbating his fear of Calida's reveal. The job offer bought and secured her silence: they both knew it.

It came about through a friend, who was assistant to a fashion photographer on East 8th. The friend was going abroad and the studio was seeking a replacement: did Brandon know anyone? Calida had already shared her photographs of New York with him—golden light falling in shafts across the Chrysler Building, the crinkled face of a storekeeper by the side of the road, the majestic, emerald Statue of Liberty like a giant aquarium ornament—and he encouraged her to put them in a portfolio.

'You're good,' said Brandon, 'seriously good.'

The studio called back and summoned her for an interview. She dressed sharp and spoke sharper, unwilling to let this chance slip through her fingers. Photography had been the one constant to draw her through the past decade, since Diego had died. Her papa had given her this gift and she had held it tight to her heart, unaware the whole time that it would become the thing that set her free. SilverLine Studios was super-league. It shot for the big guns—*Tatler*, *Elle*, *Glamour*, *InStyle*—and its owner Ryan Xiao was one of the hottest properties in America. Calida would start as a runner and welcomed the graft, the climb to the top that her sister had bypassed so regally because she was spoiled and stubborn and cared about no one but herself.

Within the week, the job was hers, and so was the elusive prize she had dreamed of since arriving in America: a work visa. The instant she turned up at SilverLine, she knew it was where she was destined to be. The place was a hub of energy. Rails of clothes were gathered along one wall, an efficiently dressed woman flicking through them and scribbling down notes. Bulb-lined mirrors appeared in a bank alongside crates of make-up, powders and lipsticks, shadows and airbrushes, pots and pastels. A collection of leather seats was positioned around a glass table, topped with neat cubes of glossy magazines; nearby a small fridge was filled with miniature bottles of Perrier and Dom Perignon, and a tray of untouched sandwiches.

Beyond the vibrant mess of preparation rolled a pure-white wasteland: the blank stage awaiting its model. The camera—a huge, handsome thing on a tripod—stood on the line between the two, like a giant punctuation mark.

'Calida Santiago?' Ryan Xiao, the most renowned photographer in New York, for bitchiness as well as brilliance, heaped a pile of fabrics in her arms. 'I'll say this once and I won't say it again, so listen up and listen good: I don't give a rat's if it's your first day, you'll haul ass at my pace, in my way, you'll do everything I damn well tell you without so much as an answer-back or you're out on the street before your first paycheck and I'm not kidding. Winona and Mags are here. Tell them they look stunning, they've never looked better, do not under any circumstances offer them breakfast, then get them into these and *only* ask Vicki for help if you *absolutely have to* because let me tell you she's doing my fucking head in today and I can't take another gripe about her workload. Do whatever the models require and do it with a smile on your face: I haven't time to crawl up their asses myself and I've already got enough shit on my nose to last ten lifetimes. Then go get Starbucks for everyone. Got it?'

Ryan strode back to the set.

'Got it,' Calida answered. Over the next few hours she moved between tasks with skill, enthusiasm, and drive. She sensed how to be useful, to have faith in her initiative and earn the trust to be given the same job next time. Her only glitch came when she was introduced to the models. Winona Glazer and Mags Lalique were two of the most in-demand cover queens of the decade: instantly she knew their faces, seen so often gazing out from newsstands across the city and billboards on Times Square. She was awed. She had never been in close proximity to such raw, unfettered beauty.

Is this what Tess Geddes is like? Is she a goddess, just like them? As Calida positioned reflectors, angled lighting, tweaked garments and cleared the scene for the next storm of images, she conceded the unbridgeable chasm between an assistant and a star, a minion and a princess, a plain-Jane and a knockout.

A sister left behind and another one taken…

Bullshit. I can be just as good as her. Better.

'Beautiful!' Ryan encouraged, as the models posed in an effortless sequence of gorgeousness, their bodies impeccably tanned and toned, the clothes hanging off them like a second skin. Over the coming weeks, Calida learned how adept Ryan was at making the women feel like a million dollars, only to wait until the door slammed behind them at the end of the day and then he'd demand a drink and a smoke and tell anyone who'd listen what an awful bunch of bitches populated the fashion industry.

'Did you know Winona *dared* criticise her headshots?' Ryan whined to her on Friday night. 'Some of the best work I've ever shot and she says her cheeks look fat? Lose some fucking weight off your cheeks then! Isn't that what surgery's for?'

Slowly but surely, Calida gained her boss's confidence. Whatever the task, from booking runway royalty to fetching his linen Armani suit from the dry-cleaner's, she made herself indispensable. Ryan wasn't one to dole out praise, but refraining from insult was pretty much the same thing. She had been at SilverLine three months when she suggested to Ryan partway through a sitting that they shoot their model from above. Brett Bennett, dashingly handsome but painfully insecure (as she was learning all models were), was anxious about the 'extra chin' he had acquired on a pool party shoot in Iceland at which he had drunk one too many Brennivín. Combined with the shadow contrasts she recommended, and the addition of a bunched-up shirt held to Brett's naked, sweat-gleaming torso, they had a win. Brett was thrilled.

Ryan didn't comment on it until the end of the day, after everyone had left.

'You were good,' he said. 'You have an eye.'

Back at the Williamsburg house, Lucy was euphoric when she heard of his approval. 'So, go on, then,' she urged, 'spill the beans! What's it like mixing with the A-list? Are they hideous? I've heard Mags is a witch.' As Calida was forming a response, Lucy barrelled on. 'Ooh! You know that six degrees of separation thing? By now you've got to be less than that away from, oh, I don't know…' her eyes fell to the table and an edition of *Vanity Fair*, which she leafed through to find the first acceptable celebrity, 'Tom Cruise! Or Anne Hathaway—or, look, Tess Geddes!'

Calida tensed. 'I guess so,' she replied.

'Did you know she's getting married?'

The room went cold. 'What?'

Lucy tapped the page. 'Tess is getting married to Steven.' She sighed. 'She'll make *such* a beautiful bride. Hey, they should hire you to photograph it!'

Somehow Calida managed to raise a smile. What she wanted to do was scream and scream until her throat bled. Seeing the pictures, she wanted to tear them up, see Tess Geddes' smile ripped corner to corner, her perfect face slashed in two. But what had she expected? Steven Krakowski was one of the richest men in the world, and there was Teresita, just as her twin had planned, her arm in his, the perfect couple.

Cheat, Calida thought.

Well, she had done it. Teresita had done it. *I'm going to make it, Calida. I hope I never see you or this dying shit-hole ever again*. And there it was in black and white: her sister's wedding day. Calida pictured Tess Geddes in her gleaming LA mansion, occupying a world in which everything was brilliant and bold, and the only thing bigger than her fleet of cars and the size of her bank account was her black soul.

Calida didn't intend to stay six degrees separated. *Bad luck, bitch. Looks like you'll be seeing me sooner than you thought.* Six degrees was about to become one.

28

Barbados

Simone Geddes knew what made a spectacular wedding—not a good one, not a great one, but a remarkable one that would be talked about in every gossip column on the planet. Despite her misgivings, she'd been adamant that her daughter should marry in style… and what style it turned out to be. Gold sand swept to the water's edge, where azure waves rolled idly to shore. White linen chairs ran in neat rows down the aisle, pastel-pink ribbons tied to their backs, fluttering in the warm breeze. A grass-capped pagoda, strung with tiny white roses, housed the minister, who appeared less like a man of God and more like an Abercrombie catalogue model. Swarms of press set up equipment on the exclusive seven-star Sundown terrace, ready to record each second this momentous day had to offer. Geddes and Krakowski: a match made in heaven.

Or so the story went. Simone wouldn't have picked this alliance in a million fucking years. She hoped Tess knew what the hell she was getting herself into. On the surface, Steven had it all; on paper, he was perfect. But beneath… Well, she could only pray the stories weren't true. Or that he had ceased to indulge in extra-curricular activities. Perhaps Tess already knew, in which case it was none of her business. But even if her beloved daughter was being kept in the dark, Simone knew her accusations would only be thrown back at her. She was hardly Wife of the Year, was she?

Guests were starting to arrive, that mingling hum of civilised conversation that Simone associated with elite dinner parties and wine tastings in the Dordogne. But she was too wired to embark on a meet and greet and instead set off to check on the Gateau de Résistance, a six-tiered creation spiked with edible pearls and sugar-spun diamonds. No sooner had she ducked into the cake's personal refrigerator, a space the size of a Harvey Nicks changing room, than she heard a familiar voice from behind.

'You've been avoiding me.'

Simone turned. The door closed with a tantalising hush and there stood Lysander like some handsome assassin, dark gaze roaming her body, hungry as a fox in a chicken coop. Her resolve crumbled like rocks into the sea. *Fuck it.* She had tried to resist her stepson. When he'd finally moved out of the mansion she had thought that might mark the end of the spell, a temptation now easier to defy... but it was impossible. Each time Brian was out she grappled for the phone like a drug addict, wild-eyed and frothing. Their combats were wordless—he showed up, they screwed right there in the hall, at the bottom of the stairs, an urgent, animal, breathless fusion.

In a dreadful, delicious way he reminded her of the boy who had got her pregnant. She knew she should hate that man, but she couldn't: her grandparents had decided he was a dropout, a degenerate, and Simone never had the chance to inform him. Each time she screwed Lysander she was taking back a piece of the frightened fifteen-year-old who had bent to her guardians' command. She was rescuing the lust she'd felt, the abandon, the rebellion, in that heady recklessness of youth.

The Chilcotts had descended yesterday. She and Lysander hadn't had a chance to be alone—until now. Knowing Brian was yards away turned her on even more.

'We mustn't—' Simone objected. She backed into a caged stand, inside which the understudy wedding cake stood in immaculate isolation, in case of any mishaps.

Something told Simone there was about to be a mishap.

Lysander's kiss hit her with delectable force, his tongue filling her mouth and his hands kneading her breasts. Together they stumbled into the chill. Her ass hit a freezer compartment and the purring buzz stung between her legs, making her throb.

'I've got to have you,' Lysander growled. 'I've got to fuck you.'

Simone hitched her skirt up—a scrupulously elegant Valentino creation for the discerning mother of the bride: none of those frumpy-pudding ensembles so many women seemed to favour, thank you very much—and parted her legs. Lysander was unbuckling. No matter how many times she saw his powerful cock, such a contrast to her husband's flagging member, it still had the ability to shock. His balls were swollen to bursting and she reached down to collect them in her hand. He groaned.

'Lysander, I…' Simone closed her eyes, lost for words as his dick ploughed into her like a battering ram. She collapsed back on the fridge. Lysander began to pump, her Valentino blazer cast aside and the peach-silk blouse beneath straining to contain her bullet-hard nipples. He tore through the buttons with deft fingers and ducked his head, drawing her nipples into his mouth. Simone cradled his head as his kisses travelled north, arriving at her neck, her collar, her earlobe, which he bit ever so gently. Sparks whizzed from her groin to the tips of her toes. Why couldn't Brian make her feel like this? He never had. These days it was like living with a monk. She was convinced her husband had started sleeping with prostitutes, but so what? It didn't bother her—at least it got him off her back, literally, at the end of a long day.

The papers were full of the marriage crisis, but let them speculate.

They would never reach the truth.

Lysander is your stepchild... your family... What are you doing? The facts should have put her off. But they didn't. If anything, they sharpened her hunger.

Simone cried out, louder than she should. Beneath the zinging coolers they could hear guests circulating, the light tinkle of harp music as people took their seats for the ceremony. Lysander fucked expertly, transporting them both to the brink.

'Oh, yes! Yes! Do it to me, yes!'

'Shh…' he hissed in her ear. '*Stay quiet, Mummy.*'

Jesus! It was too much. Simone squealed as his hard-on drove deeper, her juices spilling all over him, so wet he could hardly keep inside. She loved to watch his cock severing her, the tumescent pink of its tip like a one-eyed sea creature, or the crown of an exotic flower, captured in a botanical drawing.

'Make me come,' she moaned. 'I can't take any more!'

'Shh!' He clamped a hand over her mouth, at odds with the rampant pulse he sustained between her legs. 'Shut up, you dirty bitch, or I'll have to punish you.'

Punish me! Simone went to yell—but, before she could, a slab of something sticky and sweet landed on her tongue, filling her cheeks. She almost choked on it, on the shock, then, as Lysander's fingers chased it up, dipping between her lips as if it was the tenderest cavity he had ever explored, her tongue came alive and she tasted the familiar, sugary nectar of forbidden fruit. Moist sponge oozed creamy butter icing in her mouth and then Lysander was cramming in more, never once breaking the relentless piston of his cock as he reached into the cage to gouge out yet more of the backup cake. He wrecked it, tore it inside out, flinging hunks of vanilla loaf so it dripped and leached and seeped between his knuckles and looked as if a wild animal had been at it. Lysander brought the cake to her, rubbing icing across her breasts and then sucking it off, piling more and more into her mouth to strangle her cries, but the more he squidged the crazier she became. Sponge sprayed from Simone's mouth as her muffled screams grew savage and fraught, and, when Lysander licked his fingers and attended the insanely swollen bud above where his body was locked with hers, she shuddered hot and cold, hot and cold, and everything went black then white then black again as rapture struck and her cunt was filled with sun and rain then quiet.

Lysander ejaculated, crumpling into her arms.

'Oh, Lysander…' Simone kept saying it; his name was all she could say.

They lay there a while, skins thick and slick with crumbs and slashes of mown-down cake, hair matted with gluey icing, until reality crept back in. It was a critical situation. Lysander tackled the cake mess while at lightning speed Simone cleaned her hair and face, corrected her outfit in the Miele's reflection, and had to admit that, despite the slightly rumpled chignon and the skew-whiff button at the top of her blouse, the recently-fucked flush gave her an appealing glow that all the *laboratoires* in Paris could spend a century working on and still not come up with.

She exited without him, rounding the hotel terrace and entering a pit of press.

'Where on earth have you been?' Brian simpered; how this man had spawned such an Adonis was beyond her. 'I've been looking for you everywhere!'

Not hard enough, Simone thought. Then again, when had Brian ever been?

'I'm here now, aren't I?' she replied tartly. 'Now, let's have a wedding.'

*

Tess stepped out of the wings and took Brian Chilcott's arm. He was puffed up next to her like a stuffed quail. At the pagoda, beyond the ranks of guests, Steven waited, beaming, his handsome face alight. Harp music plucked and the sun bore down.

Admiring murmurs followed her down the aisle. Her Vera Wang scoop-back gown pooled to the floor like a rink of milk and in her arms she clutched a bouquet of jasmine and orchids, studded with miniature gemstones. Mia followed in a pretty satin silhouette that Tess had fought for, because Simone wanted her bridesmaid to wear an awful sack-like design: 'But that's what they're for, darling—to make *you* look good!' Knowing Mia was there offered comfort, for so many of the faces grinning up at her she had never seen before in her life. Simone had held final control over the invitations and her army of industry cronies outnumbered Tess's contacts ten to one.

She noticed him because his head was the only one not turned.

Alex. A scruff of black hair, facing front, and those familiar square-set shoulders; Simone had insisted she invite him— 'You know a Dalton? Christ alive, Tess, are you aware who his father is?' But she knew what he would think: that she was marrying for status. That this location was extravagant and her dress was tacky; that nobody here really knew her, the real her, so the whole thing was as fake as socialite Bette Danziger's spray tan. Well, if that's what he thought he could forget it.

Love was a trap only fools fell into. She was no fool. She had a plan.

'Darling,' Steven crooned when she reached his side, 'you look incredible.'

Brian slunk off to the front pew and Mia arranged her train. When she took Tess's bouquet, she squeezed Tess's hand and the gesture made tears rush to her eyes.

Twenty minutes later, she was married to Steven Krakowski.

*

'Congratulations.' He caught her at the champagne fountain in between photo appointments. If Steven summoned her one more time like a dog to its master's heel, or told her to, 'Slow down, darling,' she would scream. Hence the alcohol.

'Hi.' Tess swigged the remainder of her glass.

'You look great.'

It was the least embroidered comment on her appearance she had received, yet the most sincere. 'Thanks.' She waited for his caveat, and sure enough it came.

'Aren't brides meant to smile all day?'

'I am smiling.'

'Not right now.'

'Probably because I'm talking to you.'

Alex Dalton grinned. His eyes were warm, a rich, soulful brown. She felt at a disadvantage to his composure. 'I guess you disapprove of all this,' she said.

'Why?'

'I don't know. I can tell.'

Alex adjusted his tie. 'As long as you're happy, that's what counts.'

'Of course I'm happy.'

'Good. I'd hate you not to be.'

'That's very generous of you. But I'm not an idiot, Alex.'

'I never said you were.'

'You might as well have done.' All of a sudden the emotion of the day rushed at her and she wanted to lash out—not against him, necessarily, but against Steven, Simone, herself. *I'm not happy with any man. I never will be. I'm a freak.*

Alex made things worse. 'I didn't think you went in for this scene.'

'What?'

'Hollywood. This crowd. Your husband.'

Remember why you're doing this. Steven's a good man. In five years' time, pretty, rich boys like Alex Dalton will be shining your fucking shoes. So suck it up.

'You're hardly living in a cardboard box at Union Station.'

'Maybe not—but I would if it was with the right person.'

Tess snorted, ungainly and messy but the realest she had been all day. Alex had dumped Victoria's Secret and moved on to Winona Glazer, another lingerie superstar. What right did he have to talk about 'this crowd', as if he was immune?

What do you care? Tess asked herself. *Why do you even know?* But she did know that despite his censorious pontifications he was just as shallow as the rest of them.

Then she remembered his mother, who'd died. Those sympathies on Facebook she'd seen ages ago, when they were kids. The father who couldn't give a shit; Alex's attempts to be a writer and how he'd made fun of himself; the jacket he'd lent her and never picked up; the messages he'd sent her over the years. It complicated her image of him. None of it fitted with what she'd decided, so she pushed those thoughts away.

'It's like you've forgotten the person you are,' Alex went on. Tess blinked, unable to believe the words were coming out of his mouth: he was saying this *on her wedding day*?

'You can't deny where you came from. It's inside you. It's part of you.'

She was stunned. 'How dare you talk to me about what I've been through?'

'The hair isn't you.'

'Excuse me?'

'Your hair, pulled back like that—it doesn't look like you.' *Who the hell did he think he was*?

Mia bowled into them. 'Hello!' She nudged Alex. 'You know she's married now, don't you?'

'Give it up, Mia,' said Alex.

Tess found her tongue. She couldn't look at him. She was too angry with him.

'When did you two meet?' she blurted.

'On the flight over,' said Mia, linking her arm through Alex's. 'Alex shared his cinnamon brownie with me. I'd say that makes us friends, wouldn't you?'

'It's a damn sight more than we are,' said Tess, slamming down her glass and crossing to meet Steven, who was calling her for a family shot with people who weren't her family, and never would be. That was what stung. Alex Dalton was right.

*

In bed that night, she couldn't stop thinking about him.

How he infuriated her! She never wanted to see him again as long as she lived. Clearly Alex got some kick out of reminding her every time they met that despite the life she'd made for herself, despite all she had achieved, she was still that sobbing, drunk, pathetic debutante he had rescued from the ball. She *wasn't* that person and she didn't need charity—least of all from an arrogant hypocrite who thought he knew it all but in fact knew nothing. She had a husband who adored her.

Security, money, fame, social standing… A future. She had the world at her feet.

In the dark, Steven reached for her. It being their wedding night, he spent longer on the preliminaries than usual. The worst part was when he guided his erection into her mouth and asked her to suck. Afterwards, he held her in his arms.

'You thought I'd forgotten, didn't you?' he said softly.

'What?' All Tess wanted was to go to sleep. For today to end.

'Don't be coy, darling. Our honeymoon, of course…'

Tess opened her eyes.

'I know I've been busy with work,' Steven went on, stroking a lock of hair from her face, 'but it hasn't stopped me planning the trip of a lifetime.'

'Where?' She blinked.

A horrible part of her already knew.

'Argentina,' he whispered. 'You, me, a ranch…' She heard his smile. 'We leave next month. I knew you'd love it. Going back there, it'll be like you never left.'

29

New York

Calida Santiago got her break at the start of 2007.

She left SilverLine Studios a little after eight, her back aching from the set she had stayed behind to dismantle. 'Get Calida to do it,' was the line in Ryan Xiao's kingdom. 'Is Calida free?' She ensured she always was. *Graft today. Glory tomorrow.*

As she was entering the subway, she realised she had forgotten her purse.

'*Mierda*,' she muttered, heading back up East 8th, where she unlocked the studio doors and met a gust of empty darkness. Between six and six, the place buzzed with activity; at night, an abandoned creepiness settled over the ghosts of the day.

Calida was crossing back to the entrance when she heard a faint, female sobbing trickling through from one of the dressing rooms. It was an elegant sound, a sustained, mournful weep rather than an all-out cry, and so it came as no surprise that the person making it should be equally refined: a six-feet vision with tumbling syrup-blonde hair and exquisite cheekbones, sitting in a corner and sniffing into a tissue like a tear-streaked Cinderella. 'Winona?' Calida stopped. 'Are you all right?'

'Of course I'm not all right, you idiot,' came the reply. 'Do I look all right?'

'Well—'

'I'm ugly! I'm hideous! Look at me!'

There was nothing in the least bit ugly or hideous about supermodel Winona Glazer except for the verbal bullets she occasionally fired off in an unsuspecting assistant's direction. The epitome of glamour, Winona had been tagged Sexiest Woman of the Century in *USay* magazine, and regularly topped global beauty polls.

'What are you still doing here?'

'I'm hiding,' Winona snivelled. 'I'm meant to be at some fucking junket downtown but there's no way I can show my face.'

'Why not?'

'Why do you think?' Winona's features shot up at her, stained with mascara, her eyelashes clotted and her hair a nest. True, this wasn't her finest hour. 'I'm too ashamed to appear in public ever again,' she moaned. 'That's it. My career is *over*.'

Calida sat, cautiously, as if Winona were an animal about to bolt.

'How can you say that?' she tried. 'You're stunning.'

Winona produced a fistful of stills. 'See these?' She thrust them into Calida's hands. 'I've never seen anything so grotesque in my life. These are the worst pictures ever taken of me, *ever*. I might as well retire right now. Everyone says how Ryan Xiao's this fucking genius, how he makes girls look so much better than they really are—but if that's the result then what the hell do I look like in the first place? *God*!'

Calida consulted the headshots. She had to admit that Ryan had suffered an off day. For starters, the lighting was wrong. Tiny pores on Winona's forehead and chin were visible in the glare, and the shadows beneath her eyes were less sultry than sleep-deprived. She was dressed in a 1920s turban with a glittering diamond clasp, all Man-Ray pale limbs and classic sensuality, but Ryan had failed to capture that special added dimension for which his work was famous. She could only put it down to the tensions that had crackled between the pair since last year: Ryan had grown weary of Winona's emotional outbursts, while she believed a woman of her rank should be exempt from his catty sniping. One thing Calida had learned during her time at the studio was that the relationship between model and photographer was paramount.

'What are these for?' Calida asked.

'A spread in *Chic*.' Winona wiped her nose. 'It's meant to mark my five-year anniversary in fashion. It looks more like fifty years!'

'It really doesn't.'

'Ryan's bored of me. I can tell. He's a doll to every other girl who walks through these doors, then I come along and he's, like, whatever. Now I have to suffer this humiliation. All those bitches will have their claws out, just you watch.'

'What bitches?'

'Clara Steiner, Felicity Clark, Mimi Gardner—Felicity's on Twitter and she's set up this catalogue of her best shots and now they're all posting theirs too.'

Calida hadn't yet succumbed to the newest social network, but one thing was certain: it was great for compounding anxieties such as Winona's. Since its launch last year she had logged on a few times to view Tess Geddes' account, gleaning as much information as she could, fascinated and sickened by it both at once.

'What am *I* going to post?' Winona went on. 'I look like a fat pig. Next week it'll be splashed across every page—they'll be laughing so hard they'll cry out their Botox. No, that's it, I can't do it—I'll call my agent and tell him to pull the piece.'

Calida had an idea. 'I could take your picture… if you want?'

Winona pinned her with a stare that went from surprise to disbelief to humour. 'You? Thanks, sweetheart, I needed cheering up.'

'I mean it. I'm good. We'll recreate the set right now—it won't take ten minutes. I'll shoot you against the window then we'll catch you in silhouette. We can light you from above, like a spotlight, maybe use costume jewellery, and—'

'No offence, but I've been photographed by the best in the business.'

'And you're not happy with the results. You said so yourself.' Calida's words hung in the air between them, laced with treason. This was either the smartest move she'd ever made, or the most stupid. It was one thing to convince Winona on her own merit, but to sideswipe Ryan? Unwise. The girl she had been on the ranch would have run miles, afraid of upsetting or offending, of getting told off. The woman she was now understood that there were a handful of openings in life that came about once and never again. You had to be ready to take them—or else watch them sail away.

Winona narrowed ice-blue eyes. After a moment she lifted her shoulders and sighed. 'Fine,' she said. 'I suppose. Might as well see what you can come up with.'

Over the next two hours Calida worked like she had never worked before; even on Cristian Ramos's vineyard with the sun beating down on her back, or at home with the horses, reining them in on a storm-tossed day, she had never worked like this. It was exhilarating. First she sat with Winona and listened to her, really listened—what the model felt were her best assets and her worst angles, how she liked to be positioned, the frustrations she'd had in the past and how these could be rectified. Calida agreed with some and disagreed with others but didn't comment either way: the crucial thing was that Winona felt she had a voice. Once the model's concerns had been aired she began to relax, and, by the time Calida slipped behind the camera she was purring like a kitten, transformed from the wreck she had been an hour before.

Together, they settled on styling. Whenever Winona veered off-piste, Calida steered her back, all the while maintaining the illusion that Winona had arrived there herself. Beneath Calida's lens, she became playful, coy, sassy, flirtatious, timeless, romantic, austere… She became a hundred women yet stayed archetypally herself. Calida used her own camera because it was an old friend and it wouldn't let her down. She thought of all Diego had taught her, and it struck her as special that to capture a condor against the crystal-blue Patagonian sky was no different to capturing a model with an attitude problem. The thing that remained the same was her.

Calida shot in colour and black and white, in sepia and grey. She caught Winona from behind, above and beneath, until the profile she had deemed as ravishing in Ryan's photographs became something close to divine. With every shot she had it nailed. Frame after frame, Winona Glazer shone like fire.

Afterwards, Calida shared the images. Winona sat next to her and was quiet for a very long time while she went through them. Eventually, she looked up.

'I love them,' she said.

*

The next few months were a hurricane. Winona insisted on using Calida's pictures for the anniversary spread in *Chic*, and, while Calida planned to approach Ryan herself on the subject and duly requested Winona hold back, of course as soon as given the chance Winona paraded the switch, unable to keep her 'revival' under wraps.

Ryan summoned Calida for a meeting. 'You've got nerve— you know that?' he said. 'It takes some big *cojones* to go behind my back. You shouldn't have done it.'

'I'm sorry.'

'But not so sorry that you want Winona to scratch the feature?'

'No.' She met his gaze. 'Not that sorry.'

Ryan was chewing gum. He put his hands in his pockets.

'I've seen the shots,' he said, 'and I'll be frank with you, Calida, OK? I got into this business because I'm passionate about portraiture. Lately, dealing with princesses like Glazer, I've lost sight of that. Your pictures made me remember. Don't for a second imagine I'm not royally pissed at you—what you did was wrong. But I'm not standing in the way of genius. And I've a feeling you won't let me.'

After that, Ryan promoted her to his second-in-command. They spun the *Chic* item not only as Winona's celebration but also as a showcase for Ryan Xiao's newest protégée. Acclaim was unanimous. Winona's reputation as the number one catwalk queen was cemented and her nemeses on Twitter stayed notably silent.

Before long, word was spreading about the city's hottest new property. Mags Lalique requested a private session to refresh her portfolio. Brett Bennett announced he would only shoot at SilverLine if Calida Santiago was there. Within weeks their schedules had multiplied; huge names, stellar names, everyone coveted a slot. Calida soaked up all she could learn, and Ryan, not wanting to let her go, taught it.

'This business will be yours one day,' he said. 'You realise that, don't you?'

'If I decide to stay.'

He grinned. 'Now you're getting the hang of it.'

*

In July, she moved out of the Williamsburg house. Lucy had started a job at MOMA and they decided to room together in an apartment on West 86th. 'I can't afford that!' Lucy chewed her lip when they went to view the space. Calida didn't mind paying the difference. The way she saw it, if she hadn't met Lucy when she'd arrived in New York, none of this would have happened: Williamsburg, Brandon, Ryan, Winona... Besides, Lucy was her friend, and friends helped each other out.

Throughout the summer, Calida's involvement at Silver-Line grew and grew, until eventually she surpassed it. With Ryan's consent, she began taking on clients of her own. Her work was esteemed, her name whispered in dressing rooms and in private dialogues at parties—the shortened version Ryan had christened her with: 'Have you worked with Cal Santiago? Did you *see* what she did for Tilly/Catherine/Eva/Katie? I don't care what it takes, *I need a booking.*'

Ryan kept giving her raise after raise but it wasn't enough.

'I want to be partner,' she said one day. 'Existing clients we'll split seventy-thirty, but for those I bring in it's straight down the middle. I want my name on the brand: I want in on all decisions and strategies and I want to re-brand to signal the change. Here.' She showed Ryan her designs—a black square logo, stark and cool, surrounding the block white letters XS. 'It's all we need to say.'

Ryan loved it. 'Since when did you become a ball-breaker?'

Calida wondered if she hadn't always been one.

Early fall, she received a summons to Winona Glazer's birthday party. The celebrity world impressed her no more than it had as a child, but today she grasped its usefulness, the ways in which it could propel her into ever more prominent circles.

The night of the party arrived. 'I can't wait!' Lucy trilled as she rifled through her closet and flung a rainbow of clothes on the bed. 'Is Brett going? He's *gorgeous*.'

'I expect so. I'll introduce you.' Calida wore her usual black dress and gaucha boots and kept her hair loose. She applied thick eyeliner and a sweep of mascara, but no other make-up. She took ten minutes getting ready, which was about the time that Lucy emerged from the shower wearing a towel turban and not much else.

'How can it take you so long?' Calida collapsed on the mattress as Lucy embarked on the painstaking process of toning, moisturising, coiffing, and finally painting. Her friend did it all completely naked then at the last moment dropped a jade silk slip over her blonde head and, almost as an afterthought, stepped into a pair of barely-there panties. Her nipples were visible through the dress.

'You sure you want to wear that?' Calida asked.

'Why? Does it look bad?'

'It's a bit… revealing.'

Lucy snorted. 'You sound like my mom,' she said. 'It's sexy!'

They set off. Winona was toasting her twenty-fourth at the top of the Standard Hotel, in the gold-barred, glitzily lit, panoramic-viewed celebrity hangout known as The Boom Boom Room. 'This is insane,' Lucy clung to her as the elevator delivered them to the eighteenth floor. Even in Calida's line of work, she had never seen so many stunning people at once. It was like stepping into the glossy pages of *Tatler*.

'Cal! You came!' Winona fell against her like a sequin avalanche, her breath hot and sweet with pickle martinis. 'Look, everyone: Cal's here!'

Calida was led to her table. Lucy followed, nervously pulling down her dress.

'I didn't think you'd make it!' Winona slipped into the booth next to her, coked up to her eyeballs, then asked baldly: 'Who's this, your girlfriend?'

Calida introduced them. Lucy smiled, star struck, and extended her hand.

'How come we never see you out?' Winona ignored Lucy and instead draped an arm round Calida's shoulder. 'You should party more,' she purred. 'It's fun... Ooh, look who it is!' Mercifully, Winona was diverted by model-turned-actor Harry Duvall, who had just turned up with his not-so-secret boyfriend. 'I'll be back!'

When Winona had gone, Lucy made a face. 'Was she coming on to you?'

'She's high.'

'They're all banging each other anyway, you can tell.' Lucy removed the magnum from its ice bucket and poured. 'It's the ultimate narcissism, right? If they can't do themselves, they might as well do someone equally as gorgeous.'

Calida smiled. Lucy's candy-blonde, Southern-Comfort demeanour meant it was sometimes easy to forget there lay a sharp mind beneath. Looking around, she saw that Lucy was right. The models were shamelessly touchy-feely. Six-feet frames lolled over each other, a leg stroked here, a kiss planted there...

Calida downed her champagne.

Over the next few hours, despite the A-list factor in the room, it seemed that she was the person to be seen with. As she got progressively tipsy and Lucy got progressively trashed, a stream of names approached her for a photo, or just to introduce themselves. *See, Tess Geddes? You're not the only one who's good at this*.

At two a.m., the party piled into a chain of waiting cars.

'I've got a shoot in four hours,' said Calida, hailing her own cab.

'Bullshit you have!' Winona Glazer crowed, grabbing her. 'We're just getting warmed up. Brett's renting this sick place out in Glen Cove. You *have* to come!'

The mansion was an hour's drive out of NYC. Winona insisted on Calida and Lucy sharing her ride and wasted no time in producing a heap of cocaine.

'This is the best birthday ever!' Winona slurred. 'D'you know why? Because of this woman right here.' The limo turned and Winona's body slammed into hers, her hand squeezing Calida's knee. '*Cal Santiago*,' she whispered, before erupting in giggles. 'I don't know what I'd have done without you. My fucking boyfriend dumped me like two hours ago and do you know what? I don't even care! I'm invincible. Alex Dalton can go screw himself because I'm hotter than him, I'm hotter than everyone, I'm hotter than the fucking sun and it's all thanks to you!' Winona kissed her. Lucy sat opposite, flirting with a TV actor with badly dyed hair.

As Winona had vouched, the Long Island pad was unbelievable. It couldn't be smaller than the White House. Moonlight gleamed off landscaped lawns as the party of fifteen—Winona's proclaimed 'core set'—piled inside. Calida was amazed at the endless corridors and huge, polished rooms. Who lived here? It was a palace.

'Brett's renting it off some Italian dude,' said Winona. 'He's super-rich.'

'No kidding,' said Calida. A wall of photographs in the vestibule boasted a suited, dark-haired European mixing with the glitterati. The Italian was attractive but pristine: his teeth too white, his hair too oiled, his hands too smooth. Her thoughts wandered to Daniel Cabrera in his dusty T-shirt and worn blue jeans. *Don't. It hurts*.

Lucy was the first to jump in the pool. Her silk slip became transparent as she frolicked and splashed in the water, and soon the rest were joining in, peeling off their clothes and diving into the blue. Brett located the bar and the first shots were served.

'This is wild!' Lucy cried, playfully spattering the TV actor. He responded by grabbing her and kissing her. In a rush the silk slip came off and her breasts crushed against his chest. Calida decided she had seen enough. She headed inside.

The grounds were spinning. She'd drunk too much. Locating the kitchen, she drank two glasses of water and sobered up. By the time she went back outside, the pool was deserted, just several bundles of clothes lining the perimeter. Voices and music emanated from a hexagonal pool house; she crossed to it and opened the door.

Inside, it was lavishly upholstered. On the central table a collection of powder-filled bags promised the party would continue until dawn. Everyone was naked and touching each other. The word *orgy* spun in Calida's liquor-soaked brain.

She searched for Lucy. 'Hey, Cal, c'mere,' drawled Winona. The model was reclining against Brett's chest and smoking a thin cigarette. Her nipples were tight and small, light pink, and the narrow strip of hair between her legs burned amber. Keeping her eyes on Calida's, she began to touch herself, parting her thighs so Calida caught a glimpse of a silky pink flower, so similar yet so different to her own. Winona opened wider, sinking her finger and raising her hips. Brett's hands appeared from behind, lightly squeezing her breasts. People were taking their cue from Winona and kissing and fondling each other, the floor and upholstery a mass of limbs and bumps and swellings, the pink of skin and clumps of hair reaching and swaying like coral on the ocean floor. It was impossible, in places, to see where one body ended and another began; some were connected not to one other but to three or four, by hand, mouth or lower. Soft moans rose from the melee. An alarm sounded faintly in Calida's head.

Winona stretched for her, 'I'm waiting…'

A model Calida didn't recognise manoeuvred himself between Winona's legs, while another positioned himself over her, pulling himself off.

'Wait.' A voice she recognised. 'Don't. I'm not sure… I don't know if I…'

Lucy was face-down on a cushioned banquette, neck lolling and eyes bleary. The TV actor began kneading her buttocks, while Winona's friend Ursula kissed her spine from top to bottom. Lucy sighed, with pleasure or surrender or both. The actor stepped back when Ursula's kisses met the tanned ravine of Lucy's ass and parted her.

'We're going.' Calida found a shirt and threw it at her friend. 'Get dressed.'

'Chill, girl,' said the actor, with a lewd grin, pointing his obscenely big erection towards her like a cocked gun. 'Don't you want in on the action?'

By now Winona was on all fours. The guy she was with entered her from behind and drilled her like a jackhammer. 'Yeah!' she squealed. 'Oh, yeah, it's party time!' At the same moment Brett eased his penis into Winona's mouth and it vanished almost completely. She rocked between them like a dancing piston.

'Lucy, I mean it. Get dressed. Now.'

Lucy attempted to grapple forward but Ursula was eating her out like there was no tomorrow. Only when the actor tried to have sex with her did Calida pound a fist into his jaw. It cracked like wood. 'Crazy *bitch*!' he snarled. 'Are you insane?'

She grabbed Lucy and hauled her up.

'I want to go home,' Lucy blubbed, shivering and pale-faced.

'All the liquor and drugs in the world still makes that rape,' said Calida.

'Jeez, don't get heavy on my ass,' said the actor. 'It's only a freaking party!'

Out in the fresh air, Lucy promptly vomited by the side of the pool. Calida helped her get dressed. Instead of the slip, she wrapped her in a blanket, and hugged her tight to keep her warm. It was a relief when their car finally pulled up and she was able to bundle her inside. Her friend fell instantly asleep and Calida watched the Long Island mansion recede in the wing mirror like a Gothic nightmare.

What had she expected?

It proved what she had known all along about this fake, dangerous, poisonous world. Just as it had spun lies and dripped venom into her sister all those years ago, so the real version delivered. Another reminder that her twin had wished for this life, these people; she had chosen them over family, over loyalty, over everything of value.

Replaced, swapped, upgraded.

Teresita used to fear monsters, when they were six years old and lying in the bunk and could hear the old shed rattling in the wind. Calida had told her not to be afraid. She hadn't known then that the only monsters were the ones Teresita would one day pursue—and that, when she found them, she would become one herself.

Calida had read about her sister's wedding, tried to avoid it but in the end been unable to. She had seen the pictures, each one a splinter in her heart.

Had her twin thought of her? Had she even crossed her mind?

No. Of course she hadn't. Calida glanced once more at the mansion before it dissolved from sight. *Become a monster*, she told herself. *If that's what it takes*.

Lucy moaned in her sleep. 'Home… Please, take me home…'

Calida, too, closed her eyes, and prayed that the dark would come quickly.

30

Argentina

Home. The word held terror and wonder. Tess Geddes was going home.

Work commitments meant the couple were forced to delay their honeymoon, and arrived in South America two months after the wedding. Tess had hoped the trip would be put to one side once ordinary life resumed, but Steven would stop at nothing. He employed a full-time team to source their itinerary—from polo-playing to wine tasting, from an 'authentic' Pampas safari involving luxury silk-weft gazebos and a Michelin-starred chef, to an al fresco dinner party for all their friends on the final weekend. The night before they left, he presented her with a schedule.

'What do you think?' he asked, kissing the tip of her nose.

'It looks wonderful,' Tess said. All she could see was the proximity to the ranch where she'd grown up; they would be mere miles from its perimeter. *Forget it. It's a scrap of deadbeat land*. That place had abandoned her—she owed it nothing.

But as soon as she stepped off the propeller plane on that Patagonian airstrip, the heat and scent of Argentina embraced her like a lover who had broken her heart. 'This way, baby,' said Steven, who was clad in a billowing linen shirt and a camel-leather Panama, like some 1930s island explorer. He guided her towards the BMW, which squatted on the road like a growling panther. Steven preferred to maintain the illusion that this was nothing out of the ordinary, that they weren't attracting a wave of stares and a crowd of followers, that there hadn't been a cluster of tipped-off paparazzi waiting for them at the airport gates, and there wasn't a beefy security guy named Ike hovering at their back. But it was, and they were.

As they shot like a bullet through her homeland in air-conditioned luxury, the contrast gave Tess vertigo. She ought to be on horseback, barefoot and knee-scraped. Instead she wore a stark white Diane Furstenberg pantsuit with patent blue heels.

She saw herself in the tinted windows, superimposed against her rustic, sprawling birthplace, and it seemed a miracle that her country, her land, had been here all along, waiting through these years for her return, and hadn't changed. The peaks and lakes shone as bright and glorious as she remembered: more, finer, better.

You can't deny where you came from. It's inside you.

As soon as they arrived at the ranch and met its studiously rustic sign—EL PARAÍSO—Tess knew just what kind of place it was. Against all evidence to the contrary, she had both feared and hoped for a glimmer of her world, that Steven might have tapped into it. Instead this was an *estancia* purpose-built for the rich, those who wished for a sanitised Argentina and who were content to occupy the land and all its wonder, so long as a hot shower welcomed them at the end of the day and they could slip between satin sheets on a full belly and their internet access wasn't compromised.

'It's special, hey?' Steven beamed.

'Yes,' she agreed. 'It's perfect.'

*

They stayed on *El Paraíso* for two weeks, walking, relaxing, having sex, and Tess concentrated on the great things about her husband and tried to forget the rest. Now they were out of LA she saw him in a different context, and couldn't help comparing him with the rough-knuckled gauchos of her youth, who seemed daring and wild in comparison. *I'm just like my mother*, she thought. *I don't know how to be happy.*

One day, her favourite day, they took the horses out. Tess stroked her animal's flank and searched his warm, ink-glazed eye, and felt her soul slip back into place.

She put her foot in the stirrup and swung her weight up and over and it was as easy and natural as breathing. Reins in her fist, the earth below and the sky above…

Meanwhile Steven picked his way across the churned-up terrain and the rancher hauled him up; then he hung off the beast's neck, legs dangling. After a series of frustrated grunts, he righted himself, located his upper body strength, and landed on the creature's back with a loud *thwump*, his groin taking the brunt. There was a sound like ripped material and Steven's mouth slung open. His skin went bright red.

'Are you OK?' Tess asked.

Steven was quiet a moment, then said in a high-pitched voice: 'I'm fine.'

They set off. Steven put on a brave face but was clearly uncomfortable. His horse was thickset and had flatulence; each time it lifted its tail to relieve itself Steven winced as if the indignity was his, as if this were a flawless oil painting he had spent weeks constructing only to find someone had been sick all down it. The dust blew in his hair and eyes and inside the rim of his forty-five-thousand-dollar Bentley Platinum sunglasses. As they climbed across the steppe, it started to rain. Steven reached to pull a waterproof from his saddlebags and the flapping material sent his horse into a spin.

'It's having a fit!' Steven cried. 'Jesus Christ!'

The gaucho rode back. 'Stop. No clothes, no move…'

'No clothes?' Steven parroted as his animal performed a flustered circle and ducked and tossed its head. 'What the hell does that mean?'

Tess seized the bridle and soothed the horse to a stop. Steven clung to its neck, the dirt on his face streaked by rain. 'If you want to get something out of the bags,' Tess said, 'stop and dismount first. He senses the disturbance. It makes him panic.'

'I'm sorry to have troubled such a sensitive disposition,' Steven snapped. 'Does he want a scented candle and a massage with that?'

Tess stroked the horse until it calmed. It reminded her of Paco.

'You know horses,' the gaucho said to her in Spanish.

She found her mother tongue as if it had been yesterday. '*Sí. Viví aca.*'

They stopped for lunch and ate *empanadas* from the grill. By now Steven was in a comprehensively bad mood, and refused to sit on the tree logs with the others, instead spreading his waterproof as far from the horses and herd droppings as he could. Tess boiled and cooled water from the gulley, while Steven popped the top off a bottle of Evian and drank lustily, before chucking the empty plastic on the ground.

Tess could have stayed out, but her husband wouldn't entertain the idea and demanded to put the day out of its misery. As they ventured 'back to civilisation so I can wash this filth off', she could no longer fight the impulse. Telling Steven she'd be back later, Tess let her horse loose on the reins and galloped across the prairie.

It felt wonderful: the horse's hooves clattering, his mane streaming black in the choking wind. She stood in the stirrups, every motion and moment coming back to her, the familiar mould her body occupied. She could hear Steven's shouts a long way away, growing fainter and fainter as she rode faster and faster. This was her land.

And then, suddenly, it was.

Tess recognised the raised plateau, the cluster of trees, and the position of the pale day-moon in the sky, thin as a fingernail. She pulled her horse to a stop.

The light changed. The wind blew silent. *Home*.

For some time she looked at the ridge; where she and Calida had come as girls, escaping from their parents or camping out for the night. Calida would cook them supper on the fire and tell stories in the dark, about Cherokee Indians and the legend of Butch Cassidy and the Sundance Kid, and wild horses who could fly to the sun on wings made of silver, until they fell into slumber and woke up at dawn…

Beyond that ridge was her farm—or whatever was left of it. Tess dismounted and took a step, then stopped, not quite able to cross over and see the graveyard of her youth. The land wasn't theirs any more; she would be trespassing… but that wasn't the real reason she held back. She didn't trust how she would feel if she saw it again.

The wound was raw—it always would be, no matter how celebrated or prosperous she became—an unopened box of pain and rejection she had bound tight and hidden away so she never had to look inside. The absence of her twin would forever be a whistling void, made worse by Tess's inability to grieve. How could she, when the person who'd died had forsaken her so savagely? Calida had never been the person Tess believed her to be. Like Julia, she'd seen the money and run.

She hadn't cared—so why should Tess care about her?

That pain didn't go away. No matter how many banknotes she threw at it.

Tess knelt and ran her palm across the soil. Behind, her horse grunted and tugged a tuft of grass with his teeth. She let the grains run through her fingers.

A tear fell and stung a line down her cheek. The wind kissed it dry.

*

On their last weekend, the Americans descended. Steven had organised a magnificent dinner party, presumably to show off his new identity as Intrepid Adventurer.

Their guests arrived on Friday night, among them Steven's Best Man Greg Steinway and his actress wife Natalie Portis. Tess was home-baking *fugazza*, an Argentinean-style focaccia, because it gave her an excuse to hide out in the kitchen.

'Isn't it sweet? What a cute little place! How quaint!' A burble of excited chatter swept in with their guests. Tess entered the fray for the meet and greet.

'Natalie, Greg, how wonderful to see you.' She embraced them.

'Darling, you look incredible!' Natalie trilled. 'Married life suits you—and so does this place! But you're from here originally, right?'

'Nearby.'

'You should see her on horseback,' bragged Steven, 'she's a devil.'

A voice emerged from the back of the crowd. It silenced all others.

'Did someone say devils on horseback? How perfectly delicious.'

Their guests parted like a Biblical sea. The voice was absolutely sure of itself, almost offensively so, slightly accented but irresistibly refined, the kind of voice that demands to be heard. Tess caught a flash of dark hair. Crisp shirt. Blue eyes.

'Vittorio!' Steven raised his arms. 'Greg said you were unavailable!'

'You know me, Krakowski,' said the man. 'After I missed the wedding of the decade, I couldn't let another chance pass by to make your wife's acquaintance.'

The man stepped forward and lifted Tess's hand to his mouth, where he touched it ever so lightly to his lips. He held her gaze with a thrilling, potent stare.

Tess was momentarily tongue-tied. With his glistening hair and marble-square jaw, the man looked so... *European*. Like a prince in a storybook, dark and sculpted like granite. He regarded her unapologetically, hungrily, daring her gaze with his, with a stubborn tenacity she recognised in herself. *I've met my match*, she thought.

'Vittorio Da Strovisi,' the man murmured, eyes hooded. 'And you are Teresa.'

He must have read it somewhere. No one called her by her real name.

Tess's skin tingled; she experienced a physical pull in his direction. Vittorio searched her eyes, and when he found what he was looking for he smiled.

Natalie giggled. 'Vitto, *stop*! He's an awful flirt. You're both married!'

Steven joshed along with it. Tess got the impression that Vittorio could have stripped her naked and thrown her over the table and Steven would have joshed along with it. Vittorio's scent lingered, musk and sex. For once, no trace of lavender.

'How's Scarlet?' asked Steven. 'I haven't seen her since…'

Vittorio chuckled. A flash of conspiracy went between the men. 'She is back in Tuscany. We agreed I'd take this trip,' his eyebrow lifted, 'on my own.'

As the party conversed, pieces of Vittorio Da Strovisi slotted into place; Tess did know who he was. An Italian businessman often featured in the pages of *Forbes* and *Fortune*, his wife was a brittle shipping heiress named Scarlet Schuhausen and the couple were continually splashed across the press in a yacht or a super-car or boarding a jet. They had more money than Steven and his cronies combined.

Vittorio kept stealing glances in her direction. His sweater was emblazoned with the insignia *VDS* (an emblem Natalie later informed her was applied to his every possession), and his skin was so smooth that it looked as if he bathed in milk.

Back in the kitchen, while the others were showering and preparing for supper, Tess gathered herself. *What's the matter with you?*

You don't like sex anyway, remember?

'What a feast!' enthused Natalie, as they took their seats on the veranda. The dusk was lilac and sweetly fragranced, the land around them vast and quiet.

'Tess is a wonderful cook,' bragged Steven, as they dug into Provolone cheese with flatbread, followed by rich and sticky *carbonara criolla*. 'She insists on making everything from scratch. Half the time I don't know what we're paying our staff for!'

Vittorio took a slug of blood-red wine. When his plate

was put in front of him he didn't wait for anyone else, he just started. He ate like an animal.

'Where did you learn?' Natalie asked politely.

'From my sister,' said Tess. She cleared her throat; she never normally talked about her life before Simone, but Vittorio was watching her intently, as if he saw everything and there was no point in trying to hide it. 'My real sister, I mean.'

'Where is she now?' Natalie asked.

'She died,' Tess said coldly. 'She and my birth mother were murdered.'

'Oh.' Natalie put a hand over hers. 'I'm so sorry.'

'You weren't to know.'

Steven prickled in his seat, as if this really wasn't an ideal vibe for a glitzy dinner party. 'Vittorio, why don't you tell us what's new in Milan?' he encouraged.

Vittorio continued eating. He ate quickly, in big forkfuls, and when the fork wasn't adequate he tore at the food with his fingers, which was an action at odds with his neat appearance. Finally, he said: 'I want to know more about Teresa.'

'Tess doesn't like to talk about her childhood,' said Steven quickly.

'It's fine,' said Tess, 'don't make an issue of it.'

'I'm not, darling. It's just it's hardly…' Steven tried and failed to find the proper words. 'I just don't think our guests need to hear about that.'

There was an awkward silence. Tess said: 'Hear about what?'

Steven flashed her a *not now* warning. Was that it? Did she embarrass him? Was her upbringing too rough to discuss in front of his precious friends?

'It's all in the past, now, isn't it?' he said softly, and if there had been such a thing as a cap on a conversation he would have applied it with a firm, sure thumb.

Tess sat and refilled her glass. She tried not to look at Vittorio.

'So,' said Natalie, breaking the spell. 'I think I'm going to just *love* it here.'

*

Tess didn't know a great deal about relationships, but she did know that a honeymoon wasn't the best time to decide she might have married the wrong person.

Nevertheless, she persevered, masked her reservations, and threw herself into the new movie she was shooting in Canada. The role had a Best Actress award written all over it. Steven had contacts on the board and Tess had already organised a dinner party to accommodate them. She didn't care if it was shameless. While she relished the buzz acting gave her, the camaraderie onset, and the sneak peeks at the dailies, it wasn't enough. She had to keep reaching, achieving, striving for more.

Steven, meanwhile, having renewed contact with Vittorio Da Strovisi, vanished to Italy for a month. Tess banished the blue-eyed businessman from her mind, attributing her infatuation to concerns over her husband; both would pass.

Three months later, she cancelled a spontaneous getaway to Mia's new pad in Vienna due to the onset of a cold, but forgot to notify her husband. This was nothing new—for weeks they had passed like ships in the night, catching up in rushed phone calls or one-line messages (even a phase of one-picture messages, as Steven took to posting snaps of his dick with variations on the caption *We miss you*)—and Tess figured that since he was abroad again and the Santa Barbara house was empty, she would take herself there for the weekend; see if the ocean air might do her good.

On arriving at the estate, her first thought was that their security had been compromised, because the code pad had been reset and the door was unlocked. Tess advanced, her heart pounding. In the gloom of the hall, she slipped off her shoes and reached to take a vase from the cabinet. She prowled to the bottom of the stairs.

Oh no.

She could hear it now. A struggle. A skirmish. A man's muffled groans, a thump, and a cry of, 'Oh, God!' that was categorically her husband's.

Terror gripped her. *Do something. Call 911.*

But her phone was out of signal and the landline was in the dining room; by the time she reached it, it would be too late. In a flash she bounded up the stairs, two at a time, ready to strike—to kill if she had to. The air thickened, the hallway carpet turned to gloop, as shapes bloated and morphed in the pitch.

Tess slammed the door open and held the vase aloft.

For a moment she stood, numb, frozen, the scene in front of her pulsing with horrific clarity. 'Steven…?' The name flopped out of her. She thought she must be wrong—that *thing* couldn't possibly be her husband, the illustrious Hollywood producer, the successful jock with his fleet of cars and cabinet of awards and press queueing round the block to catch a spritz of his stardom… But she wasn't wrong.

It was here. It was happening.

This.

Steven was sprawled on the floor, mid-crawl, a pacifier rammed in his mouth and a diaper tied round his ass. Framing his face was a Little Miss Muffet bonnet.

His mouth opened in surprise and the dummy fell out and rolled under the bed.

'Tess—' he croaked.

Tess took in his hairy chest and the silver pins holding up his nappy. She blinked. There were ten women in the room, easily ten, all huge-breasted and lolling against the furnishings, apparently unfazed by the interruption.

Only then did she register the other man-babies. One was a senator being read a story. Another was a hard-man actor being cradled and cuddling a bear in a bow tie. Another was their lawyer, who was getting his bottom spanked. Another was model Billy Carver, who had recently divorced his wife and was now donning a baby-blue onesie with a bunny on the front and finding solace in the nipples of a hooker.

'What the *fuck*?' It could have been her that said it; it could have been someone else. Somehow, Tess kept standing. Her knees turned to jelly.

'Shit!' the senator shouted, rolling away from his night-time treat like a… well, like a giant baby. 'Shit, shit, SHIT!'

Steven clambered to his feet. He looked so funny in the diaper that she cried a short, hysterical laugh. Ripping off his bonnet, he held his arms out.

'No,' Tess said, backing away. 'No fucking way.'

'It isn't what it looks like,' Steven blabbed. 'It's my club. Just a club—a few of us, it's harmless, Tess, please.' She caught sight of an array of toys on the bed, tubes of lubricant… 'I—I have urges,' pleaded Steven. 'I was going to tell you. Men like us need outlets. It's safe, I swear, we're not hurting anyone.'

'Stay the fuck away from me.'

'I love you. These girls are just—they don't mean anything.' The big-breasted women were packing up their equipment and scooping wads of cash from the carpet; Billy Carver lay discarded in his pull-ups. 'If I could do this with you, I would,' he said. 'I'd do anything to. This is my ultimate, Tess. My fantasy. Maybe, we could—'

'Stay back, Steven.' She still held the vase. '*Stay the hell back.*'

'Darling, you're my world. This is for kicks, never doubt my devotion—' He reached for her, and missed the point. 'You give me everything I need!'

'Except a high chair and some rusks?' she spat.

'Tess, I can explain—'

'I've heard enough.' Like a cloud bursting to rainfall, her anger swelled then dissipated and all it left behind was sadness, cold and absolute. She ran.

*

He begged her not to go to the press. These men had wives and families and she would be destroying innocent lives. Horrified, Tess realised she was trapped. She tried to talk to Simone but couldn't—the humiliation was too great.

'Is everything all right?' Maximilian asked, concerned. 'You seem distracted.'

'I'm tired, that's all.'

'That husband of yours is keeping you up at night?' Her agent smiled.

She nodded. 'Can't deny it.'

Divorce was her only exit—but that door slammed, too. Going against Steven for a settlement was insanity. He and his lawyer were in cahoots; members of the same twisted society, they would stop at nothing. Her career would be in tatters. Everything she was working for: exploded. What then? What did she have then?

'You should never have walked in that day,' cried Steven.

'If you hadn't, you'd never have known. We could have carried on as normal.'

'You'll never be normal.'

Steven accepted the estrangement. He tried to wheedle back into Tess's affections but quickly realised it was futile. They took to sleeping separately—Tess couldn't bear the thought of being close to him, let alone having sex with him. She remembered their lovemaking with dismay—Steven's fascination with her breasts, how he wanted her to talk dirty, to tell him off and call him her naughty baby.

Behind closed doors, they became foreigners. In public, they maintained the lie, gracing the red carpet when required, holding hands and kissing: Hollywood's happiest couple. Tess's disgust and anger grew into throttling, poison ivy.

She did what she had vowed never to do. She took after her mama and she took to the bottle. Vodka, gin, tequila, anything she could get her hands on. Washed them down with Valium and Xanax and weed and a rattling pharmacy of prescription drugs. Anything to blot out the pain... She could no longer function sober.

All men let you down, no matter how much you think you can trust them.

'Tess, talk to me,' Maximilian urged. 'I'm worried about you.'

In the end, he contacted Simone, who got straight on a plane and arrived at the mansion to knock her into shape. 'Look at the state of you!' Simone blustered through the house. 'When was the last time you got your hair done? Have you put on weight?'

'Go home,' said Tess. 'I'm fine.'

'Well, you don't seem fine to me, young lady.' Simone pulled the blinds, surveyed the state of the room, then sat down opposite Tess, taking her hands.

'Darling,' she said gently. 'Is there something you want to talk to me about?'

'Like what?'

Simone cleared her throat. 'I don't know—work, friends, your marriage…?'

'My marriage is wonderful, thank you.'

'Because if there's anything wrong… you know, with Steven… or with anything else, you know you can talk to me. I'm always here for you.'

Tess tore her hands away. She recalled Simone's warning at the *White Candle* premiere. Did she know? It was a heinous concept. Shameful. She ran from it.

'Just because your marriage is a fuck-up doesn't mean mine has to be, too.'

Simone sat back. 'I beg your pardon?'

'Newsflash, *Simone*,' Tess blurted, drunk. 'In case you didn't realise, I know full well you're fucking Lysander. Admit it: you and Brian are dead in the water. Unlike you, I married someone who satisfies me sufficiently that I don't have to jump into bed with *a member of my family* the first chance I get. So you can keep your marital advice, thank you very much. I don't want to end up like you, shivering in a cold marriage bed then screwing my stepson in my spare time.'

Simone slapped her. It sobered Tess up a little; she even quite enjoyed it.

'Don't you ever say that again! You haven't a clue what you're talking about!'

'Neither do you. You don't care about me,' Tess rampaged. 'All you care about is your little project failing. I was always a project, wasn't I?'

'*You're my daughter*!'

'Bullshit. I've never been your daughter. Never.'

'I love you.'

'No one's ever loved me. You're no different.'

Unable to contain herself, Simone fled back to London the same day, commanding Maximilian to 'Sort her out—or else. And do it fast.'

But nothing could sort Tess out. She didn't want to be sorted. All she wanted was to lock the doors and turn the lights out and never be seen again.

*

The following week, Alex Dalton arrived in LA. Tess ignored his string of messages. The thought of his knowing her faults and secrets and what an unmitigated mess she was, was too much to bear. It would be like the *danse d'éntrée* all over again. She couldn't admit her shambolic life or her catastrophe of a marriage, proving everything he had thrown at her at the wedding, a conversation she still hadn't forgiven him for.

But in the end, fate conspired to bring them together. Maximilian had invited her to meet him at the Beverly Mounts Spa, and, as soon as she arrived, she knew it was an intervention. He interrogated her for an hour—What was wrong? Was she unhappy? Did she need therapy? Should she take a break?— then ordered her to commit to a recuperative programme. Finally, she was able to leave—where, in the foyer, she ran straight into Alex. She hadn't the energy to think up a get-out.

'Visiting your girlfriend?' she spat, knowing it was an absurd thing to bring up and hating herself for it. His latest flame was a cover girl whose favoured haunt was the Mounts. For all Alex bitched about her life, look at his, chasing one belle after another and never getting serious about any of them. Alex ignored it.

'Can we get a drink?' he asked.

'I haven't got time.'

'Where are you going?'

'Nowhere.'

'That sounds important.'

She wanted to smack the concern off his stupid handsome face. Knew that every time she opened her mouth it only added to his picture of the night they'd met. Here she was again, veering out of control—the real her, no doubt.

Was that what he'd meant at the wedding? *It's like you've forgotten the person you are*. This new version was just a pathetic excuse at papering over the cracks.

'Are you OK?' Alex asked. 'You look tired.'

'Wow, you really know how to make a girl feel good,' Tess muttered, but she let herself be steered towards a table. She *was* tired. Tired and defeated.

'It's just you look bad.'

'Again, thanks.'

Alex got up, then came round the table and hugged her. His body was warm and solid, the gesture unexpected, and for a moment there was something so achingly sheltered and familiar about being in his arms that she wanted to cry. Why didn't he yell at her? Why didn't he walk out? Why didn't he decide she wasn't beautiful, after all—that the soul he saw inside was ugly and ruined—and never bother again?

'How's Steven?' Alex asked, sitting down.

'Fine,' she answered stiffly.

'Out of town again?'

Tess's head snapped up. 'What business is it of yours?'

'What business is it of yours if I'm here to see my girl-friend?'

'None. I don't care. Are you?'

'No.'

She ordered a drink. 'Triple. On the rocks.'

'Thirsty?'

'You got a problem with that?'

Alex held his hands up. 'None at all.'

Her hair was a nest. She went to tie it up, remembered it was Alex, and didn't.

'How was your honeymoon?' he asked. 'It must have been weird going back.'

'Not really.'

'Did you see the farm…?' He searched her expression.

'No,' she said. The drinks came and Tess swallowed hers.

'You didn't see it at all?'

She lost her patience. 'Why don't you go down if you care about it so much?'

'I'm only asking.'

'Well, don't.' She motioned for the check.

'Give me a break, OK?' said Alex. 'I'm being nice here. What's your problem with me? Every time I speak to you it's as if you can't wait to leave.'

Tess grabbed her bag. 'I'm sure you've got people to see.'

'I'd rather be here.'

'Come on, isn't she upstairs right now, gasping for a fuck?' Tess regretted it as soon as she said it; she didn't know where the words had come from.

Alex looked sad. 'Talk to me, Pirate.'

'I've got nothing to say.'

'You've always got something to say.'

'Yeah, that was the problem.'

'I hope you don't regret telling me. If that's the reason…'

'Why should I? I don't care what you know.'

'It takes a lot to open up. I don't do it. You're a braver person than me.'

'What would you have to open up about? Aren't you perfect? Haven't you got it all? Go on—surprise me, Alex, tell me something I don't know.'

'I could tell you a lot of things.'

'But you won't.'

'I don't need to. Not yet.'

She pushed her chair back. He reached across and put a hand over hers.

'Don't go,' he said.

'I have to.' She lied. 'Steven's waiting for me.'

'Is he looking after you? Is he making you happy?'

'Of course he is,' she said. 'He's my husband. Isn't that what marriage is about? I guess you wouldn't know: you've never done it.'

Alex looked at her. 'No, I haven't. I guess all the good ones are taken.'

Tess stood. 'This has been fun,' she said, knowing she was being a complete bitch but unable to stop, as if she had flicked self-destruct and had to keep going until there was nothing left. 'We should do it again.' Alex went to stop her but she escaped his grasp, heels spiking the floor as she made for the door.

Outside, the street tipped and swayed. She realised she wanted him to follow her, to call out her name... and then what? He felt sorry for her—that was all. She was trapped in a nightmare that had once been a dream, imprisoned, frightened, and alone.

Hauling open the door to her Jeep, she cried for her twin. She slammed the wheel, imagining it was her sister, hitting her and smacking her just as Calida had done on the night they'd fought; the last time she had seen her.

You died thinking I hated you. I told you I hated you.

Tess swerved out of the parking lot and careened into her

lane. At the lights she skipped a red and navigated a blare of car horns and squealing tyres, though she was too out of it to know if the smell of burned rubber was her own burst wheel or another's. She gripped the steering wheel one second then let it spin loose the next.

She didn't know or care where she was headed—the mansion was unbearable but there was nowhere else. Simone despised her. She'd neglected Mia.

It would be better off if she didn't exist. What was life worth now?

Lights, other cars, hurtled towards her and rashly she ducked between them, gears grinding, the Jeep plunging onto the sidewalk. A police siren started up and that was when she saw it: the grey lamppost dashing towards her, a final full stop if only she had the courage to meet it.

She met it.

There was light and then there was dark, and not a thing in between.

31

Calida was surprised to find Lucy up so early, especially on a Saturday. Her friend was in her dressing gown, sitting at the kitchen table, her eyes glued to the TV.

'Have you seen this?' she asked, not turning round.

Calida was about to ask what, but then she didn't need to. One look at the BREAKING NEWS footage told her everything. A scarlet banner ran across the foot of the screen, each word peeling out fresh horror. *Hollywood icon Tess Geddes in high-speed crash… Tess Geddes fighting for life… Recovery needs miracle, say doctors…*

She dropped her cup of coffee.

'Shit, are you OK?' Lucy jumped up. 'Are you burned?'

'No, I—I'm fine.'

'Here, sit down. You look awful—do you have a fever?'

Calida couldn't speak. Her lips opened but she couldn't speak. She couldn't think. TV crews piled up outside a hospital. Headshots of her twin, old coverage of her gracing the red carpet, pictures of her wedding to Steven Krakowski, adorned the report. Anxious journalists spouted into mics, pressing their earpieces for updates.

'Calida…?'

'I think I'm going to faint.'

'What is it? Are you sick?'

'That's my sister.'

Lucy's expression was blank. 'Sorry?'

'Tess Geddes is my sister. She's dying. My sister is going to die.'

*

She told Lucy the truth. What choice did she have? Her friend was dumbstruck.

'You have to go to her,' she said. 'You have to.'

'Never.' Calida was shaking, her second cup of coffee cold in her hands. 'She told me how she feels about me. I'm not going. It's over between us. It has been for years.'

'Calida, listen to me. What happened in the past—'

'It's not the past. It's right now. It's a fight I've been fighting for seven years.' Her voice trembled. 'I always told myself the next time I saw her it would be to claim revenge. I'm not going now. I can't. What would I say? She doesn't want to see me.'

'How do you know?'

'Trust me.'

'Because of some letter?'

'It's more than that.'

'Whatever it is, it can't be more important than this.' Lucy touched her arm. 'Calida, what if this choice gets taken away from you? What if you never see her again because you never get the chance? Could you live with that?'

'I don't know. I could try.' But the words were hollow. She didn't mean them. All she could think about was her twin, that other, strange part of herself, as known to her as the lines on her palm but as pale and distant as the moon, struggling in a hospital bed. She strived to put her anger back together, but just as fast it came apart.

'You really don't care, then?' said Lucy. 'That's why you wear that locket around your neck every day and you never take it off, not even to get in the shower. You told me back at Brandon's your sister has one the same.'

Calida went to deny it but knew by Lucy's expression it was pointless. So many times she had wanted to tear the locket off and throw it away, but she couldn't. She told herself it was because Diego had given it to her... but in truth it was the last vestige. A gossamer-fine cord, no more than a spider's web, continued to bind them.

I hate you. I hate you. She repeated it to herself over and over again.

Lucy continued to stare at her, waiting for her to change her mind.

*

Within the hour, she was on a flight to LA. She didn't have time to think about what she was doing; it happened so fast. It was enough to put one foot in front of the other, impossible to think beyond that. What they would say to each other, how it would play out: the reunion she had imagined so many times but never like this.

The closer she got, the less possible it became for it to be too late.

Now she had made this decision, Teresita had better not back out on her. *Don't you dare do it again; you stick around for me this time.*

Landing at LAX, Calida rushed through Arrivals and dived into a cab, prompting the man who had hailed it to yell, 'Hey—!'

Streets shot past in a blur. She wanted to scream to the driver to put his foot on the gas but he was going as fast as he could. Finally, they reached the County Memorial Medical Center. A bank of press swarmed against police barriers, cameras surging to life every time the entrance swung open. Fans wept; others, less concerned with the situation than with being in proximity to the hype, stood about chatting and filming on their phones. A TV helicopter circled overhead. Calida had been aware of her sister's celebrity but had never witnessed it at such close quarters. Even back in New York, seeing the cyclone surrounding Winona and her crew, it was nothing like this. Here, at the moment of tragedy, her twin was more famous than she'd ever been.

As she came closer, she spied Simone Geddes by the door, tear-streaked and surrounded by bodyguards. The woman hadn't changed; she didn't appear to have aged at all. Still the same harsh, bitten expression, as if life had done her wrong.

'I'm utterly distraught,' Simone was prattling into a microphone. 'Tess and I are so close. We're best friends as well as family. I can't believe this has happened…'

Fake. Simone wouldn't know what family was if it bit her in the face.

Calida stood in the heaving crowd like a ball buffeted on the waves. She dared Simone to look up and meet her eye. Unbelievably, it happened. The actress's gaze flicked over her—Calida felt certain it would return, a double take, surely, but no. She was as invisible to Simone now as she had been then. The ugly sister.

Calida shoved her way to the front. 'I'm family,' she fought through the seething bodies, 'I have to get through…' Surfacing at last, she met a wall of security.

'I'm her sister,' she told them, breathless. It felt good to say it. True.

The big guy snorted. 'Yeah, you and everyone else.'

'I'm not leaving until I see her.'

'No way, lady.'

Calida fished in her bag. She brought out a photograph from her portfolio of Argentina—she and Teresita together on the farm, by the stables, innocent.

The guard took it and his expression shifted.

He glanced up at Calida, then down again. 'Wait here,' he said.

*

Tess Geddes opened her eyes to a world she didn't recognise. Everything was white. Blurred figures stood in a circle, emitting a low, continuous hum. There was a faint, mechanical *beep-beep* coming from her left side. She could smell plastic.

Her body didn't feel like hers. One moment she was inside it, looking out; the next, she was above it, looking down. Lying in bed, tiny and frail.

She tried to move but it hurt too much. Her tongue was dry and she was aware of her bones, the shape of her skeleton resting on the mattress, feather light.

*

The next time she regained consciousness, she saw a face she knew. At first, coming at her through kaleidoscopic shadow, she thought it was Calida.

Of course it wasn't Calida. Her sister was dead. *Am I dead too?*

Blinding flashes of the accident sailed through her head. The road, the slippery wheel, the lamppost hurtling towards her, and she'd known what she was doing and still made the decision to… The shadowy figure touched her arm, pulled into focus and became Simone. 'Darling, sweetheart, it's me,' she sobbed. 'Your mother.'

Another visitor took her hand. She saw Steven Krakowski as one might a stranger, and flinched from his touch before remembering he was her husband.

Steven lifted her limp hand, kissed it and cradled it, held it to his cheek. She had a sudden, nightmarish vision of him crawling about in a cot. 'The doctors say you banged your head,' he explained. 'It may be a while before your memory returns.'

You wish, thought Tess. *I can remember just fine.*

'She needs to sleep,' soothed Simone, bending to kiss her forehead. 'You'll be better soon, my angel, I promise. I'll be here when you wake up.'

*

In the event, Simone wasn't. Alex was. When Tess came round, he was sitting in a chair attempting to read. Every few seconds he would look up, and this time, when he did, he met her open eyes. 'Thank God.' He was at her side, his warm, coarse hand in hers and his dark head bent over their clasped fingers. 'It's good to see you.'

She watched his hair and thought how soft it looked. It was a head she knew well. She had known it for a long time, longer than she gave him credit for.

'I never paid,' Tess said. Words caught up with her before memory did.

Alex frowned. He wasn't quite how she remembered, somehow. 'What?'

'For my drink… I never paid.'

He held tight to her fingers and smiled. 'You can make it up to me sometime.'

She smiled back. In that instant she felt a peace she hadn't known in months—years, maybe. She wanted to stay here, in this moment, and nothing would change.

The door opened. 'Ms Geddes?' The man stepped inside. 'Is she awake?'

'Yes,' Tess said. 'I'm here.'

'There's a woman outside who claims she's your sister. Should I let her in?'

Tess allowed herself that brief glimmer of denial, of what might have been, another time and another fate in which he might actually have been talking about Calida. Instead, Emily Chilcott, that despot, that brat, usurped the title and not once stopped to consider the hurt it would cause. None of that family had. They had never imagined what it was like for her in a house full of strangers, ripped from her home.

Emily isn't my sister.

'I don't have a sister,' said Tess, turning away. 'Tell her to leave.'

*

Calida returned to New York that night.

As the plane climbed high above moon-bathed clouds, she cursed her foolish, futile mission. She knew now beyond doubt that Teresita had been driven away that day when she was fifteen and had died within the week. Tess Geddes had replaced her. Tess Geddes had written that poison letter, scaling her way from London to Paris to LA without so much as a downward glance. Tess Geddes had cut her off absolutely and without remorse. As far as Tess Geddes was concerned, Calida no longer existed.

I don't have a sister… She might as well be dead.

The next morning, Calida woke early, looked in the mirror,

and told herself she had lost nothing. She was back where she'd been two days ago: fighting for a place opposite her twin, to be stronger and harder and better than she could ever hope to be.

She had more reason for that than ever. Payback powered her every thought.

I'm going to get you. I'm going to get you where it really, truly hurts.

Weeks passed. Work continued at breakneck pace. Commissions piled in to XS Studios, more than she and Ryan could handle, and they cherry-picked their projects. Trips abroad were a welcome distraction. New people helped her forget.

In November, when Barack Obama was elected as the first black president to the White House, they turned SilverLine into a party pad and celebrated till dawn. Calida drank too much and wound up passing out in a male model's lap.

The next day, through a gruelling hangover, Ryan informed her that her biggest commission to date had arrived. 'Vittorio Da Strovisi,' he told her, barely able to keep the excitement from his voice. 'Honey, you're heading for Milan.'

32

Everybody told her that she shouldn't have survived the accident. Tess had been certain it was her time and that the world would be a better place without her in it.

The world, it seemed, had other ideas.

Early in 2009 she resumed working. The near miss had made her dynamite, and Maximilian, while exhibiting a fatherly concern, was in fact more concerned with the fact that the phones were buzzing off the hook. Tess's new movie *Grit Girl* was the perfect comeback. She was filming opposite Natalie Portis, who assumed the role of Tess's guardian until she was back on her feet. Tess protested, but Natalie heard none of it. When the project wrapped, Natalie took her for a celebratory lunch at Belfont.

'Vitto's been asking after you,' she said, once they had ordered appetisers.

'Who?'

'Vittorio Da Strovisi. Remember? You met him in Argentina.'

'Oh, yes—of course.' She had known exactly who Natalie meant, just hadn't wanted to admit it. The sound of Vittorio's name made her shiver. Since coming out of hospital, she'd had a libido for the very first time in her life. Tess thought about sex constantly, with Vittorio, with Greg, even with Lysander— with everyone, in fact, except her husband. The accident had reconnected her with her body, shown her the true nature of survival; it was as if something that was missing before had suddenly clicked into place. The memory of Vittorio's magnetism was irresistible.

'He's been worried about you,' said Natalie.

'Why?' She tried to sound casual. 'He doesn't know me.'

'My guess is he'd like to.'

Tess laughed it off, but inside she caught fire. 'I thought he and Steven were friends?' she said. 'And doesn't he have a wife?'

Natalie raised an eyebrow. 'Let's just say it's an easy-going friendship. And, I suspect, an easy-going marriage.'

At home, her partnership with Steven limped on. Tess fulfilled her part by pasting on a smile at every public outing and swooning over the care her husband had shown since her emergence from the clinic. Alone, they occupied opposite ends of the mansion and spoke only when necessary. Steven had hoped that Tess's concussion might have dislodged certain recalls, but no such luck. He refused to give her a divorce, instead plying her with gifts and toys. She felt like a goldfish at a fairground that he had resolutely decided to win, in that spoiled, entitled way of someone unaccustomed to losing. Throw enough hoops over her and she'd be unable to escape.

Her sex drive was so high that she had considered gritting her teeth and fucking him, testing her newfound capacity for gratification, but there was no way. Steven was as asexual as he'd ever been. The thought of him with a pacifier rammed in his mouth and a diaper tied round his ass was enough to make her retch over the toilet bowl. Each time he stayed out for the night, or visited friends she had never heard of, Tess did her best to ignore her suspicions. Meanwhile his fetishes rumbled silently on, the rot creeping into every crack and corner of their fake union until its infestation was complete. Some days she reasoned through the pretence and it didn't seem so bad: every couple in Hollywood cheated—Natalie had confided that both she and Greg had strayed—so what made them any different? Other days, she was reminded of Steven's outrageous perversions, that horrendous scene unfolding in the Santa Barbara house like a grim nursery rhyme, and the illusion came tumbling down.

Mia called every day. She had moved to a farm in the English countryside and was writing a book on Ford Madox Brown. 'Visit me,' she urged. 'You should see it here, Tess—you'd love it. Rolling hills, open skies, it's exactly what you need.'

It was tempting, but Tess had a life here to get in order first. Starting with Simone. She felt ashamed of the harsh words she had thrown at her adoptive mother; she should never have shown such disrespect. This was the woman who had taken her in and given her a home. She had never thought of it like that before, but there it was, the truth. Meeting death made Tess count every last blessing in her life—and Simone Geddes, surely, was the biggest of them all. What would she have done, if it weren't for her? Cast out by her own family, unwanted, unloved. She owed her everything.

'There's no need for apology, sweetheart,' Simone told her over the phone. 'Let's forget it happened. I love you, you're my daughter, nothing you say or do can change that.' When Tess thanked her, she realised there were a great many things besides that she had never thanked Simone for, and promised to make up for it.

In June, news swept through the city that Michael Jackson had died. A strange mist descended, part grief, part disbelief that a man who had escaped so many other definitions had been caught by the final one. Life was a roulette wheel, a lucky spin of the dice. It made Tess feel stupid and irresponsible for being so careless with her own, and she vowed from now on to live every moment to its absolute maximum potential.

Fired by fresh resolve, she saw her future more brightly than ever, as an unwritten map beneath her control. She alone would be responsible for her actions—no husband, no sister, nobody telling her no—and she alone would pleasure in them.

*

'I have news.' A month later, Natalie invited her for coffee. The women took their customary spot at No. 1 Townhouse and signalled the waiter for their usual. 'Vitto's having a party at his pad in New York,' said Natalie. 'He's requested your company.'

'Steven's out of town,' Tess explained.

'That's probably why he asked,' Natalie said mischievously.

Tess blushed. 'I don't know…'

'You have to get a look at this place. Seriously.'

Tess had to admit that the thought of seeing Vittorio again was intoxicating. The other day she had seen pictures of him and his wife at a gala in Boston, and vaguely wondered what Scarlet Schuhausen would make of the enormous bunch of peonies and orchids Vittorio had sent her at County Memorial. She couldn't deny that she had been thinking of him too. It was as if he had attached a thread when they'd met in South America, and every so often would tug it to remind her he was there. The more she resisted, the more she realised to which

place he had tied it: a secret, special, private place, a tingle
and a pulse, a whisper of unspoken desire…

'When is it?' she asked, as if she didn't care.

'Saturday night.' Natalie popped an olive in her mouth.
'Ooh,' she trilled, 'I *love* a Vitto virgin. Once you've been to
one of his parties, you'll *never* look back.'

Tess got an idea that Natalie might be right when, at the
weekend, Vittorio sent a plane from NYC to collect them. It
had a VDS logo splashed down one side.

'It's a bit excessive, isn't it?' Tess marvelled, scoping the
opulent interior. 'Everything about Vitto is excessive,' replied
Natalie.

When they arrived at the Glen Cove mansion, any hesita-
tions Tess might have had that this was the case were swiftly
obliterated. Vittorio's estate was nothing short of obscene—an
early-twentieth-century replica of an English country house,
complete with Corinthian columns and twenty facing windows. Through twisting wrought-iron gates their car navigated a serpentine drive to a stately portico entrance, where
a silver fountain comprised enough writhing marble bodies
to rival the Trevi. Sparkling jets shone in the floodlit night.
An array of insane sports cars was gathered, from which
impossibly beautiful creatures emerged. Sultry beats pounded
from inside.

'Shit,' said Tess.

'I know,' murmured Natalie. 'Wait until you get inside.'

In the foyer, a baronial double staircase swept majestically
between floors. Gilt-framed portraits lined the walls. Candles
burned. It was Gothic in feel, brooding and romantic, not
at all what she would have expected from Vittorio's gaudy
façade.

'Does he live here?'

'Vitto's got ten places just like this,' said Natalie wryly. 'His main home's in Italy—this is more of a... I don't know, I guess you'd call it a plaything.'

Once more, Tess felt that pull, a mischievous switch that promised to draw her to a place she had never accessed before. Vittorio Da Strovisi was shameless, his wealth was shameless, and his manners were shameless; his looks were shameless and his house and cars and private aircraft were shameless. His flirtation was shameless.

Tess wanted to be shamed. For the first time in her life, she did.

It was a while before she saw the man himself. She caught glimpses of him, tantalising as an exotic bird through a shivering tree canopy, and felt his eyes on her back, but he didn't come to say hello. He was playing with her, and with every passing second she was focusing less and less on whomever she was talking to and more and more on the red-hot burn between her legs. Several times she had to excuse herself to go to the bathroom, splash her face and wrists, and pull herself together. Something had been set free in her, dislodged, unfastened. She felt like an animal, savage and powerful. Sex wasn't about making her the victim, no, not any more. She could be in charge. She *would* be in charge. Seeing Vittorio reminded her of the men on the front of those romance novels she had devoured as a child. *The Billionaire's Mistress*...

Books Calida had told her were rubbish. People like that didn't exist. Money like that didn't exist. Men like that didn't exist. *Well, look at me now*.

At midnight, Vittorio stood before his guests and made a speech. Scarlet Schuhausen hovered close by, elegant and palely sleek as a swan, yet with the feral glare of an Alsatian guarding the homestead. It was weird to think of Scarlet and Vittorio swapping partners, if that was what they did, because the way Scarlet looked at her man implied she would claw the eyes off any bitch who dared glance at him.

Afterwards, as Natalie disappeared to take a call from Greg, Tess went alone to refresh her make-up. Away from the crowds, she crossed the open-air terrace with its shimmering blue baths and hexagonal pool house; the water twinkled invitingly and she wondered how many excessive parties it had been host to.

She padded through to the east wing, silent and empty, and descended an old stone staircase that wound like honeycomb to a lower floor. A chain of cavernous, low-ceilinged chambers greeted her, flickering with bulbs and running as far as the eye could see towards a dim inkpot of black. A draught whispered round her neck and she shivered. Her footsteps were hollow and echoing. Where did this lead?

The scent was inebriating, musty as cellars and rich as plum. Tess arrived at a chamber filled wall to wall, ceiling to floor, with dust-caked bottles of wine, their necks protruding like raised pistols and their bottoms deep and concave with age.

A wide arched door led off one wall and she went to it, pushing it open with an ancient creak, as blind in the labyrinth as Alice down the rabbit hole. Inside, she gasped as if she had stumbled across another, separate gathering; she thought she had company but then realised she didn't. Dozens of suits of armour gleamed in the moonlight, dead but somehow living. Tess stepped between the ghosts and touched the smooth, cold metal of a chest, half expecting a drum to be beating inside. Two eyes were carved from the pewter helmet, dark and sightless. She held her breath.

'Hello.'

She turned. Vittorio stood before her, as still as the army surrounding him.

'A hobby of mine,' he explained. 'I like to collect things that inspire me.'

Tess forced herself to speak. 'They're magnificent.'

'You find them unnerving.'

'A little.'

'Why?'

Vittorio took a step towards her, so she was forced to move backwards and felt her spine come up against the hard, smooth chest of a phantom soldier; caught between them, the living and the dead. Vittorio's blue eyes appeared silver.

'I don't know.'

'I always think it is because they are watching me,' he said.

'Yes.'

'Do you feel it?'

'Yes.'

'Do you like how it feels?'

'Yes.'

'I like that you like it.'

Her throat was dry. There was a long silence.

'There is energy in them,' said Vittorio at length, 'but it is quiet and unmoving. They watch but they cannot comment on the things that they see.'

'What do they see?' Tess tried for lightness but the question emerged full of promise. Vittorio's face was close to hers. His hand landed on her waist.

'What do you think your husband would say if he could see us now?'

'What would your wife say?' she countered.

Vittorio's eyes narrowed in amusement. 'Scarlet doesn't

like my extra-marital liaisons. Call me wicked, but that makes
me enjoy it more.'

Then, as if it were the most natural thing in the world,
Vittorio's hand moved down Tess's leg and his fingers crept
under the hem of her skirt. Their mouths were a pinch apart,
close enough to feel his breath, warm and sweet with a note
of brandy.

Tess's flesh trembled beneath his touch. His thumb hooked
under the elastic of her panties; he was millimetres from her
sweet spot but he didn't move.

Neither of them did. One slip and his thumb would be
inside her. Tess was pulsing with want. Every fibre yearned
to thrust on to him. Her chest rose and fell between them; she
imagined Vittorio tearing open her blouse and devouring her
breasts and she would come straight away, she would come
for the first time ever, the elusive orgasm she had heard so
much about but thought was impossible.

But Vittorio's thumb didn't move. Neither did he. The
empty suit at her back seemed to hold her from behind; the
soldier was in conspiracy with Vittorio, together they had
her pinned, they would claim her and she would fall at their
mercy.

'Steven's your friend,' she whispered. Even speaking her
husband's name had no effect; he had lost all power over her.
Vittorio's thumb stayed where it was, on an out breath grazing
her strip of pubic hair, the very edge, incidentally, as if neither
were aware it was happening. Having a conversation with a
stranger in a store, with their thumb inside her knickers. A tide
of heat surged up from her toes.

'He had sex with my wife, you know,' said Vittorio. 'Before
you.'

'Don't you care?' she asked, but only because she didn't.

She wanted sex with Vittorio. She would do anything for sex with Vittorio. She had never wanted a man like this, never thought she'd be able. His thumb eased towards her wetness but refused to indulge it. A groan escaped her lips. How could they still be fully clothed?

'We are not meant to be with one person,' Vittorio said, totally measured as his thumb came so close that she moaned. 'We are primitive. Scarlet can do as she wishes. Steven is into things that I am not. Their business is their own.'

'Do we have business, Vittorio?'

He smiled, then; at last, an acknowledgement of what was happening.

'Scarlet will not like this,' he told her. 'You are too beautiful—and you are too strong. I see myself in you.' The statement crackled between them. *In you…*

'I don't care,' he breathed. 'When I see something I want, I must have it.' His chest crushed against hers and she felt his erection through his suit pants, iron-hard and pressing her inner thigh. He was enormous. Thick. Hot. Ready to pop.

Tess's hand shook with the force of resistance it took not to reach down and seize it. She wanted it in her mouth, on her tongue, in her cunt, everywhere. She wanted Vittorio absolutely, all to herself, on tap to bring her rapture whenever she demanded it. He was the ultimate prize. The trophy she had imagined winning when she was a wide-eyed girl on a ranch in Patagonia. Though his wife wasn't with them, Tess fought that woman right now—she fought her with her beauty, her legs, her breasts, her willingness to bathe in his adulation, the contest to have him without reserve. She understood, then, Scarlet's wolf-like expression as she had stood by at Vittorio's speech, scanning the crowd for challengers, daring them to step into the fray because she would butcher them limb from limb. Tess's mind told her she was delirious with want; she had collapsed on the altar of her yearning and she wasn't thinking straight, but her body told her she would destroy any rival who tried to take him away. She had waited too long for this. Nobody was standing in her path.

'Please…'

She didn't know what she was saying any more. Unable to play the game, whatever game he had devised, she could no longer uphold her part in it. She was dripping now, dripping down the inside of her leg, dripping down his thumb.

Still he waited on her periphery, the tip of his digit taunting her, torturing her, until it struck the line between pleasure and suffering. 'Please!' she cried.

The following moments were an unbearable, intolerable, brilliant haze.

Tess didn't know what happened or what came first; her knees collapsed and she fell against him, coming and coming, shocks of pleasure rushing through her bloodstream as his thumb plunged deep, and she was so drenched with lust that when he got up to his knuckle she parted wider and his other hand came round and then there was more inside, the thickness of his wrist against her and the cold metal of his watch, and he was holding her while she came, supporting her while she cried out his name. For once, she didn't smell lavender. She didn't think of her papa. She didn't think of death, her father's death or her sister's death or her mama's death, because she had met her own and survived it. She had cheated the fate that had stolen them.

Losing all senses, Tess grappled to free Vittorio's hard-on—she needed to see it, touch it; have it inside her. But her crescendo had drained her of energy and coordination and Vittorio took a step back, watching her with interest as she moaned and panted against the suit of armour, her knickers torn around her knees.

'You are a thing of wonder,' he told her, touching her face. 'When the time is right, I will give you what you want.'

She closed her eyes and when she opened them again he was gone.

33

A week later

Calida opened her eyes to the sleeping, naked form of Vittorio Da Strovisi, and smiled, stretching luxuriously. Sunday morning in her lover's Tuscan escape, a stone-built retreat high up in the Italian hills, and there was nothing to do but have sex. She crossed the room and divided the shutters. Cypress trees formed a chain on the amber earth, strewn across the distant hillside like a bracelet. A little church glowed in tentative sunlight, over a cluster of red-roofed houses gathered on the mount.

Turning to the master bedroom, the outlook was no less sublime. Vittorio lay splayed on the linen, his chest bronzed and his cock huge, swollen even in sleep and pointing like a rod to his belly, the base of which was smattered with dark hair.

She had been sleeping with Vittorio Da Strovisi for six months.

She still couldn't really believe it. Calida knew just how exceptional and powerful he was, one of the richest, most desired businessmen in the world, a global, unstoppable powerhouse and the object of every woman's fantasy. Despite herself, how she was training herself so hard against it, Calida couldn't help but occasionally think of her twin. She imagined presenting Vittorio to Tess Geddes and gloating:

'*Surprised? I bet you never thought he'd look twice at me...*'

It had all started when she was sent to Milan to take his picture. No one had been more surprised than she at the intensity of the attraction. Heading out to his city pad, she'd had zero lead on the capitalist save for Ryan Xiao's contagious excitement. On the flight she had researched Vittorio Da Strovisi, and recognised him instantly. He was the guy who owned the flagrant mansion in Glen Cove, the one she and Lucy had been to with Winona and her set. Memories of that night were muddled and sinister, but she clearly remembered seeing his picture; not at all her type.

All the way across the Atlantic, she had sensed a force drawing her near. The coincidence felt part of a design, as if she was *meant* to meet Vittorio, meant to fall into his bed, meant to crave him every second, every minute of the day, because... Because what? By now Calida was moving in ever more influential circles; her client list was soaring; she had entered a new echelon, no longer bound to media darlings or model starlets. Now she was mixing with the big league, the truly, obscenely rich, the eccentric recluses and the icons who would abide no second best. She was hailed as 'the new Mario Testino'. But something about Vittorio was pivotal. She sensed, inexplicably, that she was being guided into this scenario—that its outcome was intended to take place and, when it did, would be of the utmost importance to her.

On the day she arrived, she had taken the tycoon's picture. Within hours, they were stripped and fucking on his bed. Calida extended her stay; they'd made love non-stop, on his sheets, in his bathroom, the veranda, the pool, the terrace, the balcony. Since then, they hooked up whenever they could, each time he visited the States or she was on commission in Europe: a hunger that could never be sated.

'You're different to other women,' Vittorio told her, after doing things to her with his hand or his tongue that had to be illegal. 'I cannot bear to be without you. Stay with me. I vow to leave my wife. We are nothing to each other.'

Vittorio was upfront about his marriage: the union with Scarlet Schuhausen was one of convenience. It wasn't that Vittorio had fallen out of love with her—it was that neither loved the other. Scarlet wouldn't care, he promised. She was out sleeping with other men. The couple rarely saw each other, seemed only to hook up for public engagements, and never exchanged calls. Vittorio told Calida they were 'seeking the right time'. She preferred not to enquire as to what happened after this—did Vittorio intend to start a relationship with her? Was that even what she wanted?

It was better than being alone. Better than thinking about Daniel Cabrera and where he was and what he was doing, the woman his arms enfolded when he fell asleep. Daniel was married. Somewhere across the world, another woman was Señora Cabrera, and, try as Calida might to deny it, much as she immersed herself in the body of another man, that fact made her sting every single day. Some nights she dreamed of him, and he appeared to her so real that when she woke it seemed impossible that he wasn't there. Her first love... her friend. *Stop. It's been too long. Let him go*.

Now, she crossed to the bed and leaned in to kiss Vittorio. At once, he grabbed her wrists. Calida screamed, delighted as he pinned her down. Holding her arms above her head, he sliced into her with a violent passion, then flipped her on to her front and did her the same from behind, until Calida hit that magic, helpless spot and climaxed, her scream stifled in the satin pillows. Vittorio came directly after.

Calida lay, breathless, hair stuck to her cheek. After a moment, Vittorio said:

'I was with Astrid last week. She's interested in you.'

It took Calida a second to register which Astrid he was referring to: partly her post-orgasm and partly because she sometimes forgot the circles in which he mixed. Astrid Engberg was the girlfriend of Prince Gustav Frederick; the Swedish papers had been speculating for months on the possibility of a forthcoming engagement.

'He is going to propose soon,' Vittorio went on, getting up and going to twist on the shower. 'Astrid knows it. He is taking her to Umbria at the weekend.'

'Why is she interested in me?'

Vittorio grinned. 'Because I recommended you, darling—and Astrid knows that when I like something, it is worth having.'

'She wants me to photograph her.'

'Not just any old sitting.' Vittorio settled next to her, the sound of running water drumming from the bathroom. 'Their engagement pictures.' His BlackBerry beeped and he scooped it up; a brief smile as he read the message and then he tucked it behind him, out of sight. Calida wanted to ask: *Who was that*? But she didn't. Just because Rodrigo Torres had twenty women on the go at once didn't mean Vitto did.

'Oh.'

'What do you think?'

She thought it was a big deal. Prince Gustav Frederick was first in line to the Swedish throne, and Astrid as his girlfriend was set to be queen. Astrid was glamorous, all tumbling blonde locks and nipped-in waist. Both in their twenties, they had done wonders for perceptions of the royal family. Photographers across the world would be vying for this gig. If Vittorio were anyone else she might doubt his conviction—as it was, she knew he would have ensured it was a done deal.

'You will meet her tomorrow,' he instructed.

'Excuse me?'

'At my studio in Stockholm.' He put an arm round her. 'That is the best place, Astrid says. She does not wish to draw attention.'

'You've already arranged this?'

'Of course.'

'Without consulting me?'

'I am consulting you now.'

'I don't like being told what to do.'

Vittorio's gaze gave no room for manoeuvre. 'I think you do,' he said, as he took her hand and led her to the steamed-up shower and turned her to face the wall.

*

Astrid Engberg glowed. She was flawless, pretty and perfect as a china doll, and appeared impossibly regal despite her lack of royal blood: a high, pale forehead, wide green eyes that were flecked with gold, and a waterfall of tresses that swirled around her shoulders. Calida thought she was one of the loveliest women she had ever seen.

But it was Astrid who was beside herself.

'I am so pleased to meet you,' she said in gently accented English. Her pastel-pink lips broke into a smile. 'I have heard so much about you.'

'From Vittorio, no doubt.' Calida smiled back.

'Oh, everywhere,' gushed Astrid. 'Everywhere I'm going,

I am hearing about Cal Santiago. Gustav is pleased, too. If I am satisfied, he tells me, we will go ahead.'

Calida's brow lifted. 'The engagement's official?'

'We have not announced it yet, but…'

'Congratulations, that's wonderful news.'

'It is confidential, you understand.'

'Of course.' Calida set down her equipment. 'Entirely safe with me.'

They were high up in Vittorio's studio, a lavish space on Lilla Erstagatan, which he used on trips to the capital. Vittorio had residences in every city going; Calida couldn't imagine how he possibly found time to make use of them all.

Fading sun spilled through the floor-to-ceiling windows. She gestured for Astrid to take a seat at the panorama and asked her to reposition herself. The soon-to-be princess had arrived with three bodyguards and been escorted through a covert entrance, but had insisted her security wait out in the hall. Calida preferred that. Other people changed the dynamic of a shoot: she wanted to reach the spirit of Astrid Engberg, to photograph her as a young woman as well as a future monarch.

Forty minutes later, they were done.

'Wow,' said Astrid, scanning the images. 'They were right.'

'It helps to have a good subject,' said Calida, who was being modest.

Astrid nodded. 'You are hired. Gustav will agree.'

'How do you know Vittorio?' she asked, as Astrid collected her coat.

'I am friends with his wife,' she replied, flicking her hair out of her collar. 'Scarlet introduced me to Gustav, as it happens, at one of Vitto's parties.'

'I didn't know.' There was a bitter taste in Calida's mouth. How easy it was to forget that Vittorio was married—and, in

spite of what he told her about his celibate marriage and separate living arrangements, she was still in on a hurtful betrayal.

'Such a lovely couple,' said Astrid, 'and so happy. Don't
you think? If Gustav and I can take one piece of that into our
lives together, we will be lucky.'

'Yes.'

Calida's voice must have given her away; that one syllable,
treacherous. Astrid gave her a sideways look. Quickly, Calida
changed the subject.

'I hear his parties are infamous,' she said. 'It must have
been fun.'

'Oh, yes—I was just at his place in Long Island last week.
He has many actor friends. Even though I am part of that
world, still I am bewitched by Hollywood.'

Bewitched. Calida liked the word, thought it interesting
that Astrid used it.

'There were so many people there,' Astrid went on. 'Natalie
Portis, Erin Fletcher, Kate diLaurentis, Tess Geddes... So
many people—and they love him!'

Calida forced a smile. The thought of Vittorio inviting Tess
to one of his homes was anathema. So they knew each other?
How well? Did Tess like him? Did she want him? Of course
she did. Every woman did—Astrid too, probably. Did Tess
covet him as she had coveted Daniel? No, she was married.
She was faithful to Steven Krakowski. *As if a detail like that's
going to stop her. She's ruthless. You know that.*

The worst part was the possibility that Vitto liked her back.
If something had happened between them... No. Even considering it was like venom in Calida's blood.

You wouldn't dare do it to me again. Just you try.

'He knows Tess Geddes?' she blurted.

'You are a fan?' Astrid asked, brightly.

'Yes,' said Calida automatically.

'You would like to take her photograph, I am sure.'

'One day.'

'I will arrange it.' Astrid headed for the door.

'Wait—'

Astrid turned. But Calida couldn't find the words.

'You gave me a wonderful gift today.' Astrid smiled. 'You made me look like me again. So many days I am surrounded by people who never know the real me and I never feel like a regular girl. I know I am lucky but I do miss her sometimes.' A beat. 'You turned me back into that girl and I am grateful. I would like to repay you.'

'You don't need to.' In all Calida's painstaking steps to access her twin's glittering world, she had always been in control. She had been the one calling the shots and deciding the moves. Now, it was running away from her, too far, too fast.

'Yes, I do.' Astrid rushed back, and embraced Calida and kissed her on the cheek. 'Leave it with me,' she said. 'I hope she is everything you wish her to be.'

Calida nodded. *I'm ready. I've been ready for nine years.*

'So do I,' she said.

34

England

Simone Geddes peeled back the loft curtain of her Kensington townhouse like someone peeking inside a boxful of cockroaches, then immediately closed it again.

'Simone! Simone! We know you're in there—come out, Simone!'

The paparazzi's cries sailed up on the damp March air. Shrouded in darkness, Simone slumped to the floor and buried her face in her hands. Downstairs, the phone rang, less than a minute since it had last stopped. She had tried disconnecting it but Brian had rigged such a complicated network that there was always at least one receiver bleating in some far corner of the mansion. *Brian.* Simone gulped.

Where was he now?

Poor, pathetic Brian, he didn't deserve any of this.

Nor did I deserve my joke of a marriage! But the words rang empty. Despite Brian's awfulness, she knew she had committed a heinous and unforgivable crime.

There was a knock at the door. 'Ms Geddes?' squeaked a voice. Vera.

'What?' Simone croaked.

'They would like to come in,' said the Spanish maid in her

stilted accent, which all of a sudden made Simone want to kick open the door and push her down the stairs. 'They ring the bell constantly. I cannot get rid of them.'

'Keep everything locked—and do *not* answer the god-damned phone!'

A brief pause, before: 'Ms Horner is at the gate. Should I let her in?'

Great. That was the last thing Simone needed: a barbed piece of Michelle's mind. Still, she couldn't get away from it. 'Fine,' she replied. 'Do it.'

Waiting for Michelle was like waiting for the guillotine. As she heard her manager's footsteps climb the loft steps, she was reminded of her grandmother—that severe, terrorising tread as it approached the attic to snatch her baby… Then, like now, she had got herself in trouble. She had done something bad. Something terrible.

Brian's face danced in her memory, that subtle shifting of expression, disbelief to horror to anger, his features contorted and crumpled until for the first time in his emasculated life he had reacted to something, punching the wall with a balled-up fist and smashing one of her prized Cretan vases on the dining room floor.

'*Anyone*,' he had raged, '*anyone else I might have got my head around—but this? My son? My own flesh and blood…?*'

Simone tried to blame him, aware as she was doing so that the claim was contemptible. '*You drove me to it! What else was I supposed to do?*'

'*Me?*' Brian had shaken like a felled tree. '*It's you who won't fucking put out! It's you who's given up on this marriage, you toxic hag!*'

'Simone?' came Michelle's whippet's yap. 'Open this door right now.'

Oh God, it was her grandmother all over again. Simone closed her eyes, tried to distance herself from the ghosts. Back then, she would gaze wistfully at the tiny square attic window and wonder if she might force herself out; it didn't matter where she landed or how, anything to be out of this room and the inevitable confrontation. Some days she fantasised that she might not land at all, just spread her arms wide and find the magic to fly. She would fly away with her newborn son and never come back.

'Right now, Simone!'

She obeyed. It wasn't like Michelle to issue commands, much less for Simone to follow them, but these were extraordinary circumstances.

'Christ alive,' said Michelle, 'you look awful!'

'What do you expect? They're baying for blood.'

Michelle followed her in. 'I was trailed all the way over. Simone, it's bad.'

'Statement of the bleeding obvious.'

'*Lysander*?'

Simone flopped on to a chaise. 'It happened. No point going over old ground.'

'How long?'

'A few years,' she mumbled.

'Bloody hell.' Michelle looked down at her, disappointment scratched all over her face—worse, *pity*. 'Do you have any idea what you've done to Brian?' she asked.

'What about what he's done to me?'

Michelle's eyes widened. 'He hit you?' she exclaimed.

'Of course bloody not.' Simone stamped out her remorse and focused on the excuse she had always given. 'He was terrible in bed. I dried up like a fucking husk.'

'Do you know where he is?'

'He went to his brother's.'

'Not Brian, Lysander.'

Simone tensed at the sound of his name; a noble, romantic poem. 'He caught on that Emily was ready to blow. Took the first flight out of London yesterday.'

'Where to?'

'Australia.'

'As far as he could get.' Michelle snorted.

'He shouldn't be here—it would only make things worse.'

'Did he say anything else to you?'

'No.' Simone's lips twisted around the lie. Lysander had said that he loved her. He'd said he'd be back, and when he was they would be together. He'd said that Emily's disclosure meant zero. If anything it proved to him beyond hesitation that he was willing to risk it all. 'Fucking Emily Chilcott!' Simone spat. 'That girl had it in for me, right from the start. I bet she couldn't wait to spill the beans. This is nothing but revenge on dear old Daddy for not loving her enough.'

'Brian dotes on his kids.'

'Not as far as Emily's concerned: she assumed he'd open the pearly gates for her and make her the next Keira Knightley. Trouble is, she's a fucking terrible actress. I suppose she had to do something to secure her moment in the sun.'

'That reminds me, today's tabloids aren't too complimentary.'

Simone scoffed. 'There's a surprise.'

Michelle stood, briskly down to business. 'OK,' she said, 'this is the plan. You'll stay *out* of the public eye, Simone. Do not speak to or see anyone. Dress demurely. Dress like a widow. Avoid anything luxurious or enjoyable and whatever you do, *never smile*. You're hurt—remember? Damaged. *You're* the victim.'

'I am?'

'You were subjected to a neglectful marriage, and, for the sake of your sanity, you were forced to be with another. I shall be sole spokesperson in this matter. Oh, and on that note, I've heard that Brian wishes to see you in court.' She raised a hand at Simone's stunned expression. 'Don't worry. I have it under control. Brian is in shock. Once he gets over that, he'll see sense. We'll eat him for breakfast.'

'Even though I was the one banging around?'

'It's moot. You didn't *choose* Lysander, you never would—what kind of creature are you?' Michelle stopped, and Simone wasn't sure if the question was rhetorical or not. She finished: 'You took comfort in the closest arms you could find.'

'Hmm, yes, OK. I like the sound of that.'

'In the meantime, you'll focus on your relationship with Tess. You're still vulnerable after her spell in hospital. This has been a tough time for you all and *she's* your priority now—not Brian, and certainly not Lysander. Remember, Tess was a venture you took on independently from Brian and she remains your achievement.'

'I'll call her.'

'Good.'

Michelle was right. Tess was the thing that would keep her going. Tess always had. With Tess, Simone could blot out those areas of her life that didn't quite fit the picture—her long-lost son, her crappy marriage, and her climbing years—and embrace the triumph of the present. Like a shot in the arm, Tess had enabled her to discover Lysander, to see that a fresh relationship was still within her grasp, even at her age.

She hadn't realised how much she'd been lacking until Tess came along.

'Michelle?' Simone whispered as her manager left. 'Will I get past this?'

Her manager didn't skip a beat. 'Yes. Simone, this is my job. By the time I've finished, you'll be a brighter star than ever: it's a question of how we present it.'

'Do you think the affair was wrong?'

'It doesn't matter what I think.'

'It does to me.'

'Then, yes. It was wrong.'

Simone nodded. 'I love him, you know.'

It was unclear whom she was talking about. Michelle decided it was irrelevant in any case, and opened the door and went downstairs.

35

Two weeks later, Tess's plane landed in London. Interest in the breakdown of Simone and Brian's marriage showed no signs of abating. The papers were full of it:

ON-THE-MEND TESS DISPATCHED INTO CRISIS ZONE.
CAN TESS FIX MARRIAGE DISASTER?
A FAMILY AFFAIR: BETRAYED BY HER OWN BROTHER!

Cameras lunged as she passed through Arrivals. 'Tess, did you know? Have you spoken to Simone? How about Brian? Lysander? Is divorce on the cards?'

It was a relief when she met her driver. The car door slammed behind her, the paparazzi's caterwauls receding into the distance. She was tired, had considered getting a hotel for the night then decided against it. An ash cloud in Europe had disrupted flights to and from the airport and places near-site were bearing the overflow. Her transport left the airport and joined the motorway going north.

Seeing Mia would be just the tonic she needed; it had been too long. Simone's scandal had been the final nudge she'd needed to leave LA: her home was bombarded with press calls day and night, and Maximilian had advised her to slip off until the frenzy cooled. Hopefully Mia's Lake District hideaway would be the perfect place.

Disgracefully, though, it hadn't been her first choice. Before booking flights to the UK, Tess had called Vittorio and appealed for sanctuary in Italy. She had expected her lover to jump at the chance—but he hadn't. Instead, he had turned her away, evasive, saying he was busy with work and it wasn't the right time.

It wasn't like Tess to lose herself over a man, but Vittorio broke the rules. Since that first erotic encounter in the armoury cellar at Glen Cove, she hadn't been able to stop thinking about him. A week later, they'd had sex in the swimming pool at his LA mansion, where, beneath a star-strewn sky, Tess had momentarily blacked out on hitting orgasm. Vittorio made her crazy. In between visits, she hungered for him.

Vittorio made her hope. She could get away from Steven. There was still time.

Her husband had no idea, as ignorant of her thoughts and feelings as he had always been. Determined to prove how much she needed him, he had taken to holding her career to ransom. He denied it, but Tess knew better. Each time she made a date with the city's big hitters—lunch with the sassiest producer in town, a meet with an eminent fashion designer, coffee with Steven's director friends—at the last moment, her appointment would back out. When she challenged Steven about it, he picked food out of his teeth and raised a lazy eyebrow and said, 'Beats me, honey.'

She was convinced it was part of his plan. *Be my wife again or I'll ruin you.*

Thank God for Vittorio Da Strovisi. His devotion softened the blow. Knowing he craved her as much as she craved him.

That he couldn't bear to be without her. He told her she was different to other women, the only one who could bring him to his knees. In the past he had bedded several lovers at a time, but not any more, he promised. She was the only one for him. As long as they were together he had need for no one else.

Which was why Vittorio's rebuff seemed strange, out of character. Tess tried not to dwell on it—he couldn't make time for her whenever she clicked her fingers.

She felt sure that Vittorio would do the right thing and break it off with his wife before too long. He had sworn it enough times. Then she could really stick it to Steven Krakowski, who imagined he was the be all and end all of her lifespan in this city. He could think again. Vittorio tore the balls from men like Steven every day of his life. Once she had Vittorio on her arm, she'd be more powerful than them all.

*

Tess slept on and off through the six-hour journey, and each time she woke the sky was a little darker and the motorway lights a little brighter.

Her phone buzzed with a message from her PA.

Bleary-eyed, she took it in:

XS Studios want to shoot you for Glamour. Interested?

Tess had heard of XS Studios—Ryan Xiao's new venture. He had a new protégée; she'd heard whispers on the grapevine of a brilliant talent, models queueing up to get snapped. Vaguely she was flattered that they had asked her—but it was bad timing. Right now the last thing she needed was to court yet more publicity. Then again… She mulled the proposition over, fiddling with the gold locket around her neck as she did so. It had been years since she had worn the necklace; she'd uncovered it the other day and decided to wear it. Had Calida's been buried with her?

Finally she tapped out a decline, read her other messages and registered faint disappointment that Vittorio hadn't been in touch. Scratch that, major disappointment.

He's married. He's with his wife.

Maybe now he was telling Scarlet. That was why he couldn't see her, because he had more important matters to attend to—matters that could enable their future together. Calmed by a shoot of hope, Tess returned to sleep and didn't wake up until the car was rumbling down a stone track, and an owl hooted on a far-off branch.

*

At the door to her cottage, Mia Ferraris embraced her as tight and as Mia-like as she had been for the past ten years. Now twenty-five, Mia had lost the puppy fat that had defined her teenage days, and had cut her hair short in a choppy, friendly bob. 'Let me get a look at you.' Her best friend stepped back. 'You look so well, Tess. You had us worried there for a while.' She squeezed her hand.

'I had myself worried,' said Tess. 'But that's over now. I'm me again.'

Mia led the way inside. The cottage smelled of a smouldering coal fire and the sweet homeliness of a freshly made cake. It was in the middle of nowhere; grey slate with twin smoking chimneys, and, from the kitchen window, Tess could see through leaves to a wild, fragrant garden, at the foot of which shone a purple lake.

'Wow, look at this place,' Tess said.

'It makes me happy,' Mia admitted. 'I've gone a bit stir-crazy, to be honest, being miles from anything and drowning in this book. But it's been good.'

Back in the kitchen, Mia brought through a battered tin, prised the lid off and dipped a hand inside. The last time Tess had seen Mia turn her hand in the cookery department were the hefty slabs of buttered toast she had fixed for them both at Sainte-Marthe, to the disgust of their twig-thin dorm-mates.

'I never knew you baked,' Tess teased.

'I'm trying.'

'Go on, then, let's have a taste of the masterpiece.'

Mia produced the cake, which wasn't quite a masterpiece, rather a toppling three-tiered mess slathered in pink icing and looking rather like the infected nipple they used to exclaim at on page 73 of Madame Labelle's Science textbook; Tess felt a welcome twinge of relief because Mia would always be Mia, and she would always love her, and Mia was the one thing that would never change.

'Delicious!' said Tess, as Mia gave her a wry smile and cut into it.

'How's Steven?' Mia asked.

'Same as ever,' Tess lied. 'I'm relieved to be out of LA, though.'

Mia nodded sympathetically. 'I bet. Can you believe it about Simone?'

'I kind of already knew.'

'You *did*?'

'Yeah. For a while.'

'Why didn't you say anything?'

Tess picked at the cake. 'The crash changed the way I see a lot of things, Mia. Simone's been good to me. She's given me so much. I was never going to rag.'

'You don't seem that freaked.' Mia wanted the gore. 'He's your *stepbrother*!'

Tess lost her appetite and pushed the plate away, remembering Emily's call after the news struck. It seemed she had got drunk, had a massive fall-out with Brian about his reluctance to support her acting career, had thrown a plant at him, then when that failed blurted out all she knew of Lysander and Simone's liaison. Brian hadn't believed it. Who would? Much as he made her skin creep, Tess felt sorry for him.

'I know,' she said bleakly.

'It's gross.'

'Tell me about it.'

'Kind of kinky, though.'

Tess flicked a cake crumb at her. 'Don't even go there.'

All night the girls exchanged news. Tess told her the truth about Steven, and didn't feel as bad as she might when Mia burst out laughing and a shower of tea exploded from her mouth. Last month the great Krakowski had declared himself a sex addict. Tess doubted he was disclosing the precise nature of his urges to the shrink—he certainly wasn't to the press—and when Mia commented that Steven ought to get offered apple rings with his coffee instead of doughnuts, she gave in and got the giggles herself. If she didn't laugh she would cry, and, besides, it was kind of funny.

Things got serious when she confided about her affair.

'Vittorio Da Strovisi is married,' Mia said gravely. 'By definition he's an asshole. I don't blame you for going elsewhere, but what about his wife?'

'Scarlet doesn't love him any more. It's a marriage of convenience.'

'Can you hear what a cliché you sound?'

'That's what he told me, and I believe him.'

'And he's promising to leave her, right?'

'That's what he says.'

'And you're the only one? No other women keeping his bed warm?'

'No.'

'Because that's what he said, right?'

Tess stood her ground. As much as Mia's words made sense, she chose not to hear them. What was she meant to do—sign on for a life of celibacy?

'Mia, you should meet him,' she said. 'He's the most amazing…'

Mia rolled her eyes. 'You don't need to finish.'

Tess knocked her arm. 'Come on,' she said, 'you must have had this before. Someone you can't keep your hands off? Someone you can never stop thinking about?' At Mia's blush, she pounced. 'There *is* someone! Who is it? Do I know him?'

Mia had gone the colour of a beetroot. 'Actually, you do.'

'Who?'

Mia waited a moment, then said quietly: 'Alex.'

'Alex?' His name didn't belong in this conversation; it seemed an anachronism, a credit card in a 1950s movie. 'As in Alex Dalton?'

'Yeah.' Mia smiled shyly.

'Oh.' Tess didn't know what to say.

'He's been up here a couple of times already. I didn't know whether to tell you—I guess I didn't want to jinx it. I mean I'm fully aware he's way out of my league. I couldn't believe when it happened once, let alone when it happened again…'

'He's not out of your league,' objected Tess. 'You're out of his.'

'Hardly!'

'When did you… When did he…?'

Why can't I get the words out?

'We got together in LA. It was over you, I suppose. We were both so worried when you were in hospital. After visiting hours, we went for dinner. It sort of seemed like… the natural thing. You know, drowning our sorrows and then one thing led to another… He's so nice, Tess.' She shook her head. 'Alex is just *so nice.*'

No, he wasn't. He was an arrogant playboy who made her feel small.

'Don't you find him up himself?'

'He's lovely.'

Tess could think of many words to describe Alex Dalton but lovely wasn't one of them. She tried to get her head around it, and couldn't.

'Are you OK?' Mia asked. 'You're cool with this?'

'I guess I just never saw you together.'

'Neither did I! He was always, like, the ultimate, wasn't he? Do you remember how Emily and Fifi used to get about him? He's so sexy,' she said dreamily, 'and clever, and kind…' She bit her lip. 'And rich! Not that that matters…'

'As long as you're happy,' said Tess. Why did she sound so tight?

'And he was always your friend. To be honest, before Steven, I thought you guys would get together for sure… We all did.'

'All?'

'Emily used to say so. Said Alex had it bad for you. Said he liked you so much he couldn't even look at you.'

'That's nonsense.'

Mia nodded. 'Alex said so, too. Which is a relief!'

Tess forced a smile.

'He adores you, though,' said Mia. 'We both do. He thinks the world of you.'

Because he feels sorry for me...

'I am happy, Tess. Happier than I've ever been.'

'I'm glad.'

Mia wore a naughty expression. 'So... I've been *dying* to tell someone, and since you've shared about Vittorio... Alex is *so* hot in bed! My God, he's, like, *the best*. I was so paranoid about all those supermodels he's been with, but he told me he only dated them because he was trying to get over someone, and anyway he loves my curves and he says I have the dirtiest laugh. We have such fun together...'

Tess tuned out. *You don't want to hear this.* And she didn't. She really didn't.

All the amazing sex she was having with Vittorio: that was what she should be focusing on. She splashed her friend with water.

'Shut up,' she said.

Mia grinned. 'OK, OK, I get it, TMI. You're sure it's not weirded you out?'

'A bit,' Tess admitted, and quashed her misgivings because a faint instinct told her they were not in Mia's interests; they were in hers. 'But I know what I want. Vittorio's the man for me—just you watch.'

Mia raised her mug for a toast.

'To happy ever afters,' she said.

Tess took a mouthful, too much at once. It burned.

36

New York

She should never have overheard the dialogue. Models gossiped—it was fuel for the dressing room, the make-up chair, often the only sustenance that kept them going—and nine times out of ten its content should be taken with a bucket of salt.

But on this occasion, she knew it was true. And that truth changed everything.

Wednesday evening and Calida had just wrapped a shoot with Samantha Pringle, renowned clotheshorse and ex-member of the world's biggest girl band. Accustomed to posing in a five-piece line-up, Samantha had been uneasy in isolation, so Calida had sourced four other beauties to stand alongside her. Afterwards, their star made a swift and glamorous getaway, while the others mingled, unhurried, in states of semi-undress. Calida was passing the wardrobe when she heard her sister's name.

'I've heard he's banging Tess Geddes…'

'No,' one of them gasped, 'really?'

'Really. They hooked up at some party. Stella says it's serious.'

'Stella talks bullshit.'

'Of course you'd say that. What's your problem with her?'

Calida stayed out of sight, her back against the wall. She held her breath.

'What about Steven? I'd give half my ass to snag a husband like him.'

'Only because your ass is insured for fifty thousand bucks.'

'I'd sooner have Vittorio,' put in the first.

'Well, nobody else stands a chance if he's sleeping with Tess.'

There was a snort of derision. 'Tess Geddes isn't *that* hot.'

'You just keep kidding yourself.'

Calida's heart thrummed. She could hear her breath, low and quick.

'His wife's not going to like it, that's for sure,' said a new voice.

'She'll never find out. She hasn't so far.'

'Yeah, but Tess is different. She's a threat. Have you seen Scarlet lately? She's like a shoelace. With eye bags.'

A mean titter, then: 'You're a bitch.'

'Don't I know it, honey.'

There followed a shuffle of bags being collected and jackets slipped on. Calida rounded the corner and watched as the models emerged. When the door swung shut behind them, her lungs expelled a whoosh of air and she sank down on to the floor.

You've been with him, she thought. *You've been with Vittorio*.

She felt as if she had been punched in the gut.

Tess and Vitto. Vitto and Tess. Rage boiled through her like flames devouring a building. She couldn't see. Could hardly breathe. It was too much to take in.

Anger pealed out of her like clanging bells.

And then the idea occurred, with the same clear ring as a note being struck. Suppose Tess *knew* he was sleeping with Calida? It would be Daniel all over again. Unwilling to accept defeat a decade ago, her twin had to exact one-upmanship now.

You saw what I had—you knew what I had—and you took it.

Fury paralysed her. Everything she despised about Tess Geddes came rushing at her like thickening, blackening thunderclouds. Only, where Calida would once have backed off, content to let her beautiful sister claim what was hers, this time she would not. She could not. Vitto was the prize, and only one of them could have him.

You want a fight? Calida thought, setting her jaw. *Fine. You've got one.*

*

The City Costume Fashion Gala on Broadway was a raging success. Ryan Xiao was in his element, cosseted in the lap of the glitterati and busy showing off his second-in-command. After dinner, cocktails, and an eye-watering charity raffle (one winner bid $245,000 for a drink with Hollywood icon Cole Steel), Calida slipped out.

Vittorio was ready to pick her up. He was tucked in a quiet road behind the venue, his car purring and the headlamps dipped. They flashed her once; she opened the door and climbed inside. Instantly she was hit by the smell of perfume— musky and sensual, with a note of lavender. *Tess?* The thought made her stomach flip.

'Drive,' Vittorio instructed, as he sealed the privacy screen and placed a hand on her thigh. Calida knew this game. Her lover remained in profile—no need for conversation. His hand crept gradually higher until it found the heat between her legs. As they whizzed through Manhattan, a palette of liquid streetlights, he moved two fingers against her. Calida spread her knees. When the car swung left and his fingers plunged into her, she thought he was going to show her mercy—but no, he kept his touch in place, refusing to move, while she worked with it as much as she could. Vittorio continued to look ahead, his expression still. Unable to bear it, Calida reached down. Vittorio caught her, gripping her fingers in his other hand.

'Not yet,' he told her.

Back in Greenwich Village, Vittorio threw her face-down on to the bed, hitched up her skirt, ripped down her panties, lifted her hips so she was on her knees, and slapped her hard on the ass. Calida bit the sheets, her cunt spread and wet.

'You want me to fuck you like I've never fucked you before?'

Vittorio stood from the bed. He came to each side, taking one wrist then the other, and tying them to the bedposts with silk ropes. Calida groaned, her lips dry. He stripped and positioned himself behind her. First, she felt his tongue, direct in her opening, licking her, and she had never felt so exposed and turned on.

With exquisite cruelty, he pulled back. The urge subsided. Then he savoured her again, lost in her this time, and she could feel the coarse grain of his stubble against her backside. She ground against him and that irreversible tingling threatened to take her for the second time. He sensed it and stopped. 'Not yet,' he said again.

Next, his fingers entered her. Building a rhythm, he withdrew and worked the liquid up to her ass. Coaxing inside that virgin orifice, she felt her knees spasm. She pulled on the cords that bound her wrists, and flushed searing hot.

'Oh!' she breathed. 'Oh, oh, oh…'

'Do you like that?' Vittorio rasped. This time he pushed further. His other hand cupped her pussy, locating her clit, and he massaged the two together.

'Yes,' she managed. 'Vitto, please,' she begged, 'fuck me there.'

Her whole body yearned to accommodate him. Even so, she wasn't prepared for the flash of blind-white pain that shot through her as he broke in.

'Ah!' she screamed—but it was short-lived. Pleasure took over instantly, his cock scorching inside her as he rocked back and forth, first slow then speeding, and this pleasure was no greater or lighter than the other pleasure, but totally unalike. She was plugged into a primitive, animal pleasure; a Freudian pleasure, one that rooted her to the solid, soiled earth. They climaxed together. Calida lost herself for those seconds, saw herself from above and below, and wasn't in her mind but out of it.

Vittorio rolled off and lay next to her, panting. She collapsed, still bound, her elbows numb now that the storm had subsided. Her legs quivered, every muscle spent. She turned to face him, marvelling at his pristine looks; the almost cruel line to his mouth, his angular jaw and chin. How many other women had he done that to?

Had he done that to Tess Geddes?

'Do it to me again,' Calida said.

Vittorio shot her a grin. 'What's up with you tonight?'

'Just do it. I want you to.'

He obeyed. This time she came more furiously than before. She wanted to go on all night, each orgasm claiming more of him, destroying another piece of her twin.

Every time Calida slept with Vittorio, it was a knife in her sister's back.

You can't deny me for ever, she thought. *When I get you face to face you won't be able to pretend I don't exist. I'll force you to admit it.*

After all, I'm fucking your boyfriend. How's that for poetic justice?

'Vitto,' she asked starkly, 'do you know Tess Geddes?'

Vittorio sighed. 'I've met her once or twice. Why?'

'Astrid Engberg mentioned it. I wondered.'

'You're not friends with her, are you?' he asked quickly.

'Astrid thought I might take her photograph. We asked but she declined.'

Vittorio pushed himself up on one elbow. 'I'm not surprised,' he mused. 'I've heard she's a stuck-up cow. Tess Geddes doesn't mix with just anyone.'

'Does she mix with you?'

He eyed her. 'Am I detecting jealousy?' he goaded.

'Never.'

He grinned. 'Good. I barely know Tess. All I know is she's a suicidal maniac who put herself in hospital. I don't want to know any more.' Vittorio leaned in.

'Now,' he murmured. 'Shall we untie you, or do you want to go again?'

*

Calida had always thought with her head—and this was no different.

She already had her shield in place, and the shield was that she didn't love Vittorio. She never would. That territory was closed. She had been there, put her heart on the line, spilled inside out for the sake of another person and had wound up being rejected. It meant she could challenge her sister without fear, without limits; it meant no weapon of Tess Geddes' could penetrate her armour. She had nothing to lose.

As the days passed, the competition obsessed her.

Ryan asked why she was distracted. Lucy couldn't understand when she cancelled plans last minute. Each time she made a date with Vittorio, it was one less date he was having with Tess. Every time his pager beeped or he told her he couldn't make a secret rendezvous, she spent the night imagining him with her sister.

Weeks after the revelation, shock still didn't do it justice. The fact that the twins had come so close, connected after all this time by the heat of another man's body, their lives crossing over so close and yet so far, was both horrible and brilliant at the same time. Every moment was bringing them closer to a head-on collision.

Two cars hurtling towards each other in the dead of night.

Time passed and she and Lucy went their separate ways: Lucy moved up at MOMA and at the same time she moved in with her architect boyfriend. Calida bought a place on Upper East, with its own studio and dark room.

Then, out of nowhere, one frosty morning in the park, her phone rang. She reached into her bag to retrieve it.

'Calida, it's me.'

It took her time to place the voice—not because she didn't recognise it but because it was the voice she had steeled herself never to hear again.

Daniel. Her cowboy. Her friend.

The only 'me' she would know besides her sister.

Hello, you.

She found her tongue. 'Hi.'

Words were insufficient to bridge the divide of time and place and hurt. Calida thought of the night she had just spent with Vittorio, and, replacing the triumph she had nursed since breakfast, a creeping uncertainty settled, something close to shame.

As if Daniel knew her better. She wasn't that person, not really, in her heart. She was the girl on the *estancia*, thousands of miles away, looking out at the sunset.

'You're doing so well, Calida,' came Daniel's voice. 'I'm proud of you.'

Unable to stop herself, Calida smiled into the phone; her eyes filled with tears. Then she imagined his wife in the background, maybe a couple of fair-haired children clinging at her skirts. The thought wounded her still-healing heart.

'Can I help you with something?' she asked formally.

'Maybe,' said Daniel. 'If I came to town... could we meet?'

The question surprised her. Of all the things he might have said, that was the last she'd expected. *Yes*, she wanted to answer. *Yes, I want to. Yes, yes, yes...*

But she stopped.

I'm too close now. I can't let this go.

I won't.

She had come so far. It had taken years to get within touching distance of Tess Geddes, and she was near enough now to reach out and...

'I can't,' she said.

There was a long quiet. 'Me and Clara didn't work out,' Daniel said at last. 'We've separated. I wanted to tell you. I had to tell you.'

Calida absorbed this information. It didn't gratify her like it might have. Instead, she worried that Daniel was hurt. Worried at what he'd been through.

'I'm sorry,' she said.

'It was my fault. I didn't love her in the way she needed. I couldn't.'

Calida remembered how she had laid herself on the line that day in Buenos Aires, humiliated when she'd asked him if he loved his new wife and unwilling to hear the answer even when she did. *Sí*. Daniel had looked her in the face and said that.

Sí. I love her. *I love her*.

'I'm with someone else now,' she said.

Calida forced herself to say it—for her, for him, for them both. For the sake of the rivalry that drove her on every day, from the instant she woke to the moment she fell asleep. Sacrificing Vittorio would mean letting it go. All she had worked for; all she had earned. 'I don't want to see you,' she said. 'I don't want to hear from you. I'm sorry for your marriage but there's nothing left for us—it's too long ago. Too much has happened. Good luck in your life, Daniel. I wish you the best. *Adios*.'

She ended the call, her hand shaking.

You've done the right thing. The only thing.

Years had passed since their encounter in Buenos Aires but the scars were still visible. Calida knew where to find them. It was better this way. Life could be lived with minimal pain and upset, if love were removed from the equation.

Part of her expected, hoped, that Daniel would ring back. He didn't.

37

December 2014
Night

She must have passed out again, because the next time she woke she was sitting upright. The gag was back in, but a new one, starched and clean and reeking of disinfectant. The scent was dizzying and sickly, rising to her nostrils.

'I'm sorry I had to do that,' said her kidnapper. 'I don't want you talking. I want you to listen. Can you listen to me?'

Limply, she nodded. Her head was drooping, her neck a cracked stalk. Her left temple throbbed, as if a hard object had clubbed it.

'I'm going to tell you a story. It's a very sad story. I hope you won't cry.'

She tried to pull her wrists apart, but they were tied too tight. A memory surged back at her—of a man, a bedroom— wild and brutal, savagely out of context.

'Once upon a time,' the person paced in front of her, moving in and out of light in familiar and unfamiliar shapes, 'I had a family. I believed in the goodness and decency of people. I thought I was secure. I was wrong.'

She shivered. The window was open; fresh air blew in.

Outside, the cold winter night sprayed snow from the sky. The moon peered in. She fought sleep.

I have to get out.

Get out. Get out. Get out.

'I had it planned, from the moment of your betrayal. Because it was a betrayal, wasn't it? Even you admit that—now, at the end of things.'

She whimpered. Tried to contain it, but it spilled out of her all the same.

'I'm sorry I had to hurt you.' The person knelt in front of her. 'You understand that I had to, don't you? I couldn't let you get away. Not again.'

She waited, eyes stinging, lungs burning. In the dark, behind her back, she worked the binds together. It was no use. They were taut and she had no strength.

'I thought I knew what love was then,' her captor said. 'Vital love, blood love, the love that lasts a lifetime—but I was fooling myself. You proved that. There were so many times I tried to reach you, tried to show you my face. But you didn't see me. You refused. You were blind. All you cared about was yourself. You still do.'

She went to shake her head but found she couldn't lift it.

'Have you ever experienced that love?' Her abductor's head cocked, interested in her response. She was unable to give it, the gag resolutely in place.

Yes, she had. Yes, she still did. With all her might, she nodded. Her assailant leaned forward. For a crazy second, she thought she was about to be kissed.

A swift slap stung her cheek.

'Liar! Don't you dare say you have. You don't know what the word means. You're a loveless, heartless bitch!'

Her throat loaded with all the things she longed to voice

but couldn't, and she wasn't sure they would make a difference even if she were able.

Suddenly, a flick of silver flourished in the pitch. A knife blade glinted.

'It's over.'

The voice was close now, all around, inescapable.

'Say good night, sister.' The blade touched her neck. She thought of Christmas unfolding outside, of joy and laughter and lights. That was the last thought she had.

'This is the end for you.'

PART FOUR

2011–2014

38

Los Angeles

Kendra was the worst of them.

Scarlet Schuhausen sat among her so-called friends and concentrated on eating her tuna ceviche as unbiologically as she could, as if she weren't a living mammal after all but a mannequin in a store window whose mouth was better designed for pouting than for accepting food. Yes, it was a dinner party—one of socialite Kendra King's exclusive soirees—but it didn't mean anyone ought to actually *eat* anything.

'So, I said to Tim, the Bahamas? Seriously? I am *so* over it. What about Capri, or Monaco, somewhere more refined? Not to mention the fact that Danny took me there for *our* honeymoon—that soon got Tim changing his mind, let me tell you…'

The seven women gathered around Kendra's table chimed obedient laughter. Kendra sat at the head like some terrible fur-drenched queen, her platinum hair scraped off a high, alabaster forehead, rather resembling Elizabeth I.

'Kendra, you are awful!' trilled Greta Sykes.

'If only my Dougie were so obliging!' sang Laura Sinclair-Beaumont.

'The thing about husbands,' Kendra went on, 'is that you've

got to keep them on a tight leash. They have to know their place—or else they'll run all over you.'

'I quite agree,' said Nancy Montefiore.

'To the outside world it appears that they make the decisions.' Kendra nodded, then added wickedly: 'Let me tell you—behind closed doors that is *not* the case!'

The women giggled. Scarlet joined in, although she was already squirming in her seat. *Say something*, she frantically thought. *Before they single you out*.

It was too late. Kendra's eyes found hers like a cat peering in a mouse hole.

'You're very quiet down there, Scarlet. Do tell: how does Vittorio match up?'

Seven heads cocked to hear her response. Or, first, view it, for her cheeks were burning up like a furnace. Scarlet hated discussing her marriage with anyone, let alone these sniping, catty, competitive wives who would gossip and bitch about her as soon as her back was turned. How was she meant to tell the truth, when she couldn't even admit it to herself? As always, she fibbed. She fibbed until her tongue hurt.

'Vittorio and I have always had an equal partnership,' she managed.

'Equal?' scoffed Kendra. 'How so?'

'He respects me.'

It was the most ludicrous thing she could have said. Intending to deny the truth, instead she had showcased it. Respect was the last thing Vittorio Da Strovisi had. He had been screwing around on his wife for years and all the ladies knew it.

'Respect is a precious thing, isn't it?' mused Kendra. 'It's hard to get back once it's lost. Tim respects me. Well, I don't know if it's respect or fear, but either one will do.' The women hummed their approval; there were a few fawning titters. 'For instance, I know he'd never *dare* stray. I'd slice his balls off in his sleep!'

Scarlet blushed. She felt Kendra's gaze bore into her. Times like this she *hated* Vittorio, really hated him. *How could you do this to me*? She had believed his gilded promises of love and security—how was she to know he couldn't keep it in his pants?

She knew he had urges. She had tried to fulfil them. She'd played nurses, teachers, air stewards, bakers; she'd surprised him on work trips wearing nothing but a pair of sky-high Louboutins; she'd taken part in threesomes with other women.

Nothing was enough. She had even attempted to make him jealous—see how he liked being a victim of his own game—and slept with heavyweights like Steven Krakowski. Well, that had been without doubt the most uncomfortable night of her life. When she had confessed Steven's travesties to Vittorio, fully expecting him to yell that if another man so much as glanced at her he would kill the motherfucker, he just nodded tolerantly and said, 'Krakowski has eclectic tastes.'

Vittorio didn't care what she did, or with whom. He had made a joke of her.

'What would *you* do,' taunted Kendra, 'if you found out Vitto was playing around?' She trailed her index finger around the rim of her glass.

Scarlet knew she would cry soon; she could feel it rising up from the point her feet met the marble-mosaic floor, and she stood and placed her napkin on the table.

'Please excuse me,' she said. 'I'm not feeling too well.'

*

For months, Kendra's dinner party stayed in her mind.

What would you do? Come on, Scarlet, what would you do…?

Her husband was away in New York. She hadn't seen him in weeks. Mostly, when Vittorio went abroad, Scarlet sought refuge in distraction, tried her best not to think about the harem of women he was making love to. No matter how accustomed she had become to it, the pain never lessened. Vitto was a master between the sheets. But, this time, his absence felt different. It felt like an opportunity.

I have to act. I can't carry on like this.

Vittorio knew he could get away with it—that was the problem. When they'd met, he had been a twenty-five-year-old entrepreneur with the world at his feet. She'd been nineteen, heir to Daddy's millions, pretty, and utterly devoted to him. After learning of his affairs, for a while she had tried to get pregnant; thought that might encourage him to stay. It hadn't worked. Vitto was militant about contraception, and though she tried to sabotage it, a pinprick here, a missed pill there, no baby arrived.

If Scarlet lost him, she didn't know what she would do. Occasionally, there were moments of reassurance—Vitto would send her flowers, or a message telling her he loved her—but, most of the time, she was filled with a bleak sense of doom. It was only a matter of time before he left her for one of his lovers. If not now, then when he realised she was unable to produce the heir he would one day require.

She could not let that happen.

Wrong as it was, foolish as it was, Vittorio Da Strovisi was her life. She was nothing without him. Whatever it took, she could not let him go.

*

In the end, the call wasn't as awkward as she'd feared. She had put it off long enough, praying as the weeks passed that her suspicions (who was she kidding, her certainties) might be mistaken. The only thing for it was to grab the phone one Friday morning and punch in the numbers before she could think twice about it. The man told her a place and a time to meet—of the utmost discretion, of course—and that was that.

The hook-up was beneath the railway arches. It was raining, and Scarlet hid beneath a wide, dark umbrella. The man approached, purposeful, striding, and smiled when he saw her. 'I hope you haven't been waiting,' he said.

'Not at all.'

'I thought this might be safer. You wouldn't want to get photographed.'

'No, absolutely.' Just imagine what a field day Kendra and Nancy would have with that! SCARLET SCHUHAUSEN HIRES PRIVATE DETECTIVE.

'Come inside.' He took her coat, flapped off the wet and did the same with his own, before hanging both up. It was a cosy cabin, a wooden desk and two chairs, a lamp, and a stack of newspapers. 'Please,' he gestured, 'make yourself comfortable.'

Scarlet sat. Henry Doric settled opposite her. He was a good-looking man, early thirties she supposed, with a crop of dishevelled brown hair.

'Whenever you're ready,' he encouraged.

She cleared her throat, wrung her hands in her lap.

'Can I get you something to drink?' Henry asked kindly. When she shook her head, he said, 'I know this is hard. No one finds it easy. Just take your time, explain it as best you can, and I promise I will do all I can to help you.'

Scarlet took a deep breath. When she exhaled, the words

came too. She explained everything in a long rush, from her marriage to Vitto right through the years of her torment. Unlike many of the people who came to see Henry, she had already resigned herself to her spouse doing the dirty. What she wanted was to find out *whom* he was screwing and how serious it was. Henry nodded and took copious notes.

'I need to know if he intends to leave me,' she concluded.

There followed a few moments' silence. Scarlet wasn't sure if she was meant to say more, but Henry continued writing and she continued sitting.

'OK,' he looked up and removed his glasses. 'I have all I need.'

'I bet you think I'm stupid, right?'

'No.'

'Still with a guy even though I know he cheats on me?'

'Love makes us do strange things, Ms Schuhausen. I understand.'

He said it so genuinely that she managed a weak smile. 'Thank you.'

'I'll be in touch as soon as I have news.'

*

Henry Doric didn't make her wait. Six days later, the envelope arrived, marked:

CONFIDENTIAL DOCUMENTS—DO NOT BEND.

Scarlet ran a nail along the seal and opened it. A dozen black-and-white prints slipped out, and immediately she recognised her husband. The prints were glossy, as if they belonged in an art gallery. Hands shaking, she flicked through them. Vitto in a café, laughing down a side street, entering a hotel then exiting hours later; holding her hands, kissing her lips, his arms around her in the rain, her face in his collar…

At first, it was unbelievable. Then, it made sense.

Her.

The same woman in every photograph, a woman Scarlet recognised with bile in her throat and hate in her heart. The woman was vivid and dark—so different from her own regal fairness—and regarded Vittorio with unabashed adoration in every frame.

It was the same woman all the way through. Would have been better if there had been a selection, a few of her husband's playthings, none that posed a real threat.

She had asked Henry to uncover any serious affair. Here was her answer.

The photographs were timed and dated. It seemed that Vitto had been busy in Italy, at the Tuscan house they'd bought together on their fifth wedding anniversary. He'd been there fucking this other woman. This *whore*.

Scarlet's tears began quietly then turned into howls. She howled her grief to the empty, loveless mansion of her hopeless marriage; she bunched the pictures in her fists and tore them into pieces and let them scatter around her like confetti. In one shard, like broken glass, she could still see the tramp's face. The confession it wore.

Love. And Vittorio loved the tramp right back.

It was over for Scarlet. There was only one thing she could do.

She stood, let herself stop crying, and then calmly mounted the stairs.

39

London

The headline ran in a blood-coloured banner across the foot of the news screen:

SOCIALITE IN SUICIDE SLASH! SCHUHAUSEN IN TRAGIC ATTEMPT!

Tess sat up in bed, alarmed. 'Vitto?' she called. Then, louder: 'Vittorio?'

In the en suite bathroom of their lavish Park Street hotel room, the shower turned off. Tess called again and the door opened. Vittorio emerged, naked, his black hair dripping. He launched himself on to the bed but she pushed him away, stricken.

'Look. Vitto. My God, *look*.'

Vittorio turned to the TV and his face went the colour of egg whites. Tess tried to take his hand but he pulled away. A reporter was talking into camera:

'*Ms Schuhausen, wife of celebrated tycoon and CEO of Tekstar Corporations Vittorio Da Strovisi, was found unconscious at her home in Los Angeles early this morning. She was taken to the Willow Central Memorial, where she is said to be in a stable condition. Ms Schuhausen had been suffering*

with depression and anxiety before her suicide attempt; our
thoughts are with her friends and family at this time.'

Vittorio stood from the bed.

'Are you going out there?' Tess asked.

'No chance,' he said, and began dressing. 'I'm getting as
far away from the city as I can. If the press catch sight of me,
I'm a dead man. They'll want to pin this on someone.' An
unpleasant snarl overtook his features. 'Scarlet's an attention
seeker,' he said. 'She's only done this to get me to come running. I won't fall for it.'

Tess was confused. 'I thought you'd told her about us. You
said you had.'

He didn't reply, just concentrated on knotting his tie.

'Isn't that where you were last week?' Tess pulled the sheet
up to cover herself. 'Back at home, explaining everything to
Scarlet? Leaving her?'

Next were his shoes, black and gleaming as a 1950s Cadil-
lac.

'Vitto?' she said coldly. 'That is where you were, isn't it?'

He sat to tie his laces, his back to her. 'I didn't get round
to it,' he muttered.

The TV continued its grisly report. Tess didn't know which
was worse—the idea that this desperate, troubled woman
should have made an attempt on her life as a result of Vittorio's aborted confession, or that she had gone to such ends
purely on the back of her misery at his affairs. Tess was part
of it. She had caused it.

'This is wrong,' she said, and the wrongness of it fell around
her like bricks.

'I'm sorry. I'll call you when I come up for air. Whenever
the hell that is.'

'I don't mean that.' For the first time since their affair began,

Tess saw the repercussions of her actions. Even if what Vittorio told her was true—that he and Scarlet had no feelings for each other any more—what she was doing was terrible.

'You haven't been honest with me,' she said. 'Or her.'

Vittorio turned at the door. 'I never said I was honest,' he replied.

'The only reason you and Scarlet hit the rocks is your infidelity. You're not estranged at all. Your wife isn't desperate to leave you. You lied.'

He laughed, meanly. 'Bit late for a conscience, Tess, isn't it?'

'I thought your marriage was as fake as mine.'

'My marriage is nothing like yours. Your husband needs therapy—and fast.'

Tess blinked at him. 'You know about Steven's club?'

'Of course I know about his club. I was invited to ride that fucked-up carousel once and I thought he was joking, laughed straight in his face. I wasn't asked again.'

'You got up to other kicks with him, though, right?' Nausea washed through her. 'Other women?' Vittorio morphed right then in front of her eyes, no longer a hero but a cheat—a nasty, conniving, manipulative cheat. She had thought he was different. He was the one who had set her free. 'I'm not the only one, am I?'

He met her gaze, then—for a long time, too long. 'No. I'm afraid you're not.'

'How many?'

'It doesn't matter.'

Tess was ready to press but didn't. He was right. It didn't matter if it was one or one hundred: once a bullshitter, always a bullshitter. Alarm bells should have sounded long ago. If he was willing to do this to Scarlet, he was willing to do it to her.

How could I have been so gullible?

She had made a point of becoming her own stronghold, surviving absolutely on her own and without support—for she could not rely on anyone or anything. *All men will let you down... no matter how much you think you can trust them.*

'Get out,' she said. The words choked out of her like knots on a length of rope. Vittorio was no better than Steven. They were one and the same. They would probably laugh about this later. He'd never had any intention of helping her out of her marriage, of raising her profile, all the things he had promised. '*Get out!*'

For a moment, she expected him to argue. Then he smiled in that way she had fallen prey to so many times. 'With pleasure,' he said, opening the door.

'Don't call me again. Call your wife. If you do one thing, call your wife.'

The door closed.

Tess sat with the silence, as she had when she was a fifteen-year-old orphan in Simone Geddes' castle, cold and alone and longing to run but having no clue where.

*

April arrived and with it the fever of a Royal Wedding. All across England, crowds gathered to watch the marriage of Prince William to Kate Middleton. Patriotism coursed through town and country; bunting and flags were erected on every street.

Simone Geddes, newly freed from the tyrannical misery of her marriage to Brian Chilcott (for that was how the press, or rather Michelle Horner, had spun it), attended the ceremony. It was her first outing since the break-up. She couldn't have chosen a more apt occasion—quintessentially British, just like

her, and reeking of more than high glamour: class, sophistication, breeding…*longevity*. Like the monarchy, Simone was an
institution. Nothing was getting rid of The Ice Queen.

'Simone, how are you?' she was asked, addressed as carefully and tenderly as if she were a brittle china doll about to
smash into a thousand pieces.

'Oh, you know,' she answered meekly. 'Bearing up.'

'You're looking so well. It must have been rotten for you,
poor thing.'

'It was. Neglect is a terrible ordeal.'

Beneath the protective shield of her pearl birdcage fasci-
nator, Simone made the perfect divorcee. At the end of the
day, people *wanted* to like her more than they did Brian; they
wanted to support her. After all, it had been she who had initi-
ated the Tess adoption; she who had been chief breadwinner;
she who attended industry engagements on her own because,
as the press told it, her husband couldn't be arsed.

'I always thought you were too good for him,' came the
hushed platitudes. Lady Penelope Isley-Brackingford touched
her arm and murmured through dog's-bottom lips, 'You did
the right thing getting out, darling. You're very brave…'

'Thank you, Penelope,' she said. 'I can always rely on you.'

'And you're still with…?'

'We're taking it a day at a time.'

'Of course, of course, I didn't mean to pry…'

The seeds had been cleverly sown. Nowadays people were
afraid to ask in case of upsetting her: after all, she was the
wronged party. Amid the furore they'd created in bitching
about poor Brian, Simone's affair with Lysander had drifted
to the backburner, no longer a raging boil but a gently agitated
simmer. Only a fool would have paraded a new lover about

over the last eighteen months, especially one who was an ex-stepson. Instead, she had kept her fragile new relationship under wraps. Lysander lived at her Notting Hill bolthole, happy in rich anonymity and screwing her ragged whenever she dropped round. It was the ideal situation. Give it another year, Simone thought, and they could emerge as a pair. The Ice Queen and her toy boy…

Was she mad with Emily Chilcott for spilling the beans? At first, she'd been incensed—but not any more: Emily had been the push she'd needed, the dodgy prawn that brought the rest of it up. Simone pitied the girl—she saw her old self in that grasping, self-serving, miserable behaviour that suddenly became irrelevant when one found peace in one's heart. Simone could not wait to cry her love for Lysander from the rooftops. The thought occurred that she might be ashamed, embarrassed somehow by her transgression—but she wasn't. She was proud of the treasure she had found.

Only she could feel the thaw at her core, the cool finally melting. Unchained from her husband, she was emerging as a new woman. She wondered if she hadn't always been this woman, hiding inside, barricading herself within blocks of frost to keep the memories at bay. Love had dissolved all that; she could feel it rushing away, like liquid. Love for Lysander, in whose hands she had softened.

Love for Tess, in whose eyes she saw her future; her immortality.

Simone did lament that Lysander and Brian were no longer talking—but what could she do? Brian was off licking his wounds in the Canadian Rockies. Knowing him, it wouldn't be long before he came creeping back to make amends with his son.

Whenever she felt guilty, she remembered Brian's love-making and instantly recovered. The thought of him with an Ottawan blonde caused her no trouble at all.

As Simone watched the highest echelons of British society swoon over each other's frocks, epiphany struck. She would share her enlightenment with the world. Michelle was pushing for a magazine spread (Simone looked better than ever: there was nothing like a bit of post-divorce anxiety to shed those extra pounds) with XS, the hottest studio in New York. What if they got Tess on board, too? What if they angled the item towards new beginnings, positive change, looking to the future? It would coincide perfectly with Tess's resurgence. Maximilian would be pleased.

In the meantime, Simone would enjoy this regal affair. She, the untoppleable queen, was resolute on her gilded throne. Let the minions come.

40

In summer 2012, Tess let herself into the Notting Hill love nest that her adoptive mother shared with Lysander and that no one was supposed to know about.

'Hey—!'

Lysander leaped up off the couch, startled. The curtains were drawn, the room shrouded in darkness, and on his Mac screen—which he flipped shut as soon as he saw her, but not quick enough—was a woman indulging in a wholehearted blowjob.

'Haven't you heard of knocking?' he seethed, clasping a cushion to his groin.

'Sorry.' Tess put down her bags. 'Is Simone back yet?'

'No.' Lysander scowled, scooping up a box of tissues and kicking a jumbo bag of Monster Munch under the sofa. 'I'll be upstairs.' He disappeared, and soon after a door slammed. Tess kept the curtains closed, and went into the kitchen to pull those blinds as well. She switched the lights off and wrapped her arms around herself.

She shivered.

It's nobody. It's nothing. It's your imagination.

But fear was hard to shake. It wasn't as if it had happened only once. Instead she was sensing it more and more, troublingly often, in LA and Paris and London, everywhere she went, this sense of being followed… She told herself not to be stupid.

Then why am I here? Why am I hiding like a fugitive?

She hadn't meant to come by unannounced, but had seen no other way. All afternoon she'd detected it. A shadow, a rhythm of footsteps; watching, waiting… That crawling sense of persecution; eyes on her, scrutinising, from the moment she left the interview to the taxi dropping her here, the only safe place she could think of.

It was hardly uncommon for a woman in her position. Stars had attention on them twenty-four/seven. But this wasn't normal. This was something else. A tingle on the back of her neck… a draught seeping under an attic door. A fatal instinct.

Last week Tess had been convinced that a man was skulking behind her as she departed a shoot in Vegas, but every time she turned, he was gone. Emerging from lunch with Natalie on Friday, she'd thought she caught her name being called. 'Did you hear that?' But Natalie heard nothing. At Steven's mansion, security lights had twice flooded the front lawns, and a warning alarm rang out like a woman's scream. Guards had assured her it was nothing, a glitch in the system, but it wasn't enough.

Am I paranoid? Has this whole thing with Scarlet made me a nervous wreck?

Admittedly, it had been a challenging time after the Vittorio split—made worse by the fact she could tell no one about it. Tess was haunted by the image of his wife lying in that hospital bed, knowing she had been the cause of such an act.

She was relieved when Simone arrived at the house, and diverted her from her thoughts. 'Darling!' Simone exclaimed, beaming. 'This is a happy surprise.'

'I thought I'd drop by.'

'It's awfully dark in here.' Simone opened the curtains with a strict flick.

'I had a headache. It's better now. Lysander's upstairs.'

'Good.' Simone smiled. Tess saw how her adoptive mother glowed at the mention of her lover's name. Lysander was a contrast to the rakishly handsome boy Tess had met when she was fifteen—these days his pallor was milky, his hair thin, and there was a comfortable paunch circling his middle—but Simone didn't notice. She was in love. With gut-wrenching envy, Tess realised she would never experience that kind of love. She would never be able to find it, even know where to look.

Simone sat on the chaise and removed her shoes. 'I have a proposal,' she said. '*NY Mode*. Michelle and I are pitching an item: "Delectable Divas". Ryan Xiao's photographing—or, rather, that partner of his that everyone's gone crazy about.'

Tess scanned through the plans on Simone's tablet. 'I don't know,' she said. She was put off by the fact that Ryan's celebrated associate was called Cal Santiago. Cal could be short for any number of names, of course, but all the same it was too weird, too close, too much a ghost of her dead twin. Clearly Simone hadn't made the connection. Her eyes were aglow.

'Why not?'

'I'd rather stay away from stuff like that…' Tess confided. 'For now.'

The suspicion of her stalker raised too many flags. She had heard horrible stories about actresses' homes being broken into, their underwear stolen, their trash raided, or worse. Assaulted. Raped. The idea of putting herself out there, being visible, was the last thing on her mind. 'I don't want the publicity,' she finished.

Simone perched next to her, concerned. 'What do you mean, you don't want it?' She asked it in incomprehension, as if Tess were a drowning woman swimming away from a raft. 'This is our life, darling. This is what we *do*. You're *Tess Geddes*.'

On impulse, Tess took her hand. 'I know I am. Thank you.'

Simone was confused. 'Darling…?'

'I never said it before and I should have. Thank you—for that and so much more: for bringing me into your family and saving me from my own. For rescuing me from my future—for taking me in when no one else did. Thank you for educating me. Thank you for putting food on my table and clothes on my back. Thank you for putting up with me when I was a brat and I'm sorry I was difficult. I know everything you did was for my benefit and I was too young to see it then, but I see it now. Thank you. Nothing can repay the generosity you've shown. I value it more than you know.'

Simone's eyes filled with tears. She hugged her. 'Oh, sweetheart…'

'I've been meaning to tell you for a while, but I never found the right time. I've done some thinking lately, and I've realised what's important. It's been hard for me to trust. I thought I'd found trust with Steven but…' She paused. 'I was wrong.'

Simone took her hands. 'You can trust me,' she said solemnly.

'But you already know. You knew about him all along.'

A sigh. 'I tried to warn you. I hoped he might have changed.'

'He hasn't. I want a divorce.'

Simone's gaze hit her again, and when it did it shone like steel. 'And you'll get one. Don't you worry for a second about that, Tess. If I can go through it and come up smelling of roses, you can too. And do you know what? It *will* make you strong. I could have crawled away with my tail between my legs, never to be seen again, but no—I kept going. I adore Lysander and I stuck to my guns. A divorced woman isn't a leper. Stand up for your rights. You must set the record straight. You're a survivor, and we'll get through it together. You and me.'

'I know. You've never let me down. Ever. You're one of the few people who have always been there for me. No secrets, no lies. You've always told me the truth.'

Simone pulled back.

'We've always been honest with each other, haven't we?' said Tess. 'That means so much. I don't know what I'd do if that was taken away.'

Simone regarded Tess seriously, as if there was something she wanted to say. Then she wiped her eyes and the moment was gone. 'Of course,' she said.

'But I'm still not doing the *Mode* piece.' Tess smiled. 'Sorry.'

Simone held her hand. She swallowed hard. 'That's OK,' she said.

*

That night, back at the Kensington mansion that had once bustled with frictions and feuds but was now empty—pictures of Brian and Simone removed, Emily's bedroom deserted and Lysander's basement gym gone—Tess Skyped Mia.

In minutes, she was given the advice she needed to hear: her stalker fears were unfounded, no one was out to get her, it was all in her head and what she needed was some time to get over Vittorio. Tess would always be grateful to Mia for not saying 'I told you so', especially since she was the only one who knew about Vitto and so bore the brunt of the break-up. Naturally, Mia had been stricken by Scarlet's actions. The poor woman was still in recuperation and hadn't been seen in public since the attempt.

'Everything you're thinking,' Tess said, 'I've already thought. I feel dreadful. It's over with him. He was lying from the start. You were right.'

Mia, as always, gave measured and impartial counsel, told her to run a hot bubble bath, watch Usain Bolt run his hundred-metre final, and get an early night.

Tess padded to the bathroom and started the taps. She switched the blind down, shuddering when she thought of someone looking in. Someone waiting.

Waiting for what?

'What's new with you?' she asked briskly. 'How's the book?'

'It's OK…' Mia trailed off into a leading silence.

Tess knew that tone in her friend's voice and sat on the rim of the tub, smiling.

'What is it?' she pressed. 'There's something you're not telling me!'

She could hear Mia's returning smile and her own widened. 'Well?'

A beat, before: 'Tess, I have news. Alex and I are getting married.'

41

New York

'Will you marry me?'

Calida put down her fork. They were at his Glen Cove retreat, naked beneath their robes and eating ice cream on the couch. Vittorio was looking straight at her.

'What?'

'You heard. I want to marry you. I want to make you my wife.'

She was shocked. 'Are you serious?'

'Scarlet's sorting herself out—or so I hear. I can begin divorce proceedings.' Vitto touched her face. 'We'll be free. I know it's fast, but what's the point in delaying? Scarlet only pulled that selfish prank because she's as miserable as I am. You believe me, don't you?'

Calida had turned that woman's plight over and over in her head. Scarlet was troubled; it wasn't Vittorio's fault. He was a victim as well, afraid to cut ties for fear of what she would do next. Calida had stuck by him through the thrashing media, staying silent in the wings, knowing the real reasons for the breakdown: mental instability, a history of psychosis. She had to trust him. 'Of course I do,' she said.

'Focusing on a wedding would be exactly the start I need.'

'Yes.'

'I know it's not the most romantic proposal,' he said, as if he were apologising for an over-cooked steak before dumping it in front of her, 'but there it is. If Scarlet sees me engaged, she might finally realise that I cannot help her any more...'

'Did you hear me, Vitto? I said yes.'

A smile broke over his face like sun across an Italian field. 'You will?'

'For the third time, yes.'

He kissed her, as ardently as he had when they had first met.

'You won't regret it,' Vittorio murmured, easing her back on the couch, the ice cream forgotten apart from the cold slip of his tongue as it found hers.

I know I won't, thought Calida, picturing Tess Geddes' face when she read the news and saw her long-lost sister's picture alongside the famous tycoon's.

The notion was electrifying. *You bet I won't.*

*

'What the hell?' Lucy asked on Friday evening, after Calida told her about the proposal. 'What is he thinking? His wife nearly died!'

'I know.'

'Calida, I mean it—I get that he's hot and rich and whatever, but *marriage*?'

'I have my reasons.'

'Is love one of them?'

'I wouldn't want to marry him if I didn't love him.'

Lucy frowned. 'That's not an answer.'

'Give Vitto a break, he's been through a tough time—'

'Nuh-uh, I'm not buying it,' said Lucy. 'I'm your best friend and I wouldn't be much of one if I weren't honest with you.

This is the rest of your life we're talking about, and you need to know where you stand. Have you even met his family?'

'Not yet.'

'His friends?' she pushed. 'Do you even know that much about him? How can you be sure he hasn't been stringing you along? That there's nobody else?'

'You're over-thinking,' said Calida. She didn't want to hear it. In her soul she already knew, but she was strapped on to the ride and there was no way she was getting off. It had taken years to secure her ticket. This was too precious to let go.

I won. You lost. He's marrying me, not you. He chose me.

'So he's left Scarlet,' said Lucy.

'He's leaving her.'

'And how exactly are you going to appear when it comes out he's got engaged two seconds later? When Scarlet's still on suicide watch?'

'She isn't.'

'I heard she was.'

'Vitto told me different.'

'Right.'

'Don't look at me like that!'

'Like what?'

'You know what.'

'If I was getting engaged to him,' said Lucy, 'what would you tell me?'

'That's not fair.'

'It's totally fair.'

'OK.' Calida thought about it. 'I'd tell you to be careful, but that it's your life and your decision, and I'd support whatever path you took.'

Lucy raised an eyebrow. 'Focus on the be careful part.'

*

Lucy's words stayed with her as she travelled across town for a shoot. All the way through the job she was unable to focus. Marrying Vitto was a means to an end. It marked deep satisfaction, a payoff at the end of a long, hard-fought match.

But then what?

She couldn't think that far ahead—but it wasn't that far, not really. After the glitz and sparkle of a wedding, Calida would have this man in her bed until the day she died. Would he be faithful to her? Would she make him content enough never again to stray? No, she admitted, probably not. And why didn't she care? Why didn't she care if Vitto slept with dozens of other women while they were together?

Because she didn't love him: she had axed love out of her life.

Love came at the expense of revenge. It was as clear-cut as that.

At the close of the day, she made a decision, and directed the cab away from her usual route and towards Central Park. Vittorio had given her a key, once, to his apartment. She headed there now, wrapping her coat around her to shield her from the cold. A harsh wind was building. In the taxi, radio reports clamoured about the incoming Hurricane Sandy, instructing citizens to stay indoors, warning of floods and electrical cuts. Calida could sense a pressure in the air, of something tense about to break.

Debris whipped and rolled and flipped on the sidewalks. Stores were bolted shut; their windows closed. The air howled like wolves.

She reached his building and turned the key. Inside, the shelter was absolute. The foyer was cool, the marble indifferent, and a glossy bank of elevators offered to take her to the penthouse suite. On floor 37, she stepped out into the carpeted hall. She came to his number and stood in front of it, looking at the gold figures: 501.

This high up, she could hear the gale take on a new pitch, like singing. A bulb flickered overhead. There was a rattling shudder from the floors below.

Calida inserted her card. For a crazy instant she expected Vitto to be here and felt a frisson shoot up her spine at the possibility—of fear, excitement? But the place was deserted. The maid had been. Through the immaculate atrium, the bed was made, linens pulled tight and pillows plumped. Calida thought of all the ways Vitto had taken her in this room and suddenly it felt sordid. Had he brought other women here?

She began in his study. Files, cabinets, desk drawers, she skimmed through them all, careful to arrange things as she had found them. What was she searching for? Evidence—for or against, it didn't matter. Knowledge. Certainty.

All was neat and meticulously ordered. Everything smelled of leather and ink. The bathroom yielded little, just a cupboard containing a toothbrush, painkillers, an empty phial of Xanax and some dental floss. In the living area, a glossy antique globe was filled with cut glass and, beyond that, a brushed granite bar boasted an array of bottled liquor. Finally she sat, exhausted, feeling foolish for her misgivings.

Supposing he's truthful… and I'm spying on him? My husband-to-be.

She resolved to go. Before she did, on a final whim, she went to the bedroom. Idly she flicked through a few drawers but was more concerned with the accelerating wind that was moaning against the windows. Spats of rain patted the panes, streaking at first then threatening to burst. Grey clouds rumbled and churned in the distance; flashes of light glowing and sparking between. It wasn't a New York sky. It looked as if New

York had been lifted and put down in another location, even on another planet. The metropolis, with its zing of cash and thrum of life, belonged to people and galleries and sushi bars. The sky, huge and Biblical, belonged to an ancient, savage anger.

Then, Calida saw it. She tugged one of the drawers too hard and something glittering spilled into view. It appeared to her like something from a dream.

A gold chain, puddled there, with an oval at its centre.

It was the size and shape of a pebble. For a weird moment Calida thought it was hers, it had to be hers, and had to touch her neck to remind her that it wasn't.

It was someone else's. A matching one, exactly the same…
A locket.

Teresita's locket.

Calida blinked. She stood still for a very long time, trying to wake from this illusion, it had to be an illusion, but each time she opened her eyes it was still there.

She experienced a flashback, bright and quick as lightning: Teresita being driven away in the car that day, her face through the window, hopeful and sad, searching for her twin's and never finding it. Calida had stayed out of sight, and then, as now, had touched the locket at her throat just as Teresita's had glinted in the light.

The question sailed towards her like paper on the wind.

Had her sister been wearing her necklace all this time?

Had she kept it, cherished it; worn it with Vitto, with Steven, with Simone?

Why hadn't she got rid of it? Why hadn't she thrown it away?

The Tess Geddes Calida knew—or rather didn't know—would have melted it to liquid and forged gold coins from the pool. *I don't have a sister*, she'd said.

But that didn't make sense. Not if she'd kept it. For this wasn't just jewellery: it was a bind, a declaration of their sisterhood, two halves of a whole, from the day Diego had given them, wrapped in tissue, and they'd helped each other tie the catch.

The locket flashed. Calida fought to join the dots, to add the sum, her brain tripping over itself to decipher what it meant. Outside, a hurricane ignited.

Pocketing the necklace, Calida fled the apartment. The elevators were out of order so she took the stairs, two or three at a time, running, unable to believe what had happened, and emerged on the street, straight into the eye of the storm.

42

Stockholm

In her parents' mansion a short drive north of the city, Scarlet Schuhausen grabbed the divorce papers that had arrived that morning and tossed them into the fire.

Good riddance. I'll sign over my dead body.

He'd like that, wouldn't he? If she'd succeeded in taking her own life. Give him a clean divorce, an easy way out, then he could resume screwing his way across Europe, across America, across every fucking continent on the globe.

Scarlet fell to her knees in front of the hearth. The family's snoozing greyhound, Pippi, peeled one eye open. She held on to Pippi's fur and cried.

Hidden behind the mantelpiece was her secret addiction. It should have been drugs; it should have been liquor—but it wasn't. She pulled out the envelope. The rest of the photographs Henry Doric had sent. Cuttings she herself had collected.

All of the same, hated woman… *That slut*.

What she longed to do to that whore! From the second she had identified Tess Geddes in the pictures, the woman had possessed her. Had Tess met him through Steven? Had she gone crying to Vitto about her husband's perversions, and together they had conjured up perversions of their own? *I'll show you perversions, you tramp.*

Scarlet had already dispatched her team of trusted moles. They were following Tess right now, tracking her moves, steering her into that final corner from which she would be unable to escape. Scarlet would meet her there. Then she'd have her fun.

The time had come to take back what was hers. Oh, yes.

Tess Geddes was going to pay.

43

England

A thousand miles away, Tess woke early and stumbled down-stairs in her stone-built Cotswold cottage. She flicked on the kettle and listened to the radio; winter sunlight streamed into the kitchen, bathing the surfaces and bouncing off the wooden floor.

Escape. She had sought it, and she had found it. Already she felt safer, no longer prickling at the slightest creak or shiver, or jumping at her cell or whenever the door buzzed. Out of the city, her paranoia eased. Her suspicions waned. Too long she had been in the vortex of the public eye. Thank God she'd got out before she'd had another breakdown. This was it, then. Peace. Anonymity. Safety.

Tess opened the door to welcome the morning. A robin landed on a nearby branch, where it hesitated a moment before darting off. Down at the gate, a cold stream of blue threaded among the rockeries, shot through with darting fish and mossy clumps of riverweed. Tess shivered, still in her nightdress, and was about to check herself for venturing into plain sight before remembering that here, in this refuge, there were no paparazzi lurking to take her picture. Who cared what she looked like?

Over breakfast she read yesterday's paper. There was a

piece at the back about Vittorio—months on from their own break-up, apparently he was divorcing Scarlet and marrying someone else. The paper made cryptic reference to 'a new woman in Da Strovisi's life', and 'the promise of marriage to this mystery belle compels him to take the leap…' Tess felt sorry for whoever had fallen prey to his advances. Vittorio had conned her, led her to believe that anyone with whom sex was that good—the first great sex of her life—had to be right. Wrong. But then Steven had been terrible at sex and he'd been wrong too.

Tess closed the paper just as her post dropped through the door. She had asked Maximilian to hold all her mail unless it was urgent, and had given this address only to a select number of people. She went to check the mat, and saw an envelope from Mia.

Inside, a plain white card was stamped with black script:

Mia Ferraris & Alex Dalton

invite

Tess Geddes

to celebrate their wedding

on: Saturday, October 25, 2014
at: Le Château de Montereau, Paris

Tess digested the words. She was thrilled for her friend; Mia was the dearest person to her and she wanted her to be happy. But something stuck. She hadn't seen Alex since before her car crash and only faintly remembered him being at the hospital—but maybe she had dreamed that part. After all, she had dreamed the part about her sister coming. Emily Chilcott had later admitted, lamely, to never having crossed the Atlantic. *'Things were super-busy…'* she'd claimed. *'But I knew you'd be all right…'*

Alex's care and concern for her had once been an aggravation—but Tess saw now, too late, that she'd liked it. Nobody since Calida had cared for her that way, the real her, the girl inside, her uncertain soul and her weakest parts. Alex had.

But he didn't care for her any more. Why should he? He had a beautiful, brilliant fiancée who deserved all his time and attention. 'We want a long engagement,' Mia had told her when she'd first shared her news. 'It has to be perfect, every detail.' Tess could only imagine how lovely it must be to plan a day like that, to take the time and care to make it right, because you knew that the person you were marrying was your forever.

Tess placed the invitation on the mantelpiece. Before leaving the room, she turned it so it was facing the wall. For some reason, she couldn't stand to look at it.

*

The New Year arrived. The land remained cold and frosty; lights glowed in windows in early evening and the trees gleamed, bare and brittle. Maximilian ramped up the pressure to get her back in LA. To appease him, Tess cited the spring.

A fortnight before she was due to leave, she received a call.

'Tess? It's Alex.'

She was stunned; said the first thing that popped into her head. 'Is Mia OK?'

'She's fine.' A pause, before: 'I'm staying in Chalmley. Mia told me you were in hiding out nearby… I thought maybe I could take you to dinner?'

'What are you doing in England?' she blurted.

'Visiting my mother.'

She was confused. 'I thought your mother was…' *How would I know anything if I hadn't been snooping on you*? 'I mean,' she tripped, 'I didn't know if—'

'Mum's buried here,' Alex said easily. 'She was British—it's where she grew up. It's her birthday next week. I always come to the UK this time of year.'

He said it so plainly that it broke her heart.

'Is your dad with you?' she asked.

Alex made a noise that sounded like a laugh. 'No.'

'Is Mia?'

'She had to fly out to Switzerland.'

'Right.'

Another beat. 'So,' he resumed, 'do you want to?' There was that tone again, the amused, entitled tone she used to find so exasperating but was now thankful to hear. They were friends, catching up; that was all. Mia had put them in touch.

'OK,' she agreed.

'There are some good places between us…' Alex said, and she waited because she sensed he hadn't finished. 'Or better still, I could cook for you at my house?'

'You have a house?'

'My aunt's—she's away.'

'You can cook?'

He laughed. 'I can try.' She felt his smile. 'I'm always willing to try, Pirate.'

*

On Saturday evening, Tess left at seven, her cab winding through pitch-black country lanes, the moon full in a ghostly sky. She felt silly for taking so long in deciding what to wear—since their phone call, if she was honest—and had eventually elected to play it casual, heels and a slip-on amber dress.

*Play it? You're not playing anything, you fool. This is Alex.
He's Mia's fiancé. He's that cocky, up-himself kid at the* danse
d'éntrée *who watched you hurl into a plant pot*. Nevertheless,
she couldn't suppress the net of butterflies whose wings fluttered in her belly. She tried to find her gold locket, wanted to
wear it, but it was nowhere. *I probably left it in LA*.

When she arrived, reaching the cobbled building and hearing the cows moo softly in the dark, she was surprised. She
had expected a grand estate to match Alex's heritage, but this
was modest—not much bigger than her own rented place. She
thought about how Alex's parents had met, what had drawn
them to each other, and which one he was most like. Tess
recognised the cavalier alpha associated with Richard Dalton's
oil empire, but there was another side, too. A deeper side; a
side she hadn't explored.

Alex looked handsome when he answered the door, in a
green-checked shirt, his hair still damp from the shower. He
didn't look vain or arrogant any more. The impression had
been a trick, and Tess felt cheated and excited at the same
time, that this person had been beneath all these years and
she hadn't seen him.

She had refused to see him. Determined to categorise Alex
Dalton as she had categorised everyone else, as a means of
containment, of keeping people away.

A fire blazed in the hall. Alex helped her out of the coat
and showed her to the living room, which was cosy; books
and papers were everywhere, a pair of muddy wellies in one
corner and tartan blankets strewn over the chairs. She could
smell chicken roasting in the Aga, and the warm scent of
thyme. Tess thought of Alex's mansions in America, of the
supermodels he entertained on his yachts.

'This is a bit simple for you, isn't it?' she said. She hadn't meant it to sound rude and, before she had a chance to qualify that she *liked* it—she liked this version of him; to hell with it, she liked *him*, and why hadn't she told him before that she liked him?—he just laughed and said: 'Always one for saying what you think.'

'I like it. It's just not what I expected.'

'You're not what I expected either.' He passed her a glass of wine.

'I've changed?'

'I mean generally. You aren't. You weren't. Shall we sit?'

Alex wore a delicious, heady aftershave. Tess fought the urge to lean into him, to feel his arms around her as she had at the Beverly Mounts. His kindness.

He's so kind, Tess.

'How's Mia?' she asked, fighting to get back on track. Her body was zinging, as it had been with Vitto but more; lower, richer, swelling in her chest as well as between her legs. It had been physical with Vitto, just physical.

'Great,' Alex nodded, 'already busy planning.'

'Are you having a big wedding?'

'Not as big as yours.'

'I know you think my wedding was shit.'

'Is your marriage any better?'

She thumped him. Decided that instead of spending her life wanting to thump Alex Dalton she should just thump him. She was sure Mia wouldn't mind.

'None of your business,' she said, but she was smiling. Suddenly she didn't care if Alex knew that her marriage had crumbled. There was no point pretending with him; he saw straight through it, he always had.

'You're way out of his league.'

'Steven gave me confidence.' Tess was startled at the

admission, the rawness of it and the fact it had spilled from her lips. 'I mean, he made me feel I was good at something. I never thought I was. He respected me. He treated me well.'

'You don't have a very high opinion of yourself, do you?'

'It's better now.'

He took her hand, held it, and didn't let go. Tess sensed there was no option to let go. He would just keep holding it, even if she struggled. 'Tess—'

'Has Mia chosen a dress?'

'Um, not yet, I don't think.'

'Are you excited? You must be really in love.'

'I am in love,' said Alex, looking straight at her.

She broke the moment, felt as if he was stripping her. *Talk about Mia; think about Mia, your best friend...* But her heart was thrashing. Her palms were hot. Still, Alex held her fingers. She reached with her other hand to collect the wine glass and it slid from her grip, splashing across the table, and she retrieved it, mortified.

'Leave it,' he said.

Alex took the glass from her and placed it on the table, which was such a small movement but spoke volumes. Tess thought it was the most exciting thing a man had ever done. That sound of that glass meeting the table... Then silence.

He kissed her. It should have come as a shock, she thought, as his lips explored hers, but it didn't. It was the inevitable thing to do.

Alex was an excellent kisser. His kiss was hot but his face was cool, as she touched a hand to his stubble-rough jaw. He tasted of the wine, rich with cherries. Electric currents sparked up and down, inside her blood, between her thighs, making her tingle. Her breasts longed to be touched; her nipples stiffened.

Oh, Alex. It's you. It's always been you.

'Wait,' she said, pulling away, 'we can't. We can't do this.'

She was transported back to that bedroom with Calida, all those years ago. Their fight, and Calida's words: '*You knew how I felt… how I feel…*'

She was doing it again. Hurting the person she loved. *Don't do it.*

'Tess,' Alex murmured, taking her chin in his hands, 'it's OK. I'll fix this. I promise you I'll fix this. But right now I can't—I mean, you're just… I can't…'

Alex's lips met hers and this time it was dangerous, tongues entwined, deep in each other's throats so she was grinding against his teeth, hungry for him, and they moaned and gasped and pulled each other's hair. Tess couldn't think of Mia. She couldn't put Mia into this equation because although it was wrong and terrible, Mia wasn't a part of this. Mia was part of a later Alex, not the one Tess had met in Paris, not the one who had spoken to her at the Plage d'Aqua, not the one who had messaged her all through the holidays, who had pissed her off at her wedding, who had held her at the spa, who had come to her in hospital… Mia's Alex wasn't Tess's Alex. It was the only way she could think of it, and in doing so fail to think of it at all.

Alex guided her waist so she was sitting on top of him, her knees either side of his lap. His hands came up to her breasts. Tess felt his hard-on against her thigh. Reaching down, she stroked it before carefully unbuttoning his fly.

'You're amazing…' Alex's cock appeared between them, swollen and thick. She drove her hand up and down the shaft, from the smooth warm tip to the rock-hard base, drawing it out, pressing lightly then gripping firmer, using both hands so she could cup and stroke his balls. The movement squeezed her breasts together, her cleavage spilling over the neckline of her dress. Alex buried his head there, savouring her, biting her, licking her, until he peeled down the fabric, shed her lace bra and sucked ravenously at her bare flesh. 'Christ,' he breathed, 'your tits…'

Tess loved the feel of his hair beneath her chin, his rough skin against her soft. They both knew this was it. There was no going back. The world would end tonight if they did not have sex. Tess had to have him inside her. She was wet and waiting for him—she had always been waiting for him, this complicated man to whom she'd been blind, unwilling to let him in because he made her feel like she needed him. So what if she needed him? It was OK to need someone, and it was OK to be needed.

'Hold on,' murmured Alex, unwilling to stop kissing her, 'don't move…'

He dragged himself away. She knew what he had gone to get and already she could imagine sliding it on and easing him into her and how miraculous that would feel, and hastily she removed the rest of her clothes. Unable to wait, she followed—and met Alex coming downstairs. A second while they took each other in, so many barriers over the years to reach this final point of not a single one, skin on skin, eyes on breasts, sweat on sweat, and never had anything been so unavoidable.

Without a word, Alex eased her on to the steps, face front, her legs spread.

'I've wanted this for so long…' he murmured.

In a paralysing bolt, he entered her. Tess screamed, her knees hitched up and spread to accommodate his girth. 'Fuck!' she cried. 'Oh, my God!'

Alex ploughed into her wetness, gripping her ass with his strong hands. The carpet stung but she wanted to bleed; she wanted to give her all to him.

He knew how to fuck. He fucked her for a long time, first on her front and then on her back and then on her front again, on her knees, his fingers in her mouth, in her ass, in her cunt; he lifted her from the stairwell, then he brought her down to the floor and fucked her on the rug in front of the fire. Just when she was ready to come, he went down on her. Tess's body was spent with bliss. She let herself be ravaged and devoured, every part of her explored and adored, every crease and crevice tasted and touched. Alex worked her with his fingers and his cock and his lips until finally he thrust into her while teasing her clit and she climaxed in a blinding storm, her head thrown back, hair plastered with sweat, gasping, her toes curled.

'Pirate…' he whispered, as he came after, rocking into her one spasm after another, as the flames cast their bodies in fire. 'I've loved you from the moment I saw you.' His statement—impossible, perfect—settled in the heat between them, requiring neither response nor elaboration; just right as it was. Alex withdrew and lay alongside her, taking her hand in his. They stayed like that for some time, not speaking.

Eventually, he turned to face her. When she met his gaze, instead of the burning guilt and anguish she knew was hours away, all she felt was joy.

There it was, her favourite face in the world. Alex Dalton's.

*

On a cold Sunday morning, Maximilian Grey-Garner III called from LA. Tess thought he was ringing to update her on the new contract with Kellaway Cosmetics, and braced herself for the return to her high-octane life. But it was nothing of the sort.

'A hate campaign has been started against you,' he warned down the phone.

She placed the note she didn't recognise in Maximilian's

voice: panic. Tess had been in a haze ever since the Alex encounter, some days devoured by conscience, others on cloud nine at the memory. Maximilian's news was like a bucket of ice.

'What?' She fumbled for her work cell. Eleven missed calls from her PR; three from her assistant; nine from Simone… and one from Vittorio.

'Scarlet Schuhausen released an open letter,' said Maximilian. 'She knows about your affair and is blaming you for her suicide attempt. According to her, you've been cheating on Steven all along. I've been up all night fielding calls and it would be an understatement to say they weren't friendly… This is bad, Tess. It's bad.'

Tess gripped the counter. 'But how did she…?'

'It doesn't matter. You've been found out.'

'Vittorio told me it was over between them. I didn't know—'

'What you did or didn't know is irrelevant. Scarlet's out for blood.'

Somehow, the thought of Alex finding out was the worst. *He'll think I'm a slut. Not enough to sabotage his engagement; I was sleeping with a married man, too.*

'Have you noticed anything odd recently?' Maximilian asked. 'Anyone following you around, dead calls, stuff like that?'

Tess gulped. 'No,' she lied.

Maximilian was silent. She thought she had lost him, then he said: 'Get back here, Tess. This letter's poison and it's going straight through the roof. Scarlet's bent on doing whatever it takes to see you fall. We have to sort this—before it's too late.'

44

Los Angeles

Tess,

I am writing to you not because I want to but because I must. You have injured me in more drastic ways than you will ever understand. How do I know that? Because a woman who sleeps with another woman's husband, aware he is married and belongs with someone else, is by definition a harlot and a whore, and incapable of grasping the meaning of love, trust, and respect. I have felt these things for my husband since our wedding day. Do you feel those things for him? I doubt it. I doubt you even feel them for yourself. Your actions make me sick. I want the world to know that I hold YOU and you alone responsible for the measure I took last year to end my life. Women across the planet should be informed that you are a slut with no esteem for others and no care for the lives you destroy. You are everything that is wrong with society, everything that is soiled, the lies, the duplicity, the rot. Did you know I was carrying his baby? Did you know that? I hope it cuts you like a knife. You stole a father as well as a husband. You are the kind of trash that women for centuries have feared. You are a bitch. An evil, toxic bitch.

Tess Geddes, you deserve your comeuppance. You deserve everything you get. You've had your golden time. Now it's my turn.

Scarlet.

Calida Santiago closed the news site and sat back in her chair.

'Everything OK?' Ryan Xiao asked, charging into her hotel room and setting down his equipment. They were in Bel Air doing a home shoot with Olympics idol Leon Sway, and were due in an hour. 'You look like you haven't slept a wink.'

'I haven't.'

'Well, get your shit together.'

'I can always count on you for sympathy.'

'Ten minutes, got it?' He left.

Calida opened her Mac and typed *Tess Geddes* into Google. In seconds she was scrolling through reams of results. Her twin was wicked, corrupt, worthless, a waste of oxygen; she should be killed, punished, made to answer for her crime…

Over the past few weeks, since Scarlet's letter was published, Tess Geddes had become the most hated woman in America. Scarlet's tirade was shared and multiplied across social media, sparking debate about marital crisis, feminism and the sorority, the crumbling of community values, of family, the exploitation of money and power. Tess became a scapegoat for everything that was immoral in the world. She was the name and face attached to every heartache, every betrayal, every wrongdoing.

Haters looked on with glee as Tess's Hollywood castle came crashing to the ground. They relished the mighty topple, at how beauty and wealth could not buy immunity, at how Hollywood's golden girl turned to copper overnight.

In one picture, Tess was flying back from England, shielding her face from a clash of cameras. There she was, emerging from her villa under a weight of coats, drawn and haunted; and here, at the premiere of her latest film, wearing a striking pearl gown and labelled: FAT COW. Calida found it sad, the things people wrote behind the cowardice of online obscurity. The treatment Tess was getting was barbaric. There was the impression that should she go out alone, she could be stoned to death on the street. Death threats flooded the forums: Scarlet's army vowed that Tess had better watch out. According to the press the actress had already been the target of direct assaults: roadkill in the mail, her car tyres slashed.

TESS GEDDES: 'FRIGHTENED FOR MY LIFE!' the headlines blared.

Calida studied pictures of her sister and saw in her eyes what she had been searching for since they were fifteen—since before then, if she were honest.

Recognition. Fear conjured the ghost of the girl Tess had been many years ago, a black-eyed child with a mischievous laugh who was scared of the dark and of snakes and of noises in the night. She wasn't this invincible movie star, this goddess beauty queen; she was the same person. Teresita. Their little Teresa…

Calida watched the drama unfold and bit her tongue to silence. Each time she heard Vittorio's name, at parties, at work, in dialogues on the street, she walked away. Anything she said or agreed on was sheer hypocrisy. Everything the press hurled at Tess could just as easily be hurled at her. Calida had committed the same offence—worse, because in Tess's latest statement she maintained she had broken off her relationship with Vitto immediately upon hearing of Scarlet's suicide attempt.

Had Calida? No. She had stayed. She had even accepted his proposal.

Now, she scanned the venomous articles with alarm. TESS GEDDES GETS ALL SHE DESERVES. KILL THE BITCH! BURY HER! MAKE HER PAY! The hashtags that spread like a rash over Twitter: #TessKarma #TessDeservesIt #Team-Scarlet.

Every woman who had ever been scorned or let down or cheated on by a man was making Tess their voodoo doll. And that doll, at last, had a face. Calida, too, had driven in a pin. She'd lost count how many. When she'd been fifteen and wished her twin would disappear. When she'd heard from Julia that Teresita had begged for the adoption. When she'd received that note, telling her Teresita was never coming home. When she'd moved to Buenos Aires and vowed to make it. When she'd hit New York and set out to match her sister's fortunes step for step. When she dreamed of meeting Teresita again, and... And what? What then? Where did they go from there?

Calida touched her locket, cool and smooth and timeless. She had been convinced all this time that her sister was rotten—had believed every scrap of dirt that the world now threw at her. But since her discovery at Vittorio's apartment, a splinter had appeared in her hate, a splinter of possibility that whispered in her ear when she lay in bed at night. *What if she still thinks about you? What if she didn't mean those things? What if she wanted to leave home but she always missed you? What if...*

Calida's phone shrilled to life. 'Where the fuck are you?' blasted Ryan.

She clicked it shut and left the room.

*

That night, she arranged to meet Vittorio.

'Thank God,' he said when they were together. 'I've had Scarlet's attorneys on the phone all afternoon stringing me up by my balls. My lawyer says now is the right time to announce the engagement. We'll issue a statement at dawn. There'll be pictures, interviews, the whole circus. OK? You're with me on this, aren't you?'

Calida watched him across the back seat of his Mercedes and shook her head.

'No,' she said. 'I'm sorry. I'm not.'

Vittorio drew a blank. Then he laughed. Then he stopped laughing.

'I know I'm not the only one,' said Calida.

Vitto slammed his fist into the leather. 'This isn't about Tess Geddes again, is it? Calida, I've *told* you. Scarlet's fabricated the whole damn thing. I've never so much as gone *near* the woman. This is classic settlement blackmail—don't you see? She even made up that crap about a pregnancy. It's lies, all of it.'

'Tess has admitted to the affair.'

'Only so she can divorce that degenerate husband of hers.'

'You're clutching at straws.'

'You're accusing me of *nothing*!'

But she didn't need Vittorio's admission to be certain. Around the time Tess claimed to have ended the affair, Calida's lover had become moody, distant, for days plummeting into black holes and snapping at her over the smallest thing. Sometimes he could only have been described as needy, which wasn't a word Calida thought she would ever associate with him. '*You won't leave me, will you*?' he'd asked more than once, running his hands through Calida's jet hair as if it reminded him of something. Someone. '*Don't be silly*,' she'd replied, kissing him and thinking as she did:

Who is this man I'm kissing?

It was probably why he had asked her to marry him. Tess's rejection had been a blow to a man like him. Vittorio Da Strovisi didn't get dumped.

'Good luck, Vitto,' Calida said now, twisting off her engagement ring and tossing it on the seat between them. 'I hope you find what you're looking for.'

She opened the car door and disappeared on to the street.

*

The following week, Calida attended a drinks reception at designer Mateo Frank's warehouse studio. Ordinarily she would share Ryan's ride home, but since he'd had obligations elsewhere, she decided to sober up by taking a walk back to her apartment. It was nine p.m. when she left and the evening was warm and calm.

Partway down Bleecker, she heard her name being called. 'Calida!'

She stopped. A woman she didn't know was rushing towards her. The woman was dressed in cheap furs and plastic jewellery, as if she had raided a second-hand clothes store. As she came closer, Calida saw her make-up was badly applied and clownish. Fake diamonds pulled her earlobes and her dress was worn and frayed.

'Calida!' the woman said again, breathless, and went to embrace her.

Calida pushed her off. It had been a bad idea to venture on to the streets alone—she wasn't recognised often, but once was once too much. 'Who are you?' she demanded.

The woman searched her eyes. Calida resumed walking.

'You mean you don't know?' came the voice.

And with it, she stood still. The stranger had spoken in

Spanish, her native Argentinian tongue. The incredible truth speared her in the back.

Calida turned.

'Mama…?'

Julia Santiago nodded, her eyes shimmering with tears. She held her arms out.

'Oh, *chica*,' their lost language rolled off her mother's tongue, 'I have waited so long for this. I have searched for you everywhere. Finally, I have found you.'

Calida's mouth filled with grit.

'How?' she managed. 'How did you find me?'

Julia's arms went down, empty, but her smile did not waver.

'I've followed my daughters' successes. I see how rich you've become. I came to New York and discovered where you worked. I went with you to the party tonight.'

It was too much to take. This person, this stranger who had abandoned her on the *estancia* as carelessly as if she were leaving for a morning's shopping, here, now, unrecognisable apart from the grasping, avaricious glint in her still-hungry eyes.

'I was outside, waiting for you,' said Julia. 'I thought I'd surprise you.'

'Congratulations,' said Calida, numb. 'I'm surprised.'

Julia's painted lips parted in a smile. Her teeth had yellowed; one of them was chipped. She had aged gracelessly, unkindly, coarse lines around her mouth and the ghosts of a scowl etched into her brow. This was her mother? Calida would have walked straight past her on the street. She nearly had. She had thought about Julia sparingly over the years, wondered about her, reviled her—but never longed for her.

'Come, *chica*, come to your mama,' said Julia. 'Be happy to see me, at least. I need looking after, *mi corazón*: the years haven't been kind. I—I lost all my money.' Her eyes glazed.

'All that lovely money… I gave you your half, but I lost my own.'

'My half?' Calida baulked.

She had been left nothing. Remembered Julia's departure, the last words her mother had spat—but no money. Julia hadn't cared. She'd left her penniless, left her for dead for all she knew, filled only with ruthless intent at building her own fortunes.

'What happened to the money?' Calida asked.

'I spent it.' Julia lifted her shoulders; the fur rose and fell. 'Money is for spending, isn't it?' Bitterness stitched into her voice. 'Oh, it wasn't enough. A couple of years it lasted me, that was all. I've tried to get more. Don't you realise I was rich, Calida, once upon a time? Before your disgusting papa came along and ruined it all.'

Calida took a step closer. 'Don't ever say anything bad about my papa again.'

'I'll say what I like,' Julia exploded, 'you don't know what your precious papa got up to right there under our roof!' Then she gathered herself, as if reminded this wasn't why she was here. 'I mean, *chica*,' she said softly, 'you must understand, it wasn't my *fault*. I didn't want to leave you that day. I had to. I knew our funds would run dry. I had to make more, for both our sakes! I was always going to come back…'

Calida watched her, this pathetic, broken, heartless woman, and felt nothing.

Nothing.

'You've found Teresita?' Calida asked, afraid of the answer.

Julia's eyes lit. 'Oh, I've tried, Lord knows I've tried. What a splendour your sister's become, Calida! She's far too important these days. I haven't been able to get close. I was hoping you might have. Have you? Do you think Teresita will see me?'

'I wouldn't know,' said Calida coldly, her mother's preference as stark and whole as it had been when they were children. 'We're not in touch.'

'I thought she could help me,' Julia babbled. 'Teresita couldn't turn her own mother away, could she? Nor could you, I suspect, not since—'

'Like I said, we're not in touch.'

Julia's disappointment was as false as her attire. 'That's a pity,' she said.

'Teresita made it clear when she left home that I meant nothing to her.'

Julia frowned. Calida wondered if her mother might be drunk. There was a dark patch down her faux-fur collar. Her words slipped over each other.

'Did she?' said Julia. 'I don't recall that.'

'You told me she begged you to let her go. She begged Simone to take her.'

'Really? Oh. Yes. Right. Of course.'

Calida's locket scalded her chest. 'Teresita did say that—didn't she, Mama?'

'Say what, *chica*?'

'That she was ready to go to England. That she was desperate. That she wanted it to be permanent. That is what she said, isn't it? Isn't it?'

Calida saw herself from outside, the rest of the city rushing by, just two friends arguing on the street. But the world was turning upside-down, slowly, slowly.

'I can't think why you're getting so upset,' said Julia, patting her nest of hair. 'How about we go for a late supper, hmm?

Your treat. I'm sure you can't wait to shower your poor mama with a taste of the high life.'

'Answer my question,' said Calida.

'What question?'

'You know damn well what question.' Blood rang in Calida's ears. Her head throbbed. People and sounds passed by like holograms, surreal and meaningless.

'Don't worry, Calida. We'll make your sister see sense. She *is* your twin, after all. We'll find her and then we can all be a family again. See? Easy.'

'Did she say those things, Mama? I need to know.'

Julia weighed her options. Calida's expression must have tipped it, knowing she wouldn't get a single thing out of her until she told the truth.

'No, she didn't,' she said. 'I thought it would be better for you if I told you that. And it was, wasn't it? Look at you now! You've got me to thank for that.'

Calida took a step back. Her knees threatened to buckle but somehow she stayed standing. Julia said: 'So, how about that dinner? Where are you taking me?'

Somehow Calida found the words. An echo of the words Julia had hit her with the last time she had seen her. 'Come now, Mama,' she whispered. 'You're an adult. I've started my new life. You can't expect me to hang around for the rest of my days playing the doting daughter.' And she turned on her heel and didn't look back.

45

New York

'Tess, are you there…? You're breaking up. I can hardly hear you.'

Tess opened the door to her newly purchased Manhattan hideout with a trembling hand, closed the door behind her, twisted the key in the lock and applied the ladder of chains. She flicked the hall light on and leaned, in relief, against the wall.

She was safe. Only then did she allow herself to speak at normal volume.

'Is that better?'

'Yes,' said Simone. 'Are you travelling?'

'I just got in.'

'I thought you had a dinner with Max.'

'We finished early. He went on to a party at Liz Goldstein's house.' Tess went through to the lounge, clicking lamps on as she went. 'I didn't feel like joining.'

Before she unhooked the blind on the final window, she spotted a figure on the sidewalk. The figure was absolutely still. Tess couldn't work out if it was facing her or facing away, so black and total was its silhouette. Fear somersaulted.

It's no one—just a guy out walking his dog.

There was no dog.

The blind fell.

'Tess, you ought to be accompanying Max to things like that,' said Simone. 'Show your face. Show them they haven't got to you.'

Why? What was the point? They had got to her. With poison and threats and the horrible, horrible things they said about her every day. That was why, as the year rolled on and the hate drilled into every part, carrying with it the threat that one day somebody might act on that hate and then where would she be, she'd had to move to New York. Nobody except Simone, Mia, and Maximilian knew the place existed. It had meant she couldn't appoint her usual security: there was nothing like two stacked guys hovering about outside a property to draw unwanted attention—but what good had they done her recently, anyway?

This time she was going it alone. Scarlet would never find her here.

'It's under control,' said Tess. 'I know what I'm doing.'

'What about Steven?'

Tess exhaled. One good thing had come of her exile, at least.

'Steven's agreed to my terms. Clean split. Clean payout.'

'Oh, darling, that's wonderful.'

Didn't she know it? As if she needed further proof, the Scarlet ordeal had exposed her estranged husband in all his true colours. Hearing of her affair with Vittorio, Steven wasted no time in joining the hate wagon against her, using Scarlet's army to fight his battles and conceal his own looming secrets. Naturally, one of the details of the divorce was that Tess could never reveal his fetishes—though now she had been exposed as a cheat and a fraud, no one was likely to believe her anyway. It had been noted in recent months that the couple were rarely seen out together, and now Steven's diligently enigmatic comments drip-fed through the media until the picture was complete: '*Tess was never easy to be with,*' he said; or '*Every time we went out, her mind was elsewhere*'; or '*She was forever making friends and refusing to let me meet them.*' Nothing so overt as to taunt her into revealing his perversions, but enough to make certain their separation had been entirely down to her shortcomings.

Still, Tess couldn't care how it was done. It was over. She was free of him.

And suddenly her ambitions to take over Hollywood, California, the States, the whole world, seemed less necessary than they had. Perhaps it was fearing for her life that had put things in perspective, perhaps it was the realisation that fame and money didn't buy peace. Perhaps it was Alex Dalton, and the memory of their night...

Alex hadn't contacted her. Could she blame him? It had been so long: there could only be one explanation. The media told him what to think and that was that: he would be disgusted by her, thankful for the purity of his bride-to-be, whom, in contrast, he would hold on to like his life depended on it. Tess was sad for what might have been, but reasoning with Alex, trying to make him understand, would shift her betrayal of Mia to new depths. One night she could reconcile as a grave mistake. Telling him she loved him was a deliberate hurt.

Time went on, and whenever Mia called, Tess's heart lodged in her throat. Had Alex confessed? Was this the showdown? But the showdown never came. Her anxiety wasn't helped by Mia's increasing indifference about the wedding, vagueness when asked about Alex, and reluctance to discuss the details of the nuptials. Tess told herself that if Mia had suspicions, she would surely know about them. Mia wouldn't keep calling her up. She wouldn't tell Tess not to care about what the papers said because the people who knew her loved her, and understood she wasn't any of those things.

I am though, thought Tess. *I am a slut and a whore. If only you knew*.

'Well,' said Simone, 'I'm coming to LA. Emily has an audition and I promised I'd go with her. I can fly out and check on you then.'

'Emily… as in *Emily*?'

'Darling, what's important to Lysander is important to me. Emily asked for my help and I told her I'd give it. Now Brian's away, I'm all that girl has.'

'Have you heard from him?'

'Brian's checked into a fat farm—and about time, too. He's mammoth—as big as a house. I mean I always knew he was prone, but now he's let go. The press here is full of it. Brian's full of it, too, by the looks of things: burgers, fries, KFC…'

'I feel for him.'

'Don't. Michelle saw his picture in *GQ*. He was at a bar opening and had some huge-titted wannabe hanging off his arm. Needless to say, he's got an appetite for those as well.' There was a tense moment before Simone asked: 'Did he ever try it on with you, Tess? I've thought about this. The notion appals me. You can be honest.'

'No!'

'I'd hate to think he did anything—all those times you were alone in the house together… Please tell me he didn't. I'll kill him. My duty was always to protect you.'

'He didn't.'

Simone's relief was audible. 'You have no idea what a comfort that is.'

In the wake of another lie—she seemed to be surrounded by them these days—Tess said goodbye and hung up. If only she could be as honest with Simone as Simone was with her. Tess trusted her completely. She'd never had reason to doubt it.

Soothed by that knowledge, that in the midst of this maelstrom there was someone upon whom she could always lean, she settled in for the night.

*

The year of Mia's wedding arrived, and with it a catalogue of disasters. Missing aeroplanes, a drowned ferry, catastrophe on the Gaza Strip… Trauma shook the world and grimly Tess looked on, frightened in the bubble of her own shrunken universe and even more frightened by what lay outside it. She thought of those days on the ranch, with Calida, when the wide earth and everything in it seemed a distant, irrelevant reality. Then, she had felt so far from danger and anger and sadness. Now, they were everywhere.

I wanted to run from that place. I wanted it every day.

But she'd had no clue, then, what she was running towards. She'd been ignorant; a child, a dreamer. If only she'd had a pinch of her twin's good sense.

I miss you, she thought.

I wish you were with me. I really wish you were.

As promised, Simone flew out to meet her, buzzing with news of Emily Chilcott's success on heavyweight Bruce 'Ace' Latimer's casting couch. Since Tess had retreated from the public eye, Simone was doing all she could to maintain the Geddes brand and keep the family on a climbing curve. Her own career had boosted after Lysander-gate, as Simone re-invented herself Demi Moore style, and tonight she was expected at an awards dinner. She persuaded Tess to accompany her.

At the party, Tess kept her head down, aware of the bitchy stares and whispers that followed her round the room. Her affair with Vittorio was leprosy, her exile a dreadful contagion that could slaughter the career of any who came too close. She wished she could find her gold locket, the weight of it round her neck gave her comfort, but to her dismay it was nowhere to be seen. *What have I done with it*? She prickled whenever she thought of it. *How could I have been so careless*?

She counted the minutes until they could leave.

'Oh, wow, Tess...?'

She was emerging from the bathroom when a face she couldn't quite place accosted her in the hall. The woman, a few years older than her, eyed her expectantly.

'Sarah Quentin,' the stranger prompted.

Tess steeled herself for an attack, some reporter who had it in for her.

'Tess—it's Sarah. Remember? From Michelle Horner's office?' The woman smiled, apparently immune to Tess's noxious reputation, and held out her hand.

Carefully, Tess took it.

'I was Michelle's assistant back in London,' Sarah elaborated, 'just after you came over from South America. It seems like an age ago now. That was my first job out of uni. God, I was petrified working for Michelle! But what a great experience.'

Tess was surprised at the connection. She thought back to when she had first landed in the UK. She must have run into Sarah Quentin from time to time during protracted meetings with Simone and Michelle, but hadn't banked her face. Vaguely, she recalled Simone blasting through the mansion and cursing Sarah's name, calling her 'incompetent' and 'a wretched liability'. Soon after, Sarah had been fired.

'Of course,' said Tess. 'What are you doing here?'

'I'm at Laney's office now.' Laney Derrickson was an

author turned screenwriter turned producer, and a great friend of Steven's; Tess had met her once.

'To anyone else Laney would be Boss-zilla,' Sarah said, lowering her voice and draining the last of her fizz. 'But after Michelle, she's a kitten. That woman was terrifying!'

'You never let on.' But Tess wouldn't know if she had or not.

'It didn't help that I kept tripping up,' Sarah continued, 'it being my first proper job and everything.' An actress-slash-model passed them in the corridor and tilted her face away, as if a bad smell had passed under her nose. Sarah didn't appear to notice. 'And Michelle kept saying, "Sarah, you do not want to make mistakes with Simone Geddes because she is my number one client! This adoption is the most important project I've ever worked on!" I was, like, OK, no pressure then!'

Tess was getting the impression that Sarah Quentin was quite loose-tongued.

'And then I messed up big style,' said Sarah. 'Well, you'll know about that. Michelle went ape. Simone demanded I got the sack. Over a fucking letter! Sorry, abysmal language, I'm working on it. But you can tell I'm over it, right? I guess you never get over being fired, and let me tell you it was hard enough convincing—'

Tess cut her off. 'Letter?' she asked, frowning. 'What letter?'

'Oh,' Sarah waved a hand, 'I can't remember. They were always really strict about stuff that got redirected from the office. Simone came in to check every day.'

Tess's mind was working. She wasn't sure towards what.

'Who was the letter from?'

Sarah squinted—then her expression changed, pulled back,

as if realising she had disclosed too much, or that Tess knew too little, or a combination of the two.

'It wasn't important,' she clarified quickly.

'Who was it from?'

Sarah took a moment. Tess saw that she was deciding whether or not to lie.

'Your sister,' she said eventually. 'That was why it was weird, you know, that you weren't allowed to see it. That's why I sent it on, because obviously I thought it was fine, and then the next thing I know Michelle's telling me Simone's thrown a shit fit and I'm packing up my desk. There were others, too, for Simone, for Michelle, but mostly for you. Michelle even got the phones re-routed to her personal line.'

There was a nagging feeling in Tess's throat. Her voice became small.

'My sister wrote to me? She wrote to Simone?'

Sarah seemed to know she had gone too far. 'I'm sorry, Tess. I really think you should talk this through with Simone. It's not any of my business.'

Down the hall, a man called her name.

'I've got to shoot,' she said. 'But let's catch up soon, yes? I'd like that.' Before she left, she hugged Tess warmly. 'Good luck,' she said. 'You deserve it.'

*

They arrived back shortly after twelve. Simone stood at the counter, making tea, her back turned, and when Tess told her she had run into Sarah Quentin, all the muscles there tensed. Simone stirred the tea carefully then put the spoon to one side.

'What did you talk about?' she asked.

'Sarah mentioned working for Michelle. All the letters

and calls she had to field at the office. A substantial number, apparently.'

'Oh?' Still, the back was turned. 'What letters were those?'

'The ones from Calida.' It was strange and magical to say her twin's name out loud after all this time. It felt amazing in Tess's mouth; it was more than words: a song.

Simone's posture changed. Hours before, she had been strutting around Paul Gerhardt's SoHo mansion like a peahen; now, she drooped like a wilting tulip.

Slowly, she turned.

'I did it for you, Tess,' she said quietly. 'I did what was best for you, to protect you. The last thing we needed was your sister wading in and complicating things.'

Tess held her breath. Every question she had kept in check on the drive home surfaced like floats, one after another after another. *Was Calida looking for me? Was she trying to find me? Did she regret what she did?* The possibility was too wonderful and tragic to trust, even for a second. It cracked her already broken heart, reminding her that it was still there, still beating, still whole, and that part of it had and would always belong to her twin alone, whom she loved with all that made her who she was.

Did Calida want me back?

'Darling,' Simone's eyes lifted to her daughter's, brimming with fear and regret, 'ask yourself: what would your life have been without me? You were born a peasant and you'd have died a peasant. I gave you the world. I saw it in that good-for-nothing mother of yours—she coveted what I had. So did you. Julia told me as much. And I said to Julia: I can give your daughter all this, I can take her for you. You said yourself how grateful you are. That you'd have been lost if I hadn't come along…'

'The adoption was your idea?'

'It was Julia's and mine. Together.'

'But not Calida's.' Tess reached for the table behind her, gripping a solid surface, needing to plant herself firm, where the force and implications of Simone's words could not blow her over. *Keep going. Don't stop. Tell me more.*

Simone's skin went blotchy, a rash of red creeping down her neck and into the silk balcony of her gown. 'Not Calida's,' she admitted, her hands splayed in a gesture to be calm. 'Your sister never knew about the arrangement, Tess. I don't know what Julia told her after you'd left but as far as she was concerned it was just a vacation.'

Tess made no sound. Cogs ground to motion in her mind, dust-caked wheels that had been left unused for years. *Calida never knew about the arrangement…*

Simone lifted her chin. 'But then I read in your diary what a terrible fight you'd both had and how in her heart Calida had wanted you gone… So I did you both a favour, didn't I? I made her wish come true—and I did the same for you!'

'You read my diary?' Tess asked in wonder.

'I had to.'

'Why?'

She had a horrifying feeling she already knew.

Simone's patience snapped. 'Because of Calida's fucking fuck-it-all-up letter, that's why!' she exploded. 'She's a tenacious madam, I'll concede her that. I had to throw her off the trail somehow. Look, Tess, I admit, it wasn't right. But I did it for you, for both of you, to put an end to this pointless contact once and for all.'

'You wrote to my sister?'

'It doesn't matter now, does it?'

'It matters to me.'

Simone was steely. 'Yes,' she said. 'I did. I wrote on your behalf.'

Tess didn't need to hear what the letter had said. She thought she would faint. If Simone had found that diary entry, the one about their fight, she'd have had an arsenal of weapons at her fingertips.

'Poor Mama never wrote you, though, did she?' Simone went on. '*She* never called. Admit it—I *was* a better mother to you than that woman! I've been a great mother—I've loved you, cared for you, all the things you thanked me for.'

'Calida didn't let me go.' Tess spoke the words she had experimented with so many times but had been too afraid and upset to sort them into this magical, game-changing sequence. 'She didn't give up. She tried to bring me home.'

'No, sweetheart,' said Simone. 'Your *home* was in London. You had a new life, with me… a new future… I knew any reminders would only upset you.'

'Calida wanted me. You told me she hated me. But she didn't.'

Even after Daniel. *I wish you'd just disappear.*

Calida hadn't meant it. She had forgiven her. They were blood: unbreakable.

What had Calida read in those letters? What had she believed Tess had said? Now, Tess would never have the chance to unpick it… because she was dead.

'She was my sister,' Tess choked. 'My *sister*.'

Simone held her arms out. 'Darling, come to me, let me make it better…'

'NO!' The force of it made Simone stop in her tracks.

'Don't you dare come near me,' Tess seethed. 'Don't you dare touch me. I swear to God, if you touch me I will kill you. You made me believe Calida sold me. That she never loved me. You took away what we had. What we had was special.'

'I know—'

'No, you don't. You can't. You never will. You don't have a sister. You don't know what it's like. She's *in* me. She's *part of* me. That will never change.'

'Sweetheart—'

'Calida died believing I had forgotten about her. That I hated her.'

Simone did stop, then. She stood for a while, observing her daughter's anger, as if she was waiting for it to change into something else, something bigger.

'Tess…' she began.

But Tess shook her head. She could hear no more.

'Get out of my house,' she said.

'You don't understand—'

'I understand perfectly.'

'It's not what you think. What I told you—'

'I don't trust a single word you say. I thought I could, I thought you were the only one, but I was wrong. You're nothing but a cheating, cruel, sad old woman.'

Simone started to cry. 'Tess, you must let me explain—'

'Get out of my house.'

'You're not listening. There's something very important that I have to—'

'GET OUT!'

Seconds passed. Then faintly, Simone nodded. She went to the door, opened it, closed it. Tess sank to the floor and waited for tears, but they didn't come.

Try as she might, she couldn't cry.

46

For somebody so famous, Tess Geddes was a surprisingly easy target.

Too easy, really—it almost took the fun out of it.

Almost.

Outside her New York building, a figure crouched, obscured by shadows. Eyes watched her—cruel, unfeeling eyes, eyes that would show her no mercy.

Like none was shown to me.

A sudden, tantalising glimpse of Simone Geddes before the blind went down. A flash—but it was enough. The figure tensed, clenched fists and cold heart.

Be patient. It will be soon… and it will be sweet.

Tess Geddes thought she was clever, making a run for another city. But she wasn't clever enough. Not to outwit him. As if running would allow the trail to go cold. This trail was hot with anger, an anger that would never cease and never die.

And now the end was close.

All it had taken was research—gratifying how simple it could be with a little ingenuity. The hardest part was the waiting…but that was nothing new. Waiting had been the name of the game for so long; since time began, it seemed. He had always been waiting, since the day he'd been born. Waiting for something that never came.

It had been a long game. He had followed her carefully, watching, discovering, until he knew her inside and out, everything about her life, every last piece. It was essential: to know his prey like he knew himself.

Soon, it would come. *Retribution*.

A few months longer made no difference. If anything, it made it better.

Every second had to be savoured, every instant cradled like a longed-for child.

What better time to do it than the anniversary of that day?

Destiny was approaching… and so was he.

47

It took weeks for Calida to move past the shock. She couldn't get the encounter with her mother out of her head. Seeing Julia again, alive, after so long, had been one thing. Seeing how she hadn't changed a bit, and was still the same selfish, uncaring woman she'd always been, had been another. But Teresita… Learning that her sister hadn't said those things. That she hadn't asked to be taken away. That her mother had lied to her face and made her believe that Teresita was wicked. That was different.

She tried to understand it. Couldn't. She spoke to Lucy.

'So Tess didn't want to go,' her friend repeated. 'Does it change anything? She still stayed in London. She still didn't get in touch in all this time.'

'But she did,' said Calida. 'That letter.'

'There you go, then.'

'Only, it doesn't add up. I wish I could show you the note, Lucy. It was… *evil*. The things she said… I thought at the time that it didn't sound like her, but I was so hurt and it kind of made sense, but now I'm thinking… God, I don't know what to think.'

'What are you getting at? That Tess *didn't* write the letter?'

'What if someone else did?' It was a long shot, a stitching together of possibly unrelated pieces, but once the idea had settled it was hard to shake. 'What if someone found out that we'd fought and wrote all that stuff to make me back off? It worked, didn't it? I decided it was over between us. I decided she'd torn it. And I never looked back... Until now.'

'You're getting ahead of yourself.'

'Am I? Suppose Simone Geddes wrote to me, Lucy. Suppose it was her.'

'That would make her a monster.'

'She'd have justified it. Got over her conscience. Then Teresita never heard from me again and figured I'd forgotten about her. Who knows what she was told?'

Lucy wasn't convinced. 'It's been fourteen years, Calida. Nothing's stopped Tess from coming to you in all that time, has it? At any point she could have returned to where she'd grown up. She could have come looking for you.'

Lucy was right. There was no explanation for her twin having failed to make contact. But she no longer knew which way was up. Her exchange with Julia changed everything. She wasn't sure what to believe.

'Tess must know your name,' said Lucy. 'Cal Santiago is everywhere.'

'And she'd know it was me...'

'Of course she'd know it was you. Why wouldn't she?'

Calida shook her head. She didn't have an answer for that.

*

The season changed, and with it the hate storm against Tess Geddes, rather than lightening, only grew worse. Her sister had vanished off grid, but that did nothing to stop the assault. Calida hoped her twin had refrained from reading what was written about her. Skipped the documentary titled *Tess: The Spectacular Fall from Grace*. Stopped listening to the vicious remarks thrown at her by the very people she had once called her friends.

Calida's heart went out to her. Not just because it was a cruel way for any person to be treated, but also because Calida herself deserved the backlash as much as her sister. She could stand by, the silent observer, no longer. She had to do something.

She had to help.

In the autumn, she made a decision. There *was* someone who could change Tess's fate... someone who could encourage Scarlet to back off.

'You said Tess was a vixen,' said Lucy, watching her pack. 'Why are you so set on protecting her? I thought you'd quit being an older sister?'

'Two minutes older.'

'You know as well as I do it doesn't matter if it's two minutes or two years.'

'This isn't about protection,' said Calida.

'What's it about, then?'

'It wasn't just her with Vittorio. It was me.'

'I think it's about that locket.' Lucy smiled. 'And how even if Tess did all those things you've accused her of, even if you'd never met Julia again and nothing had changed and Tess was still that girl who cast you off and ran away, you'd still go after her. You've always told me how different you are, but I don't think you're so different. How can you be? Life couldn't keep you apart. Vittorio's the proof.'

Calida caught sight of her reflection in the mirror. *Not so different...*

Where once she had met a plain, unexceptional girl, she now saw a woman whose hard-won poise scratched out the lingering contrasts with her twin. Not so alike as to raise suspicions, not identical, never identical, but somewhere close.

Calida's swathe of dark hair and flashing dark eyes were Teresita all over—but equally were her own. She had spent so long trying to prove that she was as good as her twin, and for what? To arrive at the conclusion that, contrary to what she had always assumed, she wasn't fifty per cent of something. She wasn't the cold one, the less attractive one, or the one who never took risks. She was Calida Santiago—a hundred per cent, absolutely, totally and unapologetically, Calida Santiago.

She zipped up her bags, left the apartment, and caught a cab to the airport.

*

The whole way to Europe she dreamed of her sister, the scent of lavender back on the *estancia*, and the wild, warm wind; the horses in the stable, the dusty rides across the prairie, and the candle in their bedroom that they had blown out before sleep.

Fears for Tess plagued her. She worried every day when she woke that she would be faced with that final print: TESS GEDDES ATTACKED.

Calida couldn't explain her feeling, but it was bad; a twin's intuition that something disastrous was coming their way. She had to stop it before it was too late.

Having landed in Stockholm, she hailed a taxi to her assignation. She had been relieved and thankful when Astrid Engberg agreed to meet. If Astrid could convince Scarlet that Tess wasn't the villain, then maybe Scarlet would quit stoking the fire. Maybe she would call her minions off their prey, her people away from the trail, whoever was working for her, terrorising Tess and forcing her from her home.

'Scarlet's hurt,' Astrid told her over their table at the Grand Hôtel. 'And what do you expect? Tess was sleeping with her husband. This is payback.'

'I know.' Calida swallowed her own shame. 'But she made a mistake. Don't you think she's suffered enough? It's been going on too long.'

Astrid sat back. 'What all this to you anyway?'

'Tess is my friend.'

The princess smiled. 'You photographed her, like I arranged?'

'Actually, no,' Calida said. 'She declined.'

Astrid, who wasn't in the habit of badmouthing people, said bitchily, 'Then she really is as stupid as she looks.'

'I want Scarlet to know that Tess is sorry.'

'She told you that?'

'I just know.'

Astrid sipped her tea. 'I'd fall apart if Gustav betrayed me.'

'That's just it, isn't it?' Calida tried. 'Vittorio's all but got away with it. Why isn't he being punished? What about him? Why should the woman get the blame?'

'What Tess did was worse.'

'How?'

'She seduced him.'

'Vitto broke his promise to Scarlet, no one else.'

Astrid made a face, but didn't have a quick response.

'Where will it end?' said Calida. 'What does Scarlet want?'

Astrid shot her a curious look. 'What do *you* want?' she demanded. 'Why are you so interested in Tess Geddes? You were when we met before.'

'It's private. I have my reasons.'

Astrid narrowed her eyes. The princess was no fool.

'Very well,' she said finally. 'I'll speak to Scarlet for you.'

48

Argentina

Daniel Cabrera prepared for his trip. He didn't need much, never had. When he'd left Europe, he had gone with only the clothes on his back. Material things meant little.

It was a risk travelling to America. She was a rich and successful woman now, had built it all from scratch—what would she want with him, still a farmhand, nothing like the men she was used to? She had told him as much. Told him she was in love with someone else. But Daniel Cabrera had said the same thing to her, once, in a café in Buenos Aires. Watched as his words tore her in two. That exchange haunted him—one of the few, precious crossroads in life from which he had taken the wrong path.

He had been lying, then.

He hoped she was lying, too.

Daniel had kidded himself getting married, should never have done it. Calida was the only girl he had ever loved. Nobody else. Nobody else had her soul. Nobody else had her skin. Nobody else had her laugh, or her spirit, or her eyes.

Whatever happened, this was a journey he had to make. Whatever she said, he had to try. He had to try.

People were what mattered. People were the things worth

fighting for: fighting to escape, or fighting to reach. Daniel's first battle had been against his father, a man who would have killed him given the opportunity—or, rather, if Daniel had let him, for his father wasn't a man who took opportunities. Daniel, however, was.

This was a different battle. His opportunity.

Maybe, his last one.

49

New York

'Can I come out and see you?' Mia asked over Skype.

Tess was taken aback by her best friend's appearance. She hadn't seen Mia in a while and thought she looked tired and restless—probably jitters at her wedding being a matter of weeks away. 'Uh, sure,' she said, although at the thought of Mia visiting she was tense. Supposing Mia could tell in her embrace, suppose something slipped, suppose it all came out? *I slept with your fiancé. And now he doesn't want to know me.*

Tess forced a smile. 'Alex won't miss you?'

Mia shook her head. 'He'll be fine.'

Did he ask after me? Does he know you're coming? Tess felt strangled by the things she longed to ask. She was desperate to talk to Alex, knew he would listen, help her, the person to whom she had first told her story, the person who understood.

Simone's treachery haunted her. The same thought kept surfacing like a body in a swamp, the same inescapable thought that could never be assuaged no matter how much time passed: putting herself in her sister's shoes—worn and tattered after hours on the land, while Tess's own were pristine and new, bought from the finest boutique in London—what had gone through Calida's mind as she had lain on that store floor, bleeding to death while the life seeped out of her? Each time Tess thought of it, she crumbled. There was no way back. She would never be able to explain… to say sorry.

'Get a flight tonight,' she encouraged.

Mia nodded, relieved. 'Thanks, Tess… I really need to talk to you.'

They said goodbye. Tess shivered. It was growing dark.

50

The engagement ring was gone. It was the first thing she noticed when Mia entered her building, and Tess's heart sank. This was it, then. The confrontation.

But Mia didn't confront her.

Instead, she accepted the drink Tess fixed, curled up on her sofa and admitted quietly: 'I didn't want to tell anyone. I was ashamed.' A breath. 'Tess, the wedding's off. It has been for ages. Alex and I broke up. I've been pretending ever since.'

Tess didn't know what to say. 'Oh, Mia…'

'It's OK. Do you know something? It's kind of a relief. Finally, to admit it, not just to everyone but also to myself. It was never right. *We* were never right—Alex and me. I knew it from the start.' She winced. 'You'd probably noticed I wasn't exactly on board with the wedding. I was hardly bride of the year, was I?'

'Mia, I'm so sorry.' That was a good place to start. Seeing Mia now, it seemed incredible that she had done those things with Alex, when Mia meant so much to her.

'Don't be. Really. I'm not.'

'What happened?'

'Alex broke up with me when he got back from England.'

Tess swallowed. 'But that was such a long time ago.'

'I know. At first, I was cut up. I didn't understand why, he just said it wasn't working. Alex moved out, took all his stuff. I told him I never wanted to see him again. Days passed and I didn't tell anyone. I was too embarrassed, like it was proof he'd always been too good for me, and the more time went by the less possible it became to admit it. So I made out like the wedding was still on, we were still madly in love—it was only behind the scenes that everything was getting cancelled. I couldn't bear to see my parents' faces, think about Emily and Fifi laughing at me...'

'Mia, don't. You're... I wouldn't change you for the world.'

'But then I realised that was all I cared about—and that was wrong... right?'

'I don't get it.'

'It wasn't *him* I was upset about.' Unexpectedly, Mia smiled. 'It wasn't Alex. I was upset about what everyone would think. I was upset that I wouldn't have this big white wedding, and it wouldn't be to a handsome billionaire whom everyone would envy me over. I was upset that I'd have to suffer the shame of being jilted. But I wasn't upset about him, because... Well, because I didn't love him. I *don't* love him. Not the basis for a lifelong partnership, is it? And if I were really honest, if Alex hadn't done it now, I would have done it down the road. I'd probably have done it on our wedding night—all the festivities finished with and then you're left with the person. Just you and them... it's a big deal, huh? That's why I insisted on the long engagement. I made out it was so everything could be right, but subconsciously, I guess, I was putting it off. I was scared.'

Tess waited. 'I thought you were crazy about him.'

'I was crazy about the idea of him. And, don't get me wrong, there's nothing at all the matter with Alex. He'll make someone a great husband—just not me. The fact is we didn't have anything in common. When I thought about the future, you know, sitting in my old age with my knitting or whatever, talking with a guy and being certain they're my best friend… well, it wasn't him. It's an artist, or a musician, or someone who writes poetry. I don't know, just not him. I sound silly.'

'You don't.'

'I was using him. I used him to get over my childhood. Being fat. Being unpopular. Being a geek. Alex was a finger up to all that. But that was all he was.'

Tess was silent. Mia turned to her.

'What do you think?' she said. 'Am I an idiot?'

Tess spoke cautiously. 'No,' she said. 'Alex wasn't for you. You'll know when the right person comes along—and they will, Mia.'

Her friend put down her drink. She looked Tess squarely in the eye.

'There was someone else,' she said.

Tess didn't breathe.

'I always knew.' Mia watched her carefully, kindly, as sweetly as she had that first day the girls had met in the medical ward at Sainte-Marthe. 'Alex never admitted it, but I knew. Someone else was always on his mind. I felt it. You can feel it, can't you? You can tell when someone isn't in the room with you, when they're looking into you but they're seeing another person, when there's just the two of you and it should feel like the closest thing in the world, but actually there's three. Alex was never into the relationship. He did all the right things and he said all the right things… but he was never in love with me. Not in the way I deserve.'

'You do deserve that.'

Mia took her hand. She was looking at her strangely,

intimately, as only a best friend can. Tess returned her gaze. They stayed holding hands.

'I know,' said Mia. 'And do you know what, Tess? You do, too. After everything you've been through, you do, more than anyone.'

She couldn't speak—and anyway, there was nothing to say.

'You just have to wait and see,' said Mia.

51

Returning to America and the circus of work, Calida found herself impotent. She could only have faith that Astrid Engberg would get through to the heiress but beyond that she had no control. Astrid took Scarlet's side, and why shouldn't she?

November arrived. The city was filled with songs and light. Christmas decorations adorned the buildings and a huge tree sparkled outside the Rockefeller.

Calida hurried through the streets, bundled up in her coat and scarf. She loved being in the thick of it, swallowed up by a flood of people; so different from her humble beginnings, when she couldn't have imagined finding solace in crowds. Now, the masses gave her anonymity. If anything, it was possible to feel more alone in the city than it had been on the ranch. She passed a hot-dog vendor, whose stand smoked salty meat, frying onions, and the sharp tang of mustard, and crossed to Ray's Diner.

Inside, it was warm, the windows damp with the heat of bodies and the bustle of waiting staff as they wound between tables. Conversation hummed and coffee was poured; a bank of TV screens chattered busily above the service counter.

Calida took a booth and ordered pancakes. She pulled out

her tablet and checked CNN. Under the latest, her attention was caught by a headline:

SCARLET SCHUHAUSEN ENTERS U.S. FOR FIRST TIME SINCE RECOVERY.

'*I'm here on a personal matter*,' the socialite was quoted as saying. '*It's time to tie up some loose ends…*' Calida read the piece with mounting apprehension. She didn't even notice when her order came, and let it go cold. Scarlet talked about exorcising her demons, about coming face to face with the people who'd hurt her. She was a woman on a mission. She had been a victim too long. She knew what she had to do in order to move on in her life. And while the rest of the world celebrated in the joy of Thanksgiving, Calida wondered what on earth that meant for her sister.

Please don't hurt her.

Don't let it be too late.

She would never forgive herself. Calida had been ablaze with animosity for so long; it was the only thing that got her up in the morning and allowed her to sleep at night—but now, at the end of things, what did she have to show for it? All that counted, all that had ever counted were the people she'd had at the start. She should never have let Daniel go. She should never have let Teresita go. Regardless of all her twin threw back at her, she should never have given her up. She should have tracked her down years ago, in London, in LA, at the wedding in Barbados, and refused to turn away; she should have stormed into that hospital, ignoring the denial and insisting on her place. She should have said to Teresita: *Here I am; I'm still me. I'm still yours.*

We're still sisters.

She should have let her stupid pride go.

Pride that had lost her Daniel as well...

The irony was that she had known all along. When Julia used to coo over money and status, Calida had known it was an illusion. It wasn't real. She had known.

Calida closed the screen and put her change down on the bar.

If the appeal to Astrid hadn't worked, she would have to face the final frontier herself. *You and me, Tess*, she thought. *It's just you and me.*

Exactly as it had been at the beginning—only this time, they wouldn't be separated. Calida had to find a way through. Find her sister, in some dark room across this city, find her and make her listen. Take her someplace safe, where she wouldn't be hurt, wouldn't be harmed, and then, maybe, just maybe, they could begin again.

52

At the start of December, Mia admitted: 'I'm dreading Christmas. Can we skip it?'

'What do you mean?'

'Just get away for a while—you and me. My parents will kill me but a family celebration is the last thing on my mind. Having to explain to everyone for the millionth time about Alex and the wedding, I'm sick of raking it over... Come on, Tess, say yes.'

Tess considered it. She was tired of being trapped in her building, frightened of going out and hating staying in, where she spent her days avoiding Simone's calls and praying for Alex's... which never came. Just because Alex had split with Mia didn't mean he wanted to be with her. Otherwise, he'd have got in touch. Wouldn't he? He'd never got in touch. His silence spoke volumes. It had all been a mistake.

New York at Christmas, with its laughter and lights and families, was an uninviting prospect. What about her family? One was dead. The other might as well be. Escaping with Mia could be the answer: string out the avoidance tactic a while longer. And then, after that, who knew? Perhaps 2015 would bring new things. New starts. She had to believe it. 'OK,' she said, warming to the idea. 'Yes.'

'Yes!' Mia grabbed her tablet. 'Where can we go?'

'We could head back to Europe. Paris, maybe, or Spain…'

Mia wrinkled her nose. 'How about this?' she said, showing Tess the screen.

Tess shrugged. 'Seems fun. Anywhere that isn't here, I'm happy.'

Her friend beamed. 'You won't regret this, Tess, I swear. One thing, though: it'll be total cut off—no phones, no internet, nothing. If I'm running away, I'm running away.'

Tess couldn't think of anything better. 'That sounds good to me,' she said.

53

The man prepared diligently. Everything had to be planned to perfection.

The luxury apartment he would use as a prison wasn't his; he would never be able to afford this kind of thing—but it seemed an appropriate place to do it, right in this living room, right in this hall. Knowing the place was vacant, he had broken in and spent hours with her belongings, using her bath salts, sleeping in her bed, the pillow pressed to his chest; scanning her photographs, photographs with that *bitch* in, and searching her expression for remorse, a glimmer of remorse, and finding none.

She would soon show remorse when he had a knife to her throat.

Now, he laid out his tools. He was shaking, which made it take longer, but there was a certain pleasure in delay. He concentrated on breathing slowly, harnessing his energy, as he might before a sexual climax. This had to be measured.

He could not blow it now—not when he was so close.

The man dressed in darkness. With each garment, he became the person he needed to be: the person who would lure her to his den. He wanted to practise ahead of the event, get a feel for his costume and what lay ahead. From inside his case, he withdrew a pair of leather gloves and strapped them on, snug as a surgeon's as they popped around his wrist. They smelled of antiseptic and the smell was delicious.

With a final glance in the dim, dusk-mottled mirror, the man turned the key in the door, as easily as if he were leaving his own home.

In a way, this was his home… It was his by rights.

All of this should have been his by rights.

He stepped outside. It started to snow.

54

Daniel landed in New York to the blaze of Christmas. Exiting the airport, a giant Santa greeted him on a bright-red billboard; trees glistened and snow lay thick on the ground; crowds swarmed and a choir of carol singers shook collection buckets.

The air was chill and bitingly fresh. He hadn't boarded a plane since fleeing Europe and had thought that was appropriate—that both times marked a pivot in his life, a springboard that led him to change. Come to think of it, both times had led him to her.

He spent the night in a cheap motel, before contacting her workplace. His English wasn't good and he knew as he made the request that it would not be granted.

Instead, he waited outside XS Studios, until on the third day he saw her.

When he did, Daniel knew he would go a whole lifetime blind for one glimpse of her face. Calida was glamorous, but in the essential ways she was the same. Still that shy girl with the horses, her soul buried on the land, her hands stained with soil, her chin lifted against the wind and rain, his wild Argentinean gaucha.

Some days Daniel rode over the mountain and visited the *estancia*, to see how it was doing. The American who'd bought it had employed a team to restore it to its former glory. He couldn't wait for Calida to see it. The way the American had rebuilt it was astonishing, faithful to its character and origins, faithful to a time, Daniel guessed, before Diego Santiago's death. Before it fell apart. It had come back to life with eternal dignity, so many details the same, as if the American had heard a whispered story about what it was like and taken it on as a personal vocation.

Daniel dreamed of one day being able to buy the ranch back for Calida. He knew that this dream was impossible. He was a good man, but he was without means.

His car pulled out after hers.

What would she say when she saw him? Would she give him a chance? Would her lover be there? Would she turn him away?

Daniel had to make her believe.

He had put his trust in her, once. Now it was her turn to do the same.

Doubt gnawed once more.

What have I got to offer her? Me... Only me.

But that was one thing he could give without reserve.

He was tense by the time they pulled up at her home. As Calida walked inside, Daniel gathered his nerve. *You'll remember this. You will.*

He was about to get out when, moments later, Calida re-emerged from the building and jumped back in her car. Daniel frowned. Where was she going?

Calida gunned the ignition. She wore an expression of sheer determination—and also fear, as if she was about to do something drastic.

The engine revved. He had no choice but to follow.

55

The man swerved his van, the steering wheel spinning in his hands before he pulled himself together and regained control. *Easy*, he told himself. *Easy does it.*

It was hard not to get carried away, to press a little firmer on the gas; try to replicate in the external world the racing adrenalin that flickered through his blood. *Crash this baby and it's over. Kaput.* No, he had to be careful. He had planned his whole life for this and finally it was here, this night, the night of his vengeance.

The night when her world came crashing down, never to be reassembled.

The man pulled up at a red light. His fingers were shaking. It wasn't like him to freak out—normally he was so composed. Everyone at work said it. The IT department where he kept himself to himself, nervous and timid, the sweet, crisp-collared data genius who was never late, who never failed to complete a task, who all the girls wanted to look after because he was so thin and pale and afraid.

Tonight, I'm invincible. You should see me tonight.

Marissa—that was the name of the girl he liked.

The man closed his eyes and inhaled sharply, imagining her next to him, urging him on. Marissa never glanced his way; she was too pretty to notice him. This worked in his favour because it meant he could follow her home—just like he had been following Tess Geddes—and watch from the gloom as she undressed for a shower, spying her naked body; a taste was enough to make him tremble and shudder. He would stagger home, exhilarated and excited, his underpants damp.

After tonight, Marissa would notice him. Yes, she would. She would call him a hero. She would climb on top of him in front of everyone and fuck his brains out.

The beep of car horns shook him from his reverie.

The lights turned green.

His van sped forward with a squeal. The man clocked a police car lurking on a corner and slowed, sweat breaking out on his brow. Now the outcome was close enough to touch, he could risk nothing in pursuit of glory. The last thing he needed was a cop pulling him over and checking his history.

Under the radar, that was his motto. *Stay hidden*.

For the hundredth time, he checked he had everything. The plan. The gloves. The rag soaked in chloroform. Everything down to the voice he would use.

Almost there.

You're mine now, Tess Geddes. You're a dead woman.

Snow whirled violently against the windscreen, diamond flakes from a dark, dark sky.

56

Calida joined the downtown traffic. Now she was actually doing it, now that the moment was here, she felt unexpectedly calm. Her sister's hideout had been easy to find. Calida had hired an agency and within twenty-four hours they delivered the address.

Who else could have found it?

Could Scarlet have found it?

Astrid had called from Sweden. '*Scarlet's plotting something. I don't know what. We have to act.*'

The thought of Vittorio's ex-wife wasn't what terrified Calida. Somehow she couldn't picture Scarlet exacting revenge; she was too frail, too wounded. It was more the thought of a hired pair of hands, some gangster deployed by Scarlet's family, or some maniacal fan wanting to act on Scarlet's behalf, his fingers closing around her twin's purple, swollen throat. Every face Calida passed sent a current up her spine.

For a while, she became convinced there was a car following her.

Don't be silly. Why would anyone be following you?

But she sped up to lose them all the same.

When she reached her sister's building, she was astonished at how ordinary it looked. Where was her security? Where were the gates and wires and spot bulbs? Was this even the right place? But the address confirmed it was. Admittedly, it drew zero attention, but how was Teresita sleeping at night? Her sister had hated the dark when they were little, scared of the monsters and shadows that hid in the corners of their simple dwelling. In some way, Teresita had returned to that simplicity. She had cast off the rich sparkle of her Hollywood life and come back to her youth.

Calida climbed out of the car and on to the abandoned street. Somewhere, a dog barked. Snow came down hard, giant flakes sweeping through the tunnel of street lamps, skimming and settling on the road. With disappointment, she realised her sister's house was deserted. The lights were off. It was still, quiet, dark.

A whistling funnel of wind howled a ghostly cry.

Calida watched the empty windows, staring back at her like unseeing eyes.

Checking behind, making sure she was alone, Calida scaled the fence. She dropped down the other side, stealthy as a cat, and felt a rush at finally being on her sister's territory. So close… but where was Teresita?

A horrid thought overtook her that someone had beaten her to it.

Be OK. Please be OK.

The same thought she'd had as when they had raced to Diego's death—but this wouldn't end like that. This couldn't. Calida would know if something bad had happened. She would feel it. She would know.

There was only one option. Calida lifted a rock and hurled it through the window. The glass smashed. She braced herself for the whine of an alarm—but none came. Breathing heavily, she advanced to the window and climbed through.

57

In the hall was a clock that had stopped. Its second hand ticked uselessly on the spot, the same instant repeated and repeated. Nine p.m. Friday, 19 December.

Calida went into the bedroom, careful not to put any lights on, and quickly her eyes adjusted to the dark. Teresita had decorated sparingly. On the dresser was a photo frame, turned down. Calida lifted it and met Simone Geddes, smiling back at her. There was a pebble on her sister's bedside cabinet. Calida picked it up and held it in the palm of her hand. Without needing confirmation, she knew it was from home.

A sound. She jumped.

But it was only the snow hitting the window, and the cool, icy gust coming from the hall, where she had broken in. The slushy rush of car tyres passing…

Calida pulled open the closet. Inside, it was scant, most of the hangers bare, as if Tess had left in a hurry. She reached in and let a fabric dress slide off its mooring.

Holding it to her face, she inhaled its scent. Washing powder on top of something else, something deeper and more obscure; a fundamental scent that belonged in Teresita's hair, behind her ears and in the hot, clinging arms that locked around Calida's waist when they hugged good night.

In the dark, Calida could almost have been her twin. Her

hair had grown out, about the same length as Tess's, curling round her shoulders and down her back. Their figures were the same, their faces similar.

Without knowing why, Calida peeled off her clothes and dropped the dress over her head. She wanted to wear Tess for a moment. See how it felt in her skin.

58

The man parked out of sight.

From the glove compartment, he seized his binoculars, held them up to his face. He cursed the snow that swirled in his vision, obscuring the apartment from view. Lights all off. *Fuck.* Was she out? He would hang tight.

What were another few minutes, after decades of hate, after years spent hunting her down?

Cunt.

His fingers tingled with the anticipation of touching her. Perhaps he would have some fun first—he hadn't decided. She was very pretty. Prettier than Marissa, even… Before Tess Geddes gave her life, she would give her body. Willingly. She would want it. It had been so long since he'd had a woman. He imagined her breasts and what they would feel like. Cupping them in his hands…

Before he slit her throat.

An involuntary gasp escaped the man's lips. Shaking, he lowered the binoculars. The anticipation was too much to bear.

Hold on. Patience.

He would catch her. It was like fishing. Endurance. Calm.

Hook her in and bring her aboard, flailing, helpless, bright-eyed with panic. He couldn't sit still with the adrenalin; his whole body was tense.

Then, there was movement. A swell of light; a door opening, a shape…

Caught off-guard, the man fumbled for his kit. There was no time to think, no time to prepare, but that was OK—he had practised this a thousand times.

He unlocked the cab and swung down on to the street.

59

The light startled Calida. On opening the front door, she must have flicked a switch, illuminating the porch. At first she panicked that a siren was preparing to shriek, but there was nothing. Just silence. A second later, the light died.

She had come away with a lead. A number scrawled on a piece of paper, found in her sister's room among a jumble of keys and notes:

Mía ☺ 444-823-9145

Calida tucked the number in her pocket and crossed the street to return to her car.

As she did so, she noticed an old man struggling to get a parcel into the back of his van. He was heaving, fighting to lift it, and stopped to lean on the tailgate.

'Are you all right?' she asked, approaching him in the dark. Her street smarts prickled but then she saw his face—it was honest and open, hopeful.

'Would you help me?' the man asked.

His voice struck an odd chord, like a flat note in a piano piece.

He was old. That was all.

In the gloom, Calida tried to make out how old. It was hard. He was hunched, almost farcically so, like a dame in a pantomime. He wore a long and heavy coat.

'Of course,' she said.

It was Christmas. If she couldn't help someone at Christmas, when could she?

'Let me take this end.' Calida heaved under the weight of the box; it was several feet long and heavy. 'What have you got in here?' she joked.

'Christmas presents.'

'For your family?'

His face was now completely engulfed by dark.

She wondered how clearly he could see her. Not very, she suspected.

'Yes,' he said. 'For my family.'

The man lifted the other end and stood in front of her. Calida's back was to the open van and it made sense for her to step inside. A tinge of unease told her not to, but she quashed it: the evening had set her on edge, and little wonder. This man was a kindly father wishing to get his kids' toys home to put under the tree.

She backed into the van.

'There,' she said, setting it down, 'got it.'

'Could you push in a little further?' the man called. He put a hand to his lower spine, as if it was hurting. 'Right in there… That's it.'

She only turned for a moment. He must have moved like a gazelle. That heavy, unambiguous tread as his foot descended on the suspension, the bulk of his presence behind her. Then the smell… The cloying smell…

A cloth was jammed to her nose and mouth. He held her

to him in an iron-vice grip and his breath was sour in her ear. 'There, there,' he groaned. 'That's the way…'

Calida collapsed. The world vanished in a pinch of absolute black.

60

Five blocks away, Daniel quit his car and wandered the streets on foot. He cursed himself for having lost Calida. She drove like the wind, weaving in and out of traffic; it had been all he could do to keep himself on the road.

Now what was he going to do?

He was beginning to lose hope when, a little way down the street, he saw a face he recognised. It was so out of context in this strange new city that Daniel did a double take, and even then thought he must be mistaken.

But, he wasn't. The face recognised him too.

'Señor Cabrera?'

The American began walking towards him.

Up close, he was just as surprised as Daniel was.

'What are you doing here?' asked the American.

The last time Daniel had seen this man was when he had sold him their farm. He had thought of the stranger so many times, sent like an angel into their lives, and now he was here, standing in front of him, a kind, inquisitive expression on his face.

'I'm looking for someone,' said Daniel.

'That makes two of us,' said the American.

Daniel wished he could remember his name—but then he

didn't need to, because the American held out his hand and offered it up.

'Alex Dalton,' he said. 'Pleased to meet you again.'

NYchronicle.com/News/US-News/Tess-Geddes-disappearance
Live Feed, 10.31AM:

Concerns are mounting over the disappearance two nights ago of Hollywood superstar Tess Geddes. Ms Geddes was last seen leaving her New York home at 21:00 on Friday 19 December and no contact has been made with her since. The vanishing is described as 'out of character', despite the actress's turbulent history. Friend and co-star Natalie Portis released this short statement yesterday: 'Tess is a fighter. We knew she'd suffered the year from hell—but she knows better than that. She wouldn't do anything stupid.'

It emerged this morning that Ms Geddes was accompanied by an unidentified female companion on the night of her disappearance. Police are now engaged in a hunt for this person, and witnesses are urged to come forward.

Calida was aware of movement. The road dashed beneath them, slick and wet, and she thought of melting snow, a running engine, rumbling and final.

Her head felt heavy and there was a strange, metallic smell. She couldn't move. Panic fluttered, fast and hectic in her ribcage like a trapped bird. Up front, a shape was hunched, a horrid set to his shoulders of uncompromising intent—and more: pleasure. Exhilaration. He could not wait to reach the place he was going. He had longish hair; she could see it against the light coming through the windshield.

Who are you? Where am I?

Calida could feel the phone in her pocket, on autopilot fumbled for it and desperately tried 911. It bleeped the disconnection. Then she remembered the other digits, the ones she had taken down as she had left Tess's place.

Easy to find, even through her addled brain. Recent additions.

Bingo.

She felt the phone spring to life.

Mia. Whoever you are, please pick up. Please pick up. Please.

Calida groaned. She tasted chemicals at the back of her throat, and retched.

He heard her. Too quick, too sudden, he reached into the back and a hard object slammed into her head. The black world consumed her whole.

63

Barcelona

In a top-floor studio off La Rambla, Tess and Mia disappeared off the face of the earth. Tess disconnected her phone, ignored the Wi-Fi and avoided going online.

Just the getaway they'd sought.

Barcelona was magical, shot through with dazzling lights. The women got lost in the teeming crowds that bustled through the city. They visited the Sagrada Familia and saw a show at the Gran Teatre del Liceu. They climbed Montjuïc and ate in late-night tapas bars, and listened to live music until the sun came up.

One morning, as the women stumbled home, Mia couldn't stop talking about a Spanish painter she had met called Gabriel. Tess said, 'You like him, don't you?'

Mia couldn't suppress the glint in her eye. 'Do you think Alex has moved on?' she asked, but it was more an appeal for permission than an enquiry.

'I don't know,' said Tess, the words leaden in her throat.

The thought of Alex moving on made her ache, the same ache she had felt when she'd seen him at her wedding, when he'd held her before her car accident, when he'd become engaged to her best friend. It was stupid. She was drunk.

Alex wasn't interested in her any more. The Vittorio scandal would have put paid to that. *Pirate, you're not the girl I thought you were...*

Alex's smile darted into her head. The firmness of his chest when she had first met him, bumping into him and spilling her drink down his shirt. Their journey back to Madame Comtois and the jacket he had left behind. She still had that jacket somewhere; it had never occurred to her to part with it.

'I do like Gabriel,' Mia confessed, unable to keep the smile off her face. 'We talked all night. You know when you meet someone and it's so easy to be yourself? Easier than you thought it could be. There must be a word for that.'

'Soul mates.'

She remembered what Alex had said to her at her wedding to Steven Krakowski. She had been so mad with him then, but the reason she'd been mad was because he spoke the truth. He spoke to something inside that no one else could see.

You can't deny where you came from. It's inside you.

It's part of you.

All this time, Tess had thought she was unable. That she would never love a man—she was too damaged. Love was a trap only fools fell into.

Then she guessed that made her a fool. Because the men had been wrong so far, not her. She had met the love of her life when she was fifteen.

Mia elbowed her. 'Don't be dumb.' But she was grinning.

The women fell asleep around six, and didn't get up until midday.

Mia had resurrected her phone short-term while she hoped that Gabriel would call. Next door, ringing silent and on the last bar of its power, it flickered to life, an unidentified number flashing across the screen.

64

New York

Usually, when Simone Geddes felt as downright abysmal as this, she would check into rehab. Now, she couldn't check into rehab. Nowhere could numb the pain.

Tess was lost.

Her daughter had vanished. Every place, every corner, was demonic.

'Simone, how are you coping? Have you heard anything?' Reporters harassed her everywhere she went—and none worse than when she touched down at JFK.

I don't know! Simone wanted to yell. *Stay away from me*!

It occurred to her what they wanted to hear: that Tess was dead. That would satisfy them, wouldn't it—the hungry, circling vultures, their appetites sated until a fresher story came along? They had driven Tess to this. They had ruined her.

It was their fault.

Simone was in hell. She was sick with worry and dogged by guilt. The last words she and Tess had spoken had been in fury. She understood her sin—oh, she knew it too well. She understood the truth and it made her weep.

Just as her child had been taken from her, so Tess had been

taken without her consent. Simone was responsible for ripping a family in two—just the same as hers.

Tess and her twin should never have been parted.

Ultimately, blood was strong as steel. It could not be broken. It could be diluted, kept apart, separated for years on end, but it would always find its way back. Blood defied death; it was the unbreakable, eternal bond, and she should know that better than anyone. She, who had given up her child, her son; her newborn baby...

I'm sorry, Simone thought. *I never meant to hurt you.*

She didn't know whether she meant it for Tess or her baby.

That letter she had written, the cunning she had been so proud of but now felt terrible about. The heinous lie she had told about Calida and Julia's death—not that Tess was any the wiser about that—and its revelation would sever them for good. What had she been thinking? She was a different woman today from the woman she'd been.

If only she could turn back time...

Back to when she visited Argentina; she would be honest with Tess, tell her the truth and on that foundation they would build their union. Because blood was only half the battle—trust was the rest. Now she had broken that, where could they go?

Where are you, Tess?

Back to her grandparents' attic: she would snatch her baby back and tell them she was surrendering him over her dead body. They would have to kill her first.

Why didn't I do that?

I was fifteen. I was scared. I was a child myself.

Nothing was any comfort. Simone had created a nightmare and was caught in its whirling, sinister epicentre; not knowing which way was up.

Please come home, Tess. Please come back.

Simone wished that Christmas and all its attendant festivities could fuck off as she made her way to the old apartment she still owned off Broadway. It wasn't much of a place, disused for most of the year, but Tess knew it. Maybe she would be there.

It was a long shot. Really, it was impossible.

But an unseen force drew Simone to that door. Blood—or something like it.

65

Alex and Daniel aided the police investigations as best they could.

'You knew Tess?'

'You grew up with Calida?'

It was always in the past tense, as if they were fielding polite enquiries at a funeral. Neither dared to voice the fear that it wouldn't be enough.

'Why were you at Tess's house?'

Both had the same reason, just different women. Love.

Calida would have been on her way there, Daniel realised, when he lost her trail. He had tried calling her but she must have changed her number.

'Do you think she's with Tess?'

'I don't know,' said Daniel.

'Has anyone heard from the twin?'

'No, chief,' said an officer. 'We didn't even know she had a twin.'

'Seems like nobody did. Get on the phones, McCarthy.'

Alex had been on his way to see Tess. They'd been together in the past, he said. He had only ever loved her. And now she was gone.

Outside the station, Daniel flicked out a packet of cigarettes and offered Alex one. 'Teresita… she's why you bought the farm, isn't she?'

Two sisters, poles apart by misunderstanding, and two men, from separate walks of life—but somehow, in this place, not so different after all.

'Yes,' said Alex.

'Why didn't you tell her?'

'I was going to. I tried. But she didn't want to know. Until the night we got together, she was… I don't know, she was stubborn—'

'She's certainly that.'

'She got married to someone else.'

There was a long silence. They both had regrets.

'What was she like as a girl?'

A smile lifted one corner of Daniel's mouth. 'Difficult.'

Alex smiled too. 'And Calida?' he asked.

The smile faded. 'She was my friend.'

The men smoked.

'I wish I could tell her,' said Alex. 'I'd do anything to tell her now, take her home and show her it's all still there—that her sister's there, too. She was so cut up about Calida. To see her, to hold her, to make it better… I know I could.'

'There are things I'd like to tell Calida, too.'

Alex put a hand on Daniel's shoulder.

'You will,' he said. 'We both will.'

66

'*Say good night, sister.*'

The blade touched the tender skin on her throat. Calida thought of Christmas unfolding outside, of joy and laughter and lights. That was the last thought she had.

Not yet.

Only it wasn't her voice, this time. It was Teresita's.

They were girls again. Outside the ranch, on the wooden veranda...

Don't go yet. Come back. Come back...

The words she had longed to yell at Teresita's departing car that day when she'd left. Forget our fight. It doesn't matter. Don't go; please, don't go...

It happened fast. Suddenly Calida's wrists were freed, worked from their ties, and with a last fist of strength she pushed against her assailant. For a second she thought she might be dead, departing her useless body and heading for the skies. The propulsion of his weight across the room told her she was not.

She was alive. She was strong.

Shock stalled him.

'*WHORE!*'

The man came towards her. In a flash, Calida's fear was replaced by fury.

How dare you do this to me? Who the hell do you think you are?

Then another question:

Who do you think I am?

In her heart, she knew. The van outside Teresita's house, the dress she was wearing from her sister's closet, the stalker her sister had sensed at her back...

The man swiped at her but he was too slow. Calida tore the gag from between her teeth and spat in his face. He was shuddering now, his eyes wide and darting, floundering at having lost control. How could she have thought he was an old man? He was barely in his fifties, still powerful, still capable of hurting her.

'You'll pay for that,' the man snarled, thrusting against her.

Calida tasted fear. She could feel the man's stiffness pressed against the inside of her thigh, and choked. 'Get off me!' she screamed. But it was no good. He was rubbing himself against her, grunting like a pig. His hand snaked under her clothes and touched her bare skin. Wildly, she recoiled. Vomit surged up her throat.

'Get away from me!'

He would not be deterred. Calida thought fast.

The knife. In his desire, he had forgotten about it.

The blade glinted on the dark floor and she pounced. Before the man could react, she slashed his leg. With a wet, stunned gurgle, he collapsed.

Calida slashed him again, and again, and again.

He had shown her no mercy.

She should kill him.

'You did a bad thing to me,' she rasped, her words—his words—spitting from her lips like fire. 'I don't like people

doing bad things to me. If someone does a bad thing to me, I
have to do a bad thing back.' She raised the knife.
  'But first,' she said, 'tell me who you are.'
  She needed to know.
  'Tell me who you are before I kill you.'

67

Barcelona

On Christmas Eve, Mia called her parents. 'They'll murder me if I don't!' she protested, but they both knew she'd powered her phone to see if Gabriel had texted.

Tess was in the shower when Mia started banging on the door.

'What is it?' Tess turned the water off.

'I'm not sure,' came Mia's voice. 'Get out here.'

Tess dried and wrapped herself in a towel. She opened the door, hair dripping.

'What's happened?' she asked. She thought of Béatrice and Anton. 'Mia?'

Mia shook her head. She was icy pale. 'I'm not sure what it is.' She handed over her phone. 'I went online. Apparently, you've been kidnapped.'

Tess scanned the item. 'Of course I'm missing,' she said. 'I'm here.'

'Yes, but look.' Mia scrolled across. 'There.'

Tess read:

MYSTERY VAN NEW LEAD IN GEDDES VANISHING.

Investigations into the disappearance of troubled Hollywood starlet Tess Geddes gained new momentum today following eyewitness reports that cited Ms Geddes climbing into an unmarked van outside her New York building on Friday night. Witnesses report a woman matching Ms Geddes' description conversing with an unknown male, before departing in his vehicle. Ms Geddes' friends and family have expressed acute concern over her disappearance five days ago, saying it is 'entirely out of character'.

'Shit,' said Tess.

'You need to go back. They think something's really happened to you!'

'But this is crazy. What are they talking about? Who got in what van?'

'Simone will be going out of her mind—you have to get in touch.'

Tess took Mia's phone, and noticed she had a series of missed calls from an unidentified number. Thinking it must be Simone, she dialled straight back.

She held the phone to her ear and waited.

Mia was right. It was time to go home.

68

New York

'*I'll* tell you.' The man choked against the knife blade, his eyes alight with wicked satisfaction: at last, a chance to assert his identity. '*If you dare...*'

Calida held the dagger to his throat, the tip tickling the thin skin covering his windpipe. He had a pronounced Adam's apple. She asked herself if she could slice through it if she must and the answer was yes. Just as Diego had slaughtered the guanaco because it was right: to put a hopeless thing out of its misery.

Her wrist cramped with her refusal to budge. The man's leg was hurt but otherwise he was strong. He hadn't been drugged, like her. He hadn't been starved, like her. But she had the weapon. She had to stay in control. '*Talk.*'

The man gulped. His throat bobbed moistly.

'My name is Martin Gallagher,' he said. There was a pause, as if this name should mean something, but it didn't. 'But that wasn't the name I was born with.'

Calida waited. The knife-tip didn't move.

'My old name was David Geddes.'

That did mean something. She just wasn't sure what.

'My mother is called Simone,' he said, and the bitterness in *his words frightened Calida more extremely than anything else he had done to her. 'She gave me away. When I was a baby, she gave me away and left me for dead. She didn't care what happened to me. She was a girl, then, and I know what excuses she would bring. Do you think those excuses mean anything to me? Do you think they make* any *fucking* difference?*' He bared his teeth. 'If anything, they make it worse.'*

Calida's mind raced. You think I'm Tess.

That's why.

This has nothing to do with Scarlet Schuhausen. It's always been you.

Simone. Tess. You.

'The people who took me were cruel and careless. They didn't want me. Nobody wanted me. And it wasn't enough that she gave me up. She helped herself to another child when it suited her. Never mind about me, or the fact I wasn't ready. I wasn't ready to be born, wasn't ready to live, but when she *was ready—that was fine. So she adopted you.' Hate infected his words. 'She gave you everything. More than I would ever have asked for. All I needed was the love of my mother.* My mother.*'*

You think I'm Tess. You think we're the same.

It was in Calida to blurt the truth—right there, waiting on the back of her tongue. But the words didn't come. She couldn't say them.

'Simone didn't love me enough to keep me,' he spat, 'but she was willing to love someone else. All that crap about giving a child a home, had she given me one? *Had she given a second thought to the home* I *ended up in? I lived with brutal people. People who made me do things I didn't want to do. I've never recovered from that.'*

Calida's grip was loosening on the knife. She felt pity, and

*with pity came weakness. 'How was I to know?' she murmured.
'It wasn't my fault.'*

*'It never is, is it, Teresa?' He sensed her waning and his
eyes hardened. 'That's your real name—just a dirty, poor little
girl who hit the jackpot. That was my jackpot. It was my prize.
Simone was my mother—not yours.'*

He moved like a snake, quick and lethal.

The knife fell from her hands.

69

Simone stepped inside her Broadway apartment. There was an awful aroma.

What on earth...?

It was so long since she'd been here. Hollywood friends occasionally used it, Lysander when he was in town and keeping a low profile—and it occurred to her that she should have taken better care of it. Installed it with a proper alarm, for starters.

I've been burgled.

Dread notes hit her one after the other—the open window, the trashed ornaments, the torn curtains and the bombsite of the living room.

Everything was wrecked. Chairs tipped over, drawers opened and emptied, shelves kicked in, picture frames smashed. Simone's eyes flew from one assault to the next, appalled at the crime. Whoever did this didn't just want her cash; they wanted to hurt her. They *hated* her. Terror washed over her, cold and prickling.

She heard a sound upstairs. A scuffle; a creak on a floorboard...

And a man's voice, a boy's voice; a voice she had never heard, and yet…

A voice she knew.

*

Calida was thrown on the floor, helpless as a ragdoll. She felt her grip desert her, and exhaustion take over. How long have I been here? *A day, two, three? She was hungry. Thirsty. Spent. Her mouth was dry and her ears were ringing.*

I need to sleep. Go to sleep now.

She could still taste the drugs, her insides raw, shutting down inch by inch.

I tried. I'm sorry. It's over.

He would think he had got her. He would leave Teresita alone.

It's over.

The man was laughing. He reclaimed the knife; glad at his confession and the effect it had wrought, mightier than ever now that the truth had spilled free.

Then, abruptly, he stopped.

His head snapped up, flat as the hood of a cobra. He could hear something.

Sounds from outside the room, all around, beneath, above, like angels.

A door clicking shut. The steady tread of footsteps.

The man turned, his attention caught.

It's too late. I need to sleep.

Calida closed her eyes. The last thing she saw was the lost expression in his eyes. Like a child to its mother's call, he turned and went towards the light.

*

A faint buzzing stirred her. It shouldn't have happened; her cell should be as dead as she was. Calida reached for it. She could barely see, barely hear, barely breathe.

The screen was lit. Mia.

Calida held it to her ear but couldn't speak.

Instead, she listened.

So did the person on the other end.

Then, the person said:

'Hello?'

*

'Mother?'

As if in a dream, he stepped out to meet her.

Their eyes met across impossible gloom. He held a knife.

Simone knew without any doubt who the man was. How could that be, when so many years had passed, when she had last seen him as a baby?

But she did.

She reached for him, but not quick enough.

'Mother… it's you…'

'It's me,' she choked.

'Where have you been?'

Simone opened her mouth. No words emerged. The scene defied definition and her addled brain worked to slot it all together—the wrecked apartment, the weapon, Tess going missing—but she was terrified of the picture it made.

'No,' she pleaded, 'what are you—?'

It was too late. As she reached him, he lifted the blade and plunged it between them, sinking through flesh. Two hearts, racing next to each other.

One of them pierced.

One of them stopped. .

Simone choked, slumped forward, the wet spill of blood as it seeped inside out, silent and scarlet, and they seemed to catch each other, together at birth and together in death, it was only the part in between they had missed.

Calida would know that voice anywhere. Any time, any place, across thousands of miles and thousands of ages, she would know it for all time in her soul and her dreams, the place she had come from and the place to which she was going.

'*Teresita*,' she whispered back.

There was a sob, solitary and deep: a sob not from the throat but the heart. Calida had never heard a heart do anything but beat and break. Hearts cried too.

'Calida?' The last part crumbled away. Then she heard crying, proper crying, the kind that only children do, uncontrolled and unembarrassed and without restraint. Disbelief ran to fear to ecstasy, and her sister sounded very far away, as if her voice, her weeping, was reaching her down a tunnel. As if Teresita was calling her across the Patagonian steppe, against the wind and dust. 'Calida, is that you?'

'It's me.'

'Say something,' she cried, 'Say anything, just talk to me—'

'It's me. It's OK, Teresita… It's me.'

Calida couldn't make out the next bit. Something about if it was a joke, if it wasn't real, it couldn't be real because Calida was…

Dead?

I'm not dead... Am I?

'Remember Paco?' Calida managed, her eyelids heavy as hot tears fell. *I'm sleeping. This is a dream.* But she wanted to dream it a while longer. 'Remember Papa? Remember the lavender? Remember the stables, and the shadows on the wall?'

'She told me you were dead.'

I am. Am I?

'I'm coming for you.' Teresita's voice was shrill, now, wet with tears but with that same determination she'd possessed since her birth. Calida pictured her crying and wanted to hold her, make the bad things go away. She always had; that would never change. 'Tell me where you are, Calida. I'll find you. Where are you?'

'I don't know.' Calida was so tired, too tired... 'It doesn't matter now.'

'Calida? Talk to me, you have to keep talking. Calida—'

'I'm in trouble,' she murmured.

'I know. It should have been me. It was meant to be me.'

'You said we weren't sisters any more. You didn't want me in your life.'

The line flickered, crackled; she thought it would cut out. 'No! It wasn't like that—after I left I never contacted you again. Because Simone told me you'd been killed. *She* wrote that letter, Calida. Not me. I don't know what it said but I promise you I never saw it. Never. I thought you'd rejected me. I thought you'd sold me.'

Calida saw the two of them, two sisters, reunited on the ranch. A paradise plain of echoed laughter and whispering trees, of rolling earth and reaching skies.

'I would never do that,' she whispered.

Teresita was shouting now, hysterical, but her shouts

reached Calida's ears as sighs, so far away, so far… 'I'm tired,' the phone slipped, 'I have to sleep.'

'No—'

'*Adios, pequeño… Te amo.*'

That was the last thing she said. She was glad she had got to say it, the single truth that eclipsed all others, before unconsciousness stole her away.

Epilogue

January, 2015

Simone was in mourning—but it was hard to know for whom.

A man she had met only twice: once, as a baby, then again, as the intruder who had stabbed himself on her stairwell days before.

The funeral took place in London. That was where he'd been born and where he should be laid to rest. Nobody except Lysander—and those present in the aftermath of the scene— knew the facts. To the rest of the world, he had been an associate, a distant acquaintance Simone had deigned to honour.

In a lifetime of courting the press, she had been spared this final intrusion. Imagine if they had caught wind of the truth… It was bad enough that she knew it.

In the Mortlake churchyard, Simone Geddes and Lysander Chilcott watched the coffin being lowered into the ground. She would have preferred him to have been cremated, gone for good, not lying under the soil, forever in this spot, so she would know he was there and be compelled to visit him. *David*. No, Martin. He wasn't the child she had given away, with his sweet, round cheeks and bracelets of fat. He was a monster, drunk on vengeance, whose warped reality had led him to that point of no return.

A psychopath had replaced her infant, and, despite Simone's countless imaginings of the person he might have become, none were anything close to this.

She had witnessed his destruction. Would never forget it, no matter how many Valium or sleeping pills or Prozac she rattled down her gasping throat.

The nights were the worst. That was when she was forced to think about that horrible final encounter, playing it on a loop until she was sick. She remembered it pace by pace, piece by piece, how she had entered the apartment, not quite normal, how she had watched him emerge and been unable to speak.

On the stairwell, they had locked in stunned silence. And then there it was, the opportunity to tell him everything she had yearned to tell him as a girl, about how sorry she was, how she would have chosen any outcome but that, how she'd had no choice. But no words came. The boy she wished to tell them to wasn't him.

Martin had lifted the dagger, glinting pure silver, and…

Simone shivered, as the frozen sky cracked and gave way to a drift of sleet. Lysander reached for her hand and held it. Thank God for Lysander.

Their critics could rot. She didn't care. The relationship had started as a short-term solution to a long-term boredom, but had grown into true and lasting affection. Into love… Together, they were plotting their retreat from the public eye. The old Simone would never have considered it. The new Simone was realising that celebrity wasn't everything. When it came to it, fame didn't matter. Family did.

She had learned the hard way.

'*In sure and certain hope of the resurrection of eternal life…*'

The priest droned on as the coffin was lowered into the wet, cold earth. Simone had paid for the funeral trimmings. It was the least she could do; give her son a proper burial when she had given him an improper birth.

How sadly it had ended… but how much worse it might have been.

Martin Gallagher had meant to kill Tess. Beloved daughter. The thought filled Simone with stark horror, even though she knew that Tess was safe. She knew he hadn't succeeded. Instead, he had unwittingly locked on to her twin.

Learning of Calida Santiago's rise through the ranks was a sobering revelation indeed. The connection with Ryan Xiao was nothing short of inconceivable; it didn't seem real. How could Simone have been so blind? She'd heard the name often enough but hadn't joined the dots. Simply, her world and that child's were utterly distinct: they could never overlap. But that child had become a giant. That unruly, wild-eyed girl on a windswept farm in Patagonia had grown into one of America's biggest names. Simone had underestimated her. Seeing what Tess had had made her fight. How tragically it had ended… that her efforts should come to this.

Simone stood a little straighter, as the cracked ground made way for her son.

'*Forgive us our sins as we forgive those who sin against us…*'

She knew she was beyond forgiveness—but that maybe, one day, Tess would think differently, and find it, buried deep, in her heart. Simone would be there.

She would wait as long as it took.

All Simone had wished for in that cold attic, the morning her grandmother took her baby away and she had wept in a heap on the floor, was a family who loved her. That family started with Lysander. She could only pray it reached out to Tess.

She wasn't letting another child go.

*

On an LA film set, Emily Chilcott waltzed off her scene and straight into the glowing praise of her jubilant director. Steven Krakowski embraced her, his hot cheek pressing against hers and a load else pressing besides—but they had to be careful.

'You were breathtaking,' Steven groaned into her hair, snatching an opportunity while the first AD was out of sight. 'Just like last night…'

Emily basked in his approval. She still couldn't believe that Steven was hers—this great, coveted man whose career could send her own into the stratosphere!

Well, he wasn't quite hers yet, because it had to stay under wraps. How could they confess to the blossoming relationship after what had happened to Tess?

They couldn't. But still…

Emily's mind reeled back to the night they had spent, the latest in a chain of illicit hook-ups. Sex with Steven took her to places she had never dared visit. He had opened up to her, confided his fetishes on the first occasion they had slept together. Emily would do anything to please him, and, while his preferences grossed her out, this was Hollywood and Hollywood was full of kinky shit, so what was the big deal?

Roll with it, she instructed herself, as she cradled six feet plus of world-famous director wearing a cosy, cotton Babygro. *Slap on a smile and get to work*, as she nursed him and sang him lullabies, pinned his nappies, and filled his bottles.

'Tess never understood,' he whined, cuddling his blanket. 'She was afraid…'

She just didn't want it as much as me! Emily decided, as she opened Steven's bedtime story and allowed him to fondle her tits. Maybe at some point she would get tired of it, but she was savvy enough to grit her teeth until she got what she wanted.

Steven had promised her a starring role in Miller & Mount's newest venture, which was tipped to be a smash. She would become a household name overnight.

Steven was the key to her future.

Emily Chilcott would do whatever, or whoever, it took to get there.

She was destined for the stars; she always had been.

*

Steven Krakowski enjoyed possessing a new plaything. It made it sweeter that Emily was Tess Geddes' stepsister—maybe one day Tess would reflect on their union and see the gifts he could have bestowed on her, and regret having let him go.

That was wishful thinking, he knew, as he watched Emily Chilcott return to set amid a gaggle of stylists. Emily was pretty, and biddable, but she was nothing against Tess. Tess was a goddess. He regretted how things had ended between them. Steven had loved her, at one point, or as close to love as he was likely to get (the only woman he had ever adored wholeheartedly was the huge-breasted nanny who looked after him as a boy: whenever she'd chided him he had spent an hour in the bathroom, rubbing himself until he was raw). It wasn't his fault Tess had turned round and stabbed him in the back. When she'd gone missing, he had half hoped that would be the end of her. While her death would have injured him, it would at least have marked the demise of a bargaining chip that was sure to haunt him to his dying day.

Instead, that freak stalker had targeted another girl, a fashion photographer who bore a remarkable resemblance to his ex-wife. It had been unfortunate for the girl, and, Steven thought, unfortunate for him. His blood ran cold at the idea that his perversions could ever be found out. Always, Tess would hold that secret against him, one she could employ at any point and however she saw fit. It was a troubling notion.

He had none of the same concerns with Emily. She was a kitten, and now they had got physical he was starting to see what she was really made of… just how far she was willing to go. The budding actress desired fame to an unreasonable degree.

What would she do to achieve it?

Steven would take great pleasure in finding out.

*

At her parents' house in the heart of Paris, surrounded by home comforts and the reassuring company of her family, Mia Ferraris kissed her boyfriend.

Officially, they had been together for only a week—but already she had brought Gabriel back to France. Weeks like the week she'd just had only reinforced that every second was precious.

Béatrice and Anton adored him. Gabriel and Mia were absolutely right for each other. While most fledgling relationships pivoted on a string of nervous first dates and anxious second-guessing, theirs had been thrown in deep from day one.

In Barcelona, Gabriel had been privy to a drama that was so enormous and so scandalous that the rest of the planet could never know about it. He was a strong, ambitious, unflappable man—and, true to form, had stayed purposefully discreet on the matter. After Tess's call to her sister, Gabriel had driven them both to the airport. He had accompanied them to America and helped sort through the aftermath.

He loved Mia for all the ways that made her unique—and she loved him back.

But her newfound happiness didn't stop her thinking about Tess. As the New Year passed and they all stepped carefully around the omission in the room, Mia couldn't help but worry. What was Tess doing? How was she feeling? They had been in touch constantly after the event, but since then Tess had asked for space. Mia had to respect it, even if she spent every second fearing Tess was alone, or sad, or afraid.

'Here,' Anton said, refilling her coffee cup over the breakfast bar, 'this'll warm you up.' Mia smiled at him. It took effort, and he sent her an enquiring look, to which she responded with a nod.

I'm OK. Bearing up.

Gabriel was helping with that, but even so the trauma would take time to work through. She recalled the stricken look on Tess's face when she had made that call, unable to fathom the voice she had heard, her features collapsing by the second, then the searing tears, part horror, part joy. The return race to America, helpless in their jet, waiting for the hours to pass and knowing by the time they got there it could be too late. The victim had been Calida all along. Calida had disappeared. Calida had got into that van. With whom? Why? What did they want? So many questions.

Maximilian cleared the airport for their return. Tess and Mia had rushed to the hospital and to Calida's bedside, where they heard that, in a final twist, Simone Geddes had been the one to find her—beaten black and blue by a psychotic fan, starved and drugged... and all along mistaken for Tess.

If only they had got there sooner.

Then things might have been different.

Some days Mia wished it had been Tess who'd found her—surely that would have been right? Others, she knew it would have been worse. At the end of their journey, the person who had stolen Tess from her home was the one to rediscover it.

Tess had gone into the hospital suite alone.

Mia would never forget her face when she came back out.

She bit back tears. Her best friend had been through so much—and then to have to go through this. She wished she could take some of the pain for her.

'Hey, come here.'

Gabriel came to sit next to her, hooking an arm round her shoulders and pulling her in close. Thanks to him, she could start looking to the future. They would face today together, then tomorrow, then the year ahead.

She only hoped that Tess could do the same.

*

In a New York bar, Julia Santiago shoved the man off and demanded that if he wanted to molest her tits he would need to buy her another drink first. Like a kicked puppy, he obeyed, sliding a five-dollar bill across the bar and burping gently. 'You wanna get out of here?' he drawled, once the brandy had arrived and Julia had necked it in one.

She ignored him, eyes glued on the TV screen, though it was difficult to focus through a quart of liquor. 'They're my daughters, you know,' she said.

The man followed her gaze. The bartender's interest momentarily piqued before he snorted a laugh and turned his attention to a nearby waitress in a short skirt.

'Oh yeah?' the man sneered. Foggily, Julia turned to him

and noticed that his hair was balding, his skin was beige and sallow, and his eyes watered unattractively.

Is this what it's come to? Julia thought. *Is this it, the sum of my life*?

'Yes,' she replied. 'I'm their mother.'

'You're wasted is what you are.'

'You don't believe me?'

The man ordered more brandy. Once again Julia chucked hers back, the liquid scalding her throat. 'No offence, lady,' he said, 'but you don't bear no similarities.'

Julia couldn't deny that. In the bar mirror she saw a saggy, withered old drunk who had thrown away a fortune and a lot more besides. *Why won't my girls give me a chance? Why won't they take me back*? Calida was dead and gone; there was no way to reconcile with her. But Teresita would come round, wouldn't she?

Wouldn't she? Then these bastards would eat their words.

Julia Santiago would rise again—she didn't care what the hell it took.

'C'mon, let's get out of here. Twenty bucks, right now, back seat of my car.'

Julia thought what twenty bucks could buy her. She followed him out.

*

At her new home in Stockholm, Scarlet Schuhausen put a hand to her growing stomach and smiled. It was a happy New Year indeed.

'Everything all right?' Henry Doric kissed her, tenderly and softly, not at all like the brusque, matter-of-fact kisses she had grown used to with her ex-husband.

Scarlet removed the last of the baubles from the Christmas

tree and returned it to its nest of white paper. It was strange how the universe worked.

She still couldn't believe it, had to say it aloud to savour its truth all over again. *I'm pregnant*. With the news, her outlook had transformed.

Henry Doric was ten times the man Vittorio had been. Since they had fallen in love he had shown her a new path, one away from her stifling parents and snooty, horrible friends. His way was honest and sensitive, decent and loyal—qualities that had been lacking so far. In turn, Scarlet had turned her life around. She had started visiting a therapist, had come off her medication, and felt stronger by the day.

Looking back, it was almost as if someone had been steering her, making the decisions, all the important ones, for her. Scarlet was a new woman, filled, quite literally, with new possibilities. Nothing could stop her now. Finally, she had the ending she deserved—and she didn't care what anyone else thought.

As was the knowledge that it hadn't been her with the fertility problem… All those times she had tried to conceive a child with Vittorio, in the hope that might make him stay. So many nights she had lain awake, fearing she was to blame—but no. It had been Vitto all along, with his proud, jutting, and ultimately useless cock.

It was surely only a matter of time before Vittorio realised that the seed he sowed so ruthlessly across so many women's sheets was defunct. When the time came, as surely it would, that Vittorio wished to produce a successor, he would find he was firing blanks. It seemed a fitting comeuppance. If it came at all…

Her relationship with Vitto seemed juvenile in comparison

with Henry—all about scoring one-ups and competition. She could hardly stand to think of it.

With Henry, she had found her reason.

And with that reason, she had abandoned her hatred of Tess Geddes.

How could she hate Tess now? Instead, she pitied her. It was preposterous that Scarlet's name had been associated with the attack and kidnap, as if she would ever have gone to such lengths to hurt the woman. Rumours had circulated for a while that Scarlet had hired a hit man, that Tess had feared some goon creeping up on her in the middle of the night and strangling her in her bed, all on Scarlet's instruction.

The notion would make her laugh if it weren't so awful. Sure, she had loathed Tess. Sure, she had imagined wreaking all manner of extreme revenge. But even if she'd had the guts to carry any of it out, her pregnancy changed everything. The truth was, she had visited America before Christmas to share her news with her extended family. It had been such a joyous disclosure that she had wished to do it in person, and, yes, before she left, she might have seemed highly strung—but where was the surprise in that? Scarlet might have slandered her, she might have reviled her, she might have targeted her as a badge for the pain she had suffered, she might even have *wanted* to give her a scare—but she could never have physically harmed Tess Geddes.

She wasn't an animal. Not like that man…

Scarlet shivered. It was finished now. She and Henry had their family to look forward to, and she didn't intend to waste another second.

*

Vittorio Da Strovisi drove into the woman like it was the last fuck of his life. He gripped her ass, slapping it so hard that she cried out in surprised pain. He fucked like there was no tomorrow. Some days, some fucks, he wished there weren't.

In Florence, he had attended a seasonal concert—candlelit and tasteful as the carols were sung in an outdoor star-strewn amphitheatre. Afterwards he was screwing in a dark alley, while the rest of his crowd mingled, the wife of one of his cronies, stripped bare of her glimmering emerald gown, her knickers caught round her ankles.

It was a bad habit he had got into, imagining any woman he nailed was Calida Santiago. He had to let go. Calida wasn't around any more. She had been beaten and starved by a suicidal maniac and the outcome had been inescapable.

Vittorio kept remembering her; he couldn't help it. The feeling he had whenever he thought of her was one of pulsing life and radiating heat. Calida had been vibrant, her anger hot and her passion sure, as if she had swallowed the sun. He had never met a woman like her—strong, independent, combative; giving him the impression that should he walk out of her life one day she wouldn't grant him a second thought. It was desperately attractive, and desperately rare.

He worried that he had been in love with her. He must have been, if he'd asked her to marry him. If he'd wanted to be with her—and still did—every second of the day. Love was a weakness, an admission of frailty; love was danger.

Vittorio wasn't in the business of being in love.

The music continued. So did Vittorio, because when he stopped it all came tumbling down: the summary of his years, empty and cold.

*

Tess opened her eyes and felt sunlight warm her aching bones.

Where was she? Somewhere familiar. Somewhere she had lost long ago, and recently found again. Somewhere old and somewhere new: a place of belonging.

The room took her back twenty years. It wasn't the room she used to sleep in. She remembered knocking softly on its door, for fear of disturbing her mama. It had wallpaper now and proper floorboards, the holes in the roof long gone and the whistling wind sealed off from outside. Her belongings filled the closet and the drawers. The window was open a fraction, letting in the scent of lavender.

She could detect it now without feeling guilt. Without thinking of her father. Its scent reminded her that while so much changed, so much else stayed the same.

Tess rolled over. The space next to her was empty. Someone had been in bed with her last night; she could feel his warmth still on the sheets, and she smiled when she recalled whom it was. His touch had put her broken body back together.

'Hello, Pirate.'

Alex Dalton was at the door. 'I didn't want to wake you,' he said.

She held her arms out. Alex, her Alex… always and forever him.

'You're beautiful when you're sleeping,' he told her, touching his lips to hers.

'And when I'm awake?' she teased.

'Not so much.'

She thumped him. Alex kissed her properly then, firmly, in the same way he'd kissed her that crazy night in England, in the same way he'd kissed her when she'd arrived back in America and visited Calida in hospital and fallen helpless into his arms. His kiss was one of absolute intent. It said everything the past fifteen years had longed to say; it was a true, eternal declaration of the love he had always kept hidden from her, and, when Tess kissed him back, she matched it word for word. It was Alex who had adored her from afar; he who had bought the farm and land from Daniel but never told her, Alex who had worked to restore it to a place where she could find home again. She could barely take in that he would do such a thing.

'I did it for you,' he said. 'I would do anything for you.'

Mia had known. She told Tess she had always known.

'I want you to be happy,' her best friend said. 'All that time with Alex, I knew it was you he was thinking of. You're meant to be, Tess. So be. Please, just be.'

For the first time in a long time, she was.

'Where's Calida?' she asked.

Alex looked at her, solemn devotion in his eyes.

She climbed out of bed and made her way through the hall, past the kitchen with its cast-iron stove, past the table they had sat at with Diego, past the pictures Alex had salvaged of their family: of Mama, Papa, Calida, and her.

Tess opened the door on to the veranda. It was hot and hazy, the peaks and dips of her heritage soaring like ice caps in the distance. The horizon melted in the blazing sun. Alex stepped up behind her and put his hands on her shoulders.

'There,' he said. 'Look.'

Two figures shimmered in the heat and Tess squinted to catch them.

'*She told me you were dead…*'

But Calida had always been living. She had been waiting, following, believing in their reunion all this time, and against all odds she had never given up.

Against the poison words she'd believed Tess had said.

At the hospital, not once had Tess let go of her sister's hand.

Not once had she stopped talking, reassuring Calida that she was here and here to stay, that she loved her and wasn't letting go. *Please wake up. Don't die. Not now. You can't.*

They had so much to make up for. So much life left to live.

I love you. I'm not going anywhere without you again.

She could not fathom that Simone had told such lies.

How could you?

Nothing Simone could say would justify it. It had been a terrible crime. No matter how Tess tried to see it from her adoptive mother's point of view, she couldn't.

But Simone wouldn't give up. She called Tess every day, and when that failed she sent missives through her people, gifts, begging letters and emails, pleading answerphone messages. '*I'm not stopping,*' Simone told her. '*You can bet the rest of your life I'll be waiting. Come back to me, Tess. Let me explain. Let me say sorry.*'

Maybe, some day, she would… but not yet.

Simone had lost two children that night. Her son, whom no one had known about and who explained so much, slumped dead in her apartment, his blood all down his mother's dress. *And me.* But Tess felt, hour by hour, a creeping sadness for Simone that, if allowed to grow, could flower into something like sympathy.

It was too soon to know how she felt. For now, Simone wasn't getting her back—and neither was Hollywood. First, she had to return to the start.

She had to realise, as she did now, watching the figures advance towards them and with the reassuring heat of Alex at her back, that without foundations no tower could ever soar. Those dreams little Teresa had nurtured with Julia, having her hair brushed, listening at her mother's knee, were castles in the sky. Floating, rudderless, inconstant as the wind. Without a counterpoint on the ground, there was nothing to catch her. Wrongly, she had thought she could cut loose her beginnings and start afresh. She had welcomed that; *wished* for it. Never stopping to ask what would happen if she fell from her castle: what or who would be there to save her?

Her twin. Always her twin, without whom the world, castles, skies, riches, fame, ambition, laughter, sadness, happiness, truth…none of it meant anything.

Money didn't matter. Fame didn't matter. There was nothing left to prove.

The figures were coming closer now. Alex planted a kiss on the back of her neck. 'There she is,' he said.

'There she is,' repeated Tess, each word a miracle.

She slipped from his grasp and ran to meet them.

*

The horses' hooves kicked up swirls of gold dust. Calida loosened the reins and rushed like fire over the earth, Daniel alongside her, their animals dashing for victory before they pulled the reins and slowed, the *estancia* finally coming into sight.

Daniel caught her. She evaded his touch and circled on her horse but then he took her and held her, their horses side by side, panting in the heat.

He kissed her. A kiss she longed for now just as much as she had when she was thirteen. A smile she loved as ardently this day as she had then.

Older now, wiser, in some ways changed—but in the vital ways the same.

Some days, she thought of all the time they had lost, on mistakes, on mix-ups, on not saying what they felt or meant. Others, Calida knew she had needed that to grow. Now, they were allies. Equals. In leaving the farm, she had learned about the world, about herself, about the great tapestry of people who kept the earth turning, but most of all she had learned that she would always hunger for home. This was where she belonged, with the horses and the land and with Daniel. With him, she had only ever had to be herself. Not her twin, nothing pretend; just her. It was enough.

'I can feel your heart,' Daniel said. It seemed to spill into his, thumping lifeblood, each recognising its counterpoint in the other.

'What does it feel like?' she asked, kissing him again, unable to stop kissing him. They had so many kisses to make up for. She could kiss him to the end of time.

'Strong.'

Calida knew that was true. Strong enough to do what she had done, to survive where others might not. But, then, she'd had something to survive for.

Calida dismounted and led her horse the rest of the way.

Through the farm gate, in the distance, she saw her twin sister.

You're there. You're real. It's you.

The words she had held tight to all the time she was sick; Teresita reaching from afar, singing to her, talking to her, wishing her back from the brink. Calida was alone on the vast savannah; and beyond the mountains, a plea had blown on the wind.

Come back... Come back... I'm here, come back...

She had known she had to live. Or she would die trying.

Even now, their phone call seemed impossible. So much of it did, from breaking into her sister's building, to the van, to her attacker, to her semi-conscious ride in the ambulance—but somehow, most of all, that phone call. She had been ready to drown when a lifeline hit the waves and she had groped for it, pressing it to her ear, and before any words were uttered she had *felt* it. She had known.

At the last moment, Teresita saved her. Calida would never forget hearing her twin's voice, and, more, the answer buried deep within it. An answer to the question she had carried since she had first wished Teresita away. *Did you leave me behind*? No. Never. The years had misunderstood them; they had misunderstood the years. In Tess Geddes' tears, Calida had heard Teresita Santiago: the girl who had never left.

One memory held sharp where others faded to shadow. Long ago, that morning they had ridden with their father, and Calida had protected her sister from the *guanaco*'s death. She had sat and held her hand, held her safe, but hadn't realised then that Teresita had been holding her safe, too. They were each other's home.

'Go to her,' said Daniel.

Calida didn't need to be told twice. She started walking but her walk broke into a run, and the sun was on her face and the dust was in her hair and the sky and earth cradled them and bathed them in the promise of the future, knowing that whatever it brought, here or afar, now or then, they would never be separated again.

She fell into her sister's arms, one heart strong against the other.

We'll always be together. Promise?
Promise.
And this time they were.

ACKNOWLEDGEMENTS

Thank you to Madeleine Milburn, Cara Lee Simpson and Anna Hogarty, the best and most brilliant team I could wish for. To Sally Williamson and everyone at Harlequin UK for bringing my books to life, and for the gorgeous covers.

To Carol Jones Cabalgatas and her gaucho Marc for an unforgettable Patagonian adventure. And to Mark Oakley for sharing it, and so much else, with me.

*A fast-paced, fun-packed rummage
through the ultimate dressing up box.*

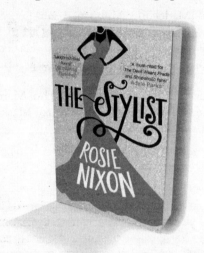

When fashion boutique worker Amber Green is
mistakenly offered a job as assistant to infamous,
jet-setting 'stylist to the stars' Mona Armstrong,
she hits the ground running, helping to style some
of Hollywood's hottest (and craziest) starlets. As
awards season spins into action Mona is in hot
demand and Amber's life turned upside down.
How will Amber keep her head?

And what the hell will everyone wear?

Bringing you the best voices in fiction
🐦 **@Mira_booksUK**

M439_TS

Loved this book?
Let us know!

Find us on **Twitter @Mira_BooksUK**
where you can share your thoughts, stay up
to date on all the news about our upcoming
releases and even be in with the chance of
winning copies of our wonderful books!

Bringing you the best voices in fiction

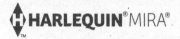